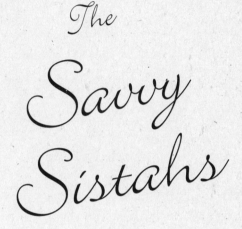

The

Savvy Sistahs

The
Savvy
Sistahs

Brenda Jackson

St. Martin's Griffin ⚮ New York

www.stmartins.com

Book design by Susan Yang

Library of Congress Cataloging-in-Publication Data

Jackson, Brenda (Brenda Streater)
    The savvy sistahs / Brenda Jackson.—1st ed.
        p. cm.
    ISBN 0-312-31512-0
        1. African American women—Fiction. 2. African American businesspeople—
Fiction. 3. Female friendship—Fiction. I. Title.

PS3560.A21165S38 2003
813'.54—dc21

                                                        2003047155

10   9   8   7   6   5

Acknowledgments

This book is dedicated to the "Savvy Sistahs" who made my birthday celebration so special: Denise Coleman, Patricia Sams, Nina Davenport, Racquel Bolden-Lott, Katherine Foster, Rita Daniels, Felicia Edwards, Tonya Knox, Brenda Johnson-Whaley, Tina Norfleet, and Tara West. I totally enjoyed our "sistahs" night out.

And to my Heavenly Father, who loves me and gives me the strength to endure all things.

Blessings on all who reverence, trust and obey the Lord.
Their reward will be prosperity and happiness.
Psalms 128: 1-2

When three fabulously fine women walked into the plush Orlando restaurant, a number of heads turned and looked their way. Individually as well as collectively, they received admiring glances and lingering gazes. Other women silently complimented the way they were dressed—glamorous, elegant, and stunning. A few necks strained to see if perhaps they were well-known celebrities who had graced the tourist city. When it was determined they weren't, everyone was satisfied in reaching the conclusion that what they saw were gorgeous, sophisticated, high-class sistahs; women who knew what they wanted; women who were accomplished in everything they did.

Brandy Bennett, a divorcée, was thirty-three and stood at a height of five-six. She had medium brown skin coloring, dark brown eyes, and wore her shoulder-length hair in braids. She was manager and sole owner of the St. Laurent, a very prestigious hotel.

Carla Osborne was thirty-two and stood five-seven. Her skin coloring was burnished bronze, the color of her eyes was dark coffee, and she wore her black hair in a short and sassy cut. She was a single parent and CEO of Osborne Computer Network, Incorporated.

Amber Stuart, also a divorcée, was thirty-two and stood five-eight.

Her black shoulder-length hair, cocoa-colored skin, and amber-colored eyes complemented her voluptuous figure. She was the proud owner of Amber's Books and Gifts.

Brandy Bennett smiled upon seeing the attention they were getting. She had a pretty good idea what everyone was thinking. Some would call them savvy and she would accept that description as a dramatic turning point in each of their lives, because before they became savvy they had been survivors of the leading destroyer of black women . . . a damn no-good brother.

She glanced over at Carla and Amber. They were here to celebrate. Their friendship had begun a year ago on this very night. At that time they had formed a sistah-circle and called it the ABCs, taken from the first letter of each of their names. The three had been victims of dog bites of the worst kind, deep wounds inflicted by doggish men who refused to do right. For a long time pride had kept them from baring the heartaches they had endured. But through the power of prayer, the grace of God, and a firm belief that no man could keep a good woman down, they had stepped out on faith and rebuilt their lives. And although they'd never shared in detail the circumstances that had brought them to this point, it hadn't been hard to figure out that it had involved mistreatment by a man. A bond had been forged between them and the support they had given one another, both personal and professional, had been priceless.

Thomas Reynolds, the owner of the Commodore Restaurant, looked up, saw them, and smiled. His gaze lingered on one of the women in particular. "Ladies, it's good seeing you again, and the room you requested is ready, if you care to follow me."

They followed as he led them to a private dining room. "Oh, Thomas, this is perfect," Brandy exclaimed, glancing around. The secluded room had a beautiful panoramic view of Orlando.

Thomas's smile widened, boosted by Brandy's compliment. "Thank you, and I'm glad I was able to please you."

He had drawn the last words out and Brandy had caught his meaning. She immediately thought of the last time he had tried pleasing her. It had been their first and last date almost two years ago. She had arrived in town not knowing a soul, and he had been eager to make her acquaintance and get her into his bed . . . and after a time she had accommodated him, only to roll away less than thirty minutes later totally disappointed. It wasn't that he hadn't tried, because Lord knows he had, but once she had lain on her back, she couldn't get past the fact that he was a man older than her father. And although the outside package was pretty damn tempting—since he didn't look the age of sixty—his techniques in the bedroom, in her opinion, were outdated and left a lot to be desired.

But what had developed between them afterward was a close friendship, and she much preferred it that way. He had been the one to tell her about the support group for professional black businesswomen called Savvy Sistahs Who Mean Business. The group's motto was: "Don't just empower sistahs—put sistahs in power." The members met monthly and offered support, advice, and the tools needed to be successful in dealing with double discrimination—both racism and sexism: maximizing strengths and downsizing weaknesses, developing business strategies and management styles, and coping with business ownership. It was there at the monthly meetings that she had met Carla and Amber.

"Can we sit down and order our food? I'm starving."

Brandy smiled at Carla, the one who always ate the most and weighed the least. "Sure." She then glanced at Amber, who was trying to hide her smile.

"Thomas, we'd like to take a look at your menu, and we would like a bottle of your best wine. We're celebrating," Brandy said excitedly.

He lifted a brow. "Oh? And what's the occasion, if I may ask?"

A beguiling smile touched the corners of Brandy's mouth. "A year of friendship and the success of our businesses."

· · ·

Their plates were cleared from the table, and Brandy reached for her wineglass while studying Carla's worried expression. "Is anything wrong?"

Carla met Brandy's gaze and smiled. She'd been caught. "No, not really. I was just wondering how Craig's doing."

Brandy took a sip and nodded, understanding completely. Craig was Carla's two-year-old son. His usual babysitter was out of town and Carla had used a backup, a girl who lived in the neighborhood. Although the teenager had come highly recommended, it was evident that Carla was still worried. "Why don't you call home and check on him."

Carla shrugged. "You think I should?"

"Yes, of course you should. You're a concerned mother and there's nothing wrong with that."

Carla smiled, relieved. "Thanks." She then glanced at Amber. "To the both of you."

Amber chuckled. "And what did we do?"

"Extending your friendships and being there for me this past year, being honorary aunties to Craig, and stepping in to help out during those last-minute business trips when Mrs. Boston or Sonya wasn't available."

Brandy nodded. "Speaking of Sonya, where is she tonight? I'm surprised she doesn't have Craig," she said about the woman who was Carla's best friend from high school and Craig's godmother.

A smile touched Carla's lips. "Sonya had a date and I couldn't ask her to change her plans on my account. I'm glad she finally met someone she likes enough to go out with. She can be so nit-picky when it comes to men."

Amber laughed as she took a sip of her own wine. "Look who's talking."

A slight frown marred Carla's smooth forehead. "I'm not nit-picky, I just choose not to date anyone seriously until Craig is older." She held Amber's gaze. "So what's your reason for being nit-picky?"

When Amber didn't answer and started studying her wineglass too long for comfort, Brandy decided to shift the attention to herself and open up a topic that the three of them had avoided since meeting.

The details of their past.

"Did I ever tell the two of you about my ex-husband, Lorenzo Ballentine?" she asked, looking at her friends from under her lashes as she sipped her wine, knowing damn well that she hadn't ever mentioned anything about Lorenzo.

When Carla and Amber simultaneously said "no," she smiled. "I think few people can recall with absolute certainty the precise moment that may have changed their lives. I can definitely remember mine."

She reached for the wine bottle to pour more wine into her glass before she continued. "It was two years ago, two days before my wedding, when I discovered that my fiancé, the man I loved completely and planned to marry, had been unfaithful with my best friend, Jolene Bradford—the woman who was maid of honor in my wedding."

Sadness and pain for Brandy reflected in both Carla and Amber's faces. "How did you find out?" Amber asked quietly.

Brandy smiled sadly. "He was stupid enough to make a videotape of their lovemaking session and hid it on a top shelf in the closet of his bedroom. I was looking for old videotapes of our past vacations that would be shown at the wedding and came across it. Since it wasn't labeled, I played it and what I saw shocked the hell out of me."

Carla shook her head, appalled. "I can imagine how you must have felt."

Brandy met her gaze. "No, I don't think anyone will ever be able to imagine the hurt and pain I endured after watching it."

After a long moment, Amber spoke up. "But you didn't call off the wedding?"

Brandy smiled. "No, although that was my first intent, but I changed my mind. That was the day that changed my life because I had help in making that decision. Three cousins who I never got along with while growing up, Alexia, Rae'jean, and Taye, showed me the true meaning of the term 'blood is thicker than water' by giving me their shoulders to cry on and sharing with me their strength. They also reminded me of the importance of family—especially in a crisis."

"They talked you into proceeding with marrying a man who'd been unfaithful to you?" Carla asked in a startled voice, clearly shocked. "Why?"

"Because financially, it made perfect sense. Lorenzo and his family are wealthy Jamaicans who made their money as real estate developers and large financial investors. They own, among other things, a number of hotels in Jamaica, the Western Caribbean, and the United States. My cousins saw no reason for me to lose out on gaining access to any of that. After I was able to put the hurt, anger, and humiliation aside, they convinced me not to get mad but to get even."

Amber chuckled. "Did you?"

"Yes."

"Good for you," Amber said laughing. "So you confronted him on your wedding night?"

"No, I arranged for the videotape to be played during the wedding reception dinner, since we'd planned to show videos of our past romantic vacations together anyway. I paid the wedding planner a little extra something to handle everything and to keep his mouth closed and do what he was told."

Carla leaned back in her chair, beside herself with laughter. "Let me get this straight. While the two of you were at the wedding reception, sitting down enjoying a wonderful meal with your wedding guests—"

"All five hundred of them," Brandy decided to cut in and add.

Carla shook her head and continued. "With all five hundred of your wedding guests watching, the videotape of your husband's tryst with your best friend began playing?"

"Yes."

Amber took another sip of her wine to keep from laughing, but ended up laughing anyway, nearly choking in the process. "What was everyone's reaction?"

"Things went crazy. I fainted, playacting of course, but according to my cousins, all hell broke loose after that. Lorenzo and I were ushered into a private room with the minister, our parents, and his attorney. Lorenzo tried to explain things but there was nothing he could say. Even his parents were appalled as well as embarrassed, since they had invited a number of important business associates to the wedding. All the while we were holed up in that private room, I'm told the tape kept playing because a number of people were enjoying watching the X-rated show Lorenzo and Jolene were putting on."

Carla's and Amber's eyes bulged, but Brandy continued, pretending not to notice. "Needless to say, to keep down the scandal and details of what happened, I was paid off very well. And although the Ballentine family—Lorenzo, in particular—didn't want to part with any of their hotels, my attorney demanded as part of the divorce settlement that I be given one of the most profitable hotels. That's how I became owner of the St. Laurent."

Brandy silently thought about the weeks following her wedding. Although she would thank God every day for letting her find out just what type of person Lorenzo was, she hadn't seemed to be able to move on with her life. Everyone thought she was doing a rather admirable job coping, but the truth was that emotionally, she'd been falling apart.

Again, it had been her three cousins who'd helped her get past Lorenzo and Jolene's betrayal and pick her life back up and move on. However, it had been her grandfather Ethan Bennett's death that had finally brought her around. During the last conversation she'd had with him, which had taken place a day before his unexpected death, he had told her that a person had to be the one to take charge of their life and seek their own happiness. Because of those words, she had decided to stop wallowing in self-pity and do exactly that.

She glanced at her watch and said to Carla and Amber, "Tonight is still early. I suggest you call home and check on Craig, Carla, then we can continue to share our wine and our secrets."

Each woman understood what she meant. The final turning point in their lives would be to finally share their past pain. They had known for the longest time that pride had kept them from owning up to the hurt they had suffered and from confiding in each other about it.

Tonight was a time to not only celebrate their success, but also to embrace their growth as women who were finally able to put to rest their deep emotional pain. When Carla placed her mobile phone back in her purse after completing her call, the three women leaned back in their seats, slipped off their shoes, and drank wine as their minds reflected what had happened in their lives to bring them to this point.

Tonight would be a night for purging their souls.

Carla was the one who spoke up next. "I haven't slept with anyone since the night I spent with Craig's father."

There was a moment of stunned silence, and then Amber spoke. "That's been almost three years, hasn't it?"

Carla smiled. "Yes, and that was my first and last time, so I only got a little taste." She felt a thickness in her throat when she immediately remembered what a nice size man he'd been. "I mean, I got a rather big taste," she said smiling sheepishly.

Brandy leaned forward, definitely interested. "And?" she asked, encouraging her.

Carla went back in time as she recalled her one and only affair. "I met him at a party. In fact, it was a birthday party that Sonya's parents had given her. Jesse Devereau was in town doing business with Sonya's father and was invited to the party. We met, were immediately attracted to each other, and made plans to spend the next day together, which was Thanksgiving."

"You made plans to spend the holiday with this guy instead of your family?" Amber asked, surprised.

"Only because my family made plans to spend Thanksgiving without me," Carla said as a bitter taste flooded her mouth. "After Dad died it became the norm for Mom to go her way on Thanksgiving and my brother Clark to go his, which left me alone with little or nothing to do."

Carla stopped speaking as she recalled the tragedy that had struck

her family a few weeks after that. "I wish things could have been different, since that was the last Thanksgiving before Clark was killed." She
took a sip of her wine, then added, "I think Mom would have preferred
it was me in that car that night instead of Clark. She's never hidden the
fact that he was her favorite."

"Thank you, Lord, that I'm an only child," Brandy said, throwing
her braids over her shoulders in a motion of bravado. "I'm blessed that
my parents have never given me grief."

It was only when Amber jerked her head around to stare at her that
it became obvious what Brandy had done. In her own usual "make it
real" way she was being the drama queen. Every so often they needed
one; especially when their talks got too somber.

"Forget about your mama for now, Carla, since we established the
fact a while back that she wasn't operating with a full deck. Let's get
back to this Jesse guy," Brandy said, gripping the edge of the table. "Why
do I get these vibes that this brother was fine, fine, fine. Maybe it's
because you've said many times that Craig took his looks from his
father, and we all know that kid of yours is going to have all the women
swooning in about fifteen years or less."

Carla smiled. "Trust me, Jesse Devereau was indeed one fine brother,
and I fell in love the moment we met. We went to a nice restaurant for
Thanksgiving dinner, went dancing, and then later went to his hotel
room. By the next morning I was no longer a twenty-nine-year-old virgin, and in the span of twelve hours I had learned bedroom techniques
that I'd never heard of before."

Amber grinned. "Sounds like a pretty good way to end an evening
to me."

Carla chuckled. "Yeah, and we used a condom, so he was either too
big or I was too small. In any case, the blasted thing didn't work and I
found out less than two months later that I was pregnant."

"Did you contact him to let him know about your condition?"
Amber asked.

"No. Although the night meant everything to me, for him it was just a one-night stand, and I didn't think he would appreciate me interrupting his life to tell him that he was going to be a father."

Carla couldn't hide the hurt in her features when she added, "I later found out that he had lied to me. I had asked him the night we met if he was involved with anyone and he said that he wasn't. I discovered that he *was* involved with someone and had been for a while. An older woman. A *rich* older woman."

A dignified snort came from Brandy. "Men are such assholes."

Amber couldn't just sit there and listen anymore. She had to finally add her past woes. "My time," she said softly. The pain in her eyes made the other two women hurt, too. "I came home from work after suffering a bad bout of morning sickness to find my husband in bed with another woman. I was three months pregnant and forgot about my condition, went ballistic and began throwing anything and everything I could get my hands on at their naked behinds. When the whore tried running down the stairs to get away from me, I took off after her, lost my balance, and fell the rest of the way . . . and lost my baby."

Amber's hand trembled from the pain she still felt as she picked up her glass of wine and finished off what was left. "Do you know that Gary not once came to the hospital to see me? And the day I came home he moved out. Before he left he looked at me and said I was one crazy-ass bitch and that I should have been more appreciative of him, since no other man wanted a size-twenty woman anyway."

She sighed deeply as she remembered his constant verbal abuse. "He would always say mean and nasty things about my weight. My self-esteem had gotten so low I didn't think that anything could ever get it up again."

Amber studied the almost empty wine bottle a moment before continuing. "More than once I wished that I had listened to my mama and never married him. Even his own mama had warned me that he was no good, but he was so good in bed that I didn't listen to anyone."

She put down her empty wineglass and reached for her glass of water, took a sip, then said, "After our divorce, I decided to leave

Nashville and start fresh here in Orlando. I saw Gary last year when I went back home for his mama's funeral. He took one look at me and saw I had slimmed down to a size sixteen and his eyes and penis got as big as his head. For some reason he thought it would be real easy to get back into my panties, but I told him that he could kiss my black—"

"Would any of you ladies care for more wine?"

The three women looked at each other and held back the laughter that threatened to pour forth. Brandy winked at Carla and Amber before clearing her throat and saying to the waiter, "No, that's all for us tonight. Thank you."

As soon as the waiter walked off, they burst out laughing. Each of them had a lot to be joyous about. They had been through some extraordinary mess with men and somehow they'd had the insight to make some positive changes.

Moments later the table got silent as they took the time to reflect on what each of them had gone through. "I think we should pray," Carla said.

Brandy smiled at her. "That's a good idea."

They joined hands, bowed their heads, and closed their eyes.

Amber prayed.

"Father, in whom are hidden all treasures of wisdom and knowledge, thank you for bringing us over. Please give us the strength not to look back, but to look forward, because we believe through you are brighter days. And we will continue to overcome whatever trials and tribulations may fall upon us, because in our hearts we believe that we can do all things through you, who will continue to strengthen us. Amen."

Book One

In whom are hid all treasures of wisdom and knowledge.

Colossians 2:3

❧ Chapter 1 ❧

Brandy

Brandy closed her eyes. She felt a headache coming on. If one more thing went wrong today she would absolutely scream. She had a million things to take care of before leaving for California, and the last thing she needed was to be on the phone listening to her mother rant and rave about what Valerie Constantine called "those damn Bennetts." She sighed deeply and reopened her eyes. Whenever she could manage to get a word in she would have to remind her mother that her daughter was one of those Bennetts and proud of it.

After a few minutes, when it became obvious her mother would not let up, Brandy had no choice but to cut in. "Mom, don't you think you're getting a little carried away?" *As usual*, she wanted to add but thought better of it. A part of her wondered if her mother and her father's family would ever get along. Sometimes Brandy had a feeling that Valerie Constantine enjoyed the rifts she always managed to cause within the Bennett family. And Brandy had to admit that for a long while, she had been right there with her mother. But that was before she had discovered what a blessing the Bennetts were. Each one of them had stepped up in some form or fashion and offered their support after what happened with Lorenzo.

"No, I am not getting carried away," Valerie Constantine snapped. "They deliberately did not invite me to your father's surprise birthday party. I have a good mind to tell him about it and ruin it for everybody. If your Grampa Ethan were alive he wouldn't stand for this. Nobody's behind this but those two heifers, Otha Mae and Cuzin Sophie. They never could stand me and they're the reason Victor never married me." After a brief pause she added, "And I don't appreciate you taking sides with them, Brandy."

Brandy shook her head. "Mom, I'm not taking sides and I think you should ask yourself why they didn't invite you. As far as everyone knows, you and Dad aren't actually a couple." *No, the two of you just get together occasionally to do the nasty*, Brandy thought as she sat in the chair behind her desk. This conversation would not be ending anytime soon.

It had always amazed Brandy how her parents seemed to enjoy sneaking around like they thought they were fooling somebody. Brandy could never forget how many times, when she was still a kid living with her mother, she would wake up to find her father sneaking out of the house, trying to leave before she woke up. It had been downright shameful. She often wondered what excuse he gave his wife about being out all night. And now her father had recently gotten a divorce from his third wife. As far as Brandy was concerned, there was no reason her parents could not go public with their thirty-two-year-old affair, but neither seemed inclined to do so. In fact, over the past year, they had seemed to be enjoying their "secret" fling more than ever. She'd been tempted on more than one occasion to ask her mother what in the heck was going on with them, then decided not to. If her parents preferred sneaking around, then it wasn't any business of hers—which her mother wouldn't hesitate to tell her even if she did say anything.

Brandy decided to change tactics. "Mom, it could have been an oversight."

"It wasn't an oversight. They just wanted to be downright nasty. No matter how they feel about me personally, I had a baby for Victor and that should count for something."

Brandy wanted to tell her mom that she wasn't the only woman to have a baby for Victor Bennett, Senior. But then she knew her mother considered herself a cut above the rest of her father's women. Strangely, Brandy knew her mother was probably right. For some reason Valerie Constantine was an addiction that Victor could not shake no matter how much he tried. And Valerie used her hold on him to make him regret that he had not married her when she'd gotten pregnant at sixteen with Brandy.

Brandy was proud to admit that her mother looked good for her age—something else her father couldn't seem to ignore. And her mother took pride in flaunting just how good she looked, and that she still held Victor's interest.

Brandy couldn't help but wonder how different things would have been if her parents *had* married when her mother got pregnant. She couldn't say things would have been better, but she had a strong feeling they would have been interesting. There was never a dull moment when her parents got together. They were very passionate, hotheaded, and stubborn individuals. There was no doubt in Brandy's mind that her mother would give any man she married pure hell. But her father was the only man she'd ever known who could actually handle Valerie Constantine.

"I can see that talking to you is useless now that you're in with that family."

Brandy sighed deeply. "Mom, I've always been 'in' with the family. I've just never appreciated it before."

"That's because you let those hellion cousins of yours talk you into making a complete fool of yourself at your wedding. I get embarrassed every time I think of what you did. Why would any woman in her right mind want the world to know that she couldn't satisfy her man physically and that he had to seek out another woman?"

Immense pain clouded Brandy's eyes. No matter what anyone thought, she felt confident there was nothing inadequate about her in bed. The only two men she'd been involved with since Lorenzo had been Grant Hoffman, a man she'd had an affair with on the rebound, and Thomas Reynolds. Neither man had complained about her performance in the bedroom. The only reason she could come up with for what Lorenzo had done was the simple reason that he was a dog.

"I think my plan was wonderful and I don't regret what I did. It cost Lorenzo plenty and he'll think twice about dogging a woman out like that again."

A few minutes later Brandy ended her conversation with her mother after promising that she would call her when she returned from California. She was about to take a few moments to inhale when her secretary buzzed. She pressed her intercom button. "Yes, Donna, what is it?"

"Miss Bennett, Mr. Ballentine is here to see you."

Brandy blinked. "Mr. Ballentine?"

"Yes. Mr. Lorenzo Ballentine."

Brandy inwardly groaned. Her ex-husband was the last person she wanted to see. The last time she had seen him had been over a year and a half ago when they'd met with her attorney and Lorenzo had grudgingly signed the St. Laurent over to her. "Send him in, Donna."

She got to her feet and watched him walk into her office, cool and confident as ever. At one point that certain arrogance about him had been a total turn-on for her. Now it was a complete turn-off.

"Why are you here, Lorenzo?" she asked bitterly, getting straight to the point and dispensing with niceties. She was upset that he had shown up unexpectedly and wondered how long it would take for him to finally accept that she didn't particularly enjoy seeing him, nor would she ever forgive him for what he'd done.

"Just hear me out, Brandy. This is strictly business," he said, taking a chair without waiting for her to invite him to do so.

"Like there's any other reason for us to have anything to say to each other," she said through gritted teeth.

He leaned back in the chair. "I want to help you out."

She crossed her arms over her chest. "Help me out in what way?"

He smiled as if her question showed definite interest on her part. "I want to buy the hotel back from you."

Brandy's anger clearly showed on her face. "This hotel is not for sale, Lorenzo, and even if it was, you would be the last person I would sell it to."

He frowned. "I can see that you still feel anger toward me."

She gave him a forced half-smile. "I don't feel anything toward you anymore, Lorenzo."

His frown deepened. "I've told you how much I regret what I did, Brandy. I was wrong to sleep with Jolene but she came on to me pretty strong at a very weak moment, so it really wasn't my fault."

Brandy could barely keep from cursing him out. That was Lorenzo for you, saying he was sorry in one breath, and in the next trying to lay the blame at someone else's feet.

"Look, Lorenzo, I'm not interested in selling the hotel. It belongs to me and I intend to keep it."

He leaned forward in his chair. "You'll ruin it."

She tried not to react to the harsh tone in his voice. "After a year and a half, I've done pretty damn good so far. And if I do ruin it, it's mine to ruin, isn't it?"

He shook his head. "And you despise me that much?"

Brandy glared at him. "Like I said earlier, I feel nothing for you. Whatever feelings I had for you were destroyed the moment I saw that videotape."

"And when was that, Brandy?"

She lifted an arched brow. "I beg your pardon?"

"I asked, when was that? I have reason to believe that you and your cousins orchestrated that entire ordeal at our reception. I started thinking about it and put two and two together. Everything that happened that day seemed a little too pat. And after talking to the guy who coordinated our wedding, he said he'd received explicit instructions from you to play a certain tape during the reception dinner. Do you know anything about that?"

Brandy smiled. "And if I did, so what? It was my wedding and I could request to show any videotape of my choosing. No one told you to be stupid enough to tape your lovemaking session with Jolene."

Anger, more than she had ever seen in him before, covered his face. "You set me up, didn't you?"

"You set your own self up by not being able to keep your pants zipped," she snapped, feeling her own anger take over. "You got exactly what you deserved."

"I don't appreciate what you did, Brandy," he said with a deep Jamaican accent that sent chills up her spine.

"And I didn't appreciate what you did either, Lorenzo. We have nothing to say to each other and I would appreciate it if you never come to this hotel again. It belongs to me and you're not welcome here."

"Not even as a paying customer?"

"Not even as a paying customer. There are plenty of hotels in this town to choose from and I'd rather you use one of them. The less I see of you the better."

Lorenzo stood slowly. "You'll regret the day you set me up, Brandy."

"And you'll regret the day you ever screwed around on me, Lorenzo. I deserved everything I got from our divorce."

Lorenzo glared at her one last time before finally walking out of the room and slamming the door behind him.

Brandy released a deep sigh, determined to pull herself together. Lorenzo was mad, angrier than she'd ever seen him before, but that was his problem and not hers.

She checked her watch. She had a number of things to check on before leaving for the airport. She would be flying to L.A. for her cousin Alexia's twin sons' birthday party. It was hard to believe they were two years old already.

Her thoughts then drifted back to the hotel. The St. Laurent was a beautiful and elegant hotel. She fully understood why Lorenzo hadn't wanted to part with it and why he wanted it back.

Not long after taking things over, Brandy had discovered that staffing was one of a hotel's most important management functions. It was essential to work with people she could depend on and trust, so Horace Thurgood, the man who had been manager for years when Lorenzo had run things, had done her a favor when he resigned, saying he didn't feel comfortable working for anyone but a member of the Ballentine family.

Thurgood's departure would have left her in a bind had it not been for Kathie Gaines, one of her college friends who happened to be a former hotel manager for the Marriott Corporation. Kathie had come highly recommended and out of friendship agreed to come work as hotel manager at the St. Laurent until Brandy was ready to take over the entire operation. Kathie had stayed on and helped out up until six months ago when she left for France to marry a guy who worked as a chef for one of the country's most renowned restaurants. Since then, Brandy had basically been on her own.

She knew that the key to her success as an entrepreneur was gaining both occupational and business skill with which to operate her business more efficiently and productively. She had taken a nine-month course, had gotten on-the-job training as a front desk clerk, housekeeper, bellhop, sports bar manager and chef. Today, before she left town, she intended to spend time with her sales director.

Brandy glanced around the room. Often she was tempted to pinch herself that this office was really hers and that she was in charge of running things. Usually things ran pretty smoothly, but it seemed that today was destined to be the day from hell.

It had started when she'd gotten up early, as she normally did, to take a tour of the hotel to see how things were going. She'd discovered that a conference room booked for a breakfast meeting for the Nurses Association of Florida had not been cleaned. With less than twenty minutes to get the room presentable or face a service breakdown or the possibility of losing the Association's future business, she had immedi-

ately placed a call to Wilbur Green, the hotel's food and beverage director. Apparently there had been some sort of mix-up in communication
with Wilbur and his staff, and the problem was rectified immediately.

A few hours later another problem had arisen when she received a
call that one of the hotel's elevators was malfunctioning. That was all
she needed with several large groups planning to check out that day. She
could only imagine the chaos of tired vacationers who were ready to go
home being delayed because an elevator was on the blink.

Brandy shook her head. Over the past year she had discovered that
customers demanded prompt and efficient service as a condition for
their continued patronage of hotels, and her aim was to please them.
She met with her staff every morning to brainstorm ways to guarantee
that her hotel would always provide a high level of service.

She flipped her calendar to the month of November. The St. Laurent
was one of the hosting hotels for the Florida Classic, the big rival football game between Bethune Cookman College and Florida A and M
University. Over a hundred thousand people were expected in town,
which meant hundreds of guests would be arriving expecting top-
notch service, which she and her staff intended to give them. Things
were going to be insane and she was going to love every minute of it.

She checked her watch again, knowing she had to get moving. She
had several meetings she needed to attend, including one with Roy Foster, her personnel manager, to discuss the extra staff she'd hired in
preparation for the Florida Classic. She also had a meeting with Perry
Hall, her security manager. He had called earlier stating there was a
matter he needed to discuss with her. She hoped nothing was wrong. If
there were any more screw-ups today, she really would scream.

Then again, she probably wouldn't. She was way too dignified, too
much of a professional to ever let loose like that. And she refused to get
stressed out over her mother. Valerie would have to deal with her own
problems with the Bennett family because Brandy had enough on her
plate. God knows her mother could be such a drama queen sometimes.

And as for Lorenzo's unexpected visit with an offer to buy the hotel, she hoped that he'd gotten her message loud and clear.

Her thoughts drifted to the dinner she'd had with Carla and Amber last week. While celebrating their individual successes, the three of them had shared moments in their pasts, and she couldn't help but admire how they had overcome very bad times in their lives. She appreciated Carla and Amber's friendship and enjoyed doing things with them like going shopping, going out to dinner, and taking in chick flicks. And they were totally honest when their opinions and thoughts were solicited. They didn't play games with each other, since they had been involved with men who'd played enough games with them to last a lifetime.

When she returned from California, it would be time for her monthly Savvy Sistahs Mean Business meeting. They tried to meet at least twice a month for their sistah-circle dinner. It was during those times that they focused on the challenges they faced in their relationships at work and at home, drawing on the experience and the wisdom they'd obtained to help each other out. Also, each time they met, someone was charged with bringing to the table some sort of principle they'd discovered for total emotional and spiritual fulfillment. It was something they had come to think of as "food for the soul." The sistah-circle was meant to uplift each of them and it always did. They talked about everything—their faith in God, their fear of failures, their fear of giving their hearts to the wrong man . . . again, and how to go about chipping away at the insecurities they each harbored.

The last time they'd met, Amber had been the one who'd brought the principle to the table, one they would dwell on for the remainder of the month and talk about again at the next meeting. The principle Amber had shared was one of true happiness. That night they had left the restaurant believing that you weren't actually free until you felt happy and secure within yourself, and that true happiness was something no one could ever take away from you.

What Brandy had told Lorenzo was true. She no longer felt anything for him. She had grown beyond that point in her life and was too busy trying to discover her own source of joy, true happiness, and contentment to waste time dwelling on all the pain he and Jolene had once caused her.

Beginning tomorrow, she would be spending a week with her cousins. As she picked up her briefcase and purse and headed for the door, a smile touched her lips. Although they made it a point to have a conference call at least once a week, it had been almost six months since she'd seen her cousins, and she was looking forward to seeing them again.

Brandy came down the stairs of her cousin Alexia's beautiful California beach home and entered the huge family room where most of the guests had gathered. She had arrived over an hour ago and had only taken time to freshen up. Alexia was a nationally known recording artist and was married to Quinn Masters, a highly successful entertainment attorney.

Glancing across the room she saw Alexia talking with some of her guests. Tall, dark, and breathtakingly stunning, Alexia Bennett-Masters looked and carried herself like a professional model and was the epitome of femininity. It was hard to believe that during her childhood there had been some family members who'd considered her the "ugly duckling," since she'd been born with skin darker than most Bennetts, and had unruly hair and a weight problem.

It was only when Brandy saw all the people in attendance that she remembered the birthday party was a joint affair. Alexia's husband Quinn's twin sister, Quinece, had also given birth to a set of twins, two beautiful girls, a week before Alexia, so the birthday party was for all four children.

Or was it a party for the adults, Brandy thought as she glanced around. In addition to a number of Bennett family members, it seemed that Quinn's entire family, the Masterses, were there. From attending Alexia and Quinn's wedding, she knew Quinn had come from a rather large family—seven siblings in all, who were spread all over the country. It seemed everyone had reunited to celebrate the birthdays of Quinn's and Quinece's offspring.

"You're all settled in?"

Brandy turned to her cousin Taye. Like Alexia and Rae'jean, Taye was her first cousin and the four of them were the same age. Michael, Taye's husband, was thirty-five and the adoptive grandson of Henry Bennett, her grandfather Ethan's first cousin. When Michael and Taye professed their love for each other almost three years ago, some members of the Bennett family had gone bonkers. Although Michael had been adopted into the Bennett family at birth, everyone had always considered him blood and in their minds a love affair between Taye and Michael was akin to incest. It was only after Grampa Ethan and Cousin Henry had given their blessings over the match that the family had accepted it and moved on.

Taye was the cousin everyone had considered "the smart one" while growing up. A math whiz, she now owned an accounting business in Atlanta. She was holding her eighteen-month-old son by the hand. She had named him Ethan Henry Bennett, in honor of Grampa Ethan and Cousin Henry.

"Yes, I finished unpacking," Brandy said in response to Taye's question. "The flight was rather rough to say the least." She looked at the little boy whose hand Taye held and studied his features, trying to determine if he looked more like Taye or Michael, and quickly decided he looked like the both of them. He had his father's forehead and lips and his mother's eyes and nose. "He's adorable, Taye."

Taye beamed proudly. "Thank you."

"How are the girls adjusting to him?" she asked of Taye's two teenage daughters, Sebrina and Monica, and of Michael's daughter, Kennedy.

Taye chuckled. "Oh, they're a big help until he poops in his diaper. Then they are quick to bring him back to me to take care of."

Brandy laughed. "You can't blame them there."

Taye shook her head. "No, I guess not."

"Don't get too close to that kid or you'll start looking like me," Rae'jean Bennett Garrison said as she joined the group.

Brandy looked at Rae'jean's pregnant state and smiled. Rae'jean had always been the one everybody in the family considered "the pretty one" with her light-skinned features and naturally straight medium brown hair. A cardiologist who lived in Boston, Rae'jean was married to Ryan Garrison, a private investigator who specialized in missing persons. The two had met when Rae'jean had begun a come-hell-or-high-water search for her biological father. Now she was happily married with a baby less than a year old and another one on the way.

"I don't think you have to worry about that," Brandy said, grinning. "I can't remember the last time I was involved with a man. I've been too busy."

"A Bennett not serious about a man? You're kidding," Alexia said, coming to join the group. "I thought I was the only Bennett who could play that game. At least until I met Quinn."

A concerned glint appeared in Taye's eyes as she gazed at Brandy. "I hope you don't plan to cut all men out of your life just because of what Lorenzo did, Brandy. I went through a similar thing after finding out that Monica's father was a married man. I thought all men were liars, cheaters, and the scum of the earth. It took me ten years to find out how wrong I'd been in thinking that way."

"I haven't become a man-hater, Taye. I'm just not ready to get seriously involved with anyone. I want to be by myself for a while, to get to know the real Brandy Bennett."

"And after you get to know the real Brandy Bennett, then what?" Rae'jean asked, eyeing her curiously.

Brandy smiled as she remembered the last conversation she'd had with her grandfather and the things he had asked her to consider. She had called to tell him she had broken off her on-the-rebound engagement to Grant and that she had accepted a teaching position in Singapore. He had told her that there was no place she could run to for happiness until she was happy with herself. After talking to him that night, she had decided not to take the teaching position and instead stay in the States and take control of her own destiny. That was when she'd made the decision to manage and operate her hotel.

"After getting to know the real me, then maybe I can find true happiness," she said, finally answering Rae'jean's question. "This has nothing to do with Lorenzo but is all about me. I need to figure out what will make me happy and content. I'm striving to become a take-charge woman, a woman who's strong, self-reliant, and, more than anything, self-confident. I don't want to be a need-a-man kind of woman," she said softly. "I've been there and done that."

"Then my prayer is that you find true happiness, Brandy," Rae'jean said, reaching out and giving Brandy a hug.

"Ours, too," Alexia and Taye chimed in, also giving her hugs.

Brandy sighed deeply when they released her. It was times like this that it was hard to believe that while growing up they didn't get along. Rae'jean, Taye, and Alexia had always been close, but thanks to her mother Valerie, Brandy had always felt like a step-cousin. That insecurity had always kept the four of them at odds with each other.

"Okay, this is not the time to get sentimental," Rae'jean said, wiping a tear.

"Yeah, but I bet Grampa Ethan and Gramma Idella are in heaven smiling from ear to ear. They'd always wanted peace, harmony, and love between us, you know."

Yes, Brandy did know, and she was glad that her grandparents' wish had truly come to pass.

A few minutes later, Brandy found herself alone when Quinn, Ryan, and Michael came to claim their wives for some task or another. She then caught sight of her brother in the swimming pool. She and Victor Junior, who was three years older than she, had the same father but different mothers. He was a married man but still managed to take the word *player* to another level. From the looks of things it seemed that he had conveniently left his wife at home.

Brandy was crossing the room to refill her punch glass when she happened to notice a man whose profile was toward her. He was standing alone on the patio watching the kids play in the pool. She wondered who he was, and when he leaned against a wall she had an unsettling thought of just how alone he appeared. He turned slightly and she got a better look at him, and the resemblance to Quinn was astounding. He was definitely a good-looking man and the woman in her couldn't help but appreciate just how good he looked.

"It's good seeing you again, Brandy."

Brandy shifted her gaze from the intriguing gentleman to the woman who'd come to stand next to her at the punch bowl. She smiled. "It's good seeing you again, too, Quinece. I can't believe how big the twins have gotten," she said of the two little girls who were sitting at the edge of the pool with their father.

Quinece smiled. "Yeah, they're growing up rather quickly. It seems like I just gave birth to them yesterday and now they're two years old already."

Brandy glanced at the man standing alone on the patio and cleared her throat. "That guy over there in the jeans and blue shirt, he has to be your brother but I don't recall meeting him at Alexia and Quinn's wedding," she said.

Quinece's gaze followed hers and a sad smile touched her lips. "Yes, that's my brother Grey. He's a year older than me and Quinn, and for the longest time everyone thought that he and Quinn were the twins since they look so much alike."

Quinece then released a sigh. "He wasn't at the wedding because a month before it took place, his wife was killed in a car accident. Grey took Gloria's death hard and hasn't been himself since then. He blames himself for her death."

At Brandy's questioning gaze, Quinece said, "Grey was a FBI agent at the time, head of an undercover operation to expose this international baby-selling ring. He'd been away from home for quite a while and his absences had always been a sore spot with Gloria. He had planned to return a few days before the accident but got detained. She was on her way to visit a friend when the accident happened. Of course Grey feels had he come home when he was supposed to, the accident wouldn't have happened."

Quinece blinked back her tears. "And although all of us have tried convincing him that that may not have been the case, he still feels responsible for her death." She smiled that same sad smile again. "Grey used to be the life of any Masters party." She shrugged. "Now, he's like a stranger. Chances are he'll be gone before the day is over."

Brandy nodded, not knowing what to say as a rush of sorrow ran through her. And here she thought she had problems.

"Excuse me for a second," Quinece was saying. "Kendall is summoning me over. Evidently one or both of the girls are in need of a potty break. I'll chat with you later."

Brandy nodded as she watched Quinece cross the patio to her husband, Kendall, who handed her one of the twins. She then turned her attention back to Grey Masters. A shiver touched her and her breath caught in her throat when she saw he had turned and was looking directly at her. His eyes were dark, penetrating, and she was suddenly flooded with a sensation that totally unnerved her.

She drew in a deep, steadying breath as her pulse began to race, and she inwardly asked herself what there was about the man that was jarring her senses, her mind . . . and her body. The undeniably disconcerting effect he had on her made her want to run for cover. He wasn't smiling nor was he frowning. His expression was unreadable, distant, and impersonal; yet she could not downplay the tingling of desire he elicited from deep within her. It may have been one-sided, but it was something she hadn't felt in a long time.

Finally he turned away, presenting his back to her. She quickly took a sip of her punch and tried to shake off the disturbing feeling that Grey Masters was definitely a dangerous man to any woman's well-being.

She heard one of the kids let out a chilling scream as they jumped into the pool, and turned to make sure no one was hurt. A few seconds later when she glanced back she noticed that Grey Masters was gone.

A week later Brandy was back in Orlando. She entered her office, kicked off her shoes, and dropped her briefcase on the floor. At the moment she didn't give a royal flip that it was a Louis Vuitton, one of a kind that she had paid well over a thousand dollars for. She was too mad to think about it.

She had just ended a lengthy meeting with Wilbur Green, her food and beverage manager. They were not seeing eye to eye. Brandy wanted the poolside snack bar's hours extended, since from the written feedback she had gotten from hotel guests, the change in hours would have made their stay at the St. Laurent more pleasurable. But Wilbur Green felt that, like in the past, they would put out more money to operate the snack bar than they would bring in.

Brandy sighed deeply. Evidently somewhere in the mix of things Wilbur had forgotten that she was the one who made the final decisions on what she wanted and didn't want for the hotel; further, it seemed the man lacked vision. Every time she made a suggestion he quickly followed it with a "But Mr. Ballentine never did it that way." She'd had to keep a firm grip on her lips to stop from saying anything that would make her openly clash with the man. She had appreciated his opinions but he had to realize that she was the one in charge, not Lorenzo. And she had the final word.

Brandy was bending down to pick her briefcase up off the floor when she saw a vase holding a single red rose sitting in the center of her desk. She smiled, thinking that someone was glad she was back from California and had been thoughtful.

Walking over to her desk, she lifted the vase and took a sniff of the red rose. It smelled heavenly. She placed the vase back down on her desk and picked up the card that had been left beside it.

She quickly opened it, and moments later her hands began to shake.

Welcome back. I've missed you. I think it's time you know that I've been watching you for quite some time and I like what I see. I want you and I will have you.

The Man

✺ Chapter 2 ✺

Carla

"Will there be anything else, Ms. Osborne?"

Carla smiled, her expression thoughtful as she tilted her head back. It had been a long day and she was looking forward to its ending. "Yes, one other thing. I still have to make a decision about James Mason's party."

Her secretary, Michelle Winthrop, nodded as she placed her writing pad aside. Michelle had started working as her secretary last year and had come highly recommended from her retiring secretary, Ora Hansberry. Ora had been with the company longer than anyone, starting out as Carla's father, Craig Osborne's, secretary right out of high school. Michelle was Ora's granddaughter, so of course she would have nothing but high praise for her. But Michelle had the goods to back up the praise. She had attended two years of junior college and was now attending night classes at the University of Central Florida to obtain a degree in Business Administration. The two of them worked well together and Michelle was turning out to be as efficient a secretary as her grandmother had been.

"Yes, you do," Michelle said, breaking into Carla's thoughts. "And I'd like to be so bold as to suggest that you attend. All the new minority business owners in the area will be attending. If you must, think of attending as an investment in Osborne Computer Network's future. But seriously, you really do need to get out and enjoy yourself more."

Carla couldn't help but chuckle. Michelle's calm, ever professional and efficient manner had slipped into that of a concerned employee as she stated a concern that a number of her other employees shared as well: the fact that their boss spent a lot of time at the office and didn't have much of a social life. But what she'd tried to convince them of for the past two years—although they refused to buy it—was the fact that her two-year-old son, Craig, provided her with all the social life she needed.

"When is the last day to send out the RSVP?" Carla asked as she toyed with her pen. Attending the affair meant leaving Craig with a sitter for an entire weekend, and although she'd done so when she'd had out-of-town business trips, she'd always seen those trips as more of a necessity. This was a beach party. Even if it was being thrown by James Mason.

"Tomorrow."

Carla smiled. "Then I'll make my decision by tomorrow and if needed, a courier can deliver it to him."

Michelle nodded as she stood. "If there's nothing else I'll get back to those reports. They'll be ready for you to review in a few hours."

"Thanks, Michelle. As always, I appreciate your hard work."

Moments later Carla took her coffee cup firmly in hand, stood, and walked over to the huge window in her office that gave her a majestic view of downtown Orlando.

As she sipped her coffee, her mind went back to cover the past two and a half years; specifically, the day the board of directors had voted her in as president to take over the day-to-day management of the business her father had started forty-five years ago. She had made a quick decision not to liquidate the company or sell out, but to roll up her sleeves and do whatever was necessary to assure the success of her father's legacy.

Like she'd told Brandy and Amber at dinner the other night, there had never been any closeness between her, her mother, and her brother, Clark. With her father it had been a totally different story. It may have been Clark who her mother always doted on, but everyone knew that Carla had been the apple of her father's eye, and even five years after his death she still missed him greatly. He'd been everything a father should be, and she had loved him dearly.

Her body shivered in anger when she remembered Clark's refusal to include her in the family business after their father's death. He had inherited the company and said she was better suited as a teacher in a classroom. Not surprisingly, her mother had agreed. But Clark's death had changed everything.

Her mother had been angered beyond belief to discover Carla had used her stock shares to vote against Dalton Gregory, the man Clark had pegged as his successor. But nothing had upset Madeline Osborne more than to discover her daughter pregnant without the benefit of a husband. But what had angered Madeline to the point that Carla thought she would have a stroke was Carla's decision not to reveal the identity of the man who had fathered her child, as well as refusing to contact the man and let him know she had gotten pregnant. For some reason Madeline felt the man had a right to know and that Carla was doing an injustice not telling him. Carla had appreciated her mother's opinion, but for the life of her she couldn't understand why Madeline had been so hell-bent on such a thing. The only reason Carla could come up with regarding this particular obsession of her mother's was that she had wanted to control Carla's every thought and decision the same way she had Clark's.

Since Craig's birth, her mother had cut ties with her. But that didn't keep Carla from hearing about her mother's activities. Last year Madeline had gotten remarried to a much younger man, one ten years younger.

Carla sighed. The way her mother lived her life was not her concern, but she couldn't accept Madeline not wanting to have a relationship with her grandson, no matter how she felt about her daughter. Turning her back on Craig was inexcusable. Carla religiously sent her mother pictures of Craig in hopes that one day Madeline would accept and embrace her grandson for the precious jewel that he was.

Carla's smile widened when she thought of her son, her pride and joy. It had been a challenge to raise Craig while working her tail off trying to get Osborne Computer Network back on its feet while retaining a position in the computer industry. But it had been well worth it. Craig was a well adjusted, much loved two-year-old and her company had shown tremendous profits over the past year. The Disney contract they'd been awarded had been a big financial boost. As a result, they had needed larger, more modern facilities. As a business move for future growth, Osborne Computer Network sold their old building and invested in a new facility right smack in the middle of Orlando's mega business district.

Thirty additional employees had been added to the staff of hardworking individuals. Everyone who worked for the company continued to be dedicated and loyal, and as their president she continued to put their welfare and best interest first, assuring that their future with Osborne remained intact.

Taking another sip of her coffee, her smile widened as she again thought of the one thing that had some of her employees concerned— her love life. She had to constantly remember that Osborne Computer Network was an old, established firm with a number of old and established employees, some of whom saw themselves as more than merely her employees. They saw themselves as honorary aunts and uncles, but always gave her the respect she deserved as their boss. However, there was some concern among them that there had not been a serious man in her life in over two years.

Her mother had been the only one who'd acted like the very idea of her being single and pregnant was the ultimate sin. Her father's former employees, rooted and firmly embedded in tradition and convention, hadn't blinked an eye at the announcement of her pregnancy, and had been there to give her support when her own mother hadn't. After all, little Craig Osborne was their former boss's grandson, and in most of their eyes her father had nearly walked on water. He had been just that loved and admired.

Carla's face softened when she again thought of Craig. Her son meant the world to her and one day she would turn the running of Osborne Computer Network over to him. She loved her role as his mother and was determined to be to him the kind of mother she'd always wanted as a child and never had.

She frowned when another person entered her thoughts, Craig's father, Jesse Devereau. She always thought of him when she looked at her son, and the one thing she remembered was that he was jaw-droppingly handsome. The force of awareness and attraction that had consumed her when she'd first seen him had been stunning. She had taken in everything about him, from the solid muscles outlined in the business suit he'd been wearing to the straight black hair that had been secured at the base of his neck. His skin tone had been that of a roasted almond, and his features were compelling and stark; it had been easy to tell that he was an interracial offspring.

The older Craig got, the more his features resembled those of Jesse, all the way down to the hazel eyes, so she could never forget her one-night fling with a man who'd made a lasting impression, both physically and emotionally, on her life.

Carla nearly jumped when she heard her phone ring. Crossing the room back to her desk she quickly picked it up. "Yes, Michelle?"

"Ms. Morrison is on the line for you, Ms. Osborne."

"Thanks, please put her through."

Carla snapped off her clip earring as she placed the phone to the other ear. Sonya was her best friend since childhood and Craig's god-mother. Everyone who knew them claimed that she and Sonya were as different as black and white, night and day, and wondered how their friendship had lasted for so many years.

Carla smiled. She had to admit that Sonya was known to do a number of wild and crazy things, but she had cherished and always would cherish their friendship. Sonya knew her better than anyone. She knew her joys and her pains, and more important, Sonya had always been there for her.

Sonya worked for a large marketing firm and her job often included a lot of travel. "Sonya? Hey, girl, what's going on?"

"A whole lot of nothing. I was calling to see if you wanted to go to the movies tonight. Mom said she would be glad to watch Craig if you're interested."

Carla lowered her gaze to the calendar on her desk. "I wish I could, but the Savvy Sistahs meeting is tonight and Brandy, Amber, and I have made plans to go somewhere afterwards for dinner and later to a movie. Of course you can join us if you'd like," she said, feeling really bad. The last couple of times Sonya had called for them to get together she'd had other plans.

"No, I don't want to go anywhere with you, Brandy, and Amber. They seem to take up a lot of your time these days and here I thought *I* was your best friend."

Aw, hell, Carla thought as she sat down in the chair behind her desk. Her friendship with Brandy and Amber continued to be a sore spot with Sonya. Sonya tried to monopolize her time and hadn't understood Carla's need to devote as much time as she could to her business, which included getting to know other business owners and networking with them. And she absolutely refused to understand Carla's friendship with Brandy and Amber. For some reason she saw Carla's close relationship with them as a threat to their friendship, which was something Carla just couldn't understand. She knew that Sonya had been going through a lot lately with the recent breakup of her parents' marriage as well as Sonya's own inability to find what she considered the perfect mate, but Carla wished her friend would just chill and stop being so possessive. Her and Sonya's friendship spanned years and as far as she was concerned was as tight as tight could be. They had always been there for each other and always would be. But if reassurance was what Sonya needed then that's what she would give her.

"Sonya, you're my best friend, you know that. There were days when I couldn't have made it without you being there for me."

"Well, you sometimes act like you've forgotten that," Sonya snapped.

"Hold on, Sonya," Carla said gently. "That's not fair. You know the hard work I've put into managing the company as well as the time I try to spend with Craig. I can't just up and drop everything whenever you call. Come on, look at things from my point of view. Just because we're close friends don't mean we have to always be in each other's pockets, does it?"

"No, but why is it that you have to spend so much time with Brandy and Amber? You know how I feel about them."

Carla rubbed her temple. "Yes, and I still can't understand why you do. They're nice people and you should give yourself the chance to get to know them."

"I don't have to get to know them. I know a lot of women like them. They're women who think they're all that and a bag of chips; women who got it going on and probably never had a bad day in their lives; women who think they're God's gift to men."

Carla shook her head, thinking just how wrong Sonya was about Brandy and Amber. She couldn't help but admire them for having the tenacity to turn things around. Like her, they were trying each day to focus their efforts on getting their lives back together, as well as running their own businesses. She knew Sonya wouldn't understand that. All her life she'd been pampered by her parents and quite frankly, at the moment, the last thing Carla wanted to hear was Sonya bitch and moan about two people she evidently knew nothing about and refused to get to know. Brandy and Amber had been more than friendly with Sonya, although more than once they had picked up on her unfriendly attitude toward them. Yet they had ignored her impoliteness, mainly because Sonya was Carla's good friend.

Whenever Sonya was in one of her funky moods there was no getting through to her. "Look, if your mother is willing to watch Craig tomorrow night then I'll be more than happy to go to the movies with you. How does that sound?"

"That's fine if that's the only time you can squeeze me into your busy schedule. There *are* some things going on in my life that I need to talk to you about."

Carla inhaled deeply. She didn't like the thought of having someone watch Craig two nights in a row, but it seemed like Sonya had a lot on her mind. "How about if we do dinner first and a movie afterwards? I can ask Michelle to keep Craig if your mother isn't free tomorrow."

"Sure . . . whatever," were Sonya's last words before she hung up the phone.

"Mommy, Mommy!"

Carla leaned down and picked up her son, who had raced to her the moment she opened the door. She hugged him tight, thinking she would never tire of holding him in her arms, although he was no longer a baby.

At two years old, Craig Osborne was as rambunctious as any child his age should be. He always amazed her with his unfailing abundance of energy.

"Were you a good boy today?"

"Yes, Mommy, I was good," he said quickly, his hazel eyes shining brightly.

Carla lifted a brow. Usually when he was that quick to respond that meant that he hadn't been good at all. "And where is Mrs. Boston?"

"She's picking up my toys."

Carla frowned. "I thought I told you that you're responsible for picking up your own toys, Craig. And how did the potty training go today?" she asked, when she noticed he was wearing a diaper. She'd heard that boys were harder to potty train than girls but felt that when it came to that task, Craig was deliberately downright lazy. People often commented on how well he was able to put together sentences for a two-year-old, but for some reason he couldn't put together the words to let her and Mrs. Boston know when it was time for him to go potty.

"All right, Craig, I want you to go help Mrs. Boston gather up your toys," she said, putting him down. Taking his hand, she allowed him to lead her to the family room.

Barbara Boston was down on her hands and knees gathering up building blocks and toy trucks. The older woman, who had once been her parents' neighbor, used to babysit Carla when she was a child and still got around pretty good for her age of sixty-eight. She was wonderful with Craig just like she'd always been wonderful with Carla; she had given her more time and attention than her own mother had.

"Mrs. Boston, I thought we agreed that Craig has to pick up his own toys. He has to learn to follow rules."

The older woman glanced up and smiled. "Yes, but he's just a baby, Carla. Besides, I don't mind doing it. However, I promise to start making him pick up after himself after he gets the potty training down."

Carla shook her head. At this rate potty training would take forever. She glanced at her watch. She would spend time with her son before getting dressed for the Savvy Sistahs Mean Business meeting. Tonight they had a guest speaker, a woman who had started her own publishing company a few years ago.

Carla watched as her son got down on the floor to help Mrs. Boston. For the second time that day she thought of Jesse, and decided that no matter how she felt about him, she would always appreciate him giving her Craig.

❧ Chapter 3 ❧

Amber

$\mathcal{A}$mber always thought that no other town could compare to Nashville, but after living in Orlando for a little over two years, she'd discovered she was wrong. There was something pleasing that could be said about the central Florida town that she now considered home. At a time in her life when she had needed to make a change and leave her problems behind, Orlando, with its friendliness and charm, had been just the place.

As she went about restocking the shelves in her bookstore, she couldn't help but remember the day her mother and sisters had approached her about coming to Florida to check on Aunt Rachel's house. Aunt Rachel, their mother's only sister, who'd never been married or had any children, had died three years before and had willed her home to her four nieces. Since neither Amber nor any of her sisters had been interested in relocating to Florida, they had rented the house out and split the proceeds between them each month. But their most recent renter had been the tenant from hell, who thought it was his right to pay his rent whenever he felt like it. After trying to work with the man for over six months, giving him as many chances as possible to catch up on the late rent payments, they'd had no choice but to take drastic steps and have him evicted.

Amber had flown to Orlando to handle the legal matters and had discovered the beautiful home was badly in need of major repairs. She had returned to Nashville with her report, along with several photographs, as well as an offer to her sisters: she wanted to buy the dilapidated piece of property and was willing to procure their share of the house to become the sole owner.

Amber had been dying a slow death in Nashville. Most of the time she was so depressed over her divorce that she'd found comfort in eating, which only escalated her health problems.

She saw moving permanently to Orlando as the answer to her prayers. Besides, she no longer wanted to remain in the same town where her ex-husband, Gary Stuart, also lived. She had never told anyone in her family but he had shown up late one night at her place, and with only a few kind words from him, she'd forgotten what a dog he was and let him get inside her panties. The next morning he'd left, acting like he had done her a favor and saying she was sex-crazed, hot between the legs. She'd felt cheap and stupid for falling off the wagon and saw distance between them as the only thing to help her get over Gary.

Although her family hadn't been happy at the thought of her leaving Nashville and moving to Orlando, they had understood her need to make a new life for herself and gave her their blessings.

Now, over two years later, she had lost over sixty pounds, which meant her health was the best it had been in years. Being overweight had not been a size issue for her but a health issue, since diabetes ran in her family. Now she maintained good physical fitness by walking at least three miles each morning, something her doctor had highly recommended.

She had done a number of major repairs to the house she now considered home and was the proud owner of Amber's Books and Gifts, which was located in the Florida Mall. Her shop sold books by and about people of African descent, various figurines, greeting cards and calendars, children's books, games, black history literature, and Masonic, fraternity, and sorority paraphernalia, as well as a number of other gift ideas. Because the mall was usually busy on any day of the week, the shop reaped the benefits of its location, and with a small business loan through the city, she'd recently expanded and had decorated it just the way she wanted. She had discovered that she was a natural at dealing with the many customers who came through her doors, some to make a purchase and others just to browse and check out her vast inventory.

Her store hours mirrored those of the mall's hours, which meant she opened at ten each morning and closed at ten each night. Those hours were no problem for her since she lived five miles from the mall. It also helped that she had two very dependable ladies who assisted her. They were older ladies, both in their sixties, who were retired librarians and loved books.

In a few weeks the store would be celebrating its second anniversary. Already she'd made plans to host a party. Nothing extravagant, but just a little something to let her customers know how much she appreciated their business. Her menu would be simple and several of the distributors she dealt with had agreed to provide free books as giveaways.

Amber glanced down at her watch. It was edging toward five o'clock and she needed to get home to shower and change. There was the monthly Savvy Sistahs Mean Business meeting tonight, as well as dinner afterward with Brandy and Carla.

She smiled when she thought of her friendship with Brandy and Carla. Someone once told her that Philadelphia was the City of Brotherly Love. If that was true then Orlando deserved an award for being the City of Sisterly Love. It had been totally refreshing at her first Savvy Sistahs meeting to become acquainted with Carla and Brandy, and to discover as their friendship progressed that they were women who enjoyed being single and weren't hard-pressed to find a man. From the beginning, they had felt an intrinsic need to bond and it had been special to get validation and support from sistahs who'd had similar circumstances in their pasts. However, it hadn't been until their dinner a few weeks ago that she had discovered what those circumstances had been and why her friends, like her, had been standoffish when it came to a brother. All three had had bad experiences with men, but instead of dwelling and wallowing in self-pity, they had found the inner strength and peace to put it behind them and move on. They enjoyed the growth of realizing that there was more to being a woman than getting wrapped up in a man.

She glanced over to where her staff members, Jennifer Claymore and Eileen Brogan, were standing, erecting a huge floor display of the latest romance novels that had arrived that week. She knew the two were die-hard romantics who usually tried to talk any customer who claimed not to read romance novels into trying one. They had even talked her into reading one, and she had to admit she'd rather enjoyed it, although while reading she kept thinking it was pure fantasy and that real life was totally different. But still, it had been a wonderful way to pass a few hours, to rest her mind and escape. She figured there was nothing wrong with wanting to believe that there was some handsome, drop-dead gorgeous man out there who could sweep a woman off her feet and who actually treated a woman like a queen.

"Don't forget I'm leaving early tonight," she called out to Jennifer and Eileen.

Eileen raised a brow. "Got a hot date?"

Amber smiled. At sixty-four the woman liked getting the scoop on Amber's love life—or lack of it. At first it had irked her but now she simply ignored it. She knew Eileen meant well and managed to take both Eileen's and Jennifer's lectures to heart. They lived by the theory that when you were young you were supposed to enjoy life to the fullest, married or unmarried—but preferably married. It wasn't until their age that you sat back and savored the memories or created some new ones.

Jennifer, at sixty, was a widow but had a constant companion by the name of Moses Lakestone and Eileen had been married for over forty years. Both women embraced life and looked upon Amber the same way they would their granddaughters.

But Amber felt that she knew more than anyone else what was best for her. Neither woman had been married to Gary Stuart, so they would never understand her reluctance to get involved with another man. Establishing a relationship took hard work and she didn't have the time or the desire to do that.

"Sorry to disappoint you but there's no date. My Savvy Sistahs meeting is tonight and later Carla, Brandy, and I are going to dinner and possibly take in a movie."

"No men?"

Amber couldn't stop the smile that began to play around her mouth. "No, there won't be any men. The three of us have sworn off the opposite sex."

"That doesn't mean you're all turning gay does it?" Eileen asked with concern etched on her face.

Amber couldn't help but chuckle. "No, it means we've all been through hell with the male species and don't need or want any more of the aggravation."

"All men aren't jerks, Amber. My Henry is wonderful," Eileen said with a firm conviction in her voice.

"Then consider yourself blessed. And I don't mean to sound like I'm grouping all men into the same category as my ex-husband, but at the moment I have a lot going on in my life and don't have the time to devote to a relationship, or at least to making one work."

"You would think differently if the right man came along," Jennifer said with a twinkle in her eye.

Amber shrugged as she grabbed her purse from behind the counter. Maybe Carla and Brandy would feel that way but she wouldn't. By staying away from men she was trying to prove a point to herself: that she was not the sex-crazed, hot-between-the-legs person Gary had accused her of being. She had been celibate for over two years and was damn proud of it. There was more to life than great sex. She had a thriving business, a neat house she enjoyed decorating, and according to her doctor she was now as healthy as an ox and had achieved the weight loss she needed to stay that way. As far as she was concerned, for the first time ever her life was in perfect order, and she didn't need a man messing things up.

❧ Chapter 4 ❧

I think I'm having a real moment here," Amber said, smiling at Carla. "I like what you just said about inner joy and peace. Just this afternoon I was talking to Jennifer and Eileen, and they're under the misconception that you need a man in your life to make you happy. But from the principle you've presented, a person is the source of their own fulfillment, right?"

Carla couldn't help but grin. "It depends on what type of fulfillment you're talking about. The only thing I'm saying is that no one, man or woman, should be dependent on anyone else to make them happy. They're accountable for their own happiness and the less dependent on others you are, then the more free as a human being you'll feel and become."

Amber's smile widened. "Hey, that's deep."

"Yeah, I thought so too while I was reading the book and I couldn't wait to share it with the two of you."

Carla then turned her attention to Brandy, who she noticed was still picking at her food. "You've been awfully quiet tonight. Is anything wrong?"

Brandy's gaze darted from her plate to Carla, then to Amber. From the look on Amber's face Brandy knew she'd been thinking the same thing, but Carla had asked first. She hadn't added much to their discussion on emotional and spiritual fulfillment, and all through the Savvy Sistahs meeting she'd been unusually quiet. She was known to stir up conversation in a group discussion. But her mind was still on the note she had found in her office that afternoon.

She sighed, wondering if she should tell Carla and Amber, and knew she had to tell someone. Once they read the note maybe they could convince her there was nothing to be concerned about—it was just a prank.

"Someone left a rose in my office today while I was out attending meetings. There was also a note." The slight tremor in her voice got both women's attention.

"What did the note say?" Carla asked softly.

Brandy reached into her purse and pulled it out. She handed it to Carla, who read it then passed it to Amber. Both women met her gaze and Brandy could tell they would not assure her that there was nothing to be concerned about.

"What did you do about this? Did you alert security? Did you call the police?" Amber's outraged voice held anger as well as concern. Before she could respond Carla hit Brandy with another question, her eyes wide and dark.

"Do you have any idea who 'The Man' is?"

Brandy shook her head. "No, I didn't alert security nor did I call the police, and I have no idea who 'The Man' is."

"I can understand why you hesitated to call the police, but why didn't you alert security?" Carla wanted to know. "This isn't your typical secret-admirer letter. This note is downright threatening, and how did this person get into your office anyway?"

Brandy rubbed her temple. That was the same question she had asked herself several times over the course of the evening. The only answer she could come up with, since there hadn't appeared to be any signs of forced entry, was that the person had a key to her office, which

meant 'The Man' could be just about anyone. There were several people, including members of the maintenance crew and housekeeping,
who had keys to her office.

"I think it's someone who's trying to scare me," Brandy said, meeting Carla and Amber's gazes. "And I hate to admit that it's working."

Carla frowned. "Why would anyone want to scare you? Who would
benefit from doing such a thing?"

"Lorenzo for one. He came to the hotel two weeks ago asking that I
sell it to him. I turned him down and told him not to come back. He
left pretty upset."

Amber nodded. "Do you think he would pull something like this?"

Brandy sighed. She wasn't real sure of anything. "I don't know,
Amber. Right now I can't think straight. That note has me off kilter."

"You should have told your security guy. This is something you
should take seriously, Brandy," Carla said in a worried tone.

"And I agree," Amber chimed in.

Brandy nodded, knowing they were both right. "I was hoping it was
just a joke and this would be the end of it."

"And if it's not?" Carla asked seriously.

"Then I'll talk with the man over security at the hotel."

Amber took a sip of her wine. "If I were you I'd watch my back.
Reading that note gave me the creeps."

"Yeah, it gave me the creeps as well," Carla added.

Brandy nodded again. It had given her more than the creeps—it
had downright scared the hell out of her. The thought that there was
some man who wanted her in a demented way was very unsettling.
"Let's not talk about it any more tonight."

"But you will alert security if anything like this happens again?"

Brandy forced a smile to her lips. "Yes, I'll alert them. I promise."

The town known as "The World's Best Playground" was certainly living
up to its name tonight, Sonya Morrison thought as she glanced around

the rowdy, crowded establishment. Sylvester's was a well-known bar and grill that served high-class drinks, and usually when a woman came in alone it meant only one thing . . . that tonight she was ripe for the picking. Two men had already approached Sonya but she wasn't a fool, and a quick look at their left hands had shown the indentation of where wedding rings were supposed to be. One thing she didn't do was married men—no matter how hard up she was.

She inwardly fumed. Tonight was not going as she had planned. When she couldn't get Carla to agree to go out with her she had decided to do a solo act. Damn, her mother was driving her bonkers. Even after a year Peggy Morrison could not believe that her husband of thirty years had left her for a much younger woman, promptly destroying her self-esteem and confidence and leaving her bitter, argumentative, mean, and hateful. And the sad thing was that Sonya had her own problems to deal with and was in no mood to deal with her mother's.

She was catching hell at work with her new boss, who seemed to find fault in everything she did; the last couple of men she'd dated had turned out to be total assholes; and she was discovering she no longer had a best friend, at least not one she could count on in times of trouble. Everything had changed since Carla had taken over her family's business. All her concentration was focused on being a good mommy and a good boss. Somewhere in the mix she had forgotten all about being a good friend.

Things had gotten worse when Carla became friends with Brandy Bennett and Amber Stuart. She wasn't any fun like she used to be and was always talking about true peace, surrendering to life's flow, your development as a human being and all that kind of crap. And to make matters worse, according to Carla the three of them had sworn off men, who they felt were the root of their problems. Hell, as far as Sonya was concerned the only thing Carla, Brandy, and Amber needed was to get laid.

She smiled wickedly. A night of good sex with the right man could clear your mind of just about anything. Who would want to stimulate their mind with words when they could stimulate their body with sexual gratification of the most provoking kind?

Sonya glanced down at her glass, wanting another drink. She'd had one too many and doubted that if she ordered another she would get it. Bars were getting downright paranoid about serving too many drinks to people who were driving, and she could tell from the look the bartender was giving her that he felt she'd had enough. Hell, he'd even offered to call her a cab. She frowned wondering what his problem was. He didn't have to worry about her getting rowdy or boisterous or anything like that. She knew how to act decorously, dignified even while in a drunken stupor.

"Fancy seeing you here tonight, Miss Morrison."

Sonya glanced up and gazed into the face of the tall man who stood over her with a beer bottle in his hand. She recognized him immediately and smiled flirtatiously. "I could say the same thing about you, Mr. Gregory."

Of all people, the last one she wanted to see tonight was Dalton Gregory. He had been college friends with Carla's brother Clark and had been brought into the family business even when Carla had been denied such a right. Everyone knew that Clark had been grooming Dalton to be the vice president of Osborne Computer Network, but upon Clark's death, the stockholders had decided otherwise and voted for Carla to take over things. Dalton was a sore loser and to this day couldn't stand the ground Carla walked on.

Dalton gave her a confident smile. He then glanced around the room. "And where's your side-kick?"

Sonya's smile widened and she decided to dig into him a little. "I guess you mean Carla, the woman who ended up getting the job you thought you had under lock and key?"

Dalton frowned. "Yeah, that's the one," he said, taking a sip of his beer.

Sonya's smile was suddenly replaced with a frown. "Oh, she ditched me tonight to have dinner with her gay friends."

Dalton lifted a brow, his curiosity piqued. "You don't say."

"Hell, yeah, I do say but forget about it. I was only joking." Sonya turned back to her empty glass. "Get lost, Dalton, and go back to whatever rock you crawled from up under. I'm not in the mood."

Dalton set his beer on the counter in front of him, then slid into the seat next to her. "Hey, a woman alone in Sylvester's usually means they *are* in the mood. You're smart enough to know that."

She turned around on the stool and met his gaze head on. "You think so?"

"Yes, I know so. You're a highly intelligent woman."

Sonya's lips tilted into a smile. "Hey, Dalton, you're an all-right guy, up-front and straightforward. I like that. And at the moment I can't rightly recall why I never liked you."

Dalton leaned back against the bar stool and met Sonya's curious gaze. "Probably because your friend doesn't like me."

Sonya chuckled. "Oh, yeah, that's right. Carla can't stand you. She thought you were a total jerk and a bad influence on Clark. And because she didn't like you, neither did I. But I've recently discovered that Carla doesn't have a good sense of character when it comes to people, so I'd like to wipe the slate clean and form my own opinion about you."

Dalton chuckled as he took another sip of his beer. "That sounds fair to me. How about if I order you another drink to celebrate our getting to know each other better?"

Sonya smiled. "Sounds like a workable plan, but Mr. Bartender won't do it. He knows I'm driving and I've had one too many already."

A smile tilted both corners of Dalton's mouth. "Don't worry about it. I'll convince him that I'll make sure you get home safely."

Sonya gave him another flirtatious smile, leaned back in her seat and crossed her legs. "Yeah, you do that."

Dalton Gregory smiled as he listened to Sonya chat endlessly away. Ply a woman with alcohol and she'll have loose lips. And he had to admit they were a nice pair of loose lips. There had been something about her that had always turned him on, but because of her rather close relationship with Carla Osborne, she'd never given him the time of day. Now he wanted more than the time of day from her. He was filled with enough sexual intensity to want her night as well, especially *this* night. And he had a feeling they were on the same page. Her dark, sensuous eyes couldn't hide what she was thinking. She was just as edgy, needy, and horny as he was. Hell, she couldn't keep her legs still. He knew what she wanted and he was more than willing to oblige.

Besides, she was full of information and it was information that he might find useful. Carla Osborne had made a fool out of him and had taken something he had worked hard to gain. He was supposed to be the one in control of Osborne Computer Network. Clark had assured him that he'd had his sister under control and there was no way she would come into the family business. Not only had she come into the business but she had made a laughingstock of him in front of everyone at that board meeting, which was something he would never forget or forgive her for. No one made a fool of him. No one.

He watched as Sonya took the last sip of her drink, draining the glass dry. He couldn't help but wonder if she made a habit of drinking like this all the time, or if tonight she'd felt the need to drown in her sorrows. So far she had ranted and raved about her parents' divorce and how her mother was driving her to drinking—and seeing was believing.

"I want another drink, Dalton."

Sonya's statement recaptured his attention. "No, I think you've had enough. It's time for me to take you home."

"I don't want to go home," she said as her mouth tilted into a pout. A damn sexy pout at that, Dalton thought. He quickly felt an erection strain against his pants. A man could explode just from looking at her lips.

He leaned toward her and whispered, "How would you like to go over to my place then?" He knew that after as many drinks as she'd had, she was pretty damn ripe for the pickin' and juicy for the screwin'. He felt his control slip a notch. He needed to get her to his place and fast.

He would give her what they both needed and he was determined to find out a couple things that he wanted to know.

His body hardened when she placed a hand on his thigh, almost too close to the area that ached. "Now why would I want to go over to your place, Dalton?" she asked, her words slurred, her gaze bright.

He leaned down and whispered an answer in her ear and almost lost it when in addition to the alcohol she had consumed, he got a whiff of her sexually frustrated flesh. The scent was hot and potent. There was no doubt about her being juicy tonight, and he had waited her out long enough. She was ready to roll and so was he.

He straightened back in his chair. "So, what do you think of that idea?" he asked, watching her eyes widen in sexual wonder.

"Oh, I think I'd like that."

He smiled. "Yeah, I figured you would."

They didn't even make it out of the parking lot before Sonya was all over him. As soon as they got inside his SUV she threw herself at him and began pulling at his clothes, popping buttons and tugging at the zipper of his pants.

Damn, double damn, he thought, when she had worked his zipper down and began fumbling inside his pants. It was a rare occurrence to find a woman this ready and eager. The rest of his thoughts left his mind when she freed him and her hot, wet, and hungry mouth quickly took him in.

Damn. Triple Damn. He shifted his body to brace against his door as he caught hold of her head and held her to him. Sonya Morrison was giving blow jobs a whole new meaning when she dispensed with pre-liminaries, skipped the licking and stroking, and went straight to suck-ing, taking as much of him inside her mouth as she could. He was grateful that Sylvester's had been crowded and the only parking space he'd been able to find was in the back, a good distance from the build-ing and in a darkened spot.

He couldn't stop the shards of sensations that ripped through him. He was out of his depth with this woman and the only thing he could do was let her have her way with him now. But he would take over later.

When he heard her moan deep in her throat he knew what was about to happen if he didn't do something. When he came he wanted to be between her legs and not in her mouth. He gave an urgent pull on her hair. "Get in the back. Quick."

She had barely landed on the back seat when Dalton followed, pulled her dress up, and parted her legs. He ripped off her panties and barely had time to sheath himself with a condom before thrusting into her and beginning to pump in and out.

Oh man, her stuff is better than good, he thought, feeling her insides clench and pull everything out of him. They were making out like rabbits and were just that out of control.

"Dalton!"

His gaze raked her features and when he felt her muscles tightening around him his rhythm increased. He held her hips in place, giving her what he hoped was the screwing of her life. The sounds of her moans were like an aphrodisiac and his breathing began coming in fast. His senses heightened with each stroke all the way up his spine.

And then it happened. A climax seized the very essence of him and he felt it all the way in his bones. He heard her cry out as his own body exploded. Thrusting hard one final time, he took them over the edge and ripped out a groan that filled the interior of the vehicle.

Fused to her, he buried his face in the curve of her shoulder, weak as water, spent, while trying to catch his breath. He slowly lifted his body and looked down at her. Her expression was just as hungry as it had been inside Sylvester's, although she was sighing with satisfaction.

He smiled. Sonya Morrison had a relentless sexual appetite that he intended to feed tonight. "Still want to go to my place?" he asked, feeling himself getting hard all over again.

She responded instantly. "Yes, and don't waste time getting there."

. . .

Brandy inhaled deeply as she walked into the coffee shop at the hotel. There was nothing like the smell of fresh roasted coffee mingling with the scent of something sweet, delicious, and sinfully wicked like a icing-coated cinnamon bun.

She had a sweet tooth tonight and since she, Carla, and Amber had taken a lot of time talking, especially after she had told them about the note, they had skipped dessert.

Brandy stood only a minute or so at the pastry counter before she was given her coffee and a huge cinnamon bun. She made it a habit to stop by the coffee shop at least once or twice a day just to take a break and sit, unwind and think.

Tonight her mind remained on the note. Talking to Carla and Amber had helped. Both had agreed that she should be cautious and until she found out the identity of the person who'd sent the note, she should be careful who she trusted. She wished she could claim that her two friends' minds were working overtime, but she'd seen enough of those police shows to know that women were often victims of 'sickos.' But a part of her believed that Lorenzo was behind this, and it was his way of getting her nervous and scared.

He knew she wouldn't take it to the police because doing so could hurt the reputation of the hotel. Business was good and she intended for it to stay that way.

An hour or so later she was catching the elevator up to her suite. When she'd taken over the hotel she'd had every stitch of furniture that Lorenzo had owned removed and had bought all new furniture. She loved her new home, which was located on the very top floor of the hotel. The elevator to the fourteenth floor had a special passkey and she was the only one who used it, with the exception of Ida Johnson, the woman who came in daily to clean up. Brandy had found the woman to be very friendly, dependable, and good at what she did.

Brandy stepped off the elevator and felt a sudden prickle of unease.

She glanced down the hallway that led to her suite, and an odd, uncomfortable sensation touched her.

She quickened her steps and glanced over her shoulders, looking all around and not seeing anything. When she made it to her suite, she scanned the area while unlocking the door. The odd sensation continued to claim her although she tried shaking it off.

It wasn't until she was inside her suite with the door closed and locked behind her that she finally breathed a relieved sigh. No matter what, she couldn't let this thing with the note get to her. There was no doubt in her mind that someone was playing with her. When she heard a sound outside her door, her heart quickened and she leaned up and tried to take a look out of the peephole, but she saw nothing. But she was more than certain that she had heard footsteps.

Checking her door again to make certain it was locked and the security chain was in place, she crossed the room and paused by the phone, thinking that maybe she should call security. But it was late and Perry Hall, her security manager, had left to go home hours ago; she didn't want to deal with his assistant.

She wrapped her arms around herself, thinking that she wouldn't be getting much sleep tonight.

Chapter 5

As she had expected, Brandy lay awake that night unable to sleep. Each time she closed her eyes she swore she heard something and each time she got out of her bed to investigate she found nothing there.

She had tried doing everything including counting sheep, and here it was nearly two in the morning and her eyes were still open like she didn't have a busy day tomorrow. Before going to bed she had reread the note again, and like before a creepy feeling had escalated up and down her spine.

And she didn't like it. She didn't like it one damn bit.

A few months ago, at one of the their sistah-circle dinner meetings, Carla had brought to the table the principle that fear would steal your livelihood, so the thing to do was to make your courage bigger and stronger than your fear. Well, tonight while quivering in bed Brandy was doing a piss-poor job of following that principle, mainly because she'd never had to encounter anything like this before.

Even after her decision to take over the running of the hotel, Kathie had warned her of the challenges she would face as a female hotel manager and that at all times she needed to walk a straight line with her male employees, not ever letting them make the assumption that she would cross over the line in her role as their boss.

Brandy sighed. She felt she had done a good job of keeping things strictly business. Oh, she was certain a number of her male employees found her attractive, since she'd caught a few of them checking her out from time to time, but she'd always maintained a high degree of professionalism between them. She had no intention of getting involved with anyone who worked for her and had sent out that message real quick. Kathie had commented to her once that she'd heard through the grapevine that some of them considered Brandy an ice princess and a couple of them had even questioned if she was gay since she never dated. But Brandy knew that most had heard the scandalous story of her and Lorenzo's wedding and brief marriage, and felt the reason she wasn't dating was because she was licking her wounds. She couldn't help wondering if that's what the person who called himself "The Man" thought? In his sick mind did he somehow think she needed him?

Brandy rolled over in bed. Tomorrow she would meet with her secretary, Donna Fields, to find out who had dropped by her office to deliver the rose. The older woman in her late fifties was sharp as a tack and her eyes didn't miss much. Until this mystery was solved, Carla and Amber were right. Brandy needed to watch her back.

Brandy was at her office before Mrs. Fields arrived. Her heartbeat escalated and she stopped when she saw her office door open. She distinctly remembered closing and locking it the night before.

Passing her secretary's desk, she took a deep breath and silently walked to the door and looked inside. Her security manager, Perry Hall, was standing at her desk with his back to her as he lifted the single rose to his nose to take a sniff.

She knew from reviewing his employment record a while back that

Perry Hall was in his late forties, married for over fifteen years with two teenage boys. He was active in a number of athletic organizations that his sons were involved in and was a die-hard Orlando Magic fan. He was also active in his church and was vice president of the PTA at the school his sons attended. He had been employed at the St. Laurent during the five years that Lorenzo had run things and for a good ten years before that under the former owners, the Rawlins Group. He had been promoted to security manager after the former security manager left to go work for a Disney hotel a few years ago. Hall had been one of Lorenzo's right-hand men, but for some reason after meeting him she'd felt he would do right by her and hadn't seen a reason not to keep him on. So far he had proven to be a highly skilled and competent individual who knew his job and kept her abreast of things she needed to know.

She'd never had a reason to suspect him of anything . . . until now. She then quickly reminded herself that a person was innocent until proven guilty.

Brandy straightened her spine and entered her office. "Mr. Hall, what are you doing here?"

He turned around, quickly putting the rose back down on her desk. "Ms. Bennett, sorry, I didn't hear you enter."

She nodded as she placed her briefcase in a chair. "I see you like that rose, Mr. Hall."

He smiled sheepishly. "Yes, I couldn't help but admire it. My wife has a fetish for roses and this one is rather unique. The petals look so soft and the color is so deep it seemed more burgundy than red."

Brandy nodded. He had yet to answer her question. "What are you doing here, Mr. Hall?"

He raised a brow after hearing the bluntness of her question. "We had a meeting this morning. I arrived a few minutes ago and thought I'd wait for you here."

"Inside my office?"

He lifted a bushy brow. "Yes, is that a problem? Mr. Ballentine always preferred that we come directly to his office instead of waiting in the lobby area where his secretary worked unless his office door was closed."

Brandy tilted her head back and looked at him. "And wasn't my office door closed when you arrived?"

Perry Hall shook his head. "It was closed but unlocked."

Brandy frowned. "I don't see how that's possible when I locked it myself before leaving yesterday."

Perry shrugged. "The maintenance crew may have inadvertently left it open after cleaning around in here last night."

She nodded. "I would appreciate if you made sure that my door is closed and locked each night, and that one specific individual is responsible for the tidying up in here. I prefer to know who's coming in and going out of here."

Perry nodded. "That can easily be arranged." He then frowned. "Is there some sort of problem you'd like to tell me about?"

Until I find out who sent that note I can't fully trust anyone. Brandy shook her head. "No, there's nothing I need to discuss with you. There are times I'll have confidential papers in my office and I prefer if my door is kept locked."

Perry nodded again. "All right. Now would you like to discuss that issue that came up yesterday about the housekeeper we had to let go because she was caught stealing?"

Brandy sighed. He had made her aware of the incident yesterday. A missing ring from one of the guest rooms had been found in the woman's locker. "And she admitted to taking it?"

"Yes, after she was questioned further."

Brandy rubbed her temple, feeling a headache coming on. This was the second person she'd had to terminate for thievery since taking over the management of the hotel. But she had made it clear from the beginning that dishonesty would not be tolerated. "All right then, is there anything else we need to discuss?"

"No, that about covers it."

Brandy took the chair behind her desk. "On your way out, if you notice that Donna has arrived, please tell her that I'd like to see her immediately." She then glanced down at the flower on her desk. "And since you're so taken with that rose you may keep it. I was going to toss it out anyway."

He looked at her strangely and said, "All right, I'd love to have it. I'll take it home to my wife."

Brandy leaned back in her chair as she watched Perry Hall leave her office with the rose, closing the door behind him.

Carla picked up the phone on the first ring. "Yes, Michelle?"

"I was finally able to reach Ms. Morrison for you, Ms. Osborne. Please hold on while I put her through."

Carla tossed the papers she'd been reading aside. She had been trying to reach Sonya all morning to confirm their dinner and movie date. She had tried calling Sonya late last night and into the wee hours of the morning. When she hadn't been able to reach her, she could only assume that Sonya hadn't come home last night.

"Yeah, Carla, what is it?" a very sluggish voice said on the other end of the line.

"Sonya? Hey, what's going on? I tried calling you several times last night and early this morning. Where have you been?"

"Out."

Carla lifted a brow. "All night?"

"Yes. And why are you trippin'? I'm not a sixteen-year-old, Carla. I'm a thirty-two-year-old woman, for Pete's sake. How about cutting me some slack here."

Carla was quiet for the longest while. Then she said, "All right. I was just concerned about you."

"Don't bother."

Again Carla didn't say anything. It was apparent that Sonya was going through some things and more than ever Carla wanted to see her and be there for her. "Look, I just wanted to check to make sure tonight is still on."

"Yeah, if you're sure you can fit me into your schedule."

Carla gritted her teeth and forced a smile. Sonya was determined to be difficult. "Hey, girlfriend, tonight belongs to us. Do you have a place you prefer going to grab a bite to eat?"

"No, you choose. Anywhere is fine with me as long as they serve seafood."

Carla couldn't help but smile. For a moment Sonya sounded like her old self. She knew that over the past year and a half their relationship had been strained but she was determined to get things back right. They had too much history to do otherwise. "Okay, I think I know just the place. How about Letos? We haven't been there in a while. Then afterwards we can catch that new Queen Latifah movie. How's that?"

"I thought you and your friends went to the movies last night."

Carla ignored the sneer in Sonya's voice. "We had planned to go after dinner but changed our minds. But even if I had gone last night there's nothing wrong with going again is there? I remember a time when we spent a lot of our evenings at the movies, sometimes seeing the same one over and over again, especially if it was one Denzel Washington starred in."

Sonya couldn't help but chuckle. "Yeah, I remember that." Then there was a long silence before Sonya let out a deep sigh. "Well, I'll see you later. I need to get some sleep."

Carla nodded. "And you're sure you're all right?"

She could hear Sonya's slight moan on the other end. "Yeah, I'm fine. I just got a hell of a hangover, but I'll be fine when I see you later. I'll meet you at the restaurant."

"All right." After Carla hung up the phone she decided that when she saw Sonya they would have a long talk. The two of them were best friends, always had been and always would be, and she couldn't understand Sonya's insecurities about their friendship.

She sighed deeply. Yes, they needed to have a long talk.

Amber placed the last book in the shelf, then stood back and admired her handiwork. She had color coordinated the books in the section of her store she called the "Kid's Corner" so they could be easily recognized. Thursdays were her light days and Eileen's day off. Jennifer wouldn't be in until noon to help with the lunch traffic. Last week Amber had hired a part-time worker, a male student from one of the local high schools, to work three days a week, mostly to unload and help put away stock. Already she found that Keith was a hard worker and the money he earned was helping to prepare him for college.

Amber looked up when she heard the bell that signaled that a customer had entered her shop. She arched her neck. From where she stood she could see the man but he couldn't see her behind the planter and Humpty-Dumpty's brick wall. His back was to her but then he slipped his hands into his pockets and slowly turned around as he studied his surroundings.

The woman in her immediately liked what she saw as her gaze slid over his face and body in one fluid sweep, and then another for good measure. His coloring was dark—a deep dark chocolate, her favorite. He was dressed casually, in a pair of jeans and a sweatshirt, and a pair of high-priced Nikes were on his feet, but from the way her body was reacting, he could have been stark naked.

A slight frown tilted her lips. Boy, she had it bad. The last thing she needed was for sexual urges to consume her mind and lead her astray, no matter how good the brother looked. But still, she couldn't help but continue to check him out, for the moment not able to control her body's response to him.

The tight fit of his jeans, the way his sweatshirt hung loosely over those jeans, not to mention the way that sweatshirt fit those muscled arms and shoulders were enough to give any woman, especially one who hadn't had sex in a long time, a reason to feel intense heat between her legs. He was a man whose bones you'd want to jump any day of the week, any time of the day. A man who could make you forget all those principles of emotion and spirit fulfillment that were discussed at the sistah-circle meetings, especially the one that said, "Everything you need to be happy is inside of you."

At the moment, in her opinion, if the man standing across the room ever got inside of her she would be more than happy, she would be thrilled right out of her bones. Just the thought of those firm, molded thighs wrapped around her, holding her in place when he made love to her was enough to make her forget that she was a woman who didn't need a man, a woman determined not to want one. But then, there was something about him that was so basic, yet at the same time so complementary. Everything about him made her think of sex, sex, and more sex.

And that wasn't good.

Amber blew her bangs out of her eyes. The room suddenly felt unbearably hot. She had to take a minute to catch her breath and to regain control of her senses. Something, probably the sound of her heavy breathing, caught his attention and he glanced her way. Their gazes met, connected, and held. She felt her heart thump against her chest and then her pulse began acting weird. His deep, dark eyes were definitely doing things to her—more specifically, doing things to her body. There was no doubt about it. Her panties were completely drenched by now.

Damn, I am simply pathetic.

"I take it that you're open."

That's not all I am, she was tempted to say. Instead she came from behind the huge planter and Humpty's wall and smiled, mainly to hide her misery. "Yes, we're open. Were you looking for anything in particular or did you come in to browse?"

He smiled and her body went bonkers again. "I came in for a little bit of both. I want to read something for pleasure. Do you have anything to suggest other than those?" he said of the huge display of romance novels that stood in the middle of the floor. "They're big sellers I assume?"

Amber's throat went dry and she swallowed hard as she closed the distance separating them. Only standing a few feet away, she could feel the warmth of his body and could smell the scent of his aftershave. It was a manly fragrance and she found herself inhaling deeply to let it consume her nostrils. When she realized just what she was doing, she forced herself to look at the display. "Well, yes, especially this time of the year, romance novels are big sellers."

He raised a dark brow. A very dark and gorgeous brow. "Why's that? I thought Valentine's Day was when people got silly and fell in love."

She raised her own brow. He sounded a bit cynical although there was a teasing smile at the corners of his lips. They were lips that looked pretty damn naughty, but oh so nice. "Actually, people who believe in true love can fall in love at any time. But the reason we have a special display is because other than the summer months, late fall is the hottest time for reading and a lot of women like to read to escape."

"Into fantasy land?"

"If you want to call it that."

"I do."

"Then what should women call it when guys become absorbed in books about superhuman heroes, creatures from the deep, Star Trek flicks, pets coming back from the dead, invisible men, and flying cars? Now that's the stuff that sounds pretty much like fantasy to me. I find nothing whimsical about two people in a committed relationship."

He bowed his head to fully meet her gaze and smiled. Then he released a deep, tumbling sound of laughter from deep within his gut. "Hey, lady, you got me there. You've definitely put me in my place."

Amber smiled. "Not at the expense of losing a potential customer, I hope."

He shook his head, still smiling. "No, not at all. I like women who speak their minds." He glanced around again. "Do you own this place?"

"Yes."

He looked at the huge sign inside the shop. "So you're Amber?"

"Yes," she responded, and wished he didn't look so appealing. His nose was straight and his mouth was full, very full yet slightly curved. And she suddenly wondered how it would feel to spread her own mouth over that mouth and tinted a darker shade of brown at the thought. His voice sounded pretty damn good too. She could feel the goosebumps forming on her arms.

"Well, from what I can see you have a real nice place here. How long have you been in business?"

"For almost two years. In fact I'm having an anniversary party in a few weeks and you're welcome to come."

"Thanks, but for now I'll just settle on that pleasure read."

She nodded and stepped closer to him. "Before I make a few suggestions of my own, do you have anything in mind?"

"A friend recommended a book by Walter Mosley."

Amber nodded. "Good recommendation. I take it you like mysteries?"

"If it will relax me, then yes."

She chuckled. "Trust me. A good book can do more than relax you. It can carry you into another world if you get that absorbed in it."

He braced his tall frame against one of the counters. "Really? I take it you like to read."

"Yes, I love books. I use to be a librarian, so that should tell you a lot. And I take it that it's just the opposite with you."

He nodded. "I only read when I have to, mainly because I usually don't have the time. I'm much too busy these days. I'm an accountant and tax season is fast approaching."

Well, I'm glad you've decided to chill awhile and do some pleasure reading. If you like this book then please come back for others. We have a vast assortment of them here."

He glanced around. "Yeah, I can see that."

After Amber had shown him a copy of Walter Mosley's latest book he agreed he would buy it. He also decided to buy a romance novel—out of curiosity and nothing else—and told her he would probably give it to his secretary since she had a birthday coming up.

When he handed Amber his credit card she glanced at the name. Cord Jeffries. "Will there be anything else for you today, Mr. Jeffries?"

"No, these two items should do it."

"All right."

After giving him his total, she presented the sales slip for his signature. She couldn't help noticing his hands, how big and strong they looked. She bet they were hands that could evoke the most stimulating kind of passion and literally drive a woman insane. Amber cleared her throat when he slid the pen and sales slip back across the counter to her. He even had a real nice signature.

A few seconds later, she handed him the bag containing his books and the receipt. "Thanks for your business, and I hope you come back."

His eyes lightened and he smiled. "I intend to."

It was late afternoon when Brandy let herself into her suite. She'd had a meeting with the committee in charge of hosting the Florida Classic. Everyone was gearing up for the game that would be played in three weeks. Plans were in place to assure that every person who stayed at her hotel was well taken care of.

She dropped her briefcase and purse down on the sofa, and plopped down beside them. She decided to just stay in tonight and watch a movie and order something from room service instead of cooking herself. She appreciated the kitchen in her suite but tonight didn't want to use it.

She stood and was just about to go in the bedroom to remove her clothes when she saw the note someone had placed on the breakfast bar counter that separated the kitchen from the living room area. She snatched it up immediately, recognizing the writing from yesterday's note.

> I stayed up late last night thinking about you and everything
> I plan to do to you. I hope you're as ready for me as I am for
> you. Every time I see you I want you more and more and it
> won't be long before I have you.
>
> The Man

Brandy frantically glanced around the room. Everything seemed in place but someone had gotten into her suite and left another note. This one was just as creepy as the one before. Cold chills immediately swept up and down her spine.

She snatched up the phone to call security.

◦ Chapter 6 ◦

So, who did you end up going out with last night?"

Sonya met Carla's gaze over her glass of water. She had declined the waiter's offer of wine since she had consumed enough alcohol last night to last her a lifetime. And even now, some of what had happened was still pretty foggy, but the one thing she did remember was leaving Sylvester's with Dalton Gregory and participating in the most intense and enjoyable sex she'd ever had in her life. And to think she'd never liked the man. Well, she certainly hadn't been thinking that last night.

"I went out by myself," she responded. There was no way she was telling Carla she had slept with Dalton.

"By yourself and you didn't come home?"

Sonya gave her a smirty smile. "Carla, a woman who goes to Sylvester's doesn't really expect to come home—at least not alone."

Carla leaned back in her chair with a deep frown on her face. Anyone living in Orlando knew the place. It was a very trendy restaurant and bar that had a not-so-glowing reputation as a pick-up place. "I guess you must have had a purpose for going there." She really didn't expect Sonya to answer and almost dropped her mouth open when she did.

"Yes, I needed to have sex with somebody last night and in a big way.

Nice, hot, sweaty, mind-boggling sex. Safe sex, of course, but sex just the same."

Carla shot her another frown. "And all because I couldn't meet you for dinner last night?"

"No, I would have been in a bad way regardless, but at least talking to you would have taken the edge off things some, since you've become such a Goody Two-shoes these days. And since you didn't have time for me, I found time for myself. Although I had to compete against all those young, hot, and easy college girls that were there. However, once it got past their bedtime then I hit gold. It felt downright sinful sitting in a bar with a bunch of men who were oozing with testosterone, knowing they were aching for something I had."

Carla shook her head. Sonya sounded like an outright slut. "I hope you know what you did last night."

Sonya smiled and thought of just how far she had gone with Dalton and just how far he had gone with her, and she had no complaints. "Hey, chill, let's not get uptight. It's not the first one-night stand I've had, and probably won't be the last. And if I remember correctly you've been involved in one yourself? Little Craig wasn't conceived with a vibrator."

Carla frowned as she took another sip of her drink. "This discussion is about you and not me, Sonya. What is with you these days? Why all this misplaced jealousy when it comes to my relationship with Brandy and Amber? Why do you see them as a threat to our friendship?"

Sonya glared across the table at her. "Mainly because they are. The last several times I needed to talk to you, you were somewhere with them."

"Yes, and no matter where we go I always invite you to come along."

"I did once and I felt totally excluded from the conversation. The three of you have things in common that I don't, like men problems."

Carla leaned back in her chair. "Yes, and we admire you for that."

Sonya lifted a brow, surprised. "Admire me?"

"Yes."

"Why?"

"Because in all the years I've known you, you've never let any man get under your skin and hurt you the way the three of us have been hurt. All we're doing is trying to overcome a difficult period in our lives, as well as trying to survive in the business world out there. That's what me, Brandy, and Amber have in common. With you and me it goes back farther than that and it's even deeper. You were my friend when my mom and Clark wouldn't give me the time of day. Then when Dad died, I don't know how I would have made it without you sticking closer to me than a blood sister. You were there with me through that ordeal with Jesse Devereau; let's not forget Mom's obsession that I let him know that I'd gotten pregnant and when I refused to do so, how she turned her back on me. A person couldn't ask for a better friend than you. I love you and I'm sorry if I let you down by not being there for you when you needed me." Carla wiped a tear from her eye.

"Damn, Carla," Sonya said, pushing back her chair and going over to Carla and giving her a huge hug, not caring that they were causing a scene in the restaurant.

"I'm sorry, too. Things have been so funky with Mom. She's about to drive me to drinking. In fact she did. Last night I got so balled over in Sylvester's that the bartender offered to call me a cab. But that was before someone offered me a ride to their place to spend the night."

Carla wiped her eyes and broke off their hug. Sonya went and sat down. "You nut. What if the person had turned out to be a mass murderer or somebody?"

Sonya smiled through her tears. "Hey, he was okay and it wasn't like he was a total stranger. He was someone I knew, although we've never hit it off before."

"Until last night?"

Sonya chuckled. "Yes, until last night. And boy, could he do the thang. He plumb wore out this little body of mine."

Carla shook her head. "You know you're downright awful, don't you?"

"Yes, and I've always been that way so don't act surprised. You know I've always depended on you to keep me straight."

Carla hugged her friend, smiling. "Well, it's a tough job but I guess somebody has to do it."

Sonya couldn't help laughing. "Yeah, you are so right."

Perry Hall glanced at Brandy. She was standing in the same spot he'd left her in when he'd started making a thorough check of her suite. He had been about to leave for the day when she had frantically summoned him telling him only that someone had been her in suite. Although she claimed nothing was missing, it was apparent she was pretty shaken up and believed her claim although he could find nothing to support it. Everything looked pretty much in order.

"I checked the entire suite and couldn't find anything. Are you sure someone else other than the cleaning lady has been here?"

Brandy met his gaze. "Yes, I'm positive." She would not tell him or anyone at the hotel about the threatening notes she'd received. "I've been back up here a couple times after she left this morning, and this evening when I returned I noticed a couple of things out of place."

He sighed. The only things she'd told him were out of place were some items on her kitchen counter. How a woman could rightly remember exactly how she'd left things beat the hell out of him. He had a gut feeling she wasn't telling him everything. "I'm going down to the front desk and cut you a new passkey and recode the security panel box in the private elevator. No one will have access to this entire floor except for you. I'll make arrangements with housekeeping to only let their person come when you're here or for you to buzz them up. The same thing will apply to room service."

"Thanks, I'd really appreciate it."

He nodded. "Are you sure you're okay?"

She sighed deeply. "Yes, I'm fine, and I'd prefer if you didn't say anything about this to anyone, Mr. Hall."

"All right, Ms. Bennett. I'll be back in a few minutes with that new key."

An hour or so later, after Perry Hall had returned and gone, Brandy was still pacing the room. She had questioned her secretary, Donna Fields, when she'd come in that morning and the older woman had told her that other than the cleaning crew no one had dropped by her office. However, Mrs. Fields said that she had left early for a dentist appointment yesterday.

Brandy couldn't shake the thought that someone was deliberately trying to scare her, and what bothered her the most was that she didn't know just who among her employees she could trust. Most of them had worked for her ex-husband and still might feel some type of loyalty to him, even Perry Hall. Lorenzo had been the one to promote Mr. Hall to his present position and she couldn't forget Lorenzo's threat to her the last time she'd seen him. He'd sworn that she would be sorry for taking the hotel away from him.

Brandy stopped in front of the window and sighed deeply. There was no use freaking out since there was absolutely nothing she could do right now other than involve the police and she'd already tossed aside that idea. But the thought that someone had been inside her suite was unnerving.

She had checked around the apartment several times to make sure none of her personal things had been tampered with. It seemed whomever had come into her suite had not used forced entry and had dropped off the note and left without touching anything else.

Twice she had started to call her cousins to brainstorm with them for ideas on how she should handle things, but each time she reached over to pick up the phone, she had changed her mind. Rae'jean, Alexia, and Taye had come up with an idea to get her out of one mess, she didn't want to depend on them to come up with another. This was going to be something that she would have to handle on her own. The hotel was hers and she refused to let anyone take it away or scare her away.

She jumped when she heard the telephone ring and for a moment almost didn't answer it, but then changed her mind. It could be room service asking when she wanted her dinner delivered. She inhaled deeply, doubting very seriously that she would be able to eat anything tonight.

Walking over to the phone she picked it up on the fourth ring. "Yes?"

"It's about time you answered." Her cousin Taye's voice came in loud and clear. "Rae'jean and Alexia are on the line, too. We thought we'd better call to let you know the latest. Cousin Sophie called a few minutes ago, hollering and screaming that your mom told Uncle Victor about his surprise birthday party just because since she didn't get an invitation."

"If you ask me, he knew about it anyway," Rae'jean piped in, laughing at the dramatics involving her family back in Macon. Living in Boston kept Rae'jean pretty isolated and she depended on Taye to keep her updated.

"Yeah, but that's what they get for not inviting Valerie," Alexia added, grinning over the line. "They should know after all these years that your mama doesn't get even, Brandy, she gets spiteful."

After a few moments Taye, Rae'jean, and Alexia noticed that Brandy had yet to make any kind of comment.

"Brandy, you still there?" Alexia asked with concern in her voice.

"Yes, I'm still here," Brandy said in a soft voice. Any chance of calming down had gone completely out the window the moment she'd heard her cousins' voices.

"What's wrong, Brandy? You don't sound like yourself," Rae'jean asked, matching Alexia's concern.

Brandy took a deep breath. "I don't feel like myself either," she answered, close to tears. She had tried being brave, but she couldn't any longer. The truth was that she had become a nervous wreck and was scared senseless.

"What is it, Brandy?" Taye asked in a direct, you'd-better-tell-me-what's-going-on voice. "What's happened?"

Brandy dropped down on the sofa and told them the only thing she could: "I'm being stalked."

Book Two

She is more precious than rubies and all the things
thou canst desire are not to be compared to her.

Proverbs 3:15

✍ Chapter 7 ✍

Grey Masters walked into the lobby of the St. Laurent Hotel and glanced around. He wasn't a man who was easily dazzled; however, he was very impressed by what he saw. He had been a special agent for the FBI for over twelve years and had spent plenty of his time in hotels, and he had to admit this was one pretty classy place, from the splendor of the atrium that overflowed with flowering plants and an abundance of greenery, to the elegance of the lobby with its custom-designed area rugs, there was something about the hotel that conveyed the sentiment that your stay here would be better than home.

And to think the place was run by a woman who was not only the head honcho in charge, but also the owner. This hotel and everything in it belonged to Brandy Bennett. According to his sister-in-law, Alexia, Brandy had received the hotel as part of her divorce settlement over two years ago and had taken on the challenge of keeping the hotel running with the same degree of success that it had achieved in the past. But someone had thrown a monkey wrench into what had been the relatively smooth sailing of her daily operations.

Someone was stalking her.

As he walked toward the registration desk he could not forget the frantic call he had received from Alexia a few nights ago. Just hearing the panic in his sister-in-law's voice had made his muscles tense and his body brace for action. Alexia had come apart at the thought that someone was stalking her cousin, and one thing he had discovered about his brother's wife was that it took a lot to make Alexia Bennett Masters come unglued. Even his brother Quinn would attest to that, which meant whatever was going on with Brandy Bennett was real serious. Or at least Alexia thought so.

After calming her down he had discovered Quinn was out of town on a business trip to London, so Grey had had to deal with getting Alexia to see reason and to talk her out of hopping the next plane to Florida to get to the bottom of Brandy's problem. And she had told him that her other cousins, Rae'jean and Taye, would join her there and that the three of them would turn the hotel inside out because nobody, and she meant nobody, messed with a Bennett.

He believed her.

Grey shook his head smiling, thinking of the time when over a cold bottle of beer, Quinn had shared with him what had happened at Brandy Bennett's wedding three years ago. At the time, Grey had needed a good laugh and after listening to his brother he had definitely gotten one. According to Quinn, up to the time of the wedding, there had been no love lost between Brandy and her three cousins. But once it had been discovered that Brandy's fiancé had screwed around on her with the maid of honor, and then had the gall to put the encounter on videotape—a tape that Brandy had found a mere two days before her wedding—the four cousins had devised a plan that set in motion the guarantee that Brandy Bennett would be financially set for life.

According to Quinn, what had gone down was classic Bennett style and had pretty much buried whatever past differences the women had had. On the day of the wedding the four Bennett cousins had united for one cause—to make damn sure that the groom knew that payback was a bitch . . . or in this case, bitches.

"Good morning, sir, and welcome to the St. Laurent. Do you have a reservation?"

The perky hotel clerk's question brought Grey out of his musings and he looked into her smiling face. "No, I'm here as a guest of Ms. Bennett."

Although the clerk's face didn't lose that smile, he did note the spark of interest in her eyes. "Are you a relative, sir?"

Keeping his smile in place, he responded, "A relative?"

She nodded. "Yes. The reason I asked is because usually we have a special floor of suites that are exclusively reserved for Ms. Bennett's relatives when they come to visit."

Grey shook his head, understanding. "No, I'm not a relative. I'm a personal friend." Again he saw the woman's eyes take on a speculative look. Evidently Brandy Bennett did not make it a habit to have male friends checking into her hotel as guests. If this clerk was a talker then news that the boss had a male visitor would spread around the hotel in no time, which was fine with him. If whoever had taken it upon themselves to harass Brandy Bennett was someone who worked for the hotel, the sooner that person knew that Brandy had a male friend visiting, the better. One thing that Grey detested more than anything was someone who preyed on women, so this all fit into his plans perfectly.

On the flight from Atlanta he had decided the best way to handle things was not to let anyone know that he intended to be Ms. Bennett's bodyguard. If word got out that someone was stalking her, business at the hotel would drop drastically. So he decided to take on the role of her lover while finding out who had sent her those messages.

Of course Alexia and the cousins had their own ideas. They figured it had to be the no-good ex-husband, Lorenzo Ballentine. According to Alexia, it was common knowledge that Lorenzo was still pissed that he'd lost the hotel to Brandy during the divorce, and that Brandy had recently asked him to stay away from the hotel. Although Grey would not discount Ballentine as a prime suspect, he wouldn't overlook anything or anyone. For some reason he had a feeling the person sending the messages was someone Brandy least suspected.

Having left the Bureau nearly three years ago, not long after his wife Gloria's car accident, he had started Masters Investigative Services in Atlanta. However, he kept his ties to the Bureau open with the many friends he'd left behind. In his employ as investigators were four very skilled former special agents, but Grey had been the one Alexia and her cousins had specifically wanted to handle this case. They had to know for certain that Brandy Bennett's life was safe and secure. Luckily, he had just wrapped up a case and had given the Bennett cousins his word that he would fly to Orlando and stick to Brandy Bennett like glue if he had to, making sure that whatever threat was hanging over her head was dealt with in a timely and efficient manner.

"I've contacted Ms. Bennett to let her know you're here and she indicated she would be right down."

Grey nodded. "Thanks, and it appears that the airline misplaced my luggage. When it's found please make sure it is delivered to Ms. Bennett's personal suite." The truth was that he had been given special clearance to transport all the high-powered surveillance equipment that he used as part of his job, equipment that had been easily detected with a security scanner at the airport. To save time as well as red tape, he had made arrangements for his luggage to be picked up by another special agent and delivered to the hotel later. Grey had contacted the local Bureau before arriving in Orlando and someone posing as an airline employee would be delivering his bags to him within the hour.

Again, a ray of interest shone in the hotel clerk's eyes. "Yes, sir. I'll make sure that's taken care of." The woman caught a movement out of corner of her eye and her smile widened. "Oh, here's Ms. Bennett now."

Grey turned slightly and met the gaze of the woman crossing the lobby. Although the two of them had never officially met, he remembered her well. He doubted that he would forget the beautiful dark eyes that had collided with his that day a few weeks ago at his nieces' and nephews' birthday party. That was one of the reasons he had hesitated when Alexia had asked him to handle things. Brandy Bennett had been the first woman who had piqued his interest, intrigued him, since Gloria's death. Even now his stomach knotted at the recollection. Days after that encounter he'd been unable to shake her image. She had flitted across his mind like some beautiful, fragile butterfly.

As he continued to watch her, it was easy to see she was as intelligent as she was beautiful, and by all accounts Brandy Bennett appeared to be a woman with not a worry in the world, one filled with self-assurance and confidence. Only someone with a trained eye such as his, who was skilled in reading people, could detect, even from a distance, the cautiousness, wariness, and troubled glint in her gaze.

He inhaled deeply as he struggled with all the things he was feeling. The attraction for her was still there, but he knew to get involved with any woman right now would be wrong. He was still trying to come to terms with what Gloria had done, what she had planned which had ultimately resulted in her death. He had shared it with no one, not even Quinn, the brother he was closer to than any of his other siblings. He wondered what the Masters family's reaction would be to know that at the time of her death, his wife had betrayed him. In fact, she had been on her way to meet her lover, the man she had planned to divorce Grey for. She had spelled out everything in the letter she had left for him to find when he returned home from his assignment. He had returned less than a day after she had written it when he'd received word she had lost her life after losing control of her automobile during a thunderstorm.

His thoughts shifted back to Brandy as he continued to watch her cross the lobby toward him. At that moment he wanted more than anything to do whatever he could to bring back calmness to her world, to get rid of whatever anxiety besieged her. He fought down that urge when he remembered that one woman, the one he'd thought he could trust above all others, had betrayed him, and the last thing he wanted was to get involved with another woman any time soon. Protecting Brandy Bennett would be a job and nothing more.

He wondered if Alexia had contacted her and scoped her on the role the two of them would be playing. She had been told that he was coming, but he wasn't sure if she knew he was going to pretend to be an exboyfriend. He shrugged; if she didn't, she would soon enough. It would be important to establish what their relationship was up front and in plain view.

When she finally reached him and was about to open her mouth and address him formally, he decided to work fast. "Hi, there, sweetheart," he murmured in a rough, low tone just seconds before he pulled her into his arms and kissed her.

He captured her startled surprise in his kiss, going beyond what was reasonably necessary by sweeping his tongue inside her mouth for a quick taste. Damn but she tasted good, he thought, releasing her mouth. He inwardly groaned in relief that she caught on quickly and had the good sense to play along. He took a step back and gazed down at her. Her lips were still parted in surprise and looked warm, inviting. Now that he knew her taste, it took everything he had not to pull her back in his arms and capture her lips with his mouth again.

Remember, Masters, this is nothing more than a job.

He sighed deeply, wondering why, if that was the case, the effects of the kiss were sending hot vibrations along his nerve endings. And he could tell, even though the kiss had been rather short in his estimation, that Brandy Bennett had been affected by the contact as well. He also knew she was trying to downplay that fact.

"Grey, it's good seeing you again, too. How was your trip?" she asked in a somewhat shaky voice.

"It was fine, but somehow they lost my luggage. I've requested for it to be brought up to your suite when the airline delivers it here." If she was stunned and confused at his insinuation that he would be sharing her suite, she didn't show it. But he had a feeling she would have a lot to say when they were alone.

"All right, come up and let me get you settled."

He immediately fell in step beside her as they walked across the lobby to the elevators. "This is a private elevator," she said of the third one in the group of six. "It will take you to the administrative offices as well as to the fourteenth floor where my suite is located. However, to get to my floor you need to know the special code."

He nodded and as soon as the elevator door opened, they both stepped inside. Once the door closed behind them she quickly turned on him, no doubt to give him hell if the frown that had suddenly marred her brow was any indication. But he quickly placed a hand to her lips and mouthed the words, "This elevator may be bugged."

That got her attention. He watched as her shoulders tensed and she looked intently at him to make sure that she had deciphered his silent message correctly. He nodded. She then took a deep breath and turned to insert her passkey into the panel box. The two of them remained silent the entire time the elevator made its way to the fourteenth floor.

Once they arrived on her floor, Grey noted that Brandy took her cue from him and remained silent as they walked down the hall to her suite. Even when they entered her suite she stood back as he looked around before gathering her hand in his and saying rather loudly, "I need a shower, baby. Come take one with me."

She didn't hesitate when he motioned for her to lead him toward the bathroom. Once inside she watched as he closed the door behind them and quickly walked over to the shower and turned it on full blast.

He then turned back to her. "All right, we can talk now but we still need to keep our voices lowered. The water will drown out our voices. If your suite is bugged, no one will be able to make out what we're about to discuss."

Brandy lifted a brow. "Honestly, Mr. Masters, do you really think someone would go so far as to bug my suite?" she whispered. "We're talking about a stalker and not a spy from another hotel wanting trade secrets. I've already told my cousins who is behind this. My ex-husband, Lorenzo Ballentine, is trying to scare me away from here."

Grey lifted his own brow. "Is that what you think?"

Brandy's forehead bunched. "Yes, although I don't believe he did it himself. I wouldn't put it past him to have someone here at the hotel, someone who used to work for him when he was in charge and who still feels loyal to him, do his dirty work."

"Are you certain of that?"

He watched her breathe in deeply. She then answered him honestly. "At the moment I'm not certain of anything."

Grey smiled, knowing it was probably hard for her to admit that. "And that's why I'm here as a favor to Alexia. I promised her I would get to the bottom of this and I will. However, until I do we can't assume anything. As soon as my luggage arrives, I'll be able to check out your apartment from top to bottom and make sure there aren't any surveillance devices in here anywhere. Whoever came inside your apartment had plenty of opportunity to leave something behind. Once I feel sure that no one is listening to anything we say then we can talk freely and you can tell me everything."

"But why would anyone be listening? Even if it's not Lorenzo, why would a stalker want to listen in on my conversations?"

"If this person is obsessed, he would do just about anything to find out about your comings and goings, so don't think a stalker wouldn't bug this place or put in some type of surveillance camera to watch your every move. I've known cases where it has happened and I won't be comfortable until I know for certain this isn't one of those times."

Brandy nodded. She really thought he was taking things a little bit too far, but then he'd been an FBI agent and certainly knew more about this sort of stuff than she did. She met his gaze. "What about that kiss downstairs? Why did you give my employees the impression that you're staying here with me instead of in the guest rooms reserved for family members?"

He crossed his arms over his chest. He had no intention of letting Brandy Bennett be difficult. "Because I will. You need a bodyguard until this matter is cleared up, Ms. Bennett, and unless you want your entire staff to know what's going on then I suggest we do things my way. If word gets out that you have a bodyguard, then business at this hotel will drop drastically. Bad news travels fast and people have a tendency not to want to stay where there might be trouble."

Brandy knew what he said was true. "But why couldn't you have said that you were a family member and used one of the suites on another floor?"

"Mainly because I promised Alexia and your other cousins that I would watch you like a hawk. And the only way I can do that is to be close to you at all times."

Brandy lifted a brow. "At all times?"

"Within reason. It shouldn't take me more than a week or so to find out who's behind this."

"You're that good?"

"I'd like to think so. The plan is for you to introduce me to everyone as a former boyfriend who's trying to make a comeback. They will readily accept the idea of the two of us getting cozy and sharing your suite for a while."

"And then?"

"And once I finish my job I will be out of your hair and you can run things, business as usual."

Brandy nodded. She hoped things would be that simple. She didn't like the thought that someone was trying to scare the wits out of her. "All right. I'll go along with your plan, but we have to decide on sleeping arrangements."

"The sofa will be fine. However we need to make sure that your housekeeper doesn't find out that we aren't sharing a bed. Until we determine what's going on, we can't trust anyone."

Brandy nodded. More than anything she wanted this nightmare to be over.

A couple of hours later, after his luggage had arrived, Grey tried not to look over his shoulder as Brandy, right on his heel, followed him from room to room as he used a device to detect if there was any type of sur-veillance equipment in her suite. The scent of her, sultry and feminine, was driving him crazy and he tried to concentrate on what he was doing and not on her. And he had been doing a pretty good job of it until he had walked into her bedroom. The large, spacious room was decorated in burgundy and mauve and the furnishings were a whitewashed oak. A king-size bed that was covered in a floral spread sat in the middle of the floor. He tried to erase from his mind thoughts of her, half naked and asleep in that big bed. The mental image was so real he had to swallow a couple of times when his breath literally got caught in his throat.

"Do you actually think something is in here?"

She had whispered the words. Her voice, soft and warm, was close to his ear as he leaned down to look under the bed. He hunched his shoulders to let her know at the moment he didn't know what to think. In fact he was doing a piss-poor job of thinking at all.

A few minutes later he was satisfied that there were no listening devices, and no hidden cameras. He leaned against her dresser. "We can talk now. You're clean."

Brandy sighed deeply. "Thank goodness for that."

Grey stared at her for a moment before asking. "Are you ready to tell me everything now?"

"Yes." Her voice was nervous.

"Then I suggest we go into your kitchen, have a cup of coffee and talk." He took her hand and led her out of the bedroom.

Grey looked down at the notes he'd taken while talking to Brandy. He had asked her a series of questions after she had told him about the first note she had found in her office and the second note that had been left in her suite.

"Do you know the name of the florist shop that delivered the rose?" he asked going back up to the first notation he'd made.

"Yes. It came from the florist shop here in the hotel. I didn't ask any questions because I didn't want to raise anyone suspicions about anything."

Grey nodded. So far on the list he had the name of her security person, Perry Hall, as well as anyone else who'd had access to the administrative floor, which included all of her staff managers, including Horace Thurgood, who had resigned when she'd taken over.

He added her secretary's name along with that of her housekeeper, although Brandy hadn't wanted him to do so. The signature of "The Man" hinted that the writer was a male, but Grey wasn't discounting anything.

"What about your other employees?"

"We employ a great number of people to take care of our guests' needs: people who answer the phones, take reservations, clean the rooms, check in the guests, cook and serve the food, as well as the maintenance guys who perform a number of duties including repairing the air conditioners. So as you can see this is a huge range of people, from manual workers to skilled professionals."

She took a sip of her coffee. "And the number of people we employ varies at different times, depending on our needs. During the busy season we have very high occupancies and as a result we need more people working for us."

Grey lifted a brow. "So you have high staff fluctuations?"

"Yes. Because of the number of colleges in town as well as those located in Daytona and Melbourne, we utilize a lot of students in various jobs whenever we can. Most of them work part time. We also hire a lot of minorities and immigrants."

"And you take the time to do background checks on everyone?"

Brandy frowned. "Yes, of course. Our human resource department does a good job of screening our applicants to make sure we hire good employees, employees who can be trusted with our guests' needs and their possessions. However, since some of the jobs, although important, require very little skill, the pay is low. And just like most other hotels, we have a relatively high turnover rate."

Grey paused as he wrote all the information down and paid close attention to the names of her employees. He then glanced back up at her. "Now I want the names of any friends you have, males or females, as well as any boyfriends, past or present."

Brandy's frown deepened. "Is all this necessary, Mr. Masters?"

"Yes, and it would make things easier if you get used to calling me Grey and I'll start calling you Brandy, all right?"

Brandy nodded, frustrated. "That's fine." She inhaled gently as she thought of the information he'd just requested of her. "My two closest friends are Carla Osborne and Amber Stuart. I've told them about the notes. I was so upset I had to tell somebody so I mentioned it to them while we were at dinner the other night."

He nodded. "Give me some info about them so I can have them checked out."

Brandy sighed. "There's no reason to suspect them."

Grey gave her a frown of his own. "Until we find out who's behind this, we will suspect everyone."

Brandy angrily stood and walked over to the sink and poured out her coffee. She turned back around and met Grey's gaze. "I trust them, Grey, and I will continue to trust them. Carla, Amber, and I have a special bond. The three of us have been bitten, and very badly I might add, by dogs."

Grey lifted a confused brow. "Bitten by dogs?"

"Yes, dogs of the most voracious and most heartless kind: the human male."

For the longest time Grey didn't say anything as he looked at her. However, he was tempted to tell her that being bitten could work both ways. His wife had definitely taken a huge chunk out of him.

"Besides," Brandy was saying, "I told them that you were coming when I spoke with them last night, and that you would be acting as my bodyguard."

Grey shook his head, wondering why women felt compelled to tell each other everything. "That's all well and good that the three of you are in some kind of sisterhood club and freely share secrets," he said curtly. "However, I'm going to have them checked out regardless, and since you trust them so much there shouldn't be anything for you to worry about." Grey glanced back down to the paper and penciled in a notation. "Now what about boyfriends?" he asked.

"I don't have one."

Grey lifted his gaze from his paper. "Are you saying there hasn't been another man in your life since your divorce?"

"None that mattered."

"Let me be the judge of that. A scorned or jealous lover can cause a lot of problems."

Brandy came back to the table and sat down. She then told Grey about her brief affair with Grant Hoffman three years ago while on the rebound, and her one-night stand over two years ago with Thomas Reynolds.

"And this Thomas Reynolds. You say that he owns the Commodore Restaurant here in town?"

"Yes, and I consider him a dear friend." She thought of all the things Thomas had done to pave the way for her to be successful. He had introduced her to the right people and had made sure she was included in the right circles—and all out of friendship. He had never tried to come on to her again since the night she'd told him that the two of them could be nothing more than friends.

"With as many friends as you have why would anyone need enemies?" Grey said sarcastically. He wondered why after what had happened with her before—being so trusting—she hadn't been taught a lesson. As far as he was concerned, she trusted *too* easily. But then, so had he at one time.

"I resent that statement, Grey."

He met her gaze. "You can resent it all you want, but the truth of the matter is that someone is either trying to scare you or hurt you, maybe even both. So in light of that reality, I don't have time to be convinced that *all* your friends and associates are trustworthy."

He stood. "Is there anyone else, present or past, that you want to tell me that you may suspect?"

Jolene's name flashed across Brandy's mind. She hadn't heard from her in almost two years. For the longest time after the fiasco at her wedding, the woman she'd considered her best friend had tried contacting her but Brandy had always refused to listen to anything she had to say. She had ranked Jolene right up there with Lorenzo—scum and trash, and the thought of either one of them always left a bad taste in her mouth.

"There's my ex-best friend by the name of Jolene Bradford."

"Ex-best friend."

"Yes. We parted ways when I found out she'd been sleeping with my fiancé."

Grey nodded. Evidently Jolene Bradford was the woman who'd found instant fame with that video Quinn had told him about. "Is this the woman who you exposed on the video at your wedding?" he asked although he already knew the answer.

Brandy raised a brow and started to ask how he knew about that, then figured Quinn must have enlightened him about everything. "Yes, she's the one."

He nodded. "When was the last time you saw or spoke with her?"

Brandy shrugged. "Almost two years ago. I understand her fiancé broke things off with her immediately after that." Especially after a few of those videotapes hit the black market, she thought, still not sure how that had happened. The only thing she could figure out was that the guy who'd coordinated her wedding had discovered a way to make a buck and had duplicated the videotape. "Jolene resigned from her position as a biology professor at Howard and I heard that she took a position at another university. But I doubt Jolene is capable of being a stalker."

"Why?"

"Stalkers spend too much time standing up. She gets more enjoyment being on her back."

Grey cleared his throat. In a way he guessed Brandy deserved to be spiteful, considering the circumstances. The woman was supposed to have been her best friend. "Is there anyone else you want to mention?".

"No."

Brandy tried to concentrate on the note taking Grey was doing and not on his physique. But she was having a hard time doing so. The man was too overwhelmingly male. His perfectly built body, along with everything else that was going wrong in her life, was frying her nerves.

She glanced down at the floor to take her eyes off him when she thought of something. She wanted to make sure her words didn't get stalled in her throat. "There was this incident that happened yesterday evening."

"And what incident was that?"

She lifted her gaze and met his as she tried to recall exactly what happened. "I worked late in my office last night and when I was getting on the elevator to leave, I noticed Wilbur Green was still in his office working."

Grey picked up the notepad off the table and scanned the list. "Wilbur Green? He's your food and beverage director, right?"

"Yes. And whomever he was talking to had him highly upset. That wouldn't be suspicious in itself other than the fact that Wilbur seldom stays late at work unless there's a big function going on and he is usually a very cool and calm man. I just thought it was strange that he was still there, and I don't think he knew I was in my office since the door was closed. I only heard bits and pieces of his conversation but he kept saying something about the person not getting another penny out of him. It made me think perhaps he was being blackmailed or something."

Brandy crossed her arms over her chest. She didn't like being leery and suspicious of her employees, employees she was just beginning to trust when she'd begun receiving the notes. "And then later that same night when I was walking down one of the vacant halls making sure things were running smoothly, I thought I heard someone following me."

"Did you see anyone?"

"No, at least not at first. But then later I ran into one of the bellmen who'd just come from delivering luggage to a guest room. I think I scared him as much as he scared me. But I'm not sure he was the person I'd actually heard."

"Do you have this bellman's name?"

"No, but I know he's one of our college students who only work part-time. I've seen him around several times and noticed that he's a hard worker."

Grey nodded. "Have any idea which college he attends?"

Brandy had to think for a minute. Then she said. "I believe the University of Central Florida. We had a masquerade party last October for Halloween and he came pretty well made up, dressed in a vampire costume. I recall someone saying he was a makeup artist in UCF's movie and production program."

"Have you fired anyone lately?"

Brandy told him about the two employees who'd worked in housekeeping that had been terminated for taking some of the guests' belongings.

Grey sighed and jotted more notations on his pad. "I think everything you've told me is worth checking out, some things more than others. And as for the way we intend to present our relationship to everyone, I suggest we do just as I planned. As far as anyone is concerned, except your two friends Carla and Amber since you've told them too much already, I am your ex-lover looking for a comeback. I will become your shadow and when the investigation is over and I leave, you can claim that things didn't work out for us because I was too domineering, jealous, and possessive and you couldn't handle that sort of relationship with me any longer. That should be simple enough."

Brandy breathed in deeply. She had a gut feeling that nothing about her association with Grey Masters would be simple.

❧ *Chapter 8* ❧

Los Angeles

Good morning, Mr. Devereau."

Jesse Devereau looked up from the newspaper he was reading when he stepped off the elevator. "Good morning, Kitty, and how are you this morning?"

"I'm doing fine, sir. I've placed your mail on your desk and Edward Shingles called twice already."

Jesse nodded, thinking what else was new? Edward Shingles had been trying to run him down all week, and he had already told the man that further discussion about the matter would be pointless. He was not interested in buying the man's company, especially after the discovery that the older man had doctored his accounting books to make it appear that Shingles Industries was in better shape financially than it really was.

"If Mr. Shingles calls back, put him through to me right away. Evidently he needs to hear the words *I'm not interested* another way."

Kitty Perkins tried hiding her smile but failed to do so. She watched as her boss entered his office and closed the door behind him. She had come to work for Jesse Devereau when he'd first started his business over eight years ago and thought he was a wonderful boss.

In a little over four years, the name Jesse Devereau spiked fear in a vast number of corporations on the west coast. Hailed as something of a corporate marauder, he had built his empire by doing whatever it took to get in on the action, whether by forcing a takeover of some successful firm that caught his eye, or going so far as to do whatever he had to do to get a seat on the board of some particular firm. He did it all and without shame, making him one of the most wealthiest African–American men on the west coast.

A few years ago, there were those who'd thought he was a gigolo when he had become the constant companion of wealthy California socialite Susan Brady, a woman twenty years his senior. They had accused him of trying to take advantage of Brady for her money since it was a known fact she had terminal cancer. But those same individuals had been shocked right out of their socks when, right before her death, Susan Brady announced publicly that Jesse Devereau was the illegitimate son she had given up for adoption. It seemed that while in college at Harvard some thirty years ago, a young Susan had fallen in love with an African-American law student and their secret affair had resulted in pregnancy. Therefore, no one was surprised at the reading of Susan Brady's will when it was announced that she had left all her money and worldly possessions to her son.

Mrs. Perkins sighed. Those who didn't really know Mr. Devereau considered him ruthless, unbending, and hard. But she saw beyond all his roughness. What she saw was a man who had achieved all of his accomplishments the hard way, and deep down beneath that tough exterior he still wanted to belong and be accepted, not as the illegitimate son of Susan Brady, but as a man who had become highly successful in his own right. But one thing she'd discovered about Jesse Devereau was that he was also a man who didn't like to be crossed. He selected his friends and business associates carefully and anyone who betrayed him had hell to pay.

The ringing of the telephone interrupted Kitty's thoughts and she quickly went about doing the work her boss was paying her a very good salary to do.

. . .

Jesse tossed all his other mail aside while studying one envelope in particular. It was postmarked from Orlando, Florida. He would never forget the last time he'd been in Orlando almost three years ago, and the woman he'd met there. Occasionally, he would allow his mind to drift back to a Thanksgiving he would never forget. Pushing aside the memories, he quickly opened the letter and read the document that was contained inside.

> I thought you would like to know that two years ago, Carla
> Osborne gave birth to your child.
>
>   An Interested Party

A frown marred Jesse's forehead as he reread the letter. A few minutes later, he leaned over and punched the intercom button on his telephone.

"Yes, Mr. Devereau?"

"Kitty, please contact Mike and tell him I need to see him immediately."

Mike Kelly watched as Jesse paced back and forth within the confines of his office. The two of them had been friends since their foster home days and Mike could claim to be the one person who knew the real Jesse Devereau.

"Stop wearing out the carpet, Jess, because it won't change a thing. As you can see from the report I gave you, you're listed as the father on Carla Osborne's child's birth certificate."

Jesse stopped his pacing and met Mike's gaze. "If I'm the child's father then why wasn't I told? I had every right to know about it."

Mike shook his head. "Look, you did say it was a one-night stand, so maybe she thought she was doing you a favor by not telling you. And there's the possibility that you would not have believed her if she had."

Jesse inhaled deeply. He would have believed her. The one thing he would never forget about that night was that Carla Osborne had been a virgin.

"And," Mike continued, "although your name is on the child's birth certificate, there's still a question as to whether the child is yours since you said that you used protection."

Jesse leaned against his desk. "Yes, but I'm not stupid enough to think a condom is a hundred percent safe," he said. Especially when he remembered the number of times they had made love that night. Somewhere in the process he could have gotten careless. He picked up the report Mike had delivered over an hour ago. Mike was not only his best friend but also his right-hand man who owned a private investigating firm in L.A.—one of the best. His clients usually included people in the entertainment industry, politicians, and other well-known individuals. As well as being someone he trusted implicitly, Mike was also someone he could always count on to bring him the facts and nothing but the facts.

"And the child's birth certificate was not part of the public records?"

"No, which I found unusual. Ms. Osborne had a special filing done by her attorney to keep the information concealed, pretty much the same way some adoptions are done."

"I want to know if the child is really mine, Mike."

Mike nodded. "If he is, then what?"

The answer to that question came easy. "If he's mine I want to be a part of his life."

Mike wasn't surprised that Jesse would feel that way, since he knew just how much family meant to Jesse. He had been given up for adoption at birth but had found himself bounced from foster home to foster home instead. "At least there's one thing you do know about Carla Osborne."

Jesse lifted a dark brow. "And what's that?"

"She's not a money grabber. If her son is really yours, she hadn't planned to use him to get to your bank account. I know a number of women who would have quickly stepped up and claimed you're their baby's daddy if they thought doing so would get them hefty child support payments each month. Evidently Ms. Osborne didn't think that way."

Jesse leaned against the desk, frowning. "Regardless, that doesn't erase the fact she didn't tell me about a child that I would have given anything to know I had. Before we parted ways, I did leave my business card with her so she knew how to contact me if she needed to."

Mike chuckled. "A business card? Oh, how romantic, Jess." He knew at the moment Jesse was too upset to see reason, but Mike had a few questions of his own, like who had sent the letter to Jess? Evidently Carla Osborne had acquired an enemy who'd known that upon receiving the letter Jesse would do one of two things: something or nothing, and they had counted on him doing something. Most men would have tossed such a letter in the trash and counted their blessings that they hadn't known about the child, but not Jesse Devereau.

Although some considered him ruthless and hard, there were those who didn't know the other side of him. It was the side that strongly believed in the principle that a man shouldered the responsibility of taking care of any child he brought into the world and should be an integral part of his child's life—from start to finish. Susan Brady's emergence into Jesse's life had come too late, although the woman had tried to make up in four months what she'd failed to do in thirty-six years.

"So what's your plan?" Mike asked, meeting Jesse's gaze.

Jesse sank slowly into the chair behind his desk. "I plan to leave for Florida immediately."

Chapter 9

"You've resorted to making office calls, Dev?"

Dr. Devin Phillips set his black bag in the middle of Cord Jeffries' desk and gave his friend a stern frown. "Yes, if that's what it will take, Cord. Janelle phoned earlier, concerned about you, and since you're determined not to keep your appointments, you left me no choice."

Cord pushed the papers he'd been working on aside, not appreciating the interruption even if it was a visit from his closest friend. "Look, Dev, Janelle had no business calling you. I'm paying her to keep my office running smoothly, not to play mother hen."

"Somebody needs to do it, Cord. You've been working too hard, nearly driving yourself into a state of exhaustion over the past six months. If you don't let things go I hate to think what might happen. Need I remind you how Dad died?"

The mention of Walter Phillips's death from a heart attack over a year ago caused a lump to form in Cord's throat. Dev's dad had been the closest thing to a father that Cord had had. The widowed man had taken him in after Cord's grandmother had died, leaving him with no other relatives at seventeen, but with a best friend who had taken him home after the funeral and said, "You might as well come live with me and Dad. He won't mind."

Not only did Walter Phillips not mind, he made things legal when he applied to become Cord's guardian through Childrens Services. Cord would always keep a special place in his heart for both Dev and his father.

"I wouldn't give Diane the satisfaction to know she's driven you to this."

The mention of his ex-wife's name reclaimed Cord's attention. He met Dev's gaze and frowned. "She hasn't driven me to anything."

"Dammit, yes, she has, Cord, and at this moment I would love to know where she is so I can forget my medical oath and put my hands around her deceitful little neck."

Cord couldn't help but replace his frown with a smile. Dev was overprotective where he was concerned. Always had been and probably always would be. And it didn't help matters that Dev had never liked Diane. In fact, he had suspected something was up long before Cord had had a clue. A year ago he had come back in town from attending the national CPA convention only to discover his wife had cleaned out every cent out of their bank account—his business account as well— and had left town with some guy she'd been having an affair with for over three months. Within a month of her departure, he had received divorce papers in the mail. He had quickly signed them and went about doing what needed to be done to get back on his feet financially. Dev, as always, had been there for him and had offered him a loan to tide him over. But he knew he had to rebuild his accounting firm to what it used to be. If word had gotten out that his wife had embezzled all of his funds, he would have lost clients for sure. So for the past year he had been working practically day and night, taking on as many new clients as possible. And with the tax season fast approaching, it seemed every-one wanted to make sure their financial books were in order. He was working even longer hours than before and had been for the past six months.

"Janelle said you're not eating properly, Cord."

Cord leaned back in his chair. "Janelle talks too much. I think I'm going to fire her."

Dev chuckled. "Yeah, right. You wouldn't know what to do without her."

Cord inwardly admitted Dev was right. His secretary was so efficient that one could look beyond her fault of having such motherly instincts. She had been a godsend when she had answered his ad for a secretary the same day it had appeared in the newspapers. For the past six months together they had rolled up their sleeves to tackle the mess Diane had left behind. Luckily, Diane hadn't had access to any of his clients' accounts or Cord would have been faced with an even bigger mess and possible jail time, all because of a greedy ex-wife.

Now he'd become a workaholic, not by design but by necessity. He usually got to work at five in the morning and didn't leave until way past seven or eight at night. Those times when he did remember to eat lunch were on the run at some fast food place, but most of the time he'd found himself skipping lunch all together. Dinner for him was even worse. When he got home he usually popped in a microwave dinner but more times than not, he was too tired to eat it and he would find the meal sitting in the microwave the next morning when he got up.

"I hope you've changed Diane as the beneficiary on your life insurance policies. Otherwise at the rate you're going you'll make her and that jerk she ran off with a happy couple, because you're definitely working yourself into an early grave."

Cord's frown returned. "You won't let up, will you?"

"Where you're concerned? No. Especially since you broke your promise to relax some."

"I have been relaxing. I'm even doing some pleasure reading like you suggested."

"Oh, and what do you think?"

Cord smiled as memories he couldn't let go of filled his mind. "I think she was something else."

Dev frowned, wondering what book Cord had read to put that sort of look on his face. "Who was something else? Just what book did you read?"

Cord met his friend's curious gaze. "I'm not talking about the book. I'm talking about the woman who sold me the book. She owns the bookstore. There was something about her that really turned me on, man."

Dev laughed. "Hell, you may be tired, but I see your libido is still kicking and in damn good working order."

Cord grinned. "Yeah. She's the first woman to pique my interest since Diane left. I hate to say it but my ex definitely left a bad taste in my mouth. A woman can really do something to a man after taking over three hundred thousand dollars out of his bank account."

Dev chuckled. "Yeah, I can imagine. But tell me some more about this woman, the one who sold you the book."

Cord smiled as he remembered. "Like I said, she owns the bookstore around the corner in the Florida Mall. It's a real nice set-up with a vast number of things, mostly books. But there was something about her, something different, and I felt it the moment I saw her."

"What? Lust?"

Cord couldn't help but chuckle, since Dev was well aware he'd gone without sex for over a year. Not only had Diane left a bad taste in his mouth but she'd also wiped clean any desire he'd had for another woman. "No, it was more than lust. At least I think it was. I admit her body turned me on and then there were her eyes. She has the most gorgeous pair of eyes I've ever seen on any woman. They're amber in color, just like her name. I bet she was named Amber because of her eyes. But her body and eyes weren't the first things that captured my interest."

"What was?"

"Her smile. And I was able to pick up two different women inside of her. One side of her seemed like a woman who got it going on, a woman who was sure of herself, someone who could probably motivate the hell out of somebody."

"And the other side?"

Cord sighed. That was the side that had him slightly confused, the side he wanted to discover. He'd detected a passionate side that was clouded by pain. She had been as aware of him as he had been of her, and he also had a gut feeling that she'd been as attracted to him as he'd been of her, but she had held back. "We were attracted to each other, Dev. I felt it. I also felt her holding back, pushing it away."

Dev nodded. "She could already be seriously involved with someone."

That comment brought a frown to Cord's face. He had thought of that, too, although she hadn't been wearing a wedding band or an engagement ring. "Yes, that could be the reason."

Dev lifted a brow. "But knowing just how tenacious you are, I guess you're going to find out the real reason, right?"

Cord smiled evenly. "Yes, that's my intent."

Dev shook his head. The woman had made one hell of a first impression on Cord. Dev didn't know whether he should be worried about Cord working himself into an early grave or him getting into something he might not yet be ready for. But he quickly decided the first was far worse than the second. After Diane, he had to trust Cord's instincts about being cautious about another involvement with a woman. He'd known that Diane Martin had been bad news from the start, but Cord had gotten caught up in her sultry voice and centerfold body before he could even blink good, and within months had announced he was getting married. It took less than a year for her to take him to the cleaners.

"All right, man, roll up your sleeve," Dev finally said, opening his black bag.

Cord sat up straight in his chair. "Ah, come on, Dev. You aren't serious, are you?"

"As serious as a heart attack, which you may eventually have if you don't slow down. But since you seem determined to work yourself to death then I guess the task of keeping you alive falls on me. First, I plan to take your blood pressure. Then I'm going to give you a blood test since I can just about bank on you not eating anything this morning anyway. If I recall, the last time I gave you a blood test, the results showed you were anemic and I bet you haven't done anything to rectify the problem. You look like you've lost a few pounds since I saw you last."

"Hell, Dev, I'm fit as a horse. Besides, there's nothing wrong with me losing a few pounds. Once I get back into the gym, I'll have more muscles on my body than you do," he said, knowing how much time Dev spent at the gym when he wasn't at the hospital. Dev wasn't married but he did have a steady girl. Briana was everything Dev needed and Cord was expecting them to announce an engagement real soon.

"Roll that sleeve up, Cord, or do I have to call Janelle in here to hold you down while I do this?"

Cord frowned as he began rolling up his sleeve. "You're getting to be a downright pain in the ass, Phillips."

"Yeah, so take care of yourself and I'll leave you alone."

Cord's frown deepened as he said, "Not damn bloody likely."

Thirty minutes later Cord stood in front of the window of his office building and looked out at Interstate 4. As usual it was backed up with everyone heading east toward Disney World. Glancing at his watch he saw it was the noon hour and Janelle would be leaving for lunch shortly.

He thought of the scolding Dev had given him and decided he may as well go out and get a bite to eat as well. But at the moment, his mind was not on food. It was firmly attached to the woman he had talked about with Dev, the woman who owned the bookstore. The woman with the beautiful eyes.

Amber.

She had been on his mind a lot lately, even during those times when he'd needed his full concentration on debits, credits, and balance sheets.

In less than ten minutes she had blown him away and there had to be a good reason other than he was hard up. And just like he'd told Dev, the attraction he felt for her went beyond sex, although he had to admit he had placed her and sex in the same thought more than once. There was just something about her full curves, rounded hips and voluptuous thighs that really turned him on. And then she had such a strikingly beautiful face. It was the kind that would catch any man's attention. And added to that was her smile. He could have talked to her all day just to see her smile. It had been a long time since a woman's smile had done anything for him but hers had done a hell of a lot.

Quickly deciding his reaction to her that day had been nothing more than a fluke, he decided to test that theory by paying another visit to her store. There was nothing wrong with telling her he had enjoyed the book and letting her know his secretary had enjoyed the romance novel as well. And it also made perfect sense for him to buy two more books: one for himself and one for Janelle.

He turned and eyed all the paperwork that was stacked on his desk, visible evidence that he would be working late again tonight. He shrugged as he headed for the door. No big deal, since it was becoming the norm anyway.

Chapter 10

*B*randy was feeling downright edgy.

She wanted the identity of her stalker revealed more than anything, but it was day seven and already Grey was wearing on her last nerve. It wasn't as if he was doing anything intentionally, but his very presence was unnerving. And although she'd always thought her suite was rather spacious, all of sudden it felt small and cramped.

And filled with a man—a damn striking one at that.

A man whose eyes were so dark they gave you a glimpse of midnight, whose features were so stark they could take your breath away at a glance, and whose body was so well defined it immediately made you think of passion—the hot spicy kind—and of sexual need, the in-your-body-all-up-your spine kind.

And if she thought she had it bad, then she felt totally awful for her female employees, who were trying hard to pretend they weren't attracted to their boss's pretend lover. More than once she'd caught a feminine eye looking at Grey with lust and looking at her with envy.

Funny that he had been the one her cousins had sent. If she didn't know for certain that they were concerned with her well-being, she would think she had been set up. But a part of her wanted to believe that wasn't the case. Taye, Rae'jean, and Alexia had careers that were just as demanding as hers and the last thing any of them had time to do was play matchmaker. But then some ingrained instinct, one that had gotten to know her cousins very well over the last three years, couldn't keep a tight lid on her suspicions.

Her thoughts fell on her and Grey's sleeping arrangements. He slept on the sofa and when she would awake in the mornings, the blankets would be neatly folded and placed back in her closet, and more often than not, he would be sitting at the kitchen table eating or drinking coffee just like it was the most natural place for him to be.

They had spent the first week going over her schedule and familiarizing him with the day-to-day operations of the hotel as well as her key employees. He had set up his equipment in the small office in the suite and kept the door locked to keep the housekeeper out. Brandy had been amazed at all the electronic devices he had brought with him, and how he had transformed her miniature office into some sort of mini-command center, which included a state-of-the-art laptop.

Each morning before they left to go to her office, he would go into her bedroom and stretch out between the covers so the bed linen could pick up his scent, thus reminding her of how important it was for her housekeeper to believe the two of them were sharing a bed.

Brandy knew it would have been a waste of her time to tell him that there was no way Mrs. Johnson, who was old enough to be their grandmother, could be a suspect, because he would not believe her. He constantly reminded her that everyone was a suspect until he found the person behind the notes.

As Brandy continued her walk away from the conference room to the elevator, her gaze darted all around her, even over her shoulder. She walked down the empty hall where a business meeting about the Florida Classic was in session. She'd had to leave to take part in an important conference call regarding another function her hotel was sponsoring.

Although she couldn't see him, had no earthly idea of just where he was, she knew Grey was somewhere close by. Twice that day he had appeared basically out of nowhere, startling her to death when he seemed to materialize right in front of her. He had told her not to worry if she didn't see him, because he was an ace at blending into walls and no matter what, he had her back. Him having her back had been a comforting thought.

It had also been an arousing one.

Brandy swallowed deeply and with urgent determination she tried pushing any thoughts of Grey Masters from her mind. He had his job to do and she had hers. He had promised he would not get in her way and she had agreed to be cooperative. He wanted everyone to think they were lovers, but not necessarily glued at the hip.

Another arousing thought.

She rounded the corner, swearing her thoughts away when she bumped into her food and beverage director, Wilbur Green. "Mr. Green, I'm sorry, I didn't see you."

"I'm sorry as well, Ms. Bennett, since I didn't see you either."

Brandy glanced up at the man who appeared to be rather nervous about something. "Mr. Green, are you all right?"

"Yes, yes, I'm fine. Now if you'll excuse me, I need to go check on things for the Lacombes' dinner party."

Brandy frowned as she watched the man's retreating back.

"He seems rather nervous about something, doesn't he?"

Brandy whirled around. Grey's sudden appearing acts were destined to give her heart failure. She placed her hand over her chest to calm her racing heart. "Grey, don't scare me like that!"

"Sorry."

After inhaling a deep breath she glanced at him; he had those deep, dark eyes aimed on her. At that moment, she suddenly felt something that was kinetically sensual.

Damn.

She turned back around to watch Wilbur Green as he rounded a corner, and used that time to let the jolt that had passed through her subside. She tried like the dickens to think of something else other than the good-looking man standing in front of her. She then recalled the comment he'd made earlier. "Yes, he did seem rather nervous."

"Is his job stressful?"

Forcing her gaze back to Grey's, she replied, "Yes, it can be. One of the things I did when I took over was increase the number of conferences we book each year, which can be rather stressful, but so far he seems to be handling things."

Brandy then glanced down at her watch. "I need to get going or I'm going to be late for the meeting and most of the city officials will be in attendance."

Grey nodded. "What are your plans for this evening?"

Brandy raised a brow. "I don't have any, why?"

"I thought it would be a good time for us to be seen together at your friend's restaurant."

Brandy shook her head, still not liking the fact that Grey considered Thomas a suspect. Besides, a part of her wanted to believe that whoever had wanted to scare her had backed off, since she hadn't received another note. "Maybe my little nightmare is over, Grey, and whoever was behind this decided to stop trying to scare me. It's been over a week and I haven't gotten another message."

Her met her gaze. "You haven't but I have."

Brandy lifted a brow and her heart escalated in beats. "You received something?"

At his nod, she then asked quietly. "From *The Man*?"

Grey smiled and even with her nervousness Brandy felt another jolt, another sensuous kinetic pull. "Yes. An envelope was left at the front desk for me a couple of days ago."

Bandy frowned. "And you didn't tell me about it?" she asked, clearly upset. She inhaled deeply and was almost afraid to voice her next question, but did so anyway. "What did it say?"

Grey's smile suddenly turned into a deep, dark frown. His eyes also changed. They became intense. "It said for me to stay away from you or I'll be sorry."

Amber stood as she arched her back, thinking she had been bending over way too long when she felt the kinks settling there. A hot bath in the Jacuzzi tub she'd had installed a few weeks ago sounded real tempting and she couldn't wait for her day to end. She thought about the store's anniversary party in two weeks and all the things she had to do to prepare for it. She had even decided to bake cookies to serve in order to cut expenses, and Jennifer and Eileen had both volunteered to bake cakes and to do the punch. The only thing left for her to take care of were the peanuts and mints and the decorating.

She had to admit she was getting rather excited thinking about it. In fact she was happier than she had been in years, which went to show that a woman could be happy without a serious relationship with a man clouding up anything.

Amber didn't look around when she heard the sound of the bell indicating someone had entered the shop, since Eileen was on duty. Besides, Amber was determined to have all the new book releases on the shelves by the end of the day, although she had to admit that things would go a lot faster if she didn't stop to read a few pages of every book she picked up.

"What you're doing looks like fun."

Amber turned at the sound of the deep, male voice and nearly gasped. It was the man who had patronized her store last week.

The man who had invaded her thoughts ever since.

She lifted a brow. He was dressed a lot differently than he had been then. The jeans, sweatshirt and Nikes had been replaced with an outfit that looked like one of Armani's top sellers. Everything he had on shouted money. She always enjoyed seeing a brother who looked good and dressed good.

With a sigh of female appreciation she smiled and tried to ignore the sensual pull she felt deep in her stomach. "Hi, it's good seeing you again. How did the reading go?"

"Wonderful, and that's why I decided to drop by to get another book."

"Oh, which one did you like? Walter Mosley or that romance novel I recommended?"

Cord chuckled. "Actually, both. I enjoyed my mystery and my secretary enjoyed the romance book."

"You mean you weren't tempted to read a few pages from that romance novel?"

He chuckled again. "Okay, I admit I did take a peek but after the first page I decided it was too sappy for my taste since there was no mention of blood or guts."

Although she didn't want to, Amber couldn't help but grin and quickly retraced her earlier thoughts. Although she knew there was more to being a woman than getting wrapped up in a man, she could definitely see a sistah getting pretty wrapped up with this brother real tight like. "You do have a point there, Mr. Jeffries."

He awarded her another easy smile and angled his head. "I'm glad you agree, and I prefer you call me Cord instead of Mr. Jeffries."

Amber placed another book on the shelf, determined not to let Cord keep her from her work. Besides, she needed something to concentrate on instead of concentrating on him, which her mind seemed intent on doing. "So, do you know exactly what book you want?" she asked, hoping that would move him on.

"Yes. I'll take another Walter Mosley novel."

Amber took out another book from the box to place on the shelf. "Do you need help finding it?" she asked without breaking her stride in what she was doing. She hoped that pretty soon he would take the hint that she was too busy to chit chat.

Or to ogle him.

"No, I remember what section it's in. And if you don't mind I think I'll browse some. I might see something else to buy."

"Another book for your secretary or for some family member?"

"I don't have any family. My grandmother was my only family and she died when I was seventeen."

"Oh, I'm sorry."

"It was years ago, but thanks anyway."

Amber nodded. A part of her felt sad that Cord Jeffries didn't have family. She'd come from a rather big family and even with the distance separating them, she knew they were there if she ever needed them. "When you're ready to check out let me know. Either me or my assistant will ring you up."

"Thanks."

She watched him walk off, thinking that he looked just as good in a suit as he did jeans and a sweatshirt. Whatever the man put on his body he wore well.

Later, when the shop had endured the furor of the lunch crowd and had a slow moment, Amber was able to sit quietly behind her desk in the back of the shop and let her thoughts dwell on Cord Jeffries.

Everything about him signaled danger, not in the real physical sense of the word but in the emotional sense. It was clearly obvious to her that he was a man that a woman could lose her heart, body, and soul to if she wasn't careful. Amber had found herself in an alluring dilemma, especially after the man's parting words were that he would be attending the bookstore's anniversary party. She wondered how much more of Cord Jeffries she could take, both physically and mentally. It had been way too long since she'd worried about this sort of thing. Mr. Jeffries was definitely a vision of reality.

Amber signed deeply, deciding that she needed to talk to someone and immediately dismissing the thought of calling one of her sisters. All three thought she needed a man and to them, the very idea that she'd been celibate for over two years was a self-imposed torture they couldn't understand. Although she knew they loved her and wanted the best for her, they just couldn't grasp the fact that she needed time to appreciate who she was before committing herself to anyone else. Unlike what everyone back home thought, she was not carrying a torch for Gary. She was carrying a torch for herself and her need for growth and development as an individual, a businessperson, and a woman.

With a long, lingering sigh, she leaned back in her chair. The only persons who understood her plight were Carla and Brandy. Like her, they'd been celibate for a while and often joked about calling their sistah-circle the Celibate Club. Well, she didn't know about Carla and Brandy but going without for over two years was just about to take its toll. But she was determined to hang tight and resist temptation, and Cord Jeffries was temptation with a capital *T*.

Picking up the phone, she decided to call Brandy and Carla to see if they wanted to do the chick flick they had put off doing the other night.

"Yes, hi, Michelle, this is Amber. Is Carla in?"

It didn't take long for Carla to come on the line. "Hey, girl, I know this is a last minute thing and you might be faced with babysitting issues, but I desperately need someplace to go tonight. How about doing a movie or dinner if you can find a sitter?"

She heard Carla's soft chuckle. "You sound rather desperate."

"I am. I need to get out tonight and work off some restless energy."

"Umm, oh, I see." There was a brief pause, then Carla asked without preamble, "Who is he?"

Amber couldn't help but grin. Brandy and Carla had gotten to know her too well. "What makes you think it's a man?"

"Hey, remember I've been there and done that, although maybe not to the extent that you and Brandy have."

Amber shook her head as she remembered what Carla had shared with them that night at dinner. Carla had been a twenty-nine-year-old virgin when she'd met and slept with a man, so Carla knew nothing about the deep yearnings a woman could feel from the need of a man.

"Yeah, but still you can just sit and listen while I tell you everything. I need a reality check right now before I'm tempted to do something really stupid." It wasn't uncommon for her, Carla, and Brandy to seek out one another's counsel, and in her mind Amber could see Carla's eyes change from amused to concerned.

"Then how about coming over for dinner tonight. I'm fixing Craig's favorite meal, spaghetti. Then after I put him to bed we can talk to your heart's content."

Amber thought about Carla's offer. "Are you sure, Carla? I don't want to impose."

"And you won't be. Besides, Craig will be glad to see you."

After a few brief moments, Amber said, "All right. Do you need me to bring anything?"

"I would suggest a bottle of wine but since both of us have to go to work tomorrow, I wouldn't dare. And I would invite Brandy to join us but she's unavailable tonight. Her bodyguard is taking her out to dinner."

"Have you met him yet?"

"No, but Brandy told me all about him when she called earlier. From what I hear, he's an absolute hunk and she's suffering the same plight as you. Overzealous hormones and sex deprivation is about to get the best of her, too."

Amber laughed. "Oh, is that how you're defining our problem."

Carla's giggle was a bright shiny spot on what Amber had begun to perceive as a rather gloomy day. "Yes, but you two have to hang tight and remember our sistah-circle principle from two meetings ago."

"Please refresh my memory."

"All right, here goes. *You have to refocus your mind in the direction you want it to go.*"

Amber rolled her eyes. That principle had sounded pretty good then, but it wasn't doing a thing for her now. Mainly because her mind was determined to be focused on Cord Jeffries' attributes and how he could use them to full potential in the bedroom.

"By the sound of your breathing, I can tell that you're wavering, Amber."

"Well, you haven't seen this guy. Trust me, he would make any woman think of lifting her dress, quickly dispensing with her panties, and taking him on."

On the other end Carla roared in laugher.

"Yeah, well you have a good laugh now, Carla Osborne, but I have a feeling that your day is coming," Amber said, before hanging up the phone.

❧ Chapter 11 ❧

Grey shook his head in an attempt to clear his mind of the desire that suddenly rammed through him the precise moment Brandy stepped out of the bedroom, dressed for dinner. Her dress, a gorgeous blue silk, clung to every curve of her body, defining perfect, high-tilted breasts and a small waist. His body reacted with every step she took and he couldn't help but stare in deep male appreciation.

"You look nice, Brandy."

"Thanks."

He finally pushed himself from where he'd been leaning against the breakfast bar and tried to focus on something else, which was easy enough when he saw her frown. She was still upset with him because he hadn't told her about the note he'd received until today. She felt he should have told her immediately. He explained in a discussion that had nearly bordered on heated that he was there to protect her and she wasn't supposed to be concerned about him. But she'd argued that it had been the principle of the thing.

He had come close, real damn close, to telling her that principles had nothing to do with anything, especially when your life was on the line. He wished he could dismiss the notes as insignificant, but he couldn't. And although he knew she was probably scared shitless, he couldn't help but admire her determination to keep her cool and remain in control. During his days as an agent he'd seen women who would literally freak out and run from their own shadow after receiving a first note, not to mention a second.

It seemed that everything he'd heard about Brandy Bennett was true. She was tough, tenacious, classy, and beautiful.

Another thing he'd been told about her was that she was a typical Bennett female, and hell knew no fury like a Bennett woman's scorn. He couldn't help but admire her spunk when she'd pulled that much-deserved fast one on her ex-husband. There were some who'd be quick to say she'd been manipulative, vengeful, and devious. And yes, he could probably think the same thing, but considering the circumstances, as far as he was concerned she'd had every right to be those things. Nothing hurt worse than finding out the person you loved had betrayed you. He knew firsthand how painful that could be.

"I'm ready to go."

Her words captured his attention, not that she hadn't had it already. She was the type of woman who would have that effect on a man the moment she walked into a room.

He slowly strode across the room to stand in front of her. He couldn't ignore the warmth that touched his skin, bringing him in full awareness of her. Her scent was a fragrance he wasn't familiar with, and it was not the same scent she'd worn that morning. This one was soft. Subtle. Woman.

He wondered, not for the first time since arriving, how her fiancé could have been such a fool to mess up the way he had. Some men were destined not to be trusted.

But then the same thing held true for some women as well.

"Do I have to go over our game plan tonight, Brandy?" he asked, deciding to get things back on the track. He didn't need to get any fanciful ideas regarding this particular Bennett. The one his brother was married to was a handful enough, but then he knew Quinn was enjoying every moment of being married to Alexia.

"No, that's not necessary, since you've done so already. But like I said, I think it's a waste. Thomas wouldn't do anything to hurt me or scare me. Why would he?"

Grey crossed his arms over his chest. He'd also heard of the Bennett women's stubbornness. "You did say the two of you had been lovers?"

Brandy rolled her eyes heavenward. "Not lovers, Grey. When I think of lovers I think of two people engaged in something long-term and definitely more substantial than a one-night stand. That's all Thomas and I had. He was lonely one night and I was grateful for his friendship. It was something that happened that I later regretted."

"And you told him that?"

"Yes. Thomas and I have an understanding that what happened that night was a mistake and it would never happen again. Since then we've accepted that our relationship is based on friendship and nothing else."

Grey wondered how she could think a man who'd had a taste of her body could ever think the two of them could just be friends. "Well, if he's not guilty of anything then you have nothing to worry about."

"Well, I don't like deceiving him," she said, making a frown form at the corners of her lips.

"Well, you *will* deceive him because right now that's what it'll take to figure out what's going on. And since this person has made a threat against me, I'm more determined than ever to find out who he is." What Grey refused to say was that he was anxious to see the man who had captured Brandy's interest, even if had been only for a night.

Brandy sighed deeply as she shoved long tendrils of braids away from her face. Grey Masters was being difficult and if he could be difficult, so could she. "Fine, just don't expect me to like it."

Grey couldn't stop the smile that touched the corners of his mouth. "I don't expect you to like it."

A sudden, involuntary shudder swept through Brandy with Grey's smile. It had actually softened the lines of his mouth, making his lips appear more . . . kissable. She'd always had a thing for locking mouths with the right man and admitted to being one of those women who enjoyed kissing as much as she enjoyed the more intimate details of lovemaking. There hadn't been a "right" man in her life in over two years and tonight her tongue was feeling rather hot and antsy.

"Do you have everything you need to get before we go?"

She tried responding to Grey's question but for some reason her hot and antsy tongue didn't want to participate. She cleared her throat and tried again. "Yes, I have everything."

Moments later the two of them walked out of her suite.

Amber sat at Carla's kitchen table waiting for her to return from putting Craig to bed. Being around Craig tonight reminded her of the child she had lost. Had the baby lived, it would have been just a few months older than Craig.

"How about if I make up a pot of coffee since we can't hit the wine bottle tonight," Carla said, reentering the room.

Amber looked up. "Coffee is fine with me. I'm going home and look through a few cookbooks for a good, simple recipe for cookies. I promised Jennifer and Eileen that I would bake a batch for the anniversary celebration. You are coming, aren't you?"

Carla smiled as she went to the sink to prepare the pot of coffee. "Of course I'll be there. We've always made it a point to be there to take a part in each other's successes, remember?"

Amber smiled. She would always be grateful for having connected with Brandy and Carla and their support. Getting their lives back in order had not been an overnight thing and they were still working at it, since it was a chipping-away process and not one to bring instant gratification or immediate satisfaction.

Satisfaction.

Thinking of that one word brought Amber's thoughts back to her present problem. She began rubbing her forehead.

Carla turned from the sink and cast a concerned eye at her friend. "What's wrong?"

Amber lifted her head and met Carla's gaze. "I need my mind stimulated."

"Are you sure that's all you need stimulated?" Carla asked, her voice deceptively light.

Amber couldn't help but chuckle. Of the three of them Carla was usually the one who tried being serious-minded most of the time. "Hell, Carla, I won't lie to you, girl. I could definitely used a good lay just about now."

Carla shook her head thinking of a similar conversation she'd had with Sonya some nights ago. Was sex the only thing on everyone's mind? "A good lay, huh? Can I guess a possible prospect?"

Amber shrugged, knowing Carla was studying her intently with those big, dark brown eyes of her. Eyes that saw everything but never placed judgment on anything. If she didn't agree with something she diplomatically told you so. "Well, what do you think?"

Carla leaned against the sink. "I think you should go back and reread those scriptures that Pastor Thomas gave us at church a couple of months ago."

Amber rolled her eyes heavenward. "Pastor Thomas can afford to talk since he has Sister Thomas. They have four kids, all under the age of eight, which means he's not missing out on anything."

Carla bit the corner of her lip to keep from smiling but failed miserably. "Amber, you're totally awful."

Amber blew out a frustrated breath. "That's not all I am." She looked up when she felt a touch on her shoulder and met Carla's eye. She hadn't known Carla had moved away from the sink. "Hey, will it be so bad for you to finally meet a guy and fall for him? Or for any of us to meet guys we might like and get serious? I think we agreed to be cautious in our next relationships, not turn into women who never want men in their lives again. If he's a nice guy and you're attracted to him then why not let yourself become interested in him?"

Amber frowned. She knew the reason she didn't want to get involved with another man: fear. Gary had stripped her of so much self-esteem that the thought that she would be setting herself up for the same thing again scared the living daylights out of her. She cleared her throat nervously as she prepared to answer Carla's question. Before she could do so, Carla's phone rang.

"Whatever you were about to say I'd like you to hold that thought until I get back."

Moments later when Carla returned Amber immediately noted the troubled look on her face. "Is anything wrong, Carla?"

Carla sank down in the chair across from Amber. "I'm not sure. That was Brandy, calling on her cell phone from the ladies room of the Commodore Restaurant. She was leaving the hotel for dinner and happen to pass the check-in desk as this man was registering."

Amber lifted an amused brow. "What's unusual about that? I'm sure plenty of men register at her hotel. What's so special about this one?"

Carla met Amber's curious gaze. "His name is Jesse Devereau."

Amber remembered the name immediately. "Aw, hell."

Sighing deeply after taking a sip of her wine, Brandy leaned back in her chair and met Grey's gaze from across the table. "I hope you're satisfied that this evening was a compete waste of both of our time."

Grey shook his head. "If you believe that then you really do have blinders on."

Brandy's cheeks tinted and a degree of fury shone in her eyes. "What do you mean by that?"

"It means Thomas Reynolds is so damn jealous that if looks could kill then I'd be dead. The look on his face when we entered this place was outright rage, although I think he downplayed it rather well." Grey leaned back in his chair. "He's old enough to be your father."

Brandy took offense at the censure she heard in his voice. "For your information, he's older than my father and what I do and who I do it with is no concern of yours, Mr. Masters."

"Thanks for reminding me of that, Brandy. And you're right. My only business is finding out who's sending those notes, and just for the record, your ex-lover stays on the list. In fact, he's moved up a notch. I can pick up on his anger from across the room."

They stared at each other for several long minutes before Brandy released his gaze. "Look, I know you're doing your job, but don't you think you've gone just a little overboard with your theory about Thomas? For the past two years he and I have been nothing but good friends. If what you think is a possibility, why would he wait until now to do anything?"

Grey shrugged. "I have no idea, but I do know there's such a thing as obsessive love and although you may feel nothing but friendship for him, it's very obvious that he's kept his feelings in check because he knows that's what you want. There's a chance he may have gotten impatient and decided to play his hand. Or," Grey said, meeting her gaze intently, "he may have come up with the idea that if you were frightened about something enough, he would be the one you would turn to for solace and protection."

Brandy lifted a brow. She really hadn't thought of that, but still what Grey was proposing wasn't convincing as far as she was concerned. "But don't you think someone would have noticed Thomas if he had caught the elevator to the administrative floor or to my suite? He's not an employee and would have stuck out like a sore thumb."

"Someone might have assumed that he was coming up to visit you. Have the two of you been seen together often?"

Brandy frowned. "No, and definitely not in the way you think, Grey. Like I said, my intimate relationship with him was only for one night. And it wasn't at the hotel but his place. Until you showed up claiming to be my long lost lover there has not been any particular man in my life. I've been way too busy to become involved with anyone. If Thomas and I were seen together it was for business and nothing more. Being an alumnus of BCC, Thomas is an important member of the Florida Classic committee. In fact, he's the one responsible for my involvement and my hotel being selected as a host hotel, which will bring in a lot of money."

Grey picked up his wine glass again to take another sip. "So he looks out for you?"

"Yes." Brandy leaned back in her chair, glad that Grey was finally getting it. Clearly sooner or later he would see that Thomas could not be "The Man." But the more he looked at her while slowly twirling the wine glass around in his hand with his penetrating dark eyes on her, the more she was beginning to think he really didn't see at all. "Why do you try so hard not to trust people, Grey?"

Her question evidently caught him by surprise, off guard. He placed his wine glass down and his gaze that was already trained on her became even more intense. "And why are you so gullible? You've been burned in the past. Didn't you learn a lesson in that?"

For the longest moment Brandy didn't say anything, and she couldn't help but think back to the time, last week in fact, when she and Grey had had a conversation about trust. It was when she had mentioned what had happened between Lorenzo and Jolene.

"What they did hurt me, Grey," she admitted softly now, wondering why she felt comfortable talking to him when he'd just called her gullible, which to her was another word for naive. "No one, not even my cousins, knew the pain I felt finding out I was betrayed that way. And then to go through the part where everyone watched that video-tape and saw the man I was to marry and my best friend, the two people I had trusted the most, being deceitful was a very difficult time for me. I got through it because my family was there for support and comfort, and to show me their love. But then when it was time for everyone to return back to their homes and I decided to do the honeymoon without the groom, I found out just how bitter, spiteful, and hateful toward men I'd become. Not only that, I felt that other than Alexia, Rae'jean, and Taye, I couldn't trust another female to get close to me as a friend."

Grey raised a brow. "What changed things?"

A small smile touched the corners of Brandy's lips. "A very wise old man by the name of Ethan Allen Bennett. My grandfather. He sat me down and told me that there were two ways to grow and change in life. You could either choose to grow and change or you could be forced to grow and change. He made me see that part of life is growth and everyone will grow because it's the purpose of us being here. But the big question is how you will grow. Will it be willingly, joyfully, or with pain? I was forced to encounter pain to grow. All through life my mother, my father, and both sets of grandparents had sheltered me. I always thought I was all of that and no one, especially my cousins whom I didn't get along with for years, had anything on me mainly because I was Valerie Constantine's daughter, and my mother in her haughty splendor had convinced me I was better than everyone."

Brandy took another sip of her wine. "It took growth on my part to realize that I wasn't. That I was human and susceptible to pain and betrayal just like anyone else. During my forced growth I also learned that although I couldn't stop the waves from coming in my life, that I could learn to surf. And that's what I've done. I had to learn to let go and move on and not see every man as Lorenzo and every woman as Jolene. I had to learn to trust all over again. I'm cautious but not cynical. It took me over two years to get to this place in my life, Grey. Even if it's proven that the person who wrote those notes is someone I thought I trusted, that's fine. I'll get over it just like I got over what happened in my life almost three years ago. What happened during that time was a lesson in disguise and I learned from it, and this time will be just the same."

Brandy stifled a long sigh. It felt good getting all of that out. She'd done so at other times with her cousins as well as with Carla and Amber, but never with a man. A part of her wished Grampa Ethan had lived to see her growth, to see how she had taken the advice he had given her and made changes in her life. Good changes. Some not easy. But changes she'd had to make for peace of mind—to survive.

Grey took a sip of his wine, saying nothing. Brandy's words explained a lot. The woman had gone through . . . and was still going through . . . a transformation of some kind, which was all well and good with him if that was her thing. But he still needed her to understand that nothing, and he meant nothing, could be accepted at face value. There were things that were meant to be checked out, scrutinized and eventually dealt with . . . like this mad, crazy person sending those notes.

And like the sudden heat of desire consuming him yet again.

He swallowed hard to keep his hormones from getting carried away, but watching her sit across from him, slowly drinking her wine, was an absolute turn-on. He cleared his throat. "Would you like to order dessert?"

Brandy shook her head. "No, thanks. I'm ready to leave." The only thing she wanted to do was to go home and go to bed. She was tired, edgy, and she *had* noticed Thomas watching her more than usual tonight. And his gaze *had* seemed angry. Had he forgotten about their agreement to be just friends? Or like Grey had suggested, had Thomas told her what she'd wanted to hear but had inwardly harbored the hope that she would eventually change her mind?

A short while later Grey had taken care of their bill and was escorting her out of the restaurant.

After Amber left, Carla went into the kitchen to pour out the cup of coffee they had never gotten around to drinking. A part of her felt awful that she had not concentrated on everything Amber had shared with her like she should have, since her mind was boggled with Brandy's phone call.

Could it be true? Was there a possibility that Jesse was in Orlando?

And if he was, did it mean anything? She wrapped her arms around herself, trying to stay calm, but the man Brandy had described sounded a lot like the Jesse she knew . . . or at one time thought she knew, at least for a night.

She stood and began pacing. What if it was him? Why was she nervous? She didn't owe him any explanation about anything, including Craig. But chances were he wouldn't want any, since he didn't know about Craig and she hoped things stayed that way. And she hoped his visit to Orlando would be a short one.

The last person she wanted to see was Jesse Devereau. And she definitely didn't want him to find out about their son.

Grey was busy making the sofa into his bed, tucking in the sheet as best he could, smoothing the comforter and fluffing the pillows. He had to admit that Brandy's sofa didn't sleep half bad. In fact, he thought it was rather comfortable. Once she went to her room each night and closed the door, she normally didn't come out. And usually in the mornings he was awake long before she got up.

He had tossed the comforter back and had stepped out of his slippers, getting ready to slide underneath the covers, when Brandy's bedroom door opened. The small light from her bedroom illuminated her form. She was standing perfectly still. He waited for her to say something.

"Grey?"

"Yes?"

"I'm thirsty. I need to go into the kitchen for a glass of water. Are you decent?"

Grey smiled. "Yes. I have clothes on, so you can come on through and turn on the lights."

After a brief pause she said, "Thanks."

He sat on the sofa as the area was bathed in bright lights and watched as she quickly crossed the room to the kitchen, heading straight for the refrigerator. She was dressed in a thick, powder blue, velour bathrobe and appeared buttoned up from her head to her toes. He smiled, wondering if she had taken the extra step to protect herself from him or to protect him from her. Whichever the case, it wasn't working, since he could still see the gorgeous curves and angles of her body that the robe couldn't hide.

He leaned back on the sofa and watched as she opened the refrigerator. At dinner she had said that over the last two to three years she had grown and had put behind her what her best friend had done to her, and he felt part of that was true, especially since she considered Carla Osborne and Amber Stuart very close friends. But if she had gotten beyond her ex-husband's wrongdoings, then why wasn't there a man in her life? For some reason he didn't buy her story that she'd been too busy to date. There was another reason she had distanced herself from men. Didn't she know anything about having balance? Most women that he knew, including his sisters, accepted that part of being a woman was including a man in your life. That didn't necessarily mean you had to get all wrapped up in one. What it meant was that a woman was supposed to be able to enjoy a healthy relationship with a man. And it didn't have to be about sleeping together either, although to a man's way of thinking, that part of a relationship always sounded pretty damn nice.

He sighed deeply, thinking that he was in no better shape than she and was finding out the hard way what not having that balance could do. It had been nearly three years since he'd gotten laid and the result of that was now taking its toll. Brandy held the distinction of being the first woman in all that time that he wanted to take to bed . . . and in a very bad way.

His attention was then drawn back to her. She had gotten a water bottle out of the refrigerator and uncapped it. He watched as she tipped the bottle up to her lips and drank, sucking on the bottle like it was the one thing she needed to survive.

He swallowed hard as he watched her, getting turned on by how her mouth sucked on the bottle. Her lips were definitely made for kissing of the most erotic kind. That water may be saturating her mouth, but at the moment, everything about Brandy Bennett was saturating his thoughts, his needs, and his desires.

Since his wife's death he had poured himself into his work, trying to make the investigative agency a success. Unlike Brandy, he couldn't claim he'd been too busy to get involved with a woman. No man could ever get *that* busy. But he hadn't wanted to become involved with any woman after Gloria's death. The pain of her betrayal was too raw. Then later, after he'd gotten over what she'd done, he hadn't been ready to become a part of the dating scene no matter how badly he felt like he needed a good lay at times. He didn't have the time or the inclination to make sure women understood that he would want to make love and not make lifetime memories. But for some reason, a part of him felt, and a part of him knew, that if he ever made love with Brandy, there would definitely be lifetime memories.

She must have felt the deep intensity of his eyes on her for at that moment she looked up and met his gaze. Her brow arched slightly. "Do you want some water, too?"

His gaze continued to hold hers and he wondered if she could perhaps handle it if he were to tell her exactly what he did want. He quickly decided it was best not to find out. Instead he stood and slowly walked to the kitchen. He saw the wariness in her eyes that she tried to keep at bay. But what got his attention more than anything were her lips. They were wet from the water she'd drunk. Wet and delicious looking.

She moved aside slightly as she turned back to the refrigerator. "There's another full bottle in here," she said reaching inside to pull out another bottle of water.

"Don't need that much to quench my thirst," he said in a voice that he knew sounded deeper than usual. "I'll just finish what you started," he said, taking the water bottle from her hand. He tipped the bottle to his lips and drank what was left, doing an awful job of drowning the heat that was consuming his stomach. But then he was getting a fairly decent taste of her as he drank from the same bottle her mouth had touched. He knew it probably was nothing compared to the real thing, but at the moment he would take what he could get.

He met her gaze as he continued to drink and saw her shiver slightly. Not from cold, since to his way of thinking it was pretty damn hot in her kitchen right now. He knew her shivers were from the deep attraction they felt for each other. It was an attraction that had been there since that first day, one they had tried to avoid, and one tonight they were acknowledging.

And one that neither would do a thing about.

Grey took the bottle from his mouth and wiped his wet lips off with the back of his hand. "That tasted good."

She forced a smile. "Water always does when you're thirsty," she said, breaking eye contact with him as she placed the unopened bottle of water back inside the refrigerator.

"Yeah, that might be true, but this tasted good because I got to savor you in the process and I like your flavor."

Brandy's gaze again met his. She pursed her lips, hesitated for a brief moment, then asked, "And what flavor is that?"

"Hot brandy."

He watched the small gasp escape her. He watched another shiver pass through her body and watched as she remoistened her already wet lips. She took a step back. "I need to go back to bed. Goodnight."

"Goodnight, Brandy."

As he continued to look at her, she quickly crossed the living room to her bedroom and closed the door behind her. He leaned against the counter and wondered if she would have as hard a time sleeping tonight as he would.

Brandy turned furiously over in bed several times and pounded her pillow with a frustrated fist. She had made a big mistake in letting Grey get into her bed that morning, like he did every morning, to make the housekeeper think they were sleeping together. His scent was everywhere in the room and not just on her bed linens. And then, earlier tonight in the kitchen, that had been the last straw—it may not have broken the camel's back but it had broken her resolve.

At least it had . . . almost.

Trying to bring a calmness to her body she lay staring at the ceiling for a long time. Every once in a while as much as she had gotten stronger over the years and as much as she had grown, she would still remember the hurt and humiliation of that day almost three years ago. For some reason tonight it had been hard to get beyond those feelings. Maybe it was because she had talked about them to Grey and her mind had relived that day. And it was only tonight while in the kitchen with him that she had to admit that all her talk had been cheap. She wasn't completely over what Lorenzo had done. Hard work and success hadn't completely eradicated his actions from her heart.

Oh, she didn't love him, that was for sure. She'd lost whatever love she had for him the moment she saw that videotape. But for a full year after that she had lived for revenge. It had been revenge for a man who didn't deserve the dirt under her shoe, and getting the hotel he'd prized so much had been sweet.

But now, almost two years later, why was she so afraid to get back into another relationship with a man? If nothing else, that episode with Grey in her kitchen had shown her just how afraid she was.

She shifted in bed, wondering if Grey was getting the sleep that she wasn't getting.

❧ *Chapter 12* ❧

*B*randy overslept.

And once she got dressed, walked out of her bedroom, and saw Grey, the first thought that came to her mind was that they both looked like hell. It was quite obvious that neither of them had gotten a good night sleep. That would have been all well and good if they'd spent the entire night making love, but that was not the case.

"Good morning," she tried to say in a cheerful tone of voice.

"What's so good about it?"

Brandy met Grey's gaze. In spite of the fact that she felt like hell this morning and probably, although she'd spent a decent amount of time in front of her mirror, looked like it, too, she couldn't help but smile. Men were rather funny when they needed to get laid. They just couldn't handle things. Whereas she had a reason for being moody and agitated, since it had been nearly a full two years for her, and to be quite honest, she couldn't even count that night with Thomas, since it had been so disastrous. She was sure it hadn't been that long for Grey. Unless, however, he was still grieving for his wife and as a result had been celibate since her death almost three years ago. Brandy shook her head finding the very thought of that ludicrous. A virile man like Grey would not be able to go without sex for three years. There was no way.

"What's so funny?"

She glanced at Grey and saw his deep frown. "Me. You. And the reason we didn't get any sleep."

Grey lifted a brow, evidently surprised at her honesty and candor. "And you find it amusing?"

"No, quite honestly I find it pathetic, but then at the same time I also find it refreshing. It's good to know at thirty-two that I can still turn a man on."

Grey leaned against the kitchen counter, the same spot she'd left him in the night before, but this morning he had a cup of coffee in his hand. He had a feeling that she would still be able to turn a man on at sixty-two. "Were you trying to turn me on?"

She tossed him a glance as she walked into the kitchen to pour her own cup of coffee. "No, and that's what so nice about it. But then you should feel good, too, since you definitely got my blood heated up pretty darn good, so consider us even."

His frown deepened. "I wasn't aware we were competing."

She lifted her head from pouring her coffee and smiled at him. "We weren't. It's this sexual chemistry thing. Trust me, I know all about it. I have parents who have a double dose of it for each other. They have never married but can't stand to be in the same room with each other for a few minutes before they blow up in smoke. It's not uncommon for them to just disappear for a while."

Brandy chuckled when she recalled how at the age of sixteen she'd finally realized what was going on with her parents. "At times they act like they hate each other but then when people aren't looking, or when they *think* people aren't looking, they can't keep their hands or eyes off each other."

Grey set his coffee cup on the counter. "Why didn't they ever marry?"

That question brought another chuckle from Brandy. "It's depends on whose story you want to believe, so over the years I've come up with my own."

She took a sip of her coffee before continuing. "Although both my mother and father would doggedly disagree with me, I think getting married was too easy for them. I believe that in the beginning my mother wanted my father to marry her since she was only sixteen when she got pregnant with me and doing so would have been the honorable thing for him to do. But I can see how right the decision was for them not to marry. While my father was in college at Morris Brown, he got a girl pregnant and her parents forced him to marry her. That meant he had to drop out of school and lose out on a football scholarship. As soon as Victor Junior was born the girl divorced my father and moved back to Ohio and finished her education at some other college and conveniently left her baby to be raised by my father and grandparents."

Brandy shifted in her chair to get more comfortable as she continued. "Three years later my father met my mother. She had slipped into this nightclub claiming to be eighteen when she was only sixteen. Anyway, she met my father there and lied about her age. Since he didn't know any different, he slept with her and she got pregnant. There were some who claimed she'd seen him around and had set her sights on seducing him and that he wasn't her baby's father, since she was known to be what everyone considered 'a fast gal.' However, any doubt that I was his child ended when I was born. I look too much like my father for anyone to claim otherwise."

Brandy took another sip. "Anyway, I think Dad would have asked Mom to marry him but she pissed him off when she tried forcing his hand. He'd already been forced into one marriage and didn't intend on getting forced into another. So he rebelled like hell and didn't marry her. He joined the army instead and when he returned two years later he brought home a Japanese wife, Tokya, which only pissed my mother off even more."

Grey shook his head, thinking her parents' history was definitely colorful as well as cultural. "Did he and the Asian woman have any children?"

"No, and I even heard that she really didn't like having sex, and that the only reason she married him was to get to America and to what she considered as a better way of life. Well, her plans backfired because my father is a man who strongly believes in having sex anytime, all the time, and when she continued to place limitations in their bed, they got a divorce and he sent her packing."

Brandy decided not to tell Grey that she'd also heard that Tokya's sister had come for a visit one year; one night after having drunk too much her father found his way into Tokya's sister's bed, the two had a night of wild sex and the woman had ended up getting pregnant. It was common knowledge within the Bennett family that her father had an Asian daughter living somewhere up north, and occasionally they would hear from her.

"But getting back to my parents' story," she said as she watched Grey refill her cup with more coffee. "Seeing my father with other women only made my mother angry and she was determined to show him just what a mistake he'd made by choosing those women over her. But in the process she forgot one major thing."

"What?"

"My mother has an addiction to my father. She hates him but she can't stand to be without him. I know that sounds rather crazy but it's true. She can give him pure hell one minute—which can last for months—but then when he comes around and throws her that lethal Bennett smile and gives off this sexual chemistry that she can't resist, she goes bonkers. But then the same thing happens to him. He's as addicted to my mother as she is to him. No matter who he marries or what woman he's with at the time, he never stays away from my mother's bed for long. So to my mother's way of thinking, she literally has him just where she wants him."

Grey rubbed his chin that was in need of a shave. "Is your father married?"

"No, he's been divorced now for almost three years, and there's no doubt in my mind that as we speak he and my mother are somewhere together." She signed heavily. "That's sad isn't it?"

"Not if your mother is satisfied with that sort of relationship."

Brandy chuckled as she set her coffee cup down. "I think she is. Besides, I don't think I could handle it if they got married." She then glanced at her watch. "I have to make a quick call to Carla, then I'll be ready to go."

"All right. When you're through, I'll walk you down."

"What did you find out, Brandy?"

Brandy heard the deep concern in Carla's voice. "I checked a few things out when I got in from dinner last night and I hate to say it but this Jesse Devereau may be one and the same. I understand he's a wealthy businessman from L.A. who's here on business. It doesn't look like he's going anywhere soon since he has his suite booked for an entire week."

Carla nodded, not liking what she was hearing. She shifted uneasily in her seat at her kitchen table. "Is he alone?" she asked.

"No," Brandy said with a heavy sigh. "But if you're asking if he's here with a woman, the answer is no. He's here with a man I assume to be a business associate by the name of Mike Kelly. They have connecting suites."

"And you're sure he's not here with a woman?"

"Positive. My female employees have been going nuts since he's been here and they watch his every move. The man is so fine. I can see how you were attracted to him the first time you saw him."

"Yeah, but that was then and this is now. If he's here on a business trip that's fine, however under no circumstances do I want him to find out about Craig."

"And you think he has?"

"No, I really don't."

"Then you don't have anything to worry about, but to play it safe I would suggest that you lay low for a while and not visit me at the hotel."

"Don't worry, I won't," Carla replied.

A short while later when Brandy and Grey walked off the elevator, her secretary gave her a big smile. "Why, good morning, Ms. Bennett, I thought you had decided to sleep in this morning."

Brandy chuckled. "No, I just overslept."

"Oh, I see."

Brandy was sure the woman thought she saw more than there really was, since Grey was standing so close to her. "Did I get any calls, Donna? Do I have any mail?"

"No calls but yes, these are for you," Donna said, handing Brandy a stack of envelopes. Brandy was surprised when Grey followed her into the office and closed the door behind them. She thought he'd only planned to catch the elevator with her to the administration floor.

"You didn't give me your agenda today," he said, taking the seat across from her desk.

"Oh, yeah, that's right, I forgot. I was too busy giving you Bennett History Lesson Number One instead," she said, flipping through the bunch of envelopes Donna had given to her.

Grey chuckled. "You mean there's more."

She looked up, met his gaze and smiled. "Believe me, I could write a book." She then glanced down at one envelope in particular as she tossed the others on her desk. A frown suddenly marred her forehead.

"Something's wrong, Brandy?"

She glanced up and met Grey's gaze again. "I'm not sure but for some reason I'm getting a funny feeling about this one letter here. I've noted all the things you told me to watch out for. There's no postage, no postmark and no return address."

Grey stood. "Let me see it."

She didn't waste any time handing it over to him, and he quickly ripped it opened and scanned the contents. "Damn."

"What is it, Grey? Let me see it."

He hesitated a moment before passing it on to her. Brandy was visibly shaken while reading the letter.

> I don't like that another man is getting what is mine. For that you will pay.
>
> The Man

As Carla swung her car into Osborne Computer Network's parking lot, the conversation she'd had earlier with Brandy was still on her mind. She hoped what she assumed was right and Jesse was in town on business and nothing more.

Juggling her keys and briefcase in one hand she closed the door to her car, turned around, and froze in place. There standing a few feet away next to a Mercedes sports car was the one man she had hoped not to see . . . ever again.

Jesse Devereau.

And he was waiting for her.

Seeing him again made her realize that he was the one and only man who had ever touched her body. And even now she could admit he was the one and only man who had once gone so far as to touch her soul as well as her heart within forty-eight hours of meeting him. But that had been before she'd found out just what type of man he was.

Seconds ticked by and Carla was unable to move. She was surprised that she was capable of breathing. After the initial shock at seeing him she quickly surmised that he was still the most gorgeous man she had ever laid eyes on. But she didn't want to think about that. What she wanted and needed to know was why he was here waiting for her.

Taking a deep breath, she walked toward him, his eyes holding hers.

He looked taller and darker, and his hair was longer and caught in ponytail at the back of his neck, Steven Seagal–style.

As she got closer she tried not to look at his mouth. She remembered that mouth well and how he had put it to use on her. All over. She moved her gaze from his mouth and met his eyes. Like his son's they were hazel, darkly intense and contrasted starkly with his dark almond complexion. But then so did the straight hair. She again wondered what he was mixed with? White? Hispanic? Some other nationality?

Her attention slid past him to the entrance of the building. She saw Sam Barnes, Osborne Network's security guard standing in front of the revolving doors, watching, looking, and making sure all was well and that the man waiting for her posed no threat and was safe.

For some reason she felt Jesse wasn't safe, especially to her peace of mind. She suddenly felt angry, annoyed that he was there. If he didn't know about Craig that meant he'd sought her out for another reason. Did he think she was willing to give him a repeat performance of what happened over two years ago? If he did then he had another thought coming.

Jesse's gaze remained fixed on Carla's face as she came closer. She was even more beautiful than he had remembered. He had thought about her often, sometimes thinking that the night they'd shared had not been real but a figment of his imagination.

He inhaled as a deep, primitive ache spread throughout every part of his body. What had it been about her that had drawn him to her like a bee to honey? They had only spent two days together, less than that if you were only counting hours; yet from the first there had been something about her that had touched him, entranced him. In his heart he had believed there wasn't a pretentious bone in her body and everything he'd seen about her that night was real and genuine. She had made an impact on him like no other woman and he'd let his guard down, which was why finding out about her betrayal had hurt tremendously, tarnishing the special memory he'd retained of her. Receiving that anonymous letter had been like a knife twisting in his heart. He didn't want to believe that she hadn't tried contacting him to let him know she'd gotten pregnant—even if their encounter had been for one night.

He distinctly remembered how she had talked at dinner about her deceased father and how close they'd been and the special bond and relationship they'd shared. If her child was his then didn't she think he deserved a chance to have that same bond and relationship with his child as well? What she didn't know but would soon find out was that family meant a lot to him since he'd never had one, other than Mike, and he needed to know if he had fathered her child; if he actually did have a son as the birth certificate claimed.

As she got closer still, he could see she looked annoyed, angry, put out, and the moment she came to a stop in front of him he could tell she was on the defensive already. The dark eyes holding his blazed and she lifted her chin. "Jesse."

He leaned back against his rental car. At least she hadn't pretended not to know him. And for a moment he still wanted to believe there wasn't a pretentious bone in her body, a body he had gotten to know quite well that night.

"Carla," he said returning a greeting just as somber as the one she'd given. He felt her discomfort, her nervousness. He also felt his blood stir and felt the blatant chemistry that flowed between them although he tried not to. Hell, he almost wanted to laugh out loud in startled disbelief. If what she'd done was true, he had every right to be angry, furious, but all he could think about was taking her into her arms and kissing her, tasting her.

"Why are you here, Jesse?"

Her question recaptured his attention. Since she'd asked he might as well get on with it. "I received a letter a couple of days ago."

She lifted a brow. "A letter?"

"Yes. It was short and to the point. In fact, I think I'll let you see it." He reached into the pocket of his jacket and pulled it out. Without wasting any time he handed it to her.

He watched as she opened the folded piece of paper and read it. She then read it again as a dark frown touched her face and her forehead bunched. She shook her head as if to clear it of the staggering effect it had on her. He watched as she finally took a deep breath before folding it back up, met his gaze, then handed it back to him. Then there was sudden stillness. Total silence.

"Well?" he asked when she stood there and didn't say anything.

"Well, what?" she all but snapped.

He reached out and lifted her defiant chin so their gazes could lock. "Did you have my child, Carla?" he asked softly.

Carla swallowed deeply. Should she tell him the truth? What right did he have to know, considering everything? But the question that burned foremost in her mind was, who had sent that letter? She breathed deeply, unsure how to deal with this. She wasn't even sure what rights he had where Craig was concerned, since she had listed him as her son's father on the birth certificate. The reason she had done so was because she'd felt she had owed that much to her son when he got older and wanted to know the identity of his father. The complete truth.

Truth.

That was the one word she had thought she and Jesse had shared that night. They had been two individuals alone on a holiday set aside to give thanks. She couldn't stop the pain she always felt when she remembered how he had lied to her, how he had looked her in the eye and told her he wasn't involved with anyone and she had believed him. So as far as she was concerned she didn't owe him anything. Not even the courtesy of answering his question.

Clearing her throat, she removed his hand from her chin and took a step back. "I won't answer that," she said bitterly, stiffly.

Jesse's eyes darkened, narrowed. "I have ways of finding out," he said curtly. He did and had thought of using those ways but had decided to meet with her first, hoping that she would admit or deny the letter's allegations. And if it was true, explain why she hadn't tried contacting him to let him know he had a son.

"Then find out, because I'm not telling you anything," she said with a stiffened spine.

"Don't you think I have a right to know?" he asked, scowling darkly.

In her mind's eyes she saw the picture that had made front page of a Los Angeles newspaper. A photograph of him and a beautiful and elegant older woman—a white woman at that—as the two of them danced together at some social function. Sonya, who'd been on a business trip to L.A., had brought the article back to show her. Even now the headlines still glared out in her mind: HEIRESS SUSAN BRADY TAKES A LOVER.

"No," she said bitterly. "You have no rights and I don't ever want to see you again."

Not waiting for him to respond, she rushed off and quickly went into the building.

Amber was not having a good day. She hadn't slept well last night but had come into the shop anyway only to find that a huge shipment of books that had been delivered were not the books she had ordered. That meant that the Reading for Fun readers group would not have their books by Saturday unless the distributor sent another order overnight.

Then there was the fact that Cord Jeffries had unexpectedly shown up that morning. Unlike the other times, he didn't have a whole lot to say. In fact, he barely said anything other than a quick hello. He had plopped down a copy of *Black Enterprise* on the counter with the correct change and before she could get the words "thank you" out, he had walked out of the shop. Well, that was just fine and dandy with her. After all, she barely knew the man . . . even if she did have a bad case of the hots for him.

She glanced down at her watch. Carla had called a half hour ago sounding rather strange and saying she needed to talk with her right away. "Eileen," Amber called out to the other woman who was putting up books. "I'll be in my office for a while. If Carla shows up she can find me there."

Once inside her office Amber decided to make a fresh pot of coffee. Even if Carla didn't want any, she sure did. She sat down, waiting for it to start brewing, and couldn't help but think of her dreams last night. Boy had they been wild! In them she and Cord Jeffries had made love in every way known to man. Even a few ways man didn't know about yet.

She couldn't help the wistful smile that touched her lips. In her dream the two of them had been so naughty, so downright sex-crazy. And then seeing him this morning, although he hadn't been talkative, had done something to her. Just the mental image of him touching and kissing her all over, taking leisurely yet greedy licks of her feminine flesh almost sent her up in smoke.

It was getting harder and harder to control her urges.

"Amber?"

Amber glanced up as Carla stuck her head in the door. "Carla, come on in. I made us a pot of coffee."

Carla came in and took the nearest chair. Amber sat up straight when she saw her friend's distraught expression. "Carla, what is it?"

Carla tried to smile. "I'm going to need something a lot stronger than coffee."

Amber raised a brow. "Why? What's wrong?"

"You know last night when I mentioned Brandy's phone call telling me that a man by the name of Jesse Devereau had checked into her hotel?"

Amber nodded. "Yes, I remember."

Carla leaned back in her chair. "Well, this morning I found out it's him. He was waiting for me in the parking lot when I got to work."

Amber's eyes widened. "He was?"

"Yes, and he had a letter someone sent to him, telling him about Craig."

Amber looked at Carla. "A letter? Who sent it?"

Carla sighed deeply. "I don't know and neither does he, but there is a letter because he showed it to me."

"Did you recognize the handwriting?"

"It was typed." Carla's throat tightened, wondering who could have sent it; the first person that came to mind was her mother, since she'd always been obsessed with having Craig's father know the truth. But her mother never knew the identity of her baby's father and the birth certificate was supposed to have been concealed.

"What did he say?" Amber asked, reclaiming Carla's attention.

"He asked me if it was true."

"And what did you say?"

Carla stood and began pacing Amber's office. Moments later she came to a stop. "I refused to answer him. He hasn't been a part of Craig's life so why should he care?"

Amber met her gaze. "But you know the reason he hasn't been a part of Craig's life, Carla. You never told him you were pregnant."

"Because he didn't deserve to know. He lied to me."

"Yes, but he's still Craig's father and with that come certain rights." Amber knew she wasn't telling Carla what she wanted to hear but she, Carla, and Brandy had agreed to always be completely honest with each other.

Carla grabbed her purse from off Amber's desk. "Look, I need to go see my attorney and get legal advice. If Brandy calls looking for me, let her know that's where I'll be." She then quickly left.

Cord Jeffries felt ill. He had awakened that morning with barely enough energy to lift his head and somehow he'd made it to the bathroom to take a shower. Even now he felt weak as water and didn't want to think about the phone call he'd received from Dev last night. Cord's test results indicated his blood pressure was high and he needed to slow down and start eating properly. Or else . . .

Cord didn't want to think of the 'or else' that he'd been presented with. He wasn't sure if Dev was kidding or just trying to scare him, but the thought of being confined in a hospital was not something he wanted. So he had promised Dev, who'd called from the airport on his way to a medical convention in Dallas, that he would take a couple of days off to relax and would start eating properly.

And he had intended to keep his promise, but when one of his biggest clients, Fred Powell, had called and said he'd received a letter from the IRS, he'd had no other choice but to get dressed and go into the office.

He had made a stop by Amber's shop on his way in, needing to see her again, if only for a brief moment. But he hadn't hung around for long, fearful that she would take one look at him and see he wasn't feeling well. He'd heard women could easily detect that sort of thing.

He looked up when a knock sounded at his door. "Come in."

His secretary stuck her head in. "I'm about to leave for today. Is there anything I can get for you before I go?"

"No, Janelle, I'm fine."

"Well, you don't look fine."

He glared at her. "Thanks for the compliment, now go and drive carefully."

"Thanks, and take my advice and stay home tomorrow."

"I'll think about it." He then thought of something. "There's something you can do, but tomorrow will be soon enough. That bookstore that I've been frequenting will be celebrating their second anniversary next week. I want an arrangement of flowers sent to the owner. Her first name is Amber but I don't know her last name."

Janelle nodded. "That won't be hard to find out. Is there any specific type of flowers you want sent?"

"No, just something nice that will last awhile."

"All right. Anything special you want on the card?"

Cord leaned back in his chair. "No, just congratulations and my name will do."

"Okay, I'll make sure it's taken care of. Now, boss, I suggest you close up shop and head on out, too. Whatever you're working on will be here when you return."

Cord forehead bunched into a frown. "Yes, but I don't particularly want to see it. Good night, Janelle."

"Good night, Mr. Jeffries."

The minute Grey heard Brandy's shower going he picked up his mobile phone and began dialing. The phone was picked up on the second ring.

"Masters here, and I hope you got something for me. Another note was left today with her secretary," he said, his tone curt and to the point. In the last week one of his investigators had been hired by the hotel as a bellman and another, a female investigator, was hired to work in house-keeping. No one knew they'd been planted there to keep their eyes and ears open. He hadn't even mentioned it to Brandy.

He'd also solicited the aid of a couple of men that he knew who were special agents working in DC to run background checks on a couple of Brandy's employees. The reports he'd gotten back earlier that day on her friends Carla Osborne and Amber Stuart were clean, and he expected to receive the report on Thomas Reynolds at any time.

He listened attentively to what the man on the other end was saying. "Umm, I find that rather interesting as well. I appreciate you uncovering that information and it may possibly be the break I need. I'll check back in with you on tomorrow."

After disconnecting the line he rubbed his chin at the information his friend, Ernie Baker, had uncovered. He found it rather interesting. It was definitely something that he doubted Brandy was aware of.

He was just about to go into the room where his laptop was set up to check to see if there were any messages for him on his computer when

Brandy's phone rang. He could still hear the shower going and decided to go ahead and answer it.

"Yes?"

"Grey, this is Alexia. It's been over two weeks and I thought you were going to check in and let me know how things were going."

Grey shook his head. His brother had definitely married an impatient woman. Beautiful, but still impatient. "There's nothing to report yet."

"Oh. Well, how is she? Rae'jean and Taye will want to know when I talk to them later tonight."

"Brandy is fine but I haven't figured out who's sending her those messages, although I've been able to piece together a few things."

"Like what?"

"That's for me to know. Right now I need to keep a lid on everything."

"And you think I'll talk?"

Grey couldn't help but laugh outright at that question. "Hell, yeah, I think you'll talk. And anything that's leaked could jeopardize this case."

"Really, Grey, it's not like I know those people."

"It doesn't matter. Just let me handle things, all right?" There was a slight pause. "Alexia," he said in a warning tone when she didn't answer him.

"Oh, all right. I guess I'll tell Rae'jean and Taye that we need to cancel our trip to Florida next week."

Grey raised his gaze to the ceiling. He'd wondered how long it would take for them to plan a trip to check up on things themselves. That's all he needed was to get tied up with the Bennett cousins. "Yeah, I think canceling that trip to Florida would be a good idea. Remember when you asked me to take this case you promised to let me handle things my way?"

"Yeah, well . . ."

"And I'm holding you to it. Trust me. Brandy is in safe hands. Now where is Quinn? I need to talk to him for a second."

Grey sighed when Alexia grudgingly told him to hold on. He didn't envy his brother one bit. In fact he didn't envy any man who married a Bennett.

"Yeah, Grey, what's going on?"

"Nothing is going on, but I believe I got some information today that may help move things along. I just need you to do me a favor."

"Sure. What?"

"Handcuff your wife to the bed or something." He could hear Quinn immediately start laughing on the other end.

"Hey, that's not a bad idea, but any particular reason that I should?" Quinn asked. "Other than a few ideas I have of my own."

Grey could just imagine his brother's ideas. "I think she and those other two cousins of hers are planning a trip to Florida and I definitely don't need that. They may decide to take matters into their own hands and heaven help us if that happens. I'll have my hands full keeping all four of them safe. The person who is sending Brandy these notes is a lunatic or he's trying hard to convince us that he is."

Quinn sighed deeply. "All right, I'll just have to come up with something to keep Alexia busy. Maybe I'll get her pregnant again." He sounded content and just a bit smug.

Grey laughed. "Hey, that's your call."

Grey had just hung up the phone when Brandy's bedroom door opened and she walked out, fresh from her shower and looking sexy as hell in the same velour bathrobe from last night.

He had stayed pretty close to her most of the day and when he wasn't around, he'd made sure the other investigators he had hired were. "Are you ready to order dinner?" he asked when she came into the living room. She sat down on the sofa, her gaze studying the floor.

"I'm not hungry," she said softly, without looking up.

He nodded. That last note had really bothered her. "You need to eat something, Brandy."

Her head snapped up and the look in her eyes was pure fire. "You don't know what I need, Grey. What I need is for the person who is sending me those damn messages to stop. If they're trying to scare me off it won't work. I won't give up my hotel, I won't."

He immediately closed the distance separating them and sat down on the sofa next to her. He reached out and tucked his thumb under her chin and raised her face to meet his. "Hey, everything's going to be all right, I promise. I told you from day one that I wouldn't let anything happen to you."

Without thinking twice about it, he pulled her into his embrace and began rubbing his hands up and down her back. "Don't let the bastard get to you, Brandy. I'll find out who he is, I promise."

He could hear her deep sigh. He could also smell her scent. The latter was beginning to drive him crazy. It was also making his body hard as a rock.

"Nothing like this has ever happened to me before, Grey. This pervert is turning me into a fraidy-cat."

Grey chuckled softly, his breath warm against her ear. "You're not a fraidy-cat. I happen to think you're brave. Only a very brave woman could have managed to continue on with her plans today like there was nothing wrong. I think you should be proud of yourself."

She leaned back and met his gaze. Her eyes, he noticed, were unusually bright and it seemed that every emotion she possessed was right there in that gaze. "You think so?"

His gaze slowly dropped to her lips. "Yes, I think so."

For the longest moment neither said anything, then in a soft, barely heard whisper, she said, "Kiss me, Grey."

When he didn't move, she leaned her body forward toward him and whispered lower still, "Go ahead, even if you don't want to kiss me, just do it to humor me. I need the kiss, Grey."

He arched a dark brow, wondering how on earth could she think he didn't want to kiss her when he was literally burning up with the need to taste her.

He folded her into his warm embrace as his mouth came down on hers. Her lips immediately parted under his and he stuck his tongue inside her mouth the exact moment he heard her long sigh of pleasure. The sound sent jolts of excitement racing down his spine. He felt vibrantly alive and passion, the red-hot kind, nipped him all over.

He made a noise that could have been a growl, he definitely wasn't sure. All he could do was to continue to suck, lick, and taste her.

The kiss was mind blowing, slow torture.

She wrapped her arms around his neck to hold on and he couldn't stop kissing her if his very life had depended on him doing so. Moments later, when breathing became a necessity, he eased back but not too far where he couldn't kiss the corner of her mouth, her cheek, nibble her bottom lip and sink his fingers into the thick mass of braids that spilled over her shoulders.

He continued to brush his mouth back and forth across hers, after not getting nearly enough of her taste. His gaze raked hers hotly. "One more kiss okay?"

Without giving him an answer, she took the initiative and covered his mouth with hers, staking her claim, continuing what he had started, and not holding back anything. He felt her shiver when his hand reached up and parted the folds of her robe, unerringly going straight to her breasts. His breath caught when he smoothed his fingers across a path that went from one nipple to the other. He made up in his mind, then and there, that the next time he would know the taste of them. He would also know the taste of her.

And there would definitely be a next time.

Once again they had to let loose for air and Grey closed his eyes and sank back against the sofa, not knowing if he would survive. He lifted a hand to pinch the bridge of his nose, in an effort—a totally wasted effort—to cut off her scent. It was stronger than ever—hot, enticing, seducing.

"Grey?"

It took all his strength to force at least one eye open to gaze at her.

Talk about a woman being easy on the eyes, she was definitely that. Her robe was still parted and he could get a glimpse of her bare breasts. He decided to open both eyes and get an eyeful—at least as much as he could get. He was definitely a breast man. Always had been and always would be, and hers were every man's dream. Even now he was tempted to lean forward, take his tongue and lick and suck her nipples until he was the ripe old age of one hundred.

"Grey?"

When she called his name a second time, he lifted his gaze from her breasts to her face. "Yes?"

"Thank you."

He lifted a brow. "What are you thanking me for?"

"For giving me what I needed tonight."

Inevitably, his gaze left hers and lingered downward, stealing a token glimpse of her breasts again. "Is there anything else you need, Brandy?" She was truly a beautiful woman, he thought. And he wanted her.

He watched as she gently swiped her lower lip with that sweet tongue of hers. If she was trying to provoke him, it was working. He felt his already hard erection get harder.

"No," she finally answered, softy. "I think that's all for now."

He met her gaze. "Are you sure?"

She smiled, the first he'd seen since she had received that letter today. "No, I'm not sure, but I'm trying to do the right thing."

He arched a brow. "Which is?"

Her smile widened. "Spare you. I've got two long years to make up for."

He sighed. She didn't know it but he had a year up on her. Mental images, most of them crystal clear, flitted across his mind. "I don't want to be spared."

Now it was her time to arch a brow. "You sure?"

"Yes, I'm positive."

She nodded as a soft chuckle escaped her throat. "I'll keep that in mind . . . the next time."

. . .

The lone figure paced the room, edgy, agitated. The plan wasn't working. Another would have to be put in place and soon. There was no time to waste. Brandy Bennett had to get what was coming to her.

↠ Chapter 13 ↞

Good morning, Grey." Brandy breezed into the kitchen with an entirely different attitude than the previous morning. Getting kissed senseless followed by a good night's sleep worked wonders for a woman.

She stopped short when she saw all the platters that were lined on her kitchen counter. "Looks like someone is rather hungry," she said teasingly, meeting Grey's gaze. It was obvious that he had called up room service.

"Yes, I'm hungry," he said, uncovering the platters to expose grits, eggs, bacon, sausage, and toast. "Care to join me?"

"Hey, why not?" she said, tossing her jacket across the chair. Brandy immediately went to the cabinet to get a plate. She was glad there was no awkwardness between them after their kiss on the sofa the night before. Evidently they both had looked at what had happened in a mature and logical way, and decided it was something that had been bound to happen sooner or later given their close proximity for the past couple of weeks, as well as the sensual vibes that had been radiating between them.

She crossed the small kitchen to the coffee pot to pour a cup of coffee. As far as she was concerned, her morning didn't officially begin until she drank her coffee.

"What's your agenda today?"

She decided to take a sip of coffee before answering Grey's question. "I have several meetings but all on site and on the fifth floor where most of the meeting rooms are located."

Grey nodded. If those were her plans today then they were his plans as well. He had no intention of letting her out of his sight unless he knew for sure his other investigators had her within their scope.

She was about to start filling her plate with food when the phone rang. "Go ahead and finish what you're doing. I'll get that," he said, hoping it was one of his men with something to report. "Hello?"

After a brief pause he said, "Yes, Brandy Bennett is at this number." There was another brief pause. Then he leaned his hip against the sofa and said. "I'll tell you who I am once you tell me who you are."

He cast a quick look across the room at Brandy. "Oh, Ms. Constantine. Please hold a minute." Grey then held out the phone to Brandy. "It's for you and I think you have a lot of explaining to do," he whispered, handing the phone to her when she reached his side.

Brandy rolled her eyes. Evidently her mother was her usual pleasant self this morning, she thought sarcastically. "Mom? Hi, what's up?" She then turned to look over at Grey who had returned to the kitchen. "Oh, that's Grey. You know, Grey Masters, Quinn's brother?"

After a brief pause Brandy said, "Grey's just a friend who came for a visit. No, Mom, the two of us aren't sleeping together." After a brief pause she added in a frustrated tone. "Yes, Mom, I'm still on the pill."

Grey, who'd been about to take a sip of coffee, stopped the cup midway to his lips when he heard Brandy's last remark. He looked over at her and she gave him with a warm smile and a shrug of her shoulders.

"Enough questions about me and my sex life, Mom," Brandy said getting a little agitated. "What I want to know is why you told Dad about his birthday party when you knew it was supposed to be a surprise?"

There was another brief pause. "I understand that, Mom, but two wrongs don't make a right and you should not have spoiled things for him and the family."

Grey couldn't help but notice there was a longer pause this time. Evidently Ms. Constantine was trying to explain her side of things and he couldn't help but smile.

"All right, Mom, but I think you owe them an apology, even if you feel you were right. I love you, too, Mom, and by the way, how's Dad?"

Brandy rolled her eyes again. "And why would I be asking you about him? Mainly because I'm sure you've seen him in the past week. And how would I know? Just call it a daughter's intuition." Brandy released a deep sigh. "Okay, Mom, I'll talk to you later and give Dad a kiss for me." Brandy hung up the phone and rejoined Grey in the kitchen. He was already eating.

"When you get time I'd like you to give me another Bennett family history lesson. Your conversation with your mother just now sounded like a doozy."

Brandy sat down at the table and immediately took a sip of her coffee. "It was."

Grey paused in biting into his toast and said, "I hate to say this and I hope it doesn't sound too disrespectful, but your mother sounds like she's a pain in the . . ."—he cleared his throat and decided to say in kindness—"rear end."

Brandy couldn't help but chuckle. "That's a nice way of putting it and yes, you're right, she is. But my father wouldn't have her any other way."

After breakfast before they left to catch the elevator, Grey decided to let Brandy in on the latest development, at least part of it. "I've decided to let the local police know what's happening, Brandy."

A dark frown deepened her brow. "Why? I thought there would not be any police involvement unless it became absolutely necessary for fear of negative publicity for the hotel, Grey."

"And that's still holds true. There won't be any involvement right now but they need to know about things just in case something major goes down. I don't like the tone of the last note that was sent."

Brandy nodded. Neither did she. "All right, Grey. I trust your judgment about all of this. All I want is for things to get back to normal and for whoever is sending those notes to stop."

Automatically, without very much thought, he pulled her into his arms in a protective embrace. "Me too, and right now I want to be cautious. And one of the positive things is that one of the agents I used to work with in D.C. knows the chief of police here. He's going to apprise him of what's going on with the understanding that we have everything under control and they won't be needed unless we call them."

Brandy nodded again. "Is there anything else I should know, Grey?"

He thought on her question and decided that it would make his job a lot easier if Brandy was kept in the dark about some things for now. "No, there's nothing else you should know."

Carla picked up her phone. "Yes, Michelle, what is it?"

"Yes, Ms. Osborne, there's a Mr. Jesse Devereau here to see you. Should I send him in?"

Carla inhaled sharply, not believing what Michelle had just said. There was no way Jesse could be here when she'd distinctly told him yesterday that she hadn't wanted to see him again. Didn't he understand that they had nothing to say to each other? The subject of whether or not Craig was his son was not open for discussion.

"Ms. Osborne?"

Sighing deeply, Carla decided to see him and try and make things clear with him once again. She would let him know that she had seen her attorney and asked that he do whatever necessary to make sure Jesse didn't try seeing her.

"Yes, Michelle, send him in but please summon security."

Carla stood as her office door swung open and Jesse Devereau walked in. "Jesse, I thought I made myself clear yesterday."

"All I want to know, Carla, is if your son is mine."

"I have no intentions of answering that."

Jesse stared at her. "If he isn't mine then why is my name on the birth certificate as his father?" When she didn't reply immediately, he lifted a brow, waited. When it became obvious that she had no intentions of answering, he frowned. "Why are you being difficult? All I want is the truth."

The truth? There was that one word again that had no place between them. How could he want to speak of truth when he had lied to her that night? "I refuse to tell you anything. And just so you know, I've contacted my attorney and he'll take whatever steps are necessary to make sure you stop harassing me."

Jesse's gaze narrowed. "Harassing you? All I've done is try to find out the truth and considering everything, I felt I should come directly to you for answers."

"I refuse to tell you anything." Carla's attention slid past him, toward the doorway where Michelle and the security guard stood.

"Is something wrong, Ms. Osborne?" Sam asked, entering her office.

"Yes," Carla said as anger seeped through her every pore. "My conversation with Mr. Devereau is over and I'd like you to escort him out of the building. And please make sure he doesn't return."

Jesse's face lit with anger. Then without saying anything, he was gone with Sam following in his wake.

"Are you all right, Ms. Osborne?" Michelle asked, in a deeply concerned voice.

Carla leaned against her desk. "Yes, I'm fine." But a part of her knew she wasn't fine. She would never forget the furious look on Jesse's face when he had walked out.

Mike watched an angry Jesse pace the confines of his suite, thinking he'd never seen him so angry.

"I can't believe the woman," Jesse said after a few minutes of constant pacing. "I've made every effort to talk to her and she refuses to have anything to do with me. She has to be the most stubborn person I know."

Mike chuckled. "Then I feel sorry for the kid if he's really your son, Jess."

Jesse stopped. "What the hell are you talking about?" His tone was as cutting as his gaze.

Mike leaned back against the sofa and ignored both. "All I'm saying is that if the kid is yours then he doesn't stand a chance, having both a stubborn mother and a stubborn father, since you're the most stubborn person that *I* know."

Jesse glared at Mike. "This isn't funny."

Mike chuckled again. "Trust me, I can very well see that and I'm curious as to what you plan to do now?"

Jesse took a seat at the desk in the room. "I spoke with John Kline a few minutes ago and things are being taken care of."

Mike's brows rose sharply. "John Kline?"

"Yes. I want to see just how stubborn she is when she's faced with losing her company."

The next morning Carla and Amber met for breakfast. Just before leaving home Carla had received a phone call from a friend who was a brilliant player on the New York Stock Exchange.

"She wanted to know what new product my company was coming out with for the recent movement in my company stock's prices," Carla told Amber, after taking a sip of coffee. "And she's heard it will really hit gold tomorrow and was calling looking for a hot tip. I told her we didn't have a new product coming out on the market. Now that has me concerned."

Amber raised a brow. "What? The fact you don't have anything new coming out?"

Carla shook her head. "No, the sudden movement of Osborne's

stock. When stock prices jump that rapidly and it can't be linked to any type of new innovation, it usually means one thing."

Amber lifted a brow. "What?"

Carla met her inquisitive gaze. "Someone is buying up a lot of shares of stock."

Two days later

"So what did you find out, Stanley?" Carla asked the man sitting across from her desk. Stanley Jerrott was Osborne's senior attorney and if anyone could find out what was happening with the company's stocks and why, he could.

"I made a few phone calls, Ms. Carla Osborne, and the news isn't good. Osborne Computer Network has become the target of a hostile takeover bid."

Color drained from Carla's face and her eyes widened in shock. "But—but, I don't understand . . . why? It's not like we're some Fortune 500 company. We're a little guy compared to other major computer companies, so why us?"

Stanley shrugged big, massive shoulders. "I wish I knew, but the only person who can answer that is the man behind the takeover. But in a way, I'm really not surprised given the current merger fever in this country. However, like you I am surprised they would want us. It's not like we make millions every year, so this doesn't make sense."

Carla nodded. She then stood and walked over to the window, not wanting to believe what Stanley had just told her about the takeover attempt. Mergers happened to big companies like IBM and Hewlett-Packard. In fact, Osborne Computer Network wasn't even listed in the top one hundred computer companies in the nation. And their clientele was basically regional, although a lot of discussion had been done lately about expanding those boundaries.

She turned back to Stanley. "Have papers been filed with the SEC?"

"Yes."

Stanley's voice had been low when he'd answered but she'd heard his response just the same. She also knew what it meant. Anyone going after more than a certain percentage of a publicly held stock had to register their intentions with the SEC. With that out of the way, whoever the person was who'd set their sights on Osborne was free to begin acquiring vast quantities of the shares on the open market. All that he needed was enough shares to give him control of the firm.

Carla sighed. She couldn't bear the thought of losing the company and not just for her sake—her main concern was her employees. If the company was forcibly taken from her, what would become of them? She'd heard numerous stories of how long-time, faithful employees got tossed out in the cold with mergers and she couldn't stand the thought of that happening. A good number of them, like Stanley, had planned to retire in a few years and now with the threat of a takeover even that was threatened, since the company's retirement plan could be eliminated.

She walked backed over to her desk but couldn't sit down. She was too angry to do so. "Who is he, Stanley? Who's the person trying to take over Osborne Computer Network?"

Stanley didn't have to open the folder he held in his hand. The man's name had been branded onto his memory. A few calls to friends he'd made on the West Coast had basically told him everything he needed to know about him. He was well known as a corporate raider; his reputation for taking over companies was legend. However, most of those Stanley spoke with were surprised he had ventured so far south for his newest acquisition. "A man by the name of Jesse Devereau."

Stanley's expression took on a high degree of concern at the sound of Carla's gasp, as well as the way she suddenly sank down in her chair. Her features appeared in shock. He immediately stood. "Carla, are you all right?"

It was awhile before she answered, and even then he noted she was trembling. "Yes, I'm fine," she said in a soft voice that had Stanley not believing her. Her reaction to Jesse Devereau's name had him curious so he pressed forward.

"Do you know Mr. Devereau?" he asked, and had a feeling she did even before she answered.

Carla nodded slowly. "Yes, Stanley, I know him."

The next morning

Carla picked up the phone. "Yes?"

"Have you seen the newspaper this morning?" Brandy asked quickly.

Carla raised a brow. "No, I just brought it in but haven't had a chance to open it yet. Why?"

"Open it, read it, and call me back."

Carla frowned. Whatever Brandy wanted her to see had to be important. "All right." Hanging up the phone she reached for the paper on the table and opened it. She inhaled sharply when she saw the headline on the front page of the Orlando Sentinel.

Wealthy West Coast Industrialist sets sights on Osborne Computer Network

After completely reading the article, Carla angrily tossed it aside. Jesse wasn't wasting any time letting his intentions be known, which left her at a disadvantage since she hadn't made any type of announcement to her employees. Seeing the article in the newspaper was a lousy way for them to find out that their jobs might be in jeopardy. To counteract the damage caused by the newspaper article, she would schedule a meeting with all of her employees once she got to work and follow it up with a brief press conference.

But what really tore her heart in two was the statement in the newspaper that her mother had sold her shares to Jesse, thus giving him enough shares in the company to control it. Angry beyond belief, Carla picked up the phone to call her mother only to be told moments later by Charles, her mother's second husband, that Madeline had left that morning for Memphis and he didn't expect her back for least three days. Carla hung up the phone thinking, *How convenient,* but she intended to confront her mother when she returned.

Although they were not what one would consider close, nevertheless Madeline was still her mother, and as far as Carla was concerned that constituted some sort of loyalty. But her mother had betrayed her and had turned her back on her in the worst possible way. She had literally yanked from under Carla's feet any financial stability she'd had for herself and Craig.

Carla inhaled deeply as she picked up the phone to call Brandy back as she'd promised she would. She needed the support of her friends now more than ever.

Book Three

Evening, and morning, and at noon, will I pray,
and cry aloud: and he shall hear my voice.

Psalms 55:17

❧ *Chapter 14* ❧

The three women in Amber's office stood in a circle, their hands joined and their heads bowed in prayer.

The sistah-circle.

They had always encouraged and uplifted each other, been supportive of one another, and in times like these they had also been there to pray together.

Today was a day to celebrate Amber's success, the second anniversary of Amber's Books and Gifts. It was also a day for the three of them to focus on their current trials and tribulations and to thank God for their friendship and faith, and to ask Him for the strength to endure whatever lay ahead and to keep their spirits high. They also asked for protection, guidance, and Divine intervention. They knew the power of prayer. It worked wonders and a person's prayers did get answered. Brandy, Carla and Amber admitted to being living witnesses of that fact.

When the praying was finished they hugged and cried while reaffirming their love for each other, their friendship and bond, and most importantly their faith and belief that no matter what, their Father would never forsake them.

. . .

Grey stood leaning against a bookcase with a steady eye on the closed office door. As soon as he and Brandy had arrived, Brandy and her two girlfriends had gone inside and closed the door behind them. That had been over twenty minutes ago and he was beginning to wonder just what was taking so long. There couldn't be that much talking in the world. He then remembered just how much yakking went on whenever the females in the Masters family got together and reclaimed that thought.

He glanced around the room. More people had arrived and most had headed straight for the tables that were loaded down with food and punch. He checked his watch again. Once Brandy came out he intended to stick to her like glue. That last note had him edgy, pissed off and in the ripe old mood to hit somebody just for the hell of it.

The call he'd gotten earlier from the Bureau in D.C. hadn't helped matters. The lead, which had looked promising yesterday, was now a dead end and he wasn't too thrilled about that. He sighed deeply. There had to be something that he was overlooking. Something was staring him straight in the face that was so damn obvious and simple he just couldn't see it for shuffling through the more complicated stuff.

He had questioned Brandy's secretary, subtly of course, to find out how she'd come in possession of that letter. The forever cheerful Donna Fields had told him that Perry Hall, the security manager, had given it to her to pass on to Ms. Bennett. Quickly following that lead he had then spoken directly with Hall, who seemed just a little bit annoyed that he was asking him anything. Grey had lied, saying that Brandy wanted to know where the letter had come from in order to thank the person who'd sent it, but unfortunately there was no return address. Hall had simply shrugged and said that someone had placed the letter in his mail slot by mistake, which was the reason he had given it to Donna Fields to pass on to Brandy.

For some reason, there had been something about the entire scenario that didn't sit well with Grey. Another thing he found rather interesting was that the man he'd hired to keep a close watch on Thomas Reynolds had reported that on occasion Reynolds would drive out of his way to the hotel after closing his restaurant. He would circle the parking lot just to see if Brandy's car was parked in its usual spot. That information didn't sit too well with Grey, either.

Before his thoughts could darken any further, the office door opened and the three women walked out. Each one could be considered gorgeous. They were women who could take a man's breath away just by entering a room, women who looked like they meant what they said and said what they meant and dared you to think differently, women who enjoyed good times but knew how to deal with the bad. To his way of thinking, there was only one word to describe the kind of women they were.

Savvy.

His gaze locked on one in particular. Brandy Bennett could make his blood heat without even trying. He swallowed deeply. Now was not the time for his thoughts to turn sexual. He needed to stay focused and keep his mind on getting the case solved and not think on how to get between Brandy's legs. But damn if the thought didn't constantly cross his mind.

A lump formed in his throat and he swallowed hard again when she glanced over in his direction. She was staring at him like there was a possibility she would need to be kissed senseless again. Soon. Maybe even right now.

He could handle that.

Grey wondered, if he breathed in deeply enough would he be able to smell her scent? As he watched, Brandy excused herself from her friends to walk over to him. The woman had a pair of legs that made him want to weep. And her skin was awfully soft too, he thought, as a flare of heat shimmered through him.

He wondered if he could convince her that tonight they needed to move beyond the kissing stage. In fact, he was game to go back to the hotel and strip naked right now if she was. He shook his head, wondering if he had suddenly lost it. He needed to concentrate on keeping her safe and not getting her in bed. Hell, getting her, period.

"Hi, Grey."

"Brandy," he acknowledged, trying to keep his gaze on her eyes and not let it drift lower to her lips. "For a moment I was beginning to wonder if I would have to come in there after you," he said, reaching out and tucking a wayward braid behind her ear. "Must have been some discussion."

"We weren't talking."

He lifted a brow. "You weren't?"

"No."

"You mean the three of you were locked up in that office all that time and weren't doing any talking?"

"Yes."

"Then what on earth were you doing?"

"Praying."

He couldn't hide his surprise. Everyone had some kind of beliefs but he hadn't expected her to be the pray-every-day-wherever-you-are kind, and found that rather interesting. He cleared his throat and asked, "Think it will help?"

She smiled at him, the kind of smile that made him appreciate being a man and doubly appreciate her being a woman, and said, "Of course. Prayer always helps. I'm a living witness of that."

He started to tell her that he was, too. As an agent he had come close to death numerous times and had had to pray himself out of several sticky situations.

Moments later Brandy said, "When I first arrived, I was really worried about Carla, especially after what I read in this morning's paper. But now I know in my heart that she'll be fine and things will somehow work out for her."

Grey nodded. He decided not to tell her that he didn't share her optimism. He had also read the article in the newspaper that morning and it didn't look good. Whether Brandy wanted to accept it or not, Carla Osborne was about to lose her company.

"This place is getting crowded. Amber has to be pleased with this turnout."

Grey nodded again, wondering how soon he could let her know that he would be *pleased* if they were to head back over to the hotel.

"Ready to mingle, Grey?"

He sighed deeply. Evidently her thoughts weren't riding the same range as his. In fact they weren't even close. "I'm ready when you are."

Together they moved into the crowd and with every step Brandy took, Grey was right by her side.

Amber's heart began pounding and her pulse began racing when the crowd shifted and she spotted Cord Jeffries.

He had come.

And he was staring right at her. A shudder swept through her under his gaze and she wondered if he felt it. She tilted her head back to continue to make eye contact. His eyes were dark, totally electrifying, and oh so sexy. He was standing next to the table with a cup of punch in one hand and a cookie in the other. It was one of the cookies that she had baked herself, carefully following the recipe her sister had given her the week before. It was a long-standing joke in her family that she couldn't cook and that anyone eating her food would be at risk, but she had been proud of how the peanut butter cookies had turned out and Cord seemed to be really enjoying his.

She thought it was a total turn-on to watch him nibble the cookie and wondered if he would nibble on her flesh the same way if given the chance. Ever since that first day he had walked into her shop she'd been trying to convince herself that she wasn't interested in a relationship, and even if she were, she lacked the confidence to handle a man like

Cord Jeffries. He had the ability to make heat flare all through her with just a smile and a glance. She didn't even want to think what his touch would do.

As she continued to watch him, deciding at some point she needed to start mingling with her guests, she saw him wipe his brow several times like he was getting extremely hot. Then he slowly loosened his tie.

Her eyes widened with concern when the empty punch cup dropped to the floor and he suddenly seemed unsteady on his feet, almost to the point of staggering backward.

She made a move to cross the room to him but found she hadn't been quick enough. He tried to grab hold of something to keep from falling but instead got thin air. Horrified, Amber watched as Cord Jeffries gave up trying to stand and crumpled lifelessly to the floor.

Chapter 15

Carla took off her shoes the moment she entered her house. Now if she could only get rid of her headache just as easily, she thought, as she immediately headed to her son's room. She felt an overwhelming sense of love when she entered and found him asleep in bed cuddling the stuffed animal Sonya had given him last Christmas.

Her gaze then shifted to Mrs. Boston, who was asleep in the rocking chair not far away from the bed. Her hands were still clutching the book she'd evidently been reading from when both she and Craig had fallen asleep.

A shudder suddenly passed through Carla when she remembered the look on Jesse's face that day when he had left her office. She was smart enough to know she had pushed him too far and now he was deliberately trying to hurt her. The question of the hour was, just how far would he go? He had already set the wheels in motion to take over her company, and she wondered what was next. Would he try and gain custody of Craig?

Her anger defused at the thought. There was no way on God's green earth she would let him or anyone take her baby away from her. She would fight him with everything she owned before she let that happen.

She would mortgage her house twenty times over if it was necessary. Craig meant everything to her and she would not lose him. He was her life and she would do anything to keep him.

Walking closer to the bed she glanced down on him. The glow from the nightlight illuminated his features. Even in sleep he looked so much like Jesse it was uncanny. Even if she had lied and said Craig was not his son, all it would take was for Jesse to see him and it would be obvious.

"Carla? I wasn't expecting you back so soon," Mrs. Boston's whispered voice floated across the room.

Carla smiled softly over at the woman who had awaken. "Yes, well it's been a very tiring day. Come join me in a cup of coffee before you leave. I need to talk with you about a few things."

Mrs. Boston had to make a stop at the bathroom and Carla used that time to call Amber's bookstore to see if there was any update on the condition of the man who had passed out in Amber's shop.

Brandy's bodyguard had swung into action and had done what was necessary while someone had the good sense to call 911. Amber had gotten so upset that she'd left the anniversary celebration to follow the ambulance to the hospital. Brandy and Grey Masters had followed in their car. Carla hoped the guy was okay, especially after finding out that he was the same man Amber had talked to her about that night. It was plain to see that Amber didn't consider him just an ordinary customer.

By the time Carla had the coffeemaker going, Mrs. Boston walked into the kitchen with a concerned look on her face. "You look tired, child. You need to get more rest."

Carla nodded. If she looked tired now she didn't want to think how she would be looking a few weeks from now while standing in the unemployment line. "I'll be fine Mrs. Boston, and thanks for your concern."

"Well, the way I see it, your mama should be here with you. That's what family is for at times like these. I still can't believe she turned her back on you that way by selling that stock. I read the article in the newspaper this morning and then watched you at that press conference on television. My heart just wanted to bleed. Your daddy has probably been rolling over in his grave all day."

Carla couldn't help but smile because she had thought the same thing several times today. In fact she had thought of her father a lot lately. She missed him so much and always would. She reached out and gently touched the other woman's hand. "Well, no matter what, I believe everything will be okay. But Jesse Devereau is making it difficult and that's what I want to talk with you about."

Mrs. Boston nodded as she took a seat at the table while Carla poured them both a cup of coffee. Carla glanced down at the older woman who had always been there for her. She then thought of her friends who were there for her now.

Carla joined Mrs. Boston at the table. "If you read this morning's paper and saw my news conference then you know that this wealthy industrialist has acquired all the shares he needs to take over Osborne Computer Network."

The older woman nodded. "Yes, and I can't believe your own mother sold him those shares to help him do it."

Carla inhaled deeply. She still was having a hard time accepting it herself.

"And who is this man who's taking over your company?" Mrs. Boston asked, interrupting Carla thoughts. "Where on earth did he come from? And for him to have that much money, why haven't I heard of him before? He certainly hasn't been featured in *Jet* magazine."

Carla's couldn't stop the small smile that touched her lips. Next to the Bible, Mrs. Boston considered *Jet* magazine as gospel. But to be quite honest, she hadn't known Jesse was all that rich either.

"He does all of his business mainly on the West Coast."

Mrs. Boston frowned. "The West Coast? Well, as far as I'm concerned he should have stayed out there. The nerve of him coming south and messing with your company."

Carla took another sip of her coffee before saying. "Mr. Devereau has what he considers a good reason for what he's doing."

Mrs. Boston lifted a brow. "And what reason is that?"

"Anger. He's pretty upset with me right now."

Mrs. Boston's brow lifted even higher. "And why is he upset with you?"

Carla sighed deeply. "Because I refused to tell him what he wanted to know about Craig."

The other woman leaned closer. "And what did he want to know about Craig?"

Like her mother, Mrs. Boston had no idea who had fathered Craig. The only persons who knew were Sonya, Brandy, and Amber. "He confronted me on two different occasions and asked if Craig was his son."

Mrs. Boston's other brow lifted and she sat back in her chair. "Is he? Is that man Craig's daddy?"

Carla moistened her suddenly dry mouth before saying, "Yes."

"Then why didn't you tell him?" Mrs. Boston asked softly.

Carla lifted her chin. "Because he doesn't need to know. He lied to me that night."

Tilting her head to the side, Mrs. Boston smiled sadly, knowingly. "And you've hardened your heart."

Carla closed her eyes for a moment, knowing that she had. From that one night she had fallen hard for Jesse, and then to find out he'd lied to her had hurt. To him it may have been just a one-night stand, but to her it had been more until she'd discovered he had lied. A wave of pain swept through her and tears she couldn't contain any longer clouded her eyes.

Mrs. Boston reached out and captured Carla's hand in hers. "I believe in my heart that everything will work out for you, Carla. I do believe that."

Amber paced back and forth in the hospital's waiting room while Grey and Brandy sat on the sofa and watched her. It had been two full hours since Cord has been admitted and they still didn't know how he was doing.

"Are you sure she just met this guy?" Grey leaned over and whispered to Brandy.

Brandy nodded as she continued to watch Amber's agitated pacing. "Yes. According to Carla, he's someone who started coming into the shop a few weeks ago. Evidently, he's a valued customer that she's really concerned about."

Grey chuckled. "Yeah. Right. There's concern and then there is concern. If you ask me, she's taking this particular customer's well being to a whole new level."

Brandy nodded. Grey was certainly right about that. She had never seen Amber this upset over anyone—especially when that person was a male. Like her and Carla, Amber had placed her full concentration on establishing her business and making it successful than on building a relationship with a man.

A few minutes later, a doctor in a white coat came through the double doors that separated the visitors from the hospital employees. "Who's a relative of Cord Jeffries?"

Amber immediately stepped forward. "I am."

The doctor nodded and then asked. "And what is your relationship?"

Amber blinked. "Excuse me?"

The doctor raised a brow. "I asked what is your relationship to Mr. Jeffries. Are you his sister, wife, cousin, fiancée . . . ?"

"Uh, I'm his fiancée." As soon as Amber said the lie, she turned and met Brandy's shocked expression and decided she couldn't worry about that now. She quickly turned back to the doctor. "How is he?"

"Nothing that a few days of rest won't cure. It seems your fiancé passed out from sheer exhaustion."

Amber raised a brow. "Exhaustion?"

"Yes, he's evidently been working himself to death and hasn't been eating properly. Your man needs to take better care of himself."

Amber nodded. "And you're sure that's the real reason he passed out?"

The doctor looked at her confused. "Yes. Why? Do you have another diagnosis that you want me to share with me?"

Amber shrugged. "Well . . . he was eating a cookie at the time he passed out. One that I baked."

The doctor looked at her for a long moment as if expecting her to tell him more and when she didn't he said. "And your point?"

"I can't cook."

The doctor chuckled. "Don't feel bad—neither can my wife, but it hasn't killed me yet. Your cookies had nothing to do with him passing out. In fact, from the look of things, your cookie is probably the only meal he's had all day. He hasn't been doing a good job of eating the right foods and what happened today is his body's way of telling him that he needs to make an improvement. Things might be worse for him the next time. If I were you, young lady, I would make sure he does whatever he has to do to improve."

Amber nodded. "Is he awake? Can I visit him?"

"I gave him something to make him sleep for a while. Forced rest you might say. And I'll be releasing him in the morning if his regular doctor, Dr. Phillips agrees. It's my understanding that Dr. Phillips is of town on business but will return later tonight."

"Can I see Cord now?" Amber asked, hopefully.

"Like I said, he's sleeping, but I guess you won't be satisfied until you see for yourself that he's fine, right?"

"Right."

The doctor smiled. "It's refreshing to see a woman who's concerned about the man she loves. I'll make sure the nurse knows I've given your permission to see him for as long as you want. I'll even have the nurse bring a cot in for you in case you want to stay all night. That way you'll be there whenever he wakes up. I'm sure he'll want to see you."

"Thanks, Doctor."

"You're welcome and good luck to you and your young man," the doctor said. He then asked, "Have the two of you set a wedding date?"

Amber swallowed as she felt her nose getting longer with each lie she told. "No, sir."

"Well, don't wait too long."

"We won't."

As soon as the doctor was no longer in sight, Amber glanced up and saw Brandy and Grey Masters approaching.

"Excuse me and Amber for just a minute, Grey." Brandy then firmly took Amber's hand and pulled her to the other side of the waiting room. "What's going on? Why did you tell the doctor that you're Cord Jeffries' fiancé? I almost choked on my Coke when you said that."

Amber shrugged. "That's the only way he was going to give me any information, and I needed to make sure the reason Cord is here isn't my fault."

Brandy raised a brow. "You mean that thing with the cookie?" she asked, since she'd heard every word of Amber's conversation with the doctor. So had Grey.

"Yes. And I'm still not sure my cookie isn't what did him in. You know that I can't cook."

Brandy nodded. Yes, she did know that. "Yeah, but only because you've never had a reason to try. There was no reason for you to learn how when your mom enjoyed doing all of the cooking, right?"

"Right."

"And cookies are rather easy and you did follow the recipe, right?"

"Right."

"And the doctor did say Jeffries passed out from exhaustion and not from eating your cookie, right?"

"Right. But I have to make sure, Brandy. I wouldn't be able to sleep tonight if there's still doubt in my mind. And that doubt won't be erased until I can speak with Cord's own personal physician tomorrow."

Brandy crossed her arms over her chest, determined to make Amber see reason. "And what if, in the meantime, his family shows up? How will you explain your existence?"

"That won't happen. In an earlier conversation we had, he happened to mention he has no family."

"What about a girlfriend? What if he really does have a fiancée and she arrives and finds out that you're impersonating her? Hell, she might be ready to kick your butt and not only are you not a cook but you're also not a fighter."

Amber hadn't thought of the possibility that there might be a woman in Cord's life and she really should have. Men who looked like him normally wasn't footloose and fancy free. "That's a chance I'll have to take."

Brandy shook her head. "And you're actually going to spend the night?"

"Yes. Please give Jennifer and Eileen a call and let them know I'm still at the hospital and to close things up for me."

Brandy took a long, hard look at her friend. "Are you sure about this, Amber?"

Amber didn't hesitate in answering. "Yes, I'm sure. Just be here to give me support, no matter what."

"Oh, girl," Brandy said, giving her friend a sistah hug. "You know I will. And I'll call Carla when I get home to give her another update. But Lord knows she has enough troubles of her own to deal with right now. Looks like we all do. But we shall overcome won't we?"

Amber smiled as she clasped Brandy's hand firmly in hers. "Yes, we will certainly do that. We have to keep the faith."

Chapter 16

Carla's doorbell rang as she began turning off all the lights for the night. Mrs. Boston had left over an hour ago and Brandy had called to give her an update on Cord Jeffries' condition and to let her know that Amber would be staying all night at the hospital with the man.

It had taken Carla a full hour to explain to Brandy what was going on with Amber and Cord Jeffries. Talking about Amber's problems had momentarily taken her mind of her own.

She headed for her front door and paused before answering it. "Yes?"

"Carla, it's me, Sonya."

Carla quickly opened the door and was immediately engulfed in her best friend's embrace. "What the hell is going on, Carla? I just got back to town and Mama told me everything. What is Jesse Devereau trying to pull?"

Carla led Sonya into her living room. "He's asking questions about Craig," she responded.

Sonya frowned. "Craig? How does he know about Craig?"

Carla sighed disgustedly. "Someone sent Jesse an anonymous letter in the mail telling him that he was Craig's father. He confronted me on two different occasions wanting to know the truth and I refused to discuss it with him."

Sonya shook her head. "But that doesn't make sense. Who would send him a letter? The identity of Craig's father is a closely guarded secret."

"I thought it was. The only persons who knew were you, Brandy, and Amber."

Sonya blinked when something suddenly stuck out in her mind. One night several weeks ago when she'd been more than slightly smashed, she'd run into Dalton Gregory. Somewhere in the back of her mind she remembered that in addition to giving her the best lay of her life, the man had also tried to pump her for information. She remembered not telling him anything at the start of the night, but hell, the only thing she remembered about the rest of the evening was reaching orgasm after orgasm after orgasm. Now she wondered if perhaps she'd flapped her jaws.

"Uh, Carla?"

"Yes."

"I need to go." Sonya quickly stood.

Carla lifted a brow. "But you just got here."

"Yes, but I just thought of something important," Sonya said, quickly heading for the door. "Look, I'll call you tomorrow. In fact, let's do lunch. By then I may have something to tell you."

Before Carla could ask her what, Sonya was out of the door.

Grey inhaled a calming breath and willed his body to relax as he entered the suite with Brandy. When that guy had dropped to the floor at the anniversary party, Grey had reacted, and immediately had been impelled into action to protect Brandy. Not knowing why the guy had passed out he had immediately thought the worst. He had sighed a deep relief when the doctor had reported that the man had passed out from exhaustion and not poison. But still the incident had reminded Grey of his purpose for being there which was to find the person who intended to do Brandy harm.

"You were awfully quiet on the ride from the hospital, Grey. Is anything wrong?"

He glanced over at Brandy as she tossed her purse on the table. "No, everything is fine. I'm just glad that guy is going to be all right."

Brandy smiled. "Well, yeah, he will be all right if he follows the doctor's orders and get some rest. He sounds pretty much like a workaholic, but then I'm sure most of us have been there before."

He nodded. He knew he sure had. He then watched Brandy as she moved toward her bedroom. "You're going to bed?"

She turned back around. "Yes. This has been a very busy day and hopefully a good night's sleep will cure everything. Good night, Grey."

"Good night." He watched as she went into her bedroom and closed the door behind her, thinking it was best that they had distance between them tonight. Even with his affirmation that he would keep his attention focused on what he was supposed to be doing, the fact remained that he wanted Brandy Bennett with a vengeance. He hadn't been aware of just how much he wanted her, how much he'd begun to care for her until that incident tonight.

Damn.

He didn't want to be, refused to be, and absolutely would not be another Masters that fell for a Bennett. Quinn had fallen and had fallen quite hard, but Grey Masters had no intensions of falling for anything or anyone. He didn't care one iota that he felt a connection to her that he didn't understand. Nor did he care that he thought she was the sexiest woman alive. The point remained that the woman had issues; she had parents who had issues; she had two girlfriends who had issues and she had cousins who were questionable, since he knew without a doubt that they would take certain matters into their owns hands if they felt they had to. Brandy Bennett was definitely not the type of woman he wanted to get involved with.

Too late. They were involved.

"Hell, no we aren't," Grey growled in a low tone as he quickly crossed the room to her office. He needed to check his laptop to see if there had been any new developments while they'd been out. He immediately noticed the blinking light on the phone, which meant someone had tried calling him. Closing the door, Grey sat down behind the desk and became absorbed in what he needed to do.

"Hell, don't break the damn doorbell, I'm coming." Dalton Gregory snatched opened his front door to find Sonya Morrison standing there. The one thing he remembered about the gorgeous woman was that when it came the sex, she was utterly insatiable.

"Hi, Dalton."

His face lit up into a wide smile. "Sonya, this is a surprise. Please come in."

Sonya smiled and sashayed into his home knowing that he was getting an eyeful from behind. She hadn't bothered going home and changing since the hour had been far spent already. She had decided that the short dress she was wearing would do the trick. It wouldn't take much to seduce a man like Dalton, and tonight without the impairment of alcohol, she intended to have the upper hand.

"So what brings you by?"

She turned slowly around. "I was thinking about you tonight."

His smile widened as he leaned against the closed door. "Really? I was beginning to think you'd forgotten me since you hadn't returned any of my calls."

She fluttered her eyes a few times and threw her braids off her shoulders to call attention to the spaghetti straps of her dress, as well as the fact that she wasn't wearing a bra. "Oh, I must have been out of town when you called. There's no way I would not have returned your call after that night we had together. Just thinking about all the things we did had my panties wet for days." She hated admitting it but it was the truth.

"Well, I'm always happy to provide a repeat performance."

Sonya smiled when she saw that he had gotten hard already. "I was hoping you would say that because there's a full moon out tonight. Have I ever told you what happens to me whenever there's a full moon?" She saw his throat tighten when he tried to swallow.

"No, what happens to you?"

"I have a tendency to want to play out my fantasies, whatever they are." She saw him swallow again. "And do you know what my fantasy is tonight, Dalton?" He had started fondling himself, right in front of her, and she wondered if he was even aware he was doing it.

"No, Sonya, what's your fantasy tonight?" he asked in a deep, husky voice.

She licked her lips. "Umm, I'd like to taste a man from head to toe and utterly blow him away." She licked her lips again. "If you know what I mean?"

She saw the smooth looking grin that came on his face and wondered how a jerk—a damn handsome jerk at that—could be so good in bed.

"Oh, yeah, I know what you mean," he said as he began unzipping his pants. "I'd love to accommodate you and we don't have to waste any time. Come over here. I got just the thing for you."

"I'm sure you do," she said as she strode over to him and reached down and caressed his erection through his pants. Boy, was he hard. She had to force herself to forget just how many hours of pleasure this particular male organ had once given her. Right now she was too damn mad for that. That night when he'd brought her here he'd done so with the intention of doing two things: pump her for sex and pump her for information.

And he had successfully done both.

Now thanks to her, Carla was in one hell of a fix and Sonya was determined to do whatever she could to correct the problem. "But I don't want to do it here, Dalton," she said in a very sultry voice.

He gazed down at her, confused. "Why not here?"

"Because it's not part of my fantasy. My fantasy includes something naughty."

He was having trouble swallowing again. "Something naughty?"

"Yes, terribly naughty. I want to do it in the school yard."

He blinked. "The school yard?"

"Yes?"

"But it's late. It's almost midnight."

"I know what time it is, but just think about it, Dalton. This is the best time. It's dark, quiet, and it's private. Haven't you ever thought about making out in the backseat of a car at night in the school yard?" She smiled knowing that even if he'd never thought about it before, he wasn't about to tell her he hadn't.

"Oh, yeah, I've thought about it lots of times. What school do you have in mind?"

"Umm, since there will definitely be a lot of drama, I thought we'd use the one Wesley Snipes graduated from, Jones High School," she said as she zipped his pants back up, then patted him. "Come on, let's hurry. My mouth is tingling. And I prefer that we use my car."

"All right, babe. I'll do anything just to get your mouth on me."

Sonya's smiled widened. The two of them were alike in a number of ways. They had a tendency to think with their friggin' body parts more so than with their heads.

Less than twenty minutes later Dalton was stretched out naked in the back seat of Sonya's Infinity. He had quickly undressed and had tossed his clothes in the front seat. "Okay, baby, come on back here and let's get this show on the road. I'm ready to get blown away," he said lifting his arms out to her. It was dark and he could barely see her, and to be on the safe side they had disconnected the interior light in the top of the car. The last thing either of them wanted was to get caught.

"Be patient, Dalton, I'm coming."

He chuckled. "Oh, you're going to be coming all right. As soon as you're through doing me, baby, then I intend to do you."

He heard her as she began climbing in the back seat. He felt her hands touching him, felt her strong, warm fingers take hold of his erection and it felt good. He was about to close his eyes when suddenly a bright light appeared, seemingly from out of nowhere. No! It wasn't a bright light—it was a ball of fire! He tried to sit up. "What the hell!"

"Don't move, Dalton, and I mean it. Don't you dare move."

He swallowed nervously. "Hey, baby, what's that? I can get kinky like the next guy but I don't believe in playing with fire. What the hell is that thing?"

"It's a flame gun. I'm sure you've seen one before. They're used to light barbecue grills, fireplaces, candles, and a number of other things."

"But what are you doing with it in here?"

"Because if you so much as move one inch without me telling you to do so, I intend to give you the blow job you've been asking for."

Dalton began getting more nervous. Sweat began pouring from his forehead. Sonya had that friggin' torch too close to vital body parts. "Look, Sonya, move that damn thing away from me before somebody gets burned."

"That's my intent, pretty boy. I don't mind being screwed but I'll be damn if I'll get screwed and used. And that night you used me, Dalton."

He tried to inch backward. "I said don't move, Dalton, or your balls get fried and I mean it!"

And Dalton believed her every word. He knew women had a tendency to get pretty emotional but he was beginning the think this broad was damn crazy. He could see her face through the flame and thought she actually looked like a she-devil. "I don't know what you're talking about, Sonya. I didn't use you. We both got what we wanted that night. You said so yourself."

Sonya frowned. "Yeah, but you got more didn't you? You got information out of me that you used to hurt Carla and for that I have a mind to set your penis on fire."

"Hey, wait a minute, let's not get stupid."

"I'm already stupid for first getting drunk that night and secondly, for going home with you. And what pisses me off even more is the fact that although I enjoyed having sex with you, I don't even like you."

Dalton had heard enough. "Put that damn flame down, Sonya, now! And back off!"

Instead of doing what he said, she moved the torch closer to his lower extremities. "Don't you dare raise your voice to me, Dalton. I'm the one with the flame so I'm calling the shots and now is not a good time to piss me off more than I already am. But I wanted you to know that I know what you did and I don't appreciate it."

"But I wasn't the one who sent that letter to Devereau. It was Carla's mother who sent it. The only mistake I made was telling her what I had found out from you, but I didn't know what the woman planned to do."

A part of Sonya wanted to believe him, but if he was telling the truth as far as she was concerned it was too late now. "Well, even if Carla's mother sent the letter, you're just as guilty and I would suggest in the future that if you see me coming you'd best go the other way. Do you understand?"

"Hell, yeah, I understand you. Now take me back home, dammit."

Sonya chuckled. "Not on your life, big guy. Get out of my car and don't try any funny business or your thing will go up in smoke because I'm keeping this torch close to it at all times. If you want take a chance and call my bluff then do it but if I were you, I wouldn't. I'm feeling somewhat crazy about now and there's no telling what I'd do. After I fry your penis and balls then I might decide to go after all that hair on your chest."

Dalton was convinced she just might do that. She had definitely shocked the hell out of him tonight. He wouldn't care if he never got another blowjob ever again from any woman.

"Now get away from my car, Dalton." He quickly did as she said, and she slid into the front seat and started the engine.

"Hey, give me my clothes, Sonya."

"Not on your life."

"You can't leave me out here naked like this."

"Wanna bet?"

And with those last words she quickly sped off and rolled up her car window to drown out the sound of Dalton's loud curses and got royally pissed when she heard him called her a stupid bitch.

When she was a few blocks away she picked her cell phone and punched in a few numbers. "Yes, hi, I'm a concerned citizen and I just passed Jones High School, and I could be mistaken but I think I saw a naked man lurking around. You may want to send a couple of your officers to check things out. Good-bye."

She pulled into the next all-night food market she came to. After gathering all of Dalton's clothes and belongings in her hands, she walked over to the garbage Dumpster and tossed them in. As she made her way home she thought of the other man she intended to visit in the morning.

Jesse Devereau.

∞ *Chapter 17* ∞

Grey glanced down the list of names he had accumulated over the past few weeks and wondered why he felt that he was omitting something vital.

The information he'd received had not been helpful other than to verify that Lorenzo Ballentine had not been in the United States within the last month. Unless he was working with an accomplice, Ballentine's name could be scratched off the list. That still left a number of people Grey wasn't ready to eliminate just yet, including Brandy's secretary. It had been discovered that the forever cheerful Donna Fields had been having a secret affair with Horace Thurgood during the years they had worked together. Why the romance had been kept a secret was anyone's guess, but Grey's investigators had been able to determine that the woman had made several trips to New York to visit Thurgood over the past six months. If the woman resented Brandy for Thurgood's decision to leave, that would give her a motive for wanting to harass Brandy. Then there was Thomas Reynolds who still occasionally drove by the hotel to check on Brandy's whereabouts.

Grey pushed back in his chair. His shoulder was beginning to ache.

So was his back. And he didn't want to think about his lower extremities but then a different kind of ache was lodged there. It was one only Brandy could relieve. He glanced over at the clock. It was after midnight.

"You're still at it I see."

Grey jerked his head up and met Brandy's gaze. She stood in the doorway wearing a bathrobe. It was similar to the other one he'd seen her in before but this one was red.

The lady in red.

And just like the night before, the sight of her took his breath away.

She moved away from the doorway and took a step into the room. "I had trouble sleeping," she said by way of an explanation as to why she was there.

Grey nodded but he didn't take his eyes from her. "Got thirsty again tonight, too?"

A smile tilted her lips. "No, I'm not thirsty but I thought I'd find something to read after I gave up counting sheep." She walked over to a magazine rack and pulled one off the stack. "Maybe this will do the trick."

He saw the title, *Hotel Management*. "I guess there's a possibility that it will."

Brandy lifted an eyebrow. "You don't sound convinced."

Grey shrugged his massive shoulders. "It depends on the reason you can't sleep. I think you need to acknowledge what's keeping you awake. What's keeping us *both* awake."

Brandy stared at him, licking her lips unconsciously. A flicker of heated desire flamed inside of her. This man had the ability to mesmerize her, turn her on without even trying. Then there was this honesty between them, no game playing. They called things as they saw them like two mature adults. But then, on the other hand, they were cautious people. They knew the score. They knew what they wanted, the price they'd have to pay if they decided to take it.

But tonight she wasn't ready to get serious about anything or anyone. Tonight she needed to feel free, uninhibited. She didn't want to remember that someone was trying to put the fear of God in her.

"Did your mother ever tell you stories?"

She blinked when she realized Grey had spoken. "Stories?"

He smiled. "Yes, bedtime stories. My mom used to tell us stories every night. Those stories would help me to sleep."

Brandy quickly remembered her childhood. "The only stories my mother would tell were about 'those damn Bennetts.' But my Gramma Idella used to read me Bible stories whenever I would visit her. Why? Do you have a good story that might put me to sleep?" she asked, amused. A bit of humor felt good right now and lightened the moment between them. Sexual tension was slowly creeping into the room. She felt it and by the darkening of his eyes knew that he felt it too.

She watched as he came around the desk to sit on the edge. Her eyes were immediately drawn to the jeans he wore and the hard erection she could make out through the denim. At that moment the lightened moment between them suddenly vanished when sexual awareness took over.

He wanted her. Just like she wanted him. He was trying like hell not to want her, but she knew there were some things your body just couldn't hide and for a man an arousal was one of them.

"I'm willing to come up with a story if you care to listen," he said lightly, and she realized he was trying to downplay their sexual attraction, their combustible hormones that wanted to do their own thing.

"Hey, I'm game," she said indulgently as she dropped down in the recliner in the room to keep her knees from wobbling. She was up against too much man and her body was letting her know it.

"All right then. Here's my story."

Brandy watched as he shifted positions so his predicament wouldn't be so obvious. "Once upon a time in the Land of Masters."

"The Land of Masters?" she asked raising a brow.

"Hey, work with me here. This is my story, right?"

She nodded. "Right, and I do apologize. Please continue."

"Once upon a time in the Land of Masters lived this boy who wanted to grow up and be a man. A very strong man. When he got older he saw there were too many bad guys out there so he decided he wanted a job that would rid the land of crooks, robbers, and thieves and make the Land of Masters safe for everyone to live. Then one day he got word that there was this damsel in distress. Some wicked person was trying to steal her crown. So the boy who had grown up to be a man decided to go do whatever he could to keep the damsel safe in the land where she lived that was called the Land of Mousketeers."

Ignoring Brandy's chuckles, Grey continued. "At first he didn't really want to go and leave the Land of Masters, but he was convinced that he was needed to help slay the damsel's dragon. However, when he got to the Land of Mousketeers, he found a damsel who really wasn't in distressed. She was just a little pissed that someone had the nerve to try and take something she owned. Something she'd worked hard to get. And the boy who had grown up to be a man also noted something else about the damsel when he got there."

Brandy noticed that Grey's voice had deepened and his gaze was searing into hers. She also saw the rise and fall of his chest and could almost hear the pounding of his heart even from across the room. The erratic beat was almost in tune with her own. And if that wasn't enough to make her draw in a shallow breath, she couldn't help but take note that the bulge of his arousal through his jeans had gotten larger and looked harder.

She nervously licked her lips and tried to ignore the perspiration that was beginning to form on her skin and the ultra hot heat that began consuming her body. "What?" she asked quietly. "What else did he find?"

He eyed her for a long moment, as if silently debating to continue. "He found that this damsel wasn't a country bumpkin, nor was she an orange grove old maiden. He discovered that she was the most beautiful woman he'd ever seen and was indeed the fairest of them all. She was a woman who, without even trying, reminded him that he was a man and made him think about mating for the first time in nearly three years."

Brandy swallowed deeply. "Mating?"

"Yes, mating. All day and all night. But not your typical mating. The boy who had grown into a man decided that typical mating wouldn't do for this damsel. She needed something way out of the ordinary since there wasn't an ordinary thing about her. She was in a class by herself. Savvy. High-class. Sexy. He thought all those things described this damsel and he suddenly found that he was the one who was in distress. Instead of concentrating on the task he'd been sent to do, he found that his mind and his thoughts were consumed with other things. They were filled with thoughts of her."

Standing, he slowly walked to stand in front of her as his gaze continued to meet hers. "He couldn't help but wonder how her breasts would taste in his mouth, how her body would fit against his and how her legs would feel wrapped tight around his waist. He also wondered just how wet her body could get when she got turned on and what sounds she would make when he entered her. He thought about taking her on the desk, the kitchen table, the floor, the wall, the shower. Anything was game. You name it, he'd thought about it. But what he thought about more than anything," Grey said, his voice low, deep, guttural. "Is how it would feel coming inside of her."

Brandy became too numb to move, too aroused to speak. Her skin suddenly became sensitive, and anything touching it served as an irritant she needed to be free of. Her clothes suddenly felt sticky, damp, and she felt the need to get out of them.

Grey took a step back when Brandy stood. He watched through desire filled eyes as she slowly began removing her clothes. First came the robe, which dropped at her feet. His breath got lodged in his throat when he saw the short, transparent nightgown that was then revealed. She released the thin straps of the gown and when it was added to the pile at her feet he stood still as his gaze feasted on her, every single part of her body that he had dreamed about for the past few weeks. The lighting from the lone lamp in the room glowed bright enough to illuminate every portion of her body and he was seeing every curve, every angle and every shade. He felt his body harden even further when his gaze locked on the area between her legs.

"Now I have a story for you, Grey."

Her words, spoke on a whisper, capture his attention and he forced his gaze to her face and met her eyes. "What's your story?" he asked, barely able to get out the words.

"There once was a lady who lived in a shoe. It was a very classy high-heeled shoe. She found she most enjoyed living in the heel section of the shoe, high away from the occasional mud that often got stepped in or slung on the shoe. But every once in a while she liked to travel to the middle of the shoe because that's where the lining was, and it was where she felt most protected, most comfortable. She had never wanted to venture to the toe area. It was the part that often got stepped on and she didn't intend for anyone to ever step on her. But one day she found herself suddenly in the toe area and she got stepped on many times and it hurt. It hurt badly. And a part of her thought she would never be able to get back to the heel again. But she was determined to make it, whatever it took. And after a while she did. So now she's back at the heel again but once in a while she remembers the middle, the lining, the area she felt most protected and most comfortable. But she was afraid to go there because it was too close to the toe where she remembered nothing but pain. She had promised herself if she ever made it back to the heel that she would never risk going back to the toe to get stepped on again. But then one day, along came this other shoe. She took a peek at it and saw it was the shoe of a man. It was black, shiny, all polished, thick soles, and wing tips. But then there appeared a roughness about it and the woman immediately got the impression that this particular shoe had once seen better days, but it was tough and had endured. The outside as well as the inside was made of thick skin, pure genuine leather of the finest quality. She quickly concluded that this was no cheap shoe. And what made it ultra special was that the man who lived in this shoe was like the shoe he wore, with all the same qualities and for the first time she didn't feel afraid of being stepped on. He gave her his protection, a chance to be comfortable. Without even realizing it he became her lining. She wanted to get to know him in a way she hadn't known another man in over two years. She wanted to know how it felt to be a woman again, without any fears. She wanted to be someone who believed it wasn't her fault that another woman had caught her man's eye, and that it had less to do with her inadequacies than his. But more than anything she wanted to become a part of this man and only this man. She wanted to go dwell with him in his shoe. She wanted to know how it felt to be engulfed in strong arms, to be skin-to-skin with someone. She wanted to know at that moment in time that he wanted her. Only her. She needed the experience of being touched, kissed and desired by him. And more than anything she wanted to know how it felt to have an earth-shaking, mind-blowing, toe-curling orgasm and scream his name from her lips."

Without pause, Grey reached out and cradled Brandy's face between both hands. "Get ready to find out," he whispered huskily before pulling her to him and letting his mouth hungrily devour hers in a tongue-tangling kiss.

It was a kiss that promised to give her everything that she wanted and her body writhed against his, needing a closeness she'd never before experienced. His kiss made her mind block out everything except him, the man claiming her body and soul, the man who was eating away at her mouth with a hunger that was driving her over the edge, and the man who with every lick of his tongue was destroying two years worth of deprivation.

Grey felt himself losing control when the need to mate with Brandy ripped through him with a blazing force and he was driven with the desire to hear her scream. He broke their kiss and began removing his own clothes, tearing off his shirt with relentless speed. He watched her eyes as he removed his jeans, pulling them down over his hips and down his legs. He tossed them aside and his briefs quickly followed.

He heard her sharp intake of breath when she saw him displayed, and the longing to be inside of her, now, buried deep, was a physical thing, sharp, potent, fierce. He reached up and picked her up into his arms and carried her over to the desk and sat her on it.

"Open your legs for me, Brandy. Wide."

She did. Automatically. Without reservation. And he went between them while she wrapped her legs completely around him and gripped his shoulders. She felt the heat of him slowly enter her, hot, large, and she took him in, inch by excruciating inch, until they were so close, connected, joined that it was hard to tell where her body ended and his began.

He groaned and the sound made her tighten her nails on his shoulder to hold on. She saw the eyes that looked at her, deep, glazed and felt the heat of him buried deep within her. He took his hands and lifted her hips off the desk surface for an even greater penetration, then opened his mouth against her throat and took a nip, leaving his mark on her skin, her body.

Branding her.

She gasped, arched her body into his, felt him going deeper, burying himself to the hilt inside of her till she could barely take anymore. And then he leaned her back and went for her breasts, opening his mouth again one dark nipple and another. Licking, laving, cherishing; she moaned deep within her throat.

He began moving his hips, pumping in and out of her in a desperate rhythm, a hot torrid mating, and with the same urgent frenzy, she met him stroke for stroke, thrust for thrust.

And when he left her breasts to capture her mouth, he mimicked the mating beat of their bodies. The intensity was too great, emotions too strong, need too overwhelming. She needed his release as much as she needed her own. She wanted to feel him as much as a woman could feel any man and she tightened her inner muscles around him, clamping and milking him. She knew just what she wanted and just what she intended to get. He'd said he wanted to come inside of her and she was going to give him his wish, which would drive her closer to her own.

She shifted her body to allow him greater penetration as he continued to kiss her long and hard. And she felt herself falling and pulled her mouth free to scream when an orgasm of gigantic proportions rammed through her at the same time she felt him shuddering with the force of his release—hot, thick—that didn't seemed to stop, flooding her insides while his deep, guttural groan filled the room.

Another scream was torn from her lips as everything exploded inside of her and she experienced the earth-shaking, mind-blowing, toe-curling orgasm she'd craved.

Bright and early the next morning Brandy woke up curled up against the hard, masculine body asleep beside her. Her body trembled from the inside out as memories flooded her mind. After they had made love on her desk, they had proceeded to do so again on the kitchen table, the floor, the wall, then finally in the shower, before they'd dried off and collapsed in her bed, where she got the best sleep of her life. They'd had a cumulative total of five years to make up for and they'd done it in grand style—even now she wasn't sure if she could move. Yet she wanted him again, this time in bed. She smiled, feeling downright insatiable, potently needy, and basking in the aura of feeling so desired. When she felt him move beside her she turned and met his sleepy gaze.

"You, Brandy Bennett, are something else," Grey whispered into the tangled mass of braids that covered her head as well as his shoulder. "Don't ever doubt your capabilities as a woman. Not ever."

Brandy nodded, unable to speak. This man, this ultra beautiful man, had reminded her over and over again all through the night just what it felt like to be a woman, a woman in the purest sensuous sense of the word. A woman made to mate with her man. A woman who could satisfy his every desire and rock his world while rocking her own.

And he'd also given her something else. A sense of worth and value. In his arms she felt cherished and possessed.

Unable to speak at the moment, she moved closer to him, his warmth, his naked body, and she then inhaled his male scent. Robust. Exhilarating. Overpowering.

Addictive.

And when he suddenly shifted positions, covering his hard thighs with hers, shifting her beneath him, she wrapped her arms around, totally prepared and willing to indulge in more fantasies with him.

For the time being they were unwilling to let reality invade this very extraordinary moment they were sharing.

Chapter 18

*E*ven before he pried open his eyes, he smelled her scent. It was a luscious fragrance that overpowered the hospital's antiseptic smell.

Cord Jeffries pulled himself from the clutches of a deep sleep and tried to mentally pull everything together in his mind to reconstruct the reason he was lying in a hospital bed with tubes and equipment hooked up to his body.

Then he remembered.

All Dev's warnings had come to pass and Cord had literally fallen on his face in exhaustion. The thought of what happened was down right embarrassing, but utterly beneficial since it had brought the woman of his dreams to his side.

He glanced across the room at her. She was asleep on a cot that had been placed in the room. The thin blanket that had intended to cover her was now on the floor, and the angle in which she lay on her side revealed the slit in the side of her dress.

His gaze ran the length of her body, lingering on the portion of thighs exposed by the split and thought it was a damn good thing he was already flat on his back or he definitely would have been knocked there. Her thighs were firm, voluptuous and well stacked. He could just imagine having those thick thighs wrapped around him in the heart of passion. In fact he had done more than just imagine it, he had dreamed it several times since meeting her.

He closed his eyes again as a question invaded his thoughts. Why was she here in his hospital room where it was apparent that she had spent the night? Granted he had taken ill in her bookstore, but still, what she'd done had gone way above and beyond mere concern for a customer and that realization warmed him inside. Other than Dev and Mr. Phillips, it had been a long time since anyone had cared about him. Even Diane hadn't shown this much interest and concern when they'd been married.

As he continued to feast his eyes on her, he noticed that one of her arms was thrown over her head in an utterly sexy pose, which made the front of her dress gape open just a little, but well enough for him to get a glimpse of the top of her breasts. Even from a distance they looked creamy, smooth, and soft, and he could imagine the palm of his hand kneading them, and the tips of his fingers caressing her nipples. Hell, he wouldn't mind getting the chance to suck on them too, since they looked like the kind he could definitely get enjoyment from.

It had been Cord's intent to study her some more while she slept, and he became somewhat disappointed when she slowly came awake. But then again, he enjoyed seeing her stretch her body and even liked the way she moaned away sleep before fully opening her amber colored eyes. He would love hearing her make a similar sound while he was planted firmly inside of her.

Then, when their gazes met and held, blatant awareness passed through them, and his body immediately became hard. The awareness they shared was the kind that neither could deny even had they wanted to. It was too potent, too overwhelming and way too staggering.

"Good morning," he somehow found his voice to say, which cost him a lot. His throat felt dry, strained and almost as thick as the erection he shifted in bed to conceal, which was a good thing when she quickly sat up then crossed the room to him.

"Good morning, Cord. How do you feel?"

Her voice sounded husky and slumberous and it immediately gave him an adrenaline rush, which in his book said a lot for a man who was in the hospital for exhaustion. "I feel all right," he murmured, his tone low and rough, and decided not to add, *especially since you're here*. "Why did you stay all night? That cot couldn't have been comfortable for you?"

She pushed a mass of hair that had flopped over in her face back and smiled with concern. "You passed out in my store, so of course I was concerned about you."

Cord nodded. If that was the story she wanted him to buy then he would do it with every penny he had. But there was no way she could convince him that she made a habit of spending the night with every man who got ill in her store.

He then glanced at the clock on the wall. It was almost seven in the morning. "How long have I been here?" he decided to ask. The happenings of yesterday were a bit foggy in his mind. The only thing he remembered before the fall was impatiently waiting for her to come out of the office where one of her employees had told him she was. And when she'd finally opened the office door and walked over, flanked by two other women, he thought seeing her again had been all that had mattered to him. He'd been like a thirsty man and she'd been the drink he craved. It was something even now he didn't understand, considering his failure in the love department. He was glad Diane hadn't completely destroyed his ability to want another woman, to engage in a meaningful relationship with someone else, or to seriously think of a solid future with a woman.

"You were brought in around six yesterday afternoon. The doctor gave you something to make you sleep," she interrupted his thoughts by saying. "He said you needed your rest."

Again Cord nodded. He could definitely agree with that. It was the best sleep he'd gotten in a long time, and to wake up to such a beautiful view was icing on the cake. Her eyes, he noted, continued to gaze at him, study him, the same way he was sure his eyes were studying her. Then suddenly, she reached out and wiped his brow, but didn't stop there. Her fingers then moved lower to caress the stubble along his cheek and jaw.

"I guess I need a shave," he managed to say. Her fingers on his face felt warm, seductive and soothing.

Instead of saying anything, she merely nodded. Her lips were parted and her mouth was slightly open and a thought that immediately came to his mind was that the place his tongue needed to be was inside her mouth. Something in his gaze must have conveyed that thought because she leaned over closer to him and he made an attempt to lean up closer to her and . . .

Harrumph.

The clearing of someone's throat had them jumping apart like two teenagers who'd been caught in the back seat of a car. Cord frowned, not appreciating the untimely interruption and his frowned deepened further when he saw it was Dev who had come into the room unannounced.

"You could have knocked," Cord grumbled, deciding to tuck the hospital blanket securely around his midsection to keep his predicament from Dev's all knowing eyes. Amber had moved away from the bed and was now standing by the cot.

"Yes, I could have," Dev said, grinning from ear to ear. "But as a doctor I really didn't think I had to. I was told by the nurse that my patient was in bed weak as water, however, from my observations, you evidently have energy to manage some things."

Dev then turned his attention to Amber and his brow lifted. "You're the fiancée, I assume?" he asked smiling.

"Fiancée?" Cord asked. Surprised by Dev's statement, he turned his full attention to Amber. "You told someone you were my fiancée?" he asked curiously.

Amber tinted in embarrassment and wished there was someway she could crawl under Cord's bed. "Ahh, yes," she said to the doctor, unable at the time being to look at Cord. "I know I shouldn't have lied but that was the only way they would tell me about his condition and I was extremely worried. He passed out in my bookstore and I was deeply concerned."

Dev nodded. "Oh, I see."

Cord raised eyes to the ceiling knowing Dev really didn't see at all. Like him, Dev was probably trying to figure out why she would be so concern to the point of spending the night on an uncomfortable cot just to be near him.

"And since I know he's doing fine I'll leave now," she quickly added when both men continued to look at her.

"Stay!"

The order was barked out simultaneously by Cord and the doctor, and it startled Amber. She jumped back in surprised.

"Sorry, we didn't mean to scare you," Cord said, trying to sit up in bed. "But I don't want you to go yet."

"And neither do I," Dev chimed in, giving her a warm smile. "I'd like to ask you more questions about what happened yesterday."

Amber's face lit in concern. "Why? Do you think it was something else other than exhaustion that brought him here?"

Dev lifted a brow. He glanced over at Cord who gave him a nod to answer Amber. By right, any discussion regarding Cord's condition was private and confidential: however, Cord had silently given the okay for him to tell her anything she wanted to know. "Since I've been concerned regarding Cord's state of health for a long time, especially the long work hours, lack of sleep and his terrible eating habits, I think I can safely say that's what brought him here, but still I need all to verify all the facts for my report."

Dev then looked at her curiously. "Why? Do you think there's something else I should check into?"

Amber shrugged. "He ate one of my cookies."

Dev raised a curious brow. "And?"

"And I can't cook although I thought I did a really good job on them. I followed my mother's recipe to the letter."

Dev chuckled. "Then I'm sure they were extremely good. But if I were you I wouldn't worry about the fact that you can't cook. Cord can't cook either, and if his own cooking hasn't killed him by now, nothing will."

"Hey, watch it. I don't appreciate being talked about like I'm not here."

Amber glanced over at Cord and saw him smile. She also took note of the affection he displayed in his eyes for his doctor and immediately knew they shared more than a doctor-patient relationship. "The two of you are friends?" she blurted out.

"Sometimes," Cord said frowning at the man.

"All the time," the doctor countered and frowned back. Dev then offered his hand to Amber. "I'm Doctor Devin Phillips, best friend of this guy who wants to be difficult, and besides being his pretend-fiancée, you are?"

"Amber Stuart, and like I said the reason I told the—"

"You explained once Ms. Stuart, there's no reason to explain again. I'm glad you cared enough to stay and check on him. I've been out of town at a medical convention and got back after midnight. And I'm about to impose some forced rest on my friend here."

"I have work to do at the office, Dev."

"Work that can wait, Cord. This here should be your wake up call. Maybe now you'll take me seriously. I've already contacted Janelle and told her that if you call and ask her to bring work to your house to refuse you and I promised her she wouldn't get fired. You need at least four solid days of rest, Cord, and I mean it. You either get it at home or I will make arrangements to keep your butt right here in this hospital for the next four days. So what's it's going to be."

Cord didn't say anything for the longest moment and then he said, "All right."

Dev lifted a brow. "For some reason I don't believe you. The other stipulation before I agree to release you is for you to hire a nurse to move in with you for the next four days. I want someone who'll make sure you take your medicine, eat properly and—"

"In other words you want someone to spy on me and report back to you with information on every little thing I do."

"Or refuse to do. You're still not well, Cord. You need the next four days to regain your strength. No man should have been working the hours you've worked over the past six months and it's time to stop. So what's it going to be? Are you willing to have a live-in-nurse for the next four days?"

"No."

"Then I have no choice but to keep you confined right here."

Amber sighed. She could see that both men were extremely stubborn and decided to offer a solution. "I can do it."

Cord's gaze left Dev and shifted to Amber. "You can do what?"

"I can make sure you do all those things."

Dev looked at Amber and frowned. "Are you saying that you're willing to move in with him for four days to—"

"Be his spy?" Cord interrupted frowning.

Amber frowned at both men. "No, I don't intend to be anyone's spy. But I am willing to help out any way I can. I can easily arrange my schedule to take off four days and make sure Cord rests and gets the proper care he needs. After all, he did pass out in my store."

Cord inwardly smiled when he knew he should feel like a downright heel. Amber was willing to come stay at his house and play nursemaid and by golly he intended to take her up on her offer. He could just see her taking care of him, feeding him, soothing him and possibly getting naughty with him. "Are you sure you want to do that?" he asked, hoping like hell that she *was* sure.

"Yes, I'm positive. And just to set the record straight, Cord. I will make sure that you follow Dr. Phillips' orders so I hope you don't think

I'm some kind of a pushover because I'm not. You will do just what you're supposed to do. Understood?"

Cord lifted a brow. Boy, the woman was downright bossy but hell he could deal with that. Besides, as soon as they got behind closed doors he intended to make her forget all about doctor orders. He planned to put another agenda in place. He smiled. "Understood."

A few moments later, Amber had stepped out of the room while Dev checked Cord over. Cord knew he should be downright embarrassed when Dev couldn't help but notice his erection that refused to go down.

"You should be ashamed of yourself, Cord."

Cord chuckled, deciding not to remind Dev of the many times he'd seen him in a similar state with his girlfriend Briana. All Briana had to do was to walk into a room and Dev's midsection would go bonkers. "I have nothing to be ashamed of. As a doctor I'm sure you know there are certain things a man doesn't have control of and arousal is one of them."

Dev raised his eyes to the ceiling. "I'm not talking about that, Cord. At least not directly. I'm talking about your eagerness to take advantage of Amber Stuart."

Cord frowned. "I'm not taking advantage of her. She volunteered."

"Yeah, and you were right there, ready and quite enthusiastic about pouncing on her offer with blatant ideas in your head of pouncing on something else. I know you have an ulterior motive behind this."

Cord smiled knowingly and had no intentions of denying that he had one. "Of course there's an ulterior motive. I want to get to know her better. I told you a couple of weeks ago that the woman fascinates me. Can I help it if someone up there heard my prayers?"

"I'm not sure it's your prayers they heard, Cord."

Cord released a deep breath. Maybe now was a good time to remind Dev how he'd met Briana. Evidently Dev had forgotten that day he had seen Briana for the first time, immediately falling in love. He had gone after her with a vengeance and dared anything and anyone to get in his way, even an old jerk of a boyfriend who'd been determined to get her back.

Dev frowned after Cord's reminder. "My situation with Briana isn't the same. She knew from day one what my intentions were, but Amber Stuart doesn't have a clue that you intend to have her flat on her back in four days or less. So I have no other choice but to protect her."

Cord's jaw clenched. Now was not the time for his best friend to play Saint Devin. "Protect her how?"

Dev smiled. "I'm including an additional restriction to my orders for you, restrictions I'm going to make sure Ms. Stuart is aware of just in case you get any ideas. But after hearing her comments there's no doubt in my mind that she's going to make sure you follow my orders to a tee."

"What additional restriction?" Cord arched his brow and waited expectantly to hear something that he knew he would not like.

Dev leaned against the closed door. "Since you need to build up your energy level, you are restricted from indulging in any sexual activity with a woman for at least two weeks."

✑ *Chapter 19* ✑

Sonya walked into the lobby of the exclusive St. Laurent Hotel thinking it comical that the hotel Jesse Devereau had chosen was one that belonged to a very good friend of Carla's. Chances were he wasn't even aware of that fact.

She strutted over to the station where a courtesy phone set and picked it up. Moments later a hotel operator came on the line. "Could you please ring Jesse Devereau's room? Yes, I'll hold."

A few minutes later the operator returned to the line and advised her that Mr. Devereau was not answering his phone. Sonya raised a brow as she glanced her watch. It was barely eight in the morning and she wondered if perhaps he'd come down to the restaurant for breakfast and decided to check out that possibility.

Moments later she walked into the restaurant. It wasn't hard picking out Jesse Devereau from what she remembered three years ago. Even from his side profile she could tell that time had definitely been kind to him. He was still a very good-looking man.

She frowned. He was dining with someone and she wondered if perhaps he was holding a business breakfast meeting. Well, as far as she was concerned that was too friggin' bad. Whatever business he was conducting had to wait. Carla came first.

She started toward his table. The blond-haired, blue-eyed man who was sitting with Jesse Devereau looked up and gave her a smile. For a heart-stopping moment she was tempted to smile back then decided she didn't want him to think she was flirting, since she was a woman who'd never been curious to know if it was true that blonds had more fun. "Mr. Devereau."

Jesse looked up from his meal and Sonya knew the moment recognition hit. Both men stood. "Ah, yes, Miss Morrison. Sonya Morrison, right?" Jesse asked, giving her one of those charming smiles that she remembered so well. But the smile wasn't working on her this morning.

"You do remember me?" she said coolly, accepting his handshake.

"I don't think I could forget." He then motioned to the man also standing. "And this is my very good friend, Mike Kelly. Mike, this is Sonya Morrison. I met her father a few years ago during my last visit to Orlando, and he was gracious enough to invite me to Sonya's birthday party while I was in town."

"Nice meeting you, Mike," she said, offering the other man her hand.

"Likewise, Miss Morrison."

Sonya frowned as a sharp sensation shot through her the moment she and Mike's hands touched. She knew he'd felt it too and appeared just as startled.

"Would you like to join us for breakfast? We're just getting started." Jesse asked, sitting back down to continue eating, leaving her and Mike standing, still holding hands like two dimwits.

She quickly dropped her hand from Mike's and gave Jesse her full attention. "What I would like is to have a private conversation with you if that's possible."

Jesse shook his head. "That's not possible if you're here to discuss your best friend. If so, then we have nothing to talk about."

Sonya pulled out a chair and sat down. "That's where you're wrong.

We have a lot to talk about since I'm the one responsible for you getting that letter."

"You're the one who sent it?"

Sonya lifted a brow. Mike, not Jesse had asked the question. Evidently Mike Kelly was privy to Jesse's business so she decided to answer. "No, I didn't send that letter but I know who did, and I feel responsible because the person who sent it got the information from someone I told. I'd promised Carla that I wouldn't tell anyone the name of Craig's father and I broke that promise."

Jesse stared at Sonya long and hard. What she'd said verified that Carla's child was his, but he wanted to hear it from Carla. She owed him the courtesy of that. "As far as I'm concerned, it should never have been a secret. I had every right to know I had fathered a child. The least Carla could have done was be up front with me when I asked."

Jesse's words pissed Sonya off. "Carla would have told you when she first found out she was pregnant had you not lied to her that night about not being involved with someone else. She found out the truth."

Jesse stopped chewing his food and glared at her. "Involved with someone else? If that's what she told you, then she's the one who lied."

That statement angered Sonya even more. "One thing Carla doesn't do is lie which is why your name is on Craig's birth certificate instead of the phony name I told her to use. I know for a fact you were involved with someone when you told her you weren't because I read it in the newspapers while on a business trip to L.A. less than a couple of months later. Carla was crushed when I brought back a copy of the newspaper for her to read. She couldn't believe you were nothing more than a gigolo and were the lover of some old wh—"

Sonya stopped, quickly remembered her audience and amended what she was about to say. "That you were the lover of some wealthy, old woman."

Both men stared at her for the longest time and said nothing. She saw blatant anger in Jesse Devereau's eyes and what appeared to be amusement in Mike's, which confused her.

That confusion was cut short when Jesse stood and threw his napkin on the table. "I refuse to sit here and talk to you a minute longer, Miss Morrison. It's Mike's business if he wants to stay and listen to what you have to say, but personally, I've heard enough. Have a good day." Without waiting for her to respond, he angrily walked off.

Sonya watched his retreating back until he was no longer in sight. Sighing deeply she then turned to Mike Kelly. "Damn, he's pretty upset, isn't he?"

Mike Kelly laughed. For some reason he liked this woman. She was cocky and had plenty of spunk. "Yes, I guess you can say that he is. He tried on two occasions to get Miss Osborne to talk to him and she refused to do so which was unfortunate. Now he intends to take drastic steps to force her to tell him what he wants to know."

Sonya frowned and tried not to be drawn in by the deep blue of Mike's eyes. "By taking away her company?"

"Yes, for starters."

Sonya sat up straight in her chair. "For starters?"

"Yes. Like you said, he's pretty upset right now and you pretty much confirmed Miss Osborne's child is his, so he's angrier than before because he feels she should have told him. There's no telling how far he'll go now."

Sonya instinctively reached across the table and grabbed Mike's hand. She almost let go of it when she felt that same sizzle of awareness she'd felt earlier. "Then we have to do something."

Mike raised a brow. "*We?*"

"Yes. He and Carla need to sit down and talk."

Mike shook his head. "Like I said, Jesse tried talking to her, but Miss Osborne refused to have anything to do with him. In fact she had him kicked off Osborne Computer Network's property. He won't make another attempt to see her. Instead he'll let their attorneys battle it out and it won't be pretty."

Sonya sighed. "You're his friend, Mike. Can't you get through to him and try deflecting some of his anger?"

Mike met her gaze. "And Miss Osborne is your friend, can't you get through to her as well?" he countered, smiling.

"I'll try."

"And so will I."

Sonya returned his smile but it faded the moment she noticed that they were still holding hands. She quickly pulled her hand back and decided it was best to address this attraction between them before he got any ideas. "Just to set the record straight, I've never liked vanilla."

"It's straight," he said grinning at her. "Because I've never developed a taste for chocolate."

She nodded and thought, *good*. Just so they understood each other.

An hour later Mike was in the suite talking to Jesse. "You heard Sonya Morrison for yourself. The reason Carla Osborne didn't contact you to let you know she was pregnant is because she assumed, like a number of other people, that you and Susan Brady were having an affair."

Jesse eyes narrowed. "Even if that was true, she still had no right to not tell me she had gotten pregnant."

"But if she thought the only thing she had meant to you that night was nothing more than a one-night stand, she would have felt she did have that right." When Jesse didn't say anything, Mike added. "But then you and I both know she was more than a one-night stand that night, don't we, Jess?"

Not waiting for him to respond, Mike turned and walked through the doorway that led to his connecting suite. He threw his sports jacket on the bed and walked over to the window and thought about Sonya Morrison and her rather frank way of putting things.

He smiled and decided for the second time that day that he liked her.

Chapter 20

*A*nd you have no idea why Thomas Reynolds makes it his business to drive by the hotel every so often, to check and make sure your car is here?"

Brandy glanced across the table at Grey and thought long and hard about his question. Once they had gotten out of bed that morning, they had showered together and ordered room service for breakfast. He had just finished telling her about what he'd found out about Thomas Reynolds.

"No, although if he's doing it, it really wouldn't surprise me. Thomas is very protective of me, Grey."

Or very jealous, Grey wanted to say but decided not to. He knew she still didn't want to consider the possibility that Thomas Reynolds might be the one sending her those messages. "What's on the agenda today?" he asked instead. It was hard to sit across from her and not think about everything they had done the night before. They had made love in just about every room in this suite, even in the kitchen on this very table. He didn't know any other woman who basked in her sensuality like Brandy, who was so open and uninhibited. Each and every time he'd come inside of her, when groans of pleasure rumbled deep in his throat, he would ride the waves of the most earth-shattering orgasm known to mankind, then he would inhale her scent, their scent, and would become thick, hard, and fully aroused all over again.

"Things are going to get pretty busy around here today," she said. "The game is next weekend so many of the committee members will check in, as well as members of the media. This is the first year the St. Laurent has been a host hotel and I'm very excited about it."

Grey nodded, deciding that with all the activities at the hotel it was going to be difficult to keep her well protected. But he was determined to do so and had even called in a few other contacts he had for backup. "I need to know where you are at all times, Brandy. Most of the time I'll be with you except for when you're involved in all that committee stuff. It won't bother me that people will began to wonder why I'm not letting you out of my sight. I'm sure they'll start thinking that I'm a very jealous and possessive lover."

Grey sighed. In a way he felt just that way. The thought of another man anywhere near her made his blood boil. But then, a part of him believed that what they'd shared last night had been unique, special and just between them.

"And it wouldn't bother me in the least if they think of you that way, too. I'll be the envy of all the women around here, and they'll wonder how I got so lucky," Brandy said smiling.

A seductive smile tilted the corners of Grey's mouth. "Do you have any regrets about last night?" he murmured questioningly.

Brandy leaned back in the chair. "No, I have none."

At that moment the phone rang and Brandy stood to pick it up. "Yes?"

She nodded. "They've started arriving already?" A few minutes later she said. "All right, that's fine. Most have been given rooms on the tenth floor except for a few. Make sure all their wishes are met." Then she quickly amended. "Within reason."

After hanging up the phone she glanced over at Grey. He was looking at her with those deep, dark eyes of his. "Don't look at me that way, Grey."

He couldn't help but smile. "And what way is that?"

"Like you want to take me back to bed."

He chuckled. She was beginning to read him so well. "But I do want to take you back to bed."

She nodded. To be completely honest, she wanted him to take her back to bed, too. But she had a lot of work to do and like she'd told him, with the Florida Classic next week things were already getting chaotic. "There's always tonight," she said saucily, as she slipped into her jacket.

He chuckled. "Yes, and I'm looking forward to it."

"The Man" looked at the vial of acid that would be used to teach Brandy Bennett a lesson. Brandy thought she had it all but would find out she was wrong when what she considered her most valuable asset, her beautiful face, was destroyed. No man would look at her with wanting and desire in his eyes, ever again.

Now all that had to be done was to calculate things just right to get her alone, which might be hard since her current lover was always hanging around her. But a way would be found around that.

It was time to make a strike.

Brandy pushed the papers on her desk aside. She knew without being told that Grey was on the other side of her closed door, probably reading a magazine or something, waiting for her to come out.

She glanced at her watch. It was almost noon and she was beginning to feel hungry. The phone on her desk buzzed and she reached over to pick it up. "Yes, Donna?"

"I have Ms. Osborne on the line for you."

Brandy sat up straight in her chair. She had tried reaching Carla earlier. "Thanks, please put her through."

A few moments later she heard Carla's voice. "Carla, you okay, girl?"

Carla sighed deeply. "Yes, I'm doing fine although stress levels and tensions are high around here. And to make matters worse, my attorney called a few minutes ago to let me know Jesse had obtained a court order to see Craig tonight."

"Tonight?"

"Yes, tonight at my place."

Brandy frowned. "When he sees Craig he'll immediately know that he's his, Carla."

"Yes, I know," Carla said, shifting uneasily in her chair, wondering what Jesse would do after finding out the truth.

"Have you spoken to your mom yet?" Brandy asked, recapturing Carla's attention.

"She's supposed to return home today and I plan to go see her later."

Brandy could clearly hear the anger in Carla's voice. Deciding to change the subject she asked, "Have you heard from Amber?"

"No, have you?"

"No, not yet," Brandy said. She looked up when Grey opened the door, walked into her office, and closed the door behind him. She watched as he sat in the chair on the other side of the room. "I'm hoping she'll give us a call with an update on Cord Jeffries' condition."

"Me, too. Well, I got to run. I'm meeting Sonya for lunch."

"Okay, you take care, and if you need me always remember I'm just a phone call away."

"Thanks, Brandy. I appreciate that."

Michelle buzzed Carla the moment she ended her phone conversation with Brandy.

"Yes, Michelle, what is it?"

"Ms. Morrison called while you were on the phone with Ms. Bennett. She said that the two of you would be doing lunch at her place instead of at a restaurant and she expected you there at noon."

Carla nodded. "All right. Anything else?"

"Yes. Mr. Devereau's attorney also called to confirm that Mr. Devereau would be at your house at six."

Again Carla nodded. "Thanks for the messages, Michelle, and when I leave for lunch I won't be back until tomorrow." She needed to go home and prepare Craig for Jesse's visit.

After ending her conversation with Michelle, Carla got up from her desk and walked over to the window. It was such a beautiful day outside, another beautiful day that the Lord had made, and no matter what, she had to believe things would work out for her.

She had to believe it.

Carla arrived at Sonya's place exactly at noon. "Hey, what gives? I thought we were meeting at Macadia for spaghetti," she said entering Sonya's condo.

"We're still having spaghetti from Macadia but I decided to do the take-out thing instead," Sonya said. "This gives us privacy. Besides, I rather not be in a public place when you kick my butt."

Carla turned around and lifted a brow. "Kick your butt? Sonya, what are you talking about?"

Sonya sighed. "You're going to find out soon enough. The question is, do you want me to tell you on a full or an empty stomach?"

Carla noticed just how nervous Sonya was, which wasn't at all like her. Maybe they needed to talk before eating. "I think you better tell me now."

"Are you sure? You may want to leave as soon as I tell you what I did."

Carla chuckled, trying to bring a lightness to their conversation. "Hey, remember I'm the one who loves to eat. No matter what you have to say, I still plan to eat my spaghetti. So come on, let's sit down and you can tell me what's going on."

The two women sat on the sofa facing each other. A few moments later, after Sonya got the nerve to speak she said. "I'm the reason Jesse Devereau is here, Carla."

Carla's forehead bunched into a curious frown. "How are you the reason? Are you saying you're the one who sent him that letter?"

Sonya shook her head. "No, but I know who did."

"Who?"

"Your mother. At least that's what I've been told."

Carla nodded. She had figured as much, although she hadn't wanted to believe that her mother would do such a thing but after reading the newspaper article about her mother selling her stock to Jesse, nothing surprised her. "And how did my mother know about Jesse? Did you tell her?"

Again Sonya shook her head. "No, I would never have done that."

"Then how did she find out?"

"She heard it from Dalton Gregory."

Carla's eyes widened. "Dalton Gregory? But—but how would he know anything about Jesse being Craig's father?"

Sonya glanced down at her hands that she had folded in her lap. "I told him."

The room got quiet and Carla thought she had misunderstood what Sonya said. "You told Dalton Gregory my secret? Our secret?"

At Sonya's nod, Carla stood. "Oh, Sonya, how could you have done such a thing? You know how that man feels about me. He thinks he had every right to take control of the company after Clark died, and you know how he and Clark as well as my mother manipulated things to keep me out."

Tears misted Sonya's eyes. "I know, I know, and my only excuse is that I was drunk that particular night that he ran into me at a Sylvester's. It was that same night I was upset because I felt you were spending more time with Brandy and Amber than you were with me.

Dalton caught me at one of my weakest moments, I was both drunk and horny and you of all people know how I have a tendency to think with my thang and not with my brain. Had I been in my right mind that night, Carla, I would have seen that he only wanted to screw me to get information about you. But I didn't see it then. I saw him as a man who wanted to spend time with me. I've always known he was a jerk but that night it didn't matter since I was so depressed about things."

Sonya inhaled and tried to stop tears. "And now that I know how much damage I've caused, as well as how much I've hurt you, I can't stand it. You've always been my best friend and now I've screwed up things and know you'll think that you won't ever be able to trust me again. I'd never do anything to hurt you or Craig; you have to believe that. And when I realized what I'd done, I confronted Dalton about it and he's the one who told me about your mother's part in it. I even tried making things right by going to see Jesse Devereau, but that man is as stubborn as they come and he wouldn't listen to anything that I had to say."

Carla breathed in deeply. Sonya was crying in earnest now, and Carla gathered her friend in a hug. "Hey, it's all right, Sonya. I know you didn't mean to tell but you're going to have to stop doing that, you know."

Sonya pulled away slightly to wipe tears from her eyes. She looked at Carla. "Doing what?"

A small smile touched Carla's lips. "Thinking with your *thang* instead of your brain."

Sonya couldn't stop laughing as she wiped her eyes. "God knows I'm working on it, believe me."

Carla nodded. "And for Pete's sake, in the future try to be more selective."

Sonya saw amusement lurking in the depths of Carla's eyes but she also saw seriousness there, too. "Trust me, I *was* drunk that night. Otherwise, I would not have given Dalton Gregory the time of day. But you're right, and I promise I'll do better." She then studied Carla. "What about us? Are we okay?"

Carla leaned back against the sofa. "Yeah, we are. I'm not saying I'm not disappointed . . . but then I've been disappointed with you before, Sonya, like the time you set me up on that blind date and told the guy that I was you."

Sonya couldn't help but laugh out loud when she remembered that. Moments later when her laughter subsided she looked at Carla. "Forgive me?"

Carla nodded. "Yes, I forgive you. No matter what, you're my very best friend who has a problem she intends to work on, right?"

Sonya smiled. "Right."

Carla nodded again. "I know you love me and Craig and wouldn't intentionally do anything to hurt us. In fact, I know how protective you are of us and I appreciate that. I always have."

After saying all of that, Carla sighed. "So come on and let's eat. I'm starving."

Sonya laughed as she and Carla embraced again.

Carla went to see her mother as soon as she left Sonya's place. She could tell by the look on her mother's face when she opened the door that she was surprised to see her. Without waiting for an invitation to come in, Carla walked passed her.

"Mom, we need to talk."

"No, we don't. In fact I'm expecting someone, Carla. Maybe some other time."

Carla met her mother's gaze. "Just answer one question for me and then I'll leave." She tightened her hand on the straps of her purse. "Why, Mom? Why did you do it? Why did you send Jesse Devereau that letter?"

Anger filled Madeline's face. "I sent it because I felt that he had every right to know. Every man should know about any child he fathered."

Carla shook her head in disagreement. "That was my decision to make and you should have respected it. You had no right to send him that letter."

"I had to tell him. I wanted to contact him and tell him about our baby but your father wouldn't let me."

Carla gazed at her mother. There was a faraway look in her eyes and Carla suddenly knew that her mother wasn't talking about Jesse Devereau any longer but about someone else.

"Who, Mother? Who did you want to contact?"

"Mark Singleton." She said the name like she expected Carla to know it. "I met Mark one night at a charity event and fell in love. We had a brief affair and I got pregnant. But I made a decision not to tell him about the baby since I was engaged to marry your father."

Carla gasped. "You had a baby from another man?"

Madeline smiled. "Of course, how on earth could you assume that Clark was Craig's child?"

Carla's head began spinning with her mother's revelation. "Did Dad know?"

Madeline chuckled. "Not for six years, then his mother told him. I decided I wanted Mark to know he had a son and wrote him a letter. Your grandmother found it and read it and took it straight to your father. He was livid and left. When he came back later that night he'd been drinking and forced himself on me and I got pregnant with you. I never wanted another child. Clark was all I ever wanted. You have always belonged to your father because he knew I never wanted you, not after what he'd done. The only man I ever loved was Mark."

"I hope I'm not interrupting anything but the front door was standing open so I walked on in."

Carla turned to see Jesse Devereau standing there. Evidently he was the person her mother had been expecting. She wondered how much of their conversation he'd heard. Right then she really didn't care. She was still in a daze over everything her mother had said. Now Carla knew the reason she and her father had been so close while on the other hand, her mother had always treated her like dirt; mainly because in her mother's mind she was dirt. And she now knew the reason her mother had been so obsessed with her telling Jesse that she'd gotten pregnant.

She needed to leave before she did something stupid like start to cry. Her mother and Jesse Devereau were the last two people who she wanted to see her tears. "No, Jesse, you aren't interrupting anything— not anything at all."

And with that final statement she walked past him and out of the house.

❧ *Chapter 21* ❧

*A*mber glanced around Cord's apartment. A bachelor definitely lived here. It was fairly neat and decorated in earth-tone colors. The living room was huge and spacious with several paintings on the wall by African-American artists as well as a wall-to-wall bookcase. For a man who claimed he didn't have time to read, he sure had a lot of books.

Cord saw what had claimed her attention and said simply, "I acquired most of those while in college, and the others are there just to impress. I heard that the intellectual type turns a woman on."

Amber arched a brow. She wondered why a man who looked like Cord thought he had to use books to impress a woman?

She had left the hospital after meeting with Dr. Phillips who had given her a list of Cord's do's and don'ts. He had given her Cord's address and told her that he would make sure Cord got checked out of the hospital and home by noon. He suggested that she take care of whatever she needed to do before arriving.

She had gone home, changed clothes, and packed a few things in an overnight bag. Then she had dropped by the bookstore to let Jennifer and Eileen know of her plans and to advise them of where she would be if they needed her.

She had also made it a point to stop by the hotel to see Brandy and tell her of her plans as well. She could tell Brandy had been surprised she would go this far to help a man she barely knew. But her friend didn't say anything other than that she would let Carla know and to call if she needed her.

"Do you want to see the guest room?"

Cord's question interrupted her thoughts. "Yes."

She followed him down a narrow hallway and came to a bedroom directly across the hall from what she assumed was his bedroom. She couldn't help taking a quick peek inside his bedroom and saw that he had a king-size bed with huge pillows.

"Think you'll be comfortable in here for the next four days?"

Again his comment recaptured her attention and she stepped into the room and glanced around. It was nicely decorated with the same earth-tone colors that seemed to flow throughout the apartment. The double bed had a comfy look and she could see herself getting a good night's sleep in it.

"I'll be fine. It's a nice room," she said when things had gotten too quiet and the air surrounding them had gotten a little too warm. Cord was dressed in a pair of jeans and an Orlando Magic T-shirt. For some reason she'd assumed he would be in pajamas since Dr. Phillips had said he needed to rest.

"Thanks. I had to get all new furniture after my divorce."

Amber swung her head around and looked at him, surprised. "You're divorced?"

"Yes."

Amber nodded. That bit of information made her realize just how little she knew about him. "For how long?" she asked, thinking she needed to know.

"A little over a year. Her name was Diane."

Amber nodded again. She wondered if he and Diane were still good friends. Some exes did remain that way. She had tried it with Gary, but found out all he wanted was the opportunity to get laid every once in a while.

"Are the two of you still pretty friendly?"

Cord chuckled, but Amber picked up on the fact there was more anger than amusement in his chuckle. "Not on your life. She left me for one of my clients and almost destroyed me and my business in the process when she emptied our personal and business bank accounts."

Amber sighed. Betrayal. Why did marriages have to end that way? She heard the bitterness in his voice and knew how if felt to be betrayed by someone you loved and trusted. "I'm divorced, too, and have been for almost three years. My ex's name is Gary and he betrayed me with another woman. I came home early from work one day and caught them . . . right in the act."

"Ouch. That must have hurt pretty damn bad."

"Yeah, it hurt like the dickens but I've gotten over it. Even after the divorce, I thought it would be best if Gary and I remained friends. But it didn't take long to see that our meaning of *being friends* was different. So, I thought the best thing to do was move away and start over. That's how I came to live in Orlando."

"From where?"

"Nashville."

Cord leaned against the dresser. The casual stance showed off his long limbs, hard muscles and manly form. "After college I lived in Atlanta but the accounting firm I was working for decided to downsize and Dev talked me into joining him here."

"How long have you and Dr. Phillips known each other?" she asked curiously.

Cord smiled. "Dev and I were friends in high school. He and his Dad took me in after my grandmother died when I was seventeen. We were living in Myrtle Beach, South Carolina at the time. After high school I went to Atlanta to attend Clark University and Dev went to

Howard, but we went home to South Carolina for the holidays." He chuckled softly. "Mr. Phillips would not have had it any other way." Then Cord momentarily got quiet and said. "He died last year of a heart attack. He was sixty and had been working too hard and refused to slow down."

"Like you?"

Cord's mouth curved into a smile. "I see that Dev has been talking to you."

"Yes, and the reason I'm here is to make sure that you follow his orders for the next four days, which has me wondering why you're not in bed."

I'll be glad to get into the bed if you get in there with me, he wanted to say. Instead he said. "I didn't think it would be proper for you to arrive and find me in my jammies."

She waved off his words. "Hey, I've seen a man in his jammies before, so the sight would not have bothered me. I stopped by the store and got you a couple of cans of soup. Dr. Phillips mentioned that your cupboards were probably bare."

"They are."

"Then I think the best thing to do is for you to get back in bed and I'll bring you a bowl of soup."

"You're not here to wait on me, Amber, and I'm not bedridden. I can relax without being glued to the bed," he said stubbornly.

"Yeah, well, I'm sure you can but I prefer that for the rest of the day you stay in bed and let me take care of you like I assured Dr. Phillips that I would." When she saw he was about to be defiant, she coaxed, "Go ahead and humor me."

He met her gaze and kept it level with hers. "All right, Amber, I'll humor you, but when the time comes I expect you to return the favor."

What had Cord meant by that? Amber thought as she poured hot soup into a bowl. After they'd left the guest room he had gone into his room and closed the door saying he planned to change into his jammies and she hadn't heard a peep out of him since.

She had continued to familiarize herself with his house and had called home to check for any messages on her answering machine. She had then gone into the living room and watched television and had gotten caught up in a movie when she'd noted it was time for Cord to eat something before he took the medicine Dr. Phillips had prescribed.

She knocked on his bedroom door twice and when she heard soft snoring decided not to wake him. Amber had made it back to the kitchen and had sat the bowl of soup on the counter when the phone rang. She quickly picked it up.

"Hello?"

"Ms. Stuart?"

Amber smiled, recognizing the voice immediately. "Dr. Phillips, yes, it's me."

"I was just calling to check on my patient. I know how difficult he can be at times."

Amber's smiled widened. "Yes, well, he's sleeping right now and has been for over a couple of hours."

Dev chuckled. "That's good since he definitely needs the rest. I increased the dosage of his medication for that reason. Besides wanting to check on Cord, I wanted to let you know that my lady friend and I plan to bring you and Cord dinner. She enjoys cooking and has made this huge pot of red beans and rice that we'd like to share."

"Umm, that sounds delicious."

"It really is," he said, and Amber could hear the admiration in his voice for his girlfriend's talent in the kitchen. "And Briana and I can stay a while with Cord if you need to go out or something. You know you don't have to be there with him every minute of the day."

"Yes, I know but being here gives me much needed rest, too. Last week was pretty hectic getting things prepared for the bookstore's anniversary party. So this way I can relax a bit. I haven't been doing much of anything since I got here but watching television, so in a way I'm glad I'm here and not at home. If I were at home there would be a million things for me to do."

"Well, I'm sure Cord appreciates you being there. I got to check on a few more patients then I'm out of here. Expect me and Briana around six."

"All right. Good-bye." She then hung up the phone.

"Was that call for me?"

Amber whipped around at the sound of the deep, husky voice. Just waking up from his nap, Cord looked as dazed as she felt. The man was standing in the kitchen doorway dressed in a pair of pajamas bottoms and had that "just slept" sexy look. Her gaze latched on the broad span of his hairy chest and masculine torso and wondered how it would feel resting against it.

She lifted a hand to push hair back from her face. Suddenly, she could feel the heat, the sensual power he radiated, evoked and provoked. Her heart began racing out of control and she could actually feel her temperature starting to rise. Cord Jeffries was definitely the type of man who could fill any woman's fantasy.

"Ahh, yes, that was Dr. Phillips. He was checking to see how you were doing," she finally found her voice to say.

Cord nodded and ran a hand down his face as if to wipe away lingering sleep. "Did you tell him I was doing fine?"

"Yes, I told him."

"Good."

Then his eyes held hers and she could see the heat in them, and it sent desire flooding through her. She decided to break eye contact and turned to the sink. "If you're ready to eat something, I can reheat the soup. Dr. Phillips said he and his girlfriend would bring something for dinner. She likes to cook."

Cord chuckled. "Yes, she does."

Amber blinked. She hadn't realized Cord had crossed the room and he was now standing directly behind her. He was so close that if she were to turn around he would pin her between his body and the sink. She decided to keep her back to him. "Like I told you this morning, I can't cook."

"It doesn't matter. I'm sure you have a number of other talents."

Amber caught her breath the moment she felt Cord slide his hands around her waist. He then took a step closer and she felt him, the outline of his hard erection against her backside. She couldn't help but pause a moment and savor the contact and was almost too ashamed to admit it was a contact she'd missed. It had been almost three years since a man had touched her and she couldn't stop the quiver of awareness that flowed through her, settling in the middle of her legs.

"I want you, Amber. I think you've known that from the first and a part of me believes that you want me, too. But I think it's more than lust here. I think we genuinely like each other, too. Right?"

She nodded, but refused to turn around. "Yes, I like you but I don't want to rush things."

"And I don't want to rush things either," he murmured, his warm breath brushing close to her ear. "According to Dev I'm not to mess around for two weeks, which I guess is fair. I'd like to use that time for us to get to know each other better. After that we need to make a decision."

Amber swallowed. "About what?"

"About where we want to go from there, if anywhere. From the sounds of things you've had a bad marriage and so have I. The question I want you to think about is will you let the past keep you from ever having a future? That's the same question I had to ask myself a while back and decided I wouldn't let Diane take away my joy for living."

He leaned over and touched his lips to that space on her neck, just under her ear. She began to tremble. She leaned back against him and he shifted forward to cup her curvaceous bottom. The feel of it was driving him insane. He didn't want to think of how it would feel when they were skin to skin.

"Can I kiss you?" he asked, his tone low and deep.

The husky sound of his voice made her squirm and clench her thighs together. "Yes," she whispered, barely able to catch her breath.

"Turn around and give me your mouth, Amber."

Slowly, she turned to face him and immediately locked her gaze with his. His eyes were dark and filled with a wanting she'd never seen in a man eyes before, at least not with such intensity. When he lowered his head and captured her mouth with his, he didn't try to hide the hunger he felt.

Neither did she.

She closed her eyes when his lips touched hers and then she was lost. He plundered her mouth from corner to corner, side to side, top to bottom, licking, stroking, sucking, and then his tongue captured hers, held it captive and mated, relentlessly, greedily, sending her into oblivion where the only thing she could do was moan. Her breasts were beginning to ache, the area between her thighs felt needy, and she shifted so she could cradle his erection there in her center, although what she craved was more intimate contact.

And when Cord suddenly pulled his mouth away, she bit her lip against a whimper of protest and slowly opened her eyes. He was looking at her with deep desire. His lips were still wet and his breathing uneven. She immediately became concerned that he might have overexerted himself.

She braced herself against the sink, allowing her own breathing to return to normal. The kiss had left her entire body aching for more. "You weren't supposed to overwork yourself," she said softly, lifting her gaze to his when she could finally speak.

"I didn't overwork myself, Amber. What I got is overcharged. There is a difference." When she was about to say something he covered her mouth with his fingers.

"No, I won't let you regret what we just shared. I won't." Then he replaced his fingers with his lips and kissed her slow and easy, with a sweetness that almost brought tears to Amber's eyes as her mouth clung to his, taking everything he was offering.

When he broke the kiss and stepped back she knew. There had been a reason she had been drawn to him from the beginning, and although she wasn't sure what that reason was, she was willing to find out.

"I don't regret anything, Cord."

A slow, easy smiled tilted his lips. "Good, and I appreciate you being here with me, Amber. It means a lot to me."

She nodded. It meant a lot to her as well.

Chapter 22

Jesse stood back after ringing the doorbell, trying to put out of his mind the episode he'd witnessed earlier that day with Carla and her mother. What he'd heard had taken him aback.

But then it had shocked the hell out of Carla Osborne.

That much had been evident on her face when her mother had dropped her little bombshell. How could a child accept that she had not been wanted by one of her parents? For him it had been fairly easy growing up in a foster home most of his life. Most of the kids there had been in the same boat he'd been in. Every single one of them had been either given up for adoption or had been taken away from their parents because the parents hadn't cared enough to look out for their welfare. He would never forget the day he had met Mike and the two had bonded and had become the best of friends. It was their dream, their plan to grow up not wanting or needing anyone, and so far that's the way they'd always kept things. They had each other and they hadn't needed anyone else. He would never forget that day when Susan Brady's private investigator had tracked him down, claiming he was her long lost son—the one she'd given up for adoption. After meeting her, she'd told him the long story of how she, a white woman, had fallen in love with this African-American law student and had gotten pregnant.

His thoughts returned to the present when he heard the sound of footsteps approaching the door. Although he didn't want it to, his heart had gone out to Carla. Her mother's words had been brutal and cruel. But then, he quickly decided, what was between Carla and her mother was their business. His only concern was his son, which was the reason he was here.

He would get to see and meet his son for the first time.

He tried not to be nervous at the thought of how his child would react to him. He intended for this to be the first of several visits. If Carla had a problem with him coming to her home then he would make arrangements for him to spend time with his child elsewhere. But come hell or high water, he intended to be a permanent fixture in his child's life. He refused for his son to find out about his parent the way he had.

Or the way Carla had found out about hers.

He wondered which was worse, growing up not knowing your parents or knowing the one you had had never loved you?

Before he could ponder that question any further, the door opened and he stared at Carla standing there, looking beautiful as ever. His gaze rolled over her, taking in her pullover blouse and jeans. Jeans never looked so good on a woman and desire quickly spread through him. He remembered another time he had stood on Carla's doorstep when she'd opened the door. Thanksgiving night nearly three years ago.

His hand tightened into fists at his side. Now was not the time to be captivated by a beautiful face. He had to remind himself that this was the woman who'd had his child and hadn't had the decency to tell him. It would have been different if she'd not known how to reach him but she had. He'd made certain of that. In fact after returning to California he'd wanted her to call and for the first couple of months had hoped that she would, for any reason, even if it was to institute a long-distance affair. But . . . according to Sonya Morrison, Carla thought he had lied to her and was involved with someone else when they had slept together. He wondered how she would react to know that person had been his mother.

"Jesse."

Her voice was cool, detached, and he knew she wished he was not there, but as far as he was concerned that was her problem and not his. "Carla, you know why I'm here."

"Yes. Please come in. Craig is just finishing up dinner."

He entered her home and immediately felt its warmth and homeyness. He glanced around and it was evident that a child lived there. Not because of any toys scattered about, but because of the number of photographs everywhere, as well as the child safety locks he quickly noticed. There was no doubt that she had taken every precaution to keep her child—their child—safe.

"If you care to have a seat, I'll go get Craig."

Jesse nodded as he sat down on a leather couch. It was obvious she planned to give him the cold shoulder and have very little to say to him. That was fine with him if she wanted to use that approach, since any time her mouth moved he remembered the taste of it. It was a taste he doubted he would ever forget.

"He was named after your father?" he asked before she could leave the room.

"Yes." Carla met his gaze and decided to say, "Craig and I had a long talk today and I told him you were coming for a visit. He'll be somewhat shy at first, which is understandable, but once he gets to—"

"Who did you tell him was coming?"

Carla sighed as she gathered herself. There was no use denying what would soon be the obvious. "His daddy."

Jesse's breath got caught in his lungs. "Am I, Carla?" he asked, wanting her to tell him what he'd wanted to hear directly from her all along. "Am I your son's father?"

Everything in Carla went still. She knew what he wanted. He wanted to hear her admit it and there was no way she could not. She looked at him for a long moment, accepting his right to know, a right she had refused him for almost three years. "Yes, Craig is your son," she said quietly, finally. "Please excuse me while I go get him."

Jesse's throat tightened when Carla left the room. Carla. *The woman who was the mother of his child.* That single thought had more of an impact than he wanted it to. All along he'd known there was a strong possibility it was true, but hearing her admit it had a sudden calming effect on him.

"Jesse, this is Craig."

Jesse's head swung around and his gaze fixed on the little boy whose hand Carla held. His breath caught. It was like looking at a miniature of himself. Everything was there, practically the same. The skin tone, the eye color, the hair texture, his features. Even if Carla never acknowledged it with words, the total package clearly showed this was *his* son.

Half his.

He couldn't deny that although his son had the majority of his features, he also belonged to Carla. He was *their* son.

"Craig, this is your daddy. I told you that he was coming by. Say hello."

Jesse watched as the little boy's gaze shifted from staring at the floor to him. "Hello," he said softly, shyly.

Jesse's heart almost stopped but he forced it to keep beating as he slowly crossed the room and crouched down in front of his son, meeting his direct gaze on his level. He became overwhelmed when hazel eyes met hazel eyes and for a moment he couldn't get out the words he had intended to say when an insurmountable degree of emotions surged through him. "Hello, Craig. How are you?" he asked when he was finally able to speak.

The little boy glanced up at his mother as if seeking her permission to answer. At her nod, he said, "Fine."

Jesse stood as he cleared the tightness in his throat. "Would you like to sit on the sofa and talk to me a while?"

His son frowned. "Can Mommy come, too?"

Jesse heard fear in his son's voice and understood. He shot a glance at Carla. "Yes, she can if she wants."

Carla didn't want to. "You're a big boy, Craig. You can sit on the sofa with your daddy all by yourself. Mommy will be right here. All right?"

Craig looked at her with pleading eyes. "You won't go away?"

She smiled down at the son she loved more than life. "No, I won't leave the room so go ahead."

She then took her son's hand and placed it in Jesse's and sensed the emotional impact Craig was having on him. When Jesse walked Craig over to the sofa, she crossed the room to look out the window, needing the distance from the man who had fathered her child.

She glanced back over her shoulder and saw that Craig was sitting in Jesse's lap and could see the look of awe and surprise on Jesse's face to see just how much his son looked like him.

"So tell me, Craig, are you a good boy?"

Craig shook his head no. Carla couldn't help but smile. At least her son was honest.

"And why not?" Jesse asked as if surprised by the little boy's response.

"Because I still wet my pants."

Jesse smiled and Carla tried not to be captured by that smile. "But it is something you're getting better at, right?" Jesse asked.

"Wetting my pants?"

Jesse lifted a brow. "No, not wetting them."

Craig seemed to ponder that question then said, "Mrs. Boston said I'm getting better."

Jesse lifted his gaze to Carla. "Who's Mrs. Boston?"

"She's the lady who keeps him every day while I'm at work."

"She's nice," Craig said, giving his father a toothless grin.

For the next few minutes Carla stood by the window and watched Jesse talk to their son as the two got to know each other. She was surprised that he hadn't shown up with some extravagant gift to win Craig over. She really had expected him to. Instead, he was offering himself to his child without any fancy frills. He evidently wanted to build a place in his son's heart without any material inducements, and she couldn't help but appreciate that.

"Are you glad to see my mommy, too?"

Craig's question caught Carla's attention. Jesse had just finished telling him how glad he was to see him.

"Yes, I'm glad to see your mommy, too."

"Will you live with us?"

Carla swallowed. Craig had asked her that very same thing when she'd told him about Jesse earlier that day, and she had told him no, his daddy would be living elsewhere. Evidently her son had decided to ask Jesse for himself.

"No, but I'll never be far away and I'll come see you every chance I get. Maybe you can even come and visit me."

Craig smiled. "Will Mommy come, too?"

Jesse glanced across the room at Carla, and before he could answer, she did. "No, sweetheart, Mommy won't be coming. Whenever you and your daddy spend time together it will be just the two of you and you will have lots of fun."

Craig looked at his mother and thought on her answer. He pondered it for a while then said in a pout, "No. I won't go if Mommy don't go."

Carla opened her mouth to argue the point but Jesse shook his head sending her a silent message that it was okay. Building a relationship with his son would take time and he knew, understood, and accepted that.

"Can you color?"

Craig's question recaptured Jesse's attention and he couldn't help but laugh. "Yes, I can color."

"Will you color with me?"

"Yes, if that's what you want to do."

No sooner had Jesse answered than Craig scrambled out of his arms and took off.

Carla couldn't help but shake her head as a grin touched her lips. "You may have made a big mistake. That's Coloring Craig and he'll have you stretched out here on the floor coloring with him for hours."

Jesse chuckled. "I don't mind."

The way Jesse suddenly looked at her with odd intensity made her uncomfortable. It also reminded her that the two of them were still at odds with each other. He was trying to hurt her and was willing to destroy the livelihood of her employees in the process. Tomorrow would be the day the board met to decide the fate of Osborne and chances were she, along with a number of other employees, would be given their walking papers.

"Well, I mind," she said coolly, deciding to reset the tone between them. They weren't friends and she refused to pretend that they were. "Your attorney said you would only be here for an hour and an hour is all you're getting."

He narrowed his gaze at her. Before he had a chance to respond to her statement, Craig raced back into the room carrying several coloring books under his arms.

"Come on, get down on the floor with me to color."

Without wasting any time and mindless of the expensive suit he was wearing, Jesse stood and took off his jacket. With the agility of a man who made getting down on the floor seem like a common occurrence, Carla watched Jesse join his son on the carpeted floor and although she didn't want to, she couldn't help the tears that misted her eyes as she watched the two similar faces drawn together over the open coloring book. It was truly a Kodak moment.

A couple of hours later as Jesse entered his hotel room, closing the door behind him, he could still hear the sound of his son's laughter ringing in his ears. He'd gone well over the allotted time. He'd known it and Carla had known it. But he'd been having so much fun spending time with his son that in the end she'd had the decency to let things be.

After they'd finished coloring at least three pictures, Craig had wanted to bring out a few of his other toys and in no time at all, the living room had gotten cluttered. Somehow during that time, Carla had managed to sneak out of the room and leave them alone and Craig hadn't seemed to notice.

When she'd returned and glanced around, Craig had looked at all the toys they'd scattered. He'd then looked at Jesse sheepishly and whispered, "Mommy's not going to be happy with the mess you made, Daddy."

At that particular moment Jesse couldn't do anything but pull his son to him. Craig's acceptance of him as his father had been the most awarding experience he'd ever encountered. Even now he was still touched and knew he would remember that moment for the rest of his life.

He had just taken his jacket off when there was a knock on the connecting door. Knowing it was Mike, he quickly said, "Come in."

Mike entered. "How did things go?"

Jesse smiled. "I saw him, Mike, and it's obvious that he's mine. And I held him. You don't know how good that felt. I got nearly three years to make up for and I want to give him everything, especially my name."

"Did you and Carla get a chance to talk about that?"

Jesse snorted. "No. Although she was cordial, she's still acting unapproachable and reserved."

"How else do you expect her to act when she'll be losing her company to you tomorrow?"

Jesse's eyes narrowed. "She gave me no choice."

Mike nodded slowly as he met Jesse's gaze. "There's something about that word *choice*. All of us have choices, Jess. Have you taken the time to consider that Carla had a choice of whether or not she wanted to give birth to your son? What if she'd chosen to have an abortion instead?"

Jesse flinched. His son's cherubic face loomed in his mind. After seeing Craig, his own flesh and blood, he couldn't imagine such a thing, and a part of him was profoundly grateful that Carla hadn't taken that route.

"I'm going downstairs and browse the gift shop for a new razor. I'll check you out later," Mike said. And as he closed the door behind him he hoped that he had left Jesse with something to think about.

❧ *Chapter 23* ❧

Grey hung up the phone after talking with his friend at the Bureau in D.C. A handwriting analysis had confirmed what Grey had suspected for a while. There was an eighty percent chance that the messages had been written by a female not a male. Now with this most recent information, he needed to go back down the list and check out every female whose name he had recorded, starting with Brandy's secretary.

He rubbed a hand across his face. Today had almost been a nightmare with all those people checking into the hotel for the Florida Classic. It had been hard as hell to keep up with Brandy and on a few occasions he'd had to depend on his backup to make sure she was being covered. She had been forced to make several last-minute changes to her schedule and no doubt she would be doing the same thing again tomorrow, which meant he needed to bring this to an end and soon.

He glanced up when Brandy came out of the bedroom and his gaze immediately locked on hers. His throat tightened and the palms of his hands suddenly felt warm. Dressed in a long flowing white silk robe, she was a sight to behold and his sharply male gaze held her within its scope, tight. This was a woman made for loving a man, he thought as his body became unbearably hard. He began to ache all over, especially in certain parts and when he breathed in and his nostrils pulled in her scent, he knew he had to have her.

Now.

Brandy stopped walking when she saw how Grey was staring at her. The heat of his gaze trailed fire all across her body, starting with her breasts then slowly moved downward. When she began feeling this ferocious burning sensation between her legs, she almost gasped out loud. His raw need was reaching out to her, pulling her within its clutches and arousing her in a way she had never been aroused before.

He was going to make love to her again.

That had been a foregone conclusion when she'd awakened that morning in his arms after having spent the better part of the night and predawn hours making love. She had thought about him most of the day when she should have been busy getting ready for the coming week's festivities. But all she'd been able to think about was Grey and how he had found pleasure in her body and had given her pleasure in return. He hadn't lied when he'd said he had three years to make up for, and it seemed he would continue making up for it again tonight.

He stood and the hunger she saw in his eyes excited her as well as incited her. Without waiting, without being asked, she untied her robe and let it fall to her feet. His eyes widened when he saw that she'd been completely naked underneath. He slowly crossed the room and when he stopped before her, she inhaled gently, as if letting the aroma of an aroused man fill her senses.

He reached out and his hand automatically went to her breasts, which seemed to come alive with his touch. His fingers gently tugged at her nipple before leaning forward and taking it into his mouth, sucking and making her arch her back to give him more. Without breaking contact with her breasts, his hand automatically went between her legs and found her wet, ready. He hadn't used a condom and hadn't given much thought to using one since he had remembered her conversation with her mother that day confirming she was on the pill. For some reason he had needed to come inside of her, ejaculate as much as he could. He had needed to know his release was actually filling her and not a piece of latex. The thought quickly flashed through his mind that his obsession had been extreme and one he'd never encountered with a woman before. Unprotected sex had never been the norm for him. That thought startled him, but not enough for him to put on a condom now. He wanted to feel himself come inside of her again.

Brandy suddenly found herself swept into his arms as he took her back into the bedroom. He gently placed on her the bed and stepped back, almost tearing off his shirt and quickly stepping out of his pants. Moments later he was just as naked as she and just as she had last night, Brandy marveled how beautifully made he was, with his sleek shoulders, broad chest, and firm, flat stomach. His skin was a dark brown and glowed from the moonlight flowing in through the window. But what really held her interest more so than anything was his aroused body part, large, thick, and muscular as it boldly and proudly jutted from the apex of his thighs. He was a man who was made to bring a woman pleasure, and as he took a step forward she knew that like last night, she would be the recipient.

Brandy's breathing quickened when he got in bed with her, moved his body over hers, began licking her neck and gliding his body tormentingly slowly over hers. He wanted her to feel just what he had for her, what he planned to give her.

In a surprise move he lifted up his body to turn her over, pulling her hips back against him. He wanted her this way and his body slowly pressed against her, seeking her entry. She arched her back, strained back against him, letting him know she wanted it this way as much as he did. And when he entered her, going through the wet folds of her swollen, hot flesh, she moaned, and the sound sent tremors through his body.

He ran his hand over the delectable curves of her backside before firmly gripping her hips and stroking her deeply, moving in and out while he clenched his teeth to stop from screaming his pleasure.

Brandy had no such intentions. She thought, the hell with it, they had an entire floor to themselves and she planned to scream until she couldn't scream anymore.

And she did. The moment she felt him come inside of her, drenching her insides with his release, she tightened her muscles, pulling more, wanting more and getting her wish when he continued to buck against her, smacking his thighs against her backside penetrating deeper, holding her body pressed close to his, allowing her to take everything his body was giving her, sweeping her off into ecstasy while a feeling of intense pleasure filled her, illustrating and demonstrating just how much he had wanted her and needed her.

When there was nothing left in him to give, when she had literally taken everything, he locked his arms around her and pulled her down to him, keeping their bodies connected and savoring in the moments they had just shared.

Grey slowly opened his eyes, feeling totally depleted of strength. He had never taken a woman with such urgency before. Never before had reaching a climax been so powerful, so gut wrenching satisfying. Even now while holding her against him spoon-style, his body still locked to hers, he felt himself getting hard inside of her all over again.

He needed more.

Slowly lifting her leg over his he saw the minute she became awake and realized what he was about to do. He leaned over and kissed her, elated with the passion he could evoke in her so quickly. And when she began returning his kiss, he began moving inside of her, in and out, making love to her all over again. This woman he now claimed as *his* in every way a man could claim a woman.

His woman.

That revelation made pleasure rip through his body; joy filled his soul and love overflowed in his heart.

Love?

No, he refused to surrender to the power of love ever again. And when the crushing waves of ecstasy came crashing down on them, he deepened the kiss and somewhere in the back of his mind, the only thing he could think about was that he would not be another Masters who let a Bennett get under his skin. He wouldn't go there.

His head came up sharply and his gaze narrowed on her face. She had fallen asleep with a satiated smile on her lips. His gut clenched.

Too late, he thought. He was gone.

"Tell me about Jolene Bradford."

Brandy raised a brow over her cup of coffee. She looked at him as if surprised he had brought up the name.

After she and Grey had made love for three solid hours, they had showered together and then while she'd slipped into a nightgown, he'd made a pot of coffee and said he needed to talk with her. She frowned. Jolene was not someone she wanted to talk about.

"Brandy?"

She met Grey's gaze. "What made you think of her?"

Drawing a deep breath he said, "As I lay there holding you in my arms and thinking what a damn fool Lorenzo Ballentine had to be, I couldn't help remembering what he did. Then it occurred to me I hadn't checked Jolene Bradford out, as closely as maybe I should have. So tell me what you know about her."

Brandy sighed. "There's nothing to tell other than she was a woman I had considered my closest friend until I found out she'd been screwing my fiancé behind my back."

Grey nodded. "How did the two of you meet?"

"We became professors at Howard about the same time and hit it off. I never thought of her as a threat or someone I could not trust with my man. After all, she had her own boyfriend, a very handsome guy with a promising career in politics."

Grey nodded again. "Why do you think she went after your fiancé?"

Brandy chuckled. "I'm not absolutely sure she went after him, Grey.

It might have been the other way around. Lorenzo may have gone after her and she was too weak to resist. The reason I say that is because after my divorce, Alexia confided that Lorenzo had tried hitting on her while we were engaged."

Grey leaned back in his chair. "So you don't blame Jolene for not being able to keep her legs closed?"

Brandy shook her head and studied the contents of her coffee. "I blame Jolene for betraying my trust."

Grey took a sip of his coffee. "Do you think she knew she was being videotaped?"

She lifted her gaze to his. "No. I may be wrong but I really don't think she knew. She tried to talk to me afterwards but I refused to talk to her. And then when copies of that videotape surfaced on the Howard campus, she resigned, completely humiliated."

"Copies of the videotape surfaced?"

"Yes. I don't know exactly who was responsible for that. I made only two copies: one for my attorney and the other to give to my brother, since he'd been so taken with Jolene. Victor Junior swears he knows nothing about the copies that started being distributed. If he told me the truth then I can only assume the guy who coordinated my wedding decided to take advantage of what he saw as a good thing. Copies of that videotape began spreading like wildfire."

Grey set his coffee cup down. "Final question."

"What?"

"Do you know where she is now?"

"Yes. After she left Howard she got a teaching job at Bethune Cookman College."

Jolene Bradford was not teaching at BCC, Grey discovered later after Brandy had gone to bed. With a promise to join her later, he had made a call to a friend in DC to run Jolene Bradford's social security number through the system. The report indicated that Jolene had been asked to leave a year and a half ago when copies of the videotape began circulating on BCC's campus. After leaving BCC she worked at the University of Central Florida here in Orlando, but only for a few months. The report did not provide a reason as to why she left, but it did indicate that she had not used her social security number since leaving UCF.

Grey couldn't help wondering if Jolene was still living in Orlando and if she was employed, then where?

He was determined to find out everything there was to know about the woman.

Chapter 24

Unable to sleep, Cord slipped out of bed and pulled on his jeans. It was way past midnight and he felt restless, agitated, and horny. He couldn't remember the last time he felt this intense about having a woman. Even now his body throbbed just thinking about Amber.

Dev and Briana's visit had somehow relieved some of his edginess, but only temporarily. He had enjoyed spending time with them and could tell that Amber had enjoyed their visit as well. She had seen Dev in a less professional light and by the end of the evening she was no longer calling him Dr. Phillips.

Amber and Briana had hit it off, too. They had talked for hours about various books they had read, movies they had seen, and places they had shopped, while he and Dev had gotten engrossed in a football game on the tube.

Knowing his way around the apartment in the dark, Cord strolled down the hall and through the living room—his destination was the terrace. Opening the glass sliding door, he stepped out and inhaled the scent of orange blossoms and realized that it was Amber's scent that filled his nostrils.

He leaned against the wall and watched as a full moon lit the predawn sky. Satisfaction filled him that the woman he'd been thinking about for the past three weeks, literally nonstop, was sharing his home, asleep in his guest room. And she had agreed to get to know him.

But for some reason he felt as if he had known her for years and the next two weeks of getting to know her were just a formality. There was something between them and whatever it was, it bound them together. If he had his way he would be in bed with her this very minute, between her legs, planted firmly inside of her, thrusting in and out until—

"Cord, are you all right?"

Her voice startled him. He hadn't heard her approach. He half-turned to find her standing in the doorway wearing a full-length robe. The moonlight reflected the smooth curves of her voluptuous figure and his body hardened even more. "Yes, I'm fine. I couldn't sleep."

She walked toward him and when she stopped in front of him, her incredible amber-colored eyes scanned him from head to toe while a concerned frown touched her brows. "Are you sure you're okay?"

Oh, yeah, I'm okay, but this hard-on is something of a nuisance, he thought, but instead he said, "Yes, I'm fine. Like I said, I couldn't sleep."

She worried her lips nervously. "I shouldn't have let you kiss me. You were already exhausted and needed your rest."

He reached out and took hold of her hand and a heated sensation tore through him, but he refused to let her hand go. "Hey, we said no regrets, remember?"

"Yes, but—"

"No buts, Amber. I wanted that kiss. Hell, I needed that kiss. If anything that kiss relaxed me in a way bed rest never could have."

She searched his face uncertainly. "You mean it?"

He smiled. "Yes, I mean it. Come here." Before she could stop him he pulled her into his arms, needing to hold her.

She tipped her head back, her expression guarded. "I'm usually a very level-headed person."

Cord smiled. "And you think being here with me means that you're not?"

"I really don't know you."

"And I don't know you and that's why we've agreed to get to know each other. But in a way I think that we do know each other, Amber. We know each other in a way that truly matters right now, and one thing I do know is that you cared enough for a virtual stranger to be here with him to make sure he got well, and to me that says a lot."

She frowned and stepped back from him, pulling herself from his embrace. She had to be completely honest with him. "I'm not here out of the goodness of my heart, Cord. I'm here because I want you. The woman in me is attracted to you. I haven't been with a man for over two years. I guess you can say I'm about at the end of my rope."

Cord stiffened in surprise. He wasn't shocked at the fact that she wanted him, he'd picked up on that, but he was surprised that she hadn't been with a man in over two years. "Why?"

She arched a brow. "Why what?"

"Why haven't you been with someone in over two years? Weren't you lonely? Didn't you date any after your divorce?"

"No."

"Why not?"

Amber leaned back against the railing and rubbed her arms. "Mainly because I didn't want to. I needed time to get my head on straight and once I moved here I got caught up in getting my business up and running."

He nodded, remembering the number of hours he had spent in those early days getting his business off the ground. But still he had dated. Spending time with the opposite sex was something a person made time to do. "Men asked you out?" He was pretty sure that they had. Men didn't routinely ignore women who looked like Amber.

"Yes, guys asked me out."

"And you turned them down?"

"Yes. Like I said, I wasn't ready to devote the time it took to build a relationship with a man."

His gaze narrowed on her face. "And do you have the time to build a relationship with a man now, Amber?"

She met his gaze and again decided to be honest. "No."

Cord's body tensed. "So being here is only about sex to you, is that it? You need someone to take off that two-year edge?"

The tone of his voice had gone as cold as ice. Amber looked at him steadily. "I thought so in the beginning but now I don't know. I'm confused. I guess you can tell that I'm not good at any type of a casual relationship."

Cord let out a silent sigh of relief. He was glad she wasn't. It appeared she was just as confused about what was happening between them. Initially, the thought that she'd intended to use him just for sexual pleasure had made him angry, but now he saw hope.

What he saw was a chance to show her that there was more between them than sex, although as fiercely drawn as he was to her, he'd do just about anything to get her into his bed now. But he was willing to wait it out and let that part come later. He wanted to get to know her in all the ways a man got to know a woman. He would take things slow with her, build her trust then capture her heart, the way he could now admit she was beginning to capture his.

"So you agree that getting to know each other is the best approach, no matter what our hormones are saying?" he asked hoarsely, reaching out and covering her hands with his. He waited for her response. Every muscle in his body tensed.

Amber pulled in a deep breath. Should she even think about pursuing a serious relationship with Cord like he wanted, instead of something more casual? She had been so wrong about Gary and had put her heart and pride on the line. Could she do so again? For the past year she had been living under the concept of "conditional growth." One of the principles for that growth was to grow and work on yourself as long as you remained in your comfort zone. Getting seriously involved with

Cord would take her out of the comfort zone she'd been in for over two years. Maybe it was time for her to realize that when you grow conditionally, you run the risk of robbing yourself of many opportunities and blessings.

She didn't want that. She had to believe that all growth and accomplishments involved taking risks. Sometimes it meant finding the courage to leap into the unknown. Hadn't she done that when she'd left Nashville and moved to Orlando, and again when she'd taken out a small business loan to open her bookstore?

She met Cord's gaze and finally gave him her response. "Yes, Cord. I agree."

Book Four

Let us not love merely in theory or in speech but in deed
and in truth—in practice and in sincerity.
I John 3:1

∞ Chapter 25 ∞

Carla entered the crowded board room and inhaled deeply when she saw the look of anxiety on a number of her employees' faces. Today would be the day that Jesse played his winning hand if he had succeeded in obtaining all the outstanding stock he needed.

"You're all right, Carla?"

She smiled when Stanley Jerrott approached. Even now, he was more concerned with her well-being than his own. No matter what, she would land on her feet even if she had to relocate elsewhere to find a job. But at sixty-two it would be almost next to impossible for Stanley to start over someplace else unless he went into private practice.

The lump in her throat thickened at the thought that she had let her employees down. They had given her their confidence and loyalty by making her their chief executive officer. But now most of them would probably be losing their jobs. She had phoned Jesse's attorney that morning asking that Jesse meet with her before today's board meeting. She had wanted his assurance that her employees would be dealt with fairly when the merger went into effect. The attorney, surprisingly, had been rather pleasant and had stated that Jesse would get back in touch with her. She was disappointed but not really surprised that Jesse had not.

Speak of the devil, she thought, when she turned the moment Jesse and his attorney walked in. She didn't see the slightest flicker of emotion in his features and thought how much different he appeared today than last night. Emotions of joy and love had shone in his face each and every time he had looked at Craig. They had been so openly displayed it had taken her breath away.

And they had been genuine.

She had seen it and felt it. In a way her heart went out to Jesse. With all his wealth, he was still a man with no one, but last night he had been a man with a son and she couldn't help but marvel at the difference. Craig had brought laughter and warmth to Jesse's hard, cold eyes. And at that moment she was hit with something very elemental, an eye-opener.

Jesse needed his son in his life.

No sooner than that thought came to her mind, Jesse's eyes met hers and held, and something she saw reflected in their dark hazel depth made her breath catch. She wasn't certain but she could swear she saw pain and regret. She shook her head and almost chuckled to herself. Jesse Devereau had no reason to be in pain or regret anything. He was getting his wish. He had wanted to teach her a lesson and he was about to do just that.

"I think we should go ahead and get started now that everyone's here," Stanley said, recapturing her attention.

"Yes, of course." Carla took her place at the head of the long oak table. Smiling sadly, Michelle sat next to her with her steno pad ready.

The first thirty minutes or so passed in a nervous haze for Carla as she went through the routine of calling the meeting to order and asking for the reading of the last minutes. She then gave her report that showed the increase in profits for Osborne Computer Network and how their recent expense management campaign had already saved the company well over a half a million dollars that year. She tried not to notice that every time she looked around the table, Jesse's gaze was glued to her, and she couldn't help but wonder if he was deliberately trying to make her nervous.

With all other business matters aside, the next item on the agenda was a list of nominations for officers for the coming year and of course the first office was that of president. Stanley immediately stood and cast out Carla's name and some other person in the room, someone that Carla figured was from Jesse's group nominated Jesse. She was about to request that someone offer a motion to close the nominations on those two names when Jesse's attorney raised his hand asking to be recognized.

"Yes, Mr. Kline?"

"Ms. Osborne, I know this is breaking procedure, but my client, Jesse Devereau, wishes that his name be removed from the list of nominees."

A murmur of voices swelled around the room and Carla had to regain order. She restated Mr. Kline's request to make sure she had heard the man correctly.

"Yes, and I have a statement that Mr. Devereau would like me to read which I believe will speed things up a bit."

Trying not to show her startled expression, she nodded, giving her consent.

Mr. Kline opened an envelope and took out a legal document. "What I have is a stock transfer. My client is transferring ownership of all the stock he has obtained by legal acquisition to his son, Craig Osborne, upon the changing of his son's name to Craig Osborne Devereau. Carla Osborne, mother and legal guardian of said child, is to have total control of these transfers to handle as she sees fit in the best interest of Craig Osborne Devereau until his twenty-first birthday."

Murmured voices, louder than before swept around the room. Mr. Kline had just announced to everyone present that Jesse was the father of her son and a quick glance indicated their shock. None of them had been aware of her past relationship with Jesse. But at the moment, she was too overwhelmed to care about any of that. She was in a daze over the fact that Jesse had transferred all of his stock over to her to control until Craig turned twenty-one. That meant the company remained hers. In fact, things were better than before since she now had in her control all outstanding stock including that which her mother had owned. Why had Jesse done such a thing?

The rest of the meeting moved rather quickly after that. With no one opposing she was again named as president of the company. Once she had adjourned the meeting, Jesse and his attorney walked out with the same air of calmness they'd had when they'd walked in.

Later that night Carla was strolling around her home, still overwhelmed with what had transpired in the stockholders meeting earlier that day. She'd been more ecstatic for her employees than for herself, and the moment the meeting was over she'd had Stanley look over the stock transfer papers to make sure everything was legitimate.

"Yes, everything seems to be as it should be," Stanley had said, smiling from ear to ear, clearly astonished and just as elated as her other employees. "The only glitch is that everything hinges on you agreeing to give your son Devereau's last name." Stanley raised a dark, bushy brow and asked, "Do you have a problem doing that?"

She had let out an unconscious sigh and replied that she didn't have a problem with it. She had denied Jesse his right to be Craig's father long enough.

The ringing of the doorbell caught her attention and she quickly moved toward the door thinking it was Sonya, Brandy, or Amber. She had called all three earlier to share her good news and plans were made for them to get together later that week to celebrate.

She looked through the peephole and was surprised to find Jesse standing on her doorstep. Taking a deep breath, she opened the door. "Jesse, what are you doing here?"

He was leaning against the doorjamb with his suit jacket thrown over his shoulder and his free hand stuck into the pocket of his slacks.

The first two buttons of his shirt were undone and his tie was hanging loosely around his neck. Carla quickly concluded that of all the times she'd seen him, this was the only time he'd looked so unkempt.

"Carla, may I please come in?"

Something inside of her made her hesitate. "If you want to see Craig, I've put him to bed for the night."

Jesse shook his head. "No, I'm here to see you."

Carla met his gaze. The look she'd gotten a glimpse of earlier was again there in his eyes and even though she didn't want to feel anything for him, not anything at all, she did. Standing before her was the one and only man she had ever shared her body with, and the man who had given her the most precious gift she possessed, her son.

"All right," she said as she stepped back. The scent of his aftershave, a very manly, seductive scent, lingered in the air when he walked past her. She closed the door behind him.

"We can sit in my living room or you can join me in the kitchen for a cup of coffee." Initially, a part of her wanted him to say whatever it was he had on his mind and leave, but then she decided she had a few questions she wanted to ask him. If they were going to have to deal with each other on a pretty regular basis because of Craig, then they needed to get a few matters straight.

"Although the offer of coffee sounds good, I think it would be best if I said what I have to say then leave."

She nodded then walked over to the sofa and sat down. For some reason it seemed that he preferred standing. She watched as he removed his jacket from across his shoulder and the tie from around his neck and placed them both on a chair. He then surprised her by crossing the room and coming to sit next to her on the sofa. He leaned back, tilted his head to one side, and met her gaze.

"I wanted to hate you when I found out there was a possibility that I had a son. Mainly because family means a lot to me, which is one of the reasons I've made sure I never engage in unprotected sex. Because I was given up for adoption and went from foster home to foster home, it had always been my intent to be married to the mother of my child. I never wanted my child not to know me as their father. I wanted to always share with my child all the things that I never had: male guidance, love, protection, support, and a number of other things. It's always been my belief that any man could be a daddy. But being a father took work— work that I'd always looked forward to doing."

He sighed deeply before he continued. "And when you refused to be cooperative and tell me what I wanted to know, what I needed to know, I wanted to lash out and hurt you, the same way you had hurt me, and was still hurting me by not telling me the truth. But then I discovered you thought you had a good reason. Thanks to your friend Sonya who came to the hotel to see me, I know you thought I'd lied that night about not being involved with anyone. But I had told you the truth, Carla."

Carla frowned as she recalled reading the newspaper article Sonya had brought back from Los Angeles. It had detailed Jesse's trip abroad to Paris with a much older woman. Carla stood and silently crossed the room and opened the drawer to her curio and pulled out a section of a newspaper she hadn't been able to throw away.

She returned to the sofa and sat down. "Then how do you explain the article about you and this woman, Jesse?" As much as she had tried to keep the anger out of her voice, Carla knew she had failed to do so when she saw Jesse lift his dark brow and look at the paper she held in her hand. Moments later he eased back so he could look at her at an angle that had direct eye contact.

"And just what did you read, Carla?"

Carla broke eye contact with him and looked down at the paper in her hand, seeing a photo of the beautiful blond-haired older woman over whose shoulders Jessie had draped his arms. "It doesn't matter," she said quietly.

"Yes, perhaps it does," he said softly. "Especially since you think I did lie to you."

Carla swung her gaze back to his. "According to this article you were involved with her for about six months, which meant you were also involved with her when we slept together."

A short, potent silence hung between them for a moment as they looked at each other. Carla was about to break eye contact with him again when he suddenly reached up, caught her chin, and forced her to look at him.

"To be quite honest with you, that article was wrong. Actually, my relationship with Susan Brady had begun more than six months before." At the anger that flared in her eyes, he added, "But it was not the sort of relationship the newspaper had painted it to be, in fact it was far from it. All they saw was a wealthy white woman—who happened to be terminally ill—being escorted around by a man half her age, and who was African-American. Of course the media assumed the worst and the articles they printed reflected that until they learned the truth."

"And just what was the truth, Jesse?" Carla asked.

"The truth is that Susan Brady was my mother."

Shock froze the hell out of Carla and for the second time that day she found herself speechless. "Your mother!"

He nodded, letting go of her chin and easing back against the sofa once again. "Yes, she was my mother, and Craig's grandmother. So my relationship with her began from the day I was born. It just took us that long to find each other."

Carla gave herself a mental shake but doubted that would do the trick. She was momentarily struck speechless. Jesse evidently took pity on her obvious state of mind and explained. "While attending college at Harvard, Susan Brady met and fell in love with this African-American law student. Of course their relationship was taboo and was kept a secret. When she got pregnant both she and the man went home to deliver the news to her parents and was immediately met with disapproval and rejection. She had never been one to stand up against her parents and they were able to convince her that any thoughts of being party to an interracial marriage was out of the question as well as her giving birth to a mixed child. Because they were Catholics, abortion was out of the question. However, they did send her away to Paris to have the child with the understanding that she was to give it up for adoption."

Carla took a deep, steadying breath then asked, "And what about the baby's father? Your father?"

"Susan's parents led her to believe that the man had taken the money they offered him to disappear. And naively, she believed them. It was only when she saw him again, years later, at a fund-raiser in Washington, D.C., that they got a chance to talk and discovered the lies her parents had told. He had become an affluent attorney and had gone all those years thinking that she had gotten an abortion, and she had gone through all those years believing he'd been bought out. Together they decided it was important to find their child."

He didn't say anything else for a brief moment and Carla found herself holding her breath as she waited for him to continue. "Unfortunately," he finally said moments later, "their search was initiated too late. My biological father died the following year of prostate cancer and Susan was diagnosed a few years later with breast cancer. But the private detective they both hired was diligent in finding me and eventually he did. So I got to spend the last six months of Susan's life with her. The month before she died we decided to make the announcement of our true relationship public since the newspapers were having a field day speculating. Needless to say, the truth shocked the hell out of the media."

Carla smiled sadly. "Yes, I can imagine."

"Yes, but the sad thing is that in just six months I discovered just what a classy woman she was, and all those years I spent hating the person who'd given me away dissolved. Although I didn't want to, I understood the circumstances that she and my father had been placed in. An interracial relationship back in the late sixties was not acceptable."

Carla nodded again. She was glad things had somewhat changed since then. Most people now were marrying for love and not for color. "Did either of them have family?"

"No, neither of them had siblings or kids of their own, so I still don't have any family other than Craig and my friend Mike Kelly. Mike and I met when we were fifteen and spent time in the same foster home. In fact we ran away together one night and have basically been together since. We learned to live off the streets together, learned to hustle together and we both learned the hard way that crime didn't pay and having a good education was the key to our future success."

Carla's heart suddenly did a flip when it went out to the child that Jesse had once been. The child who'd had no one he could count on other than this friend who had stuck by his side, pretty much the way she and Sonya had stuck by each other while growing up. But then, unlike him, she had known at least one parent's love. Although her mother may not have wanted her, she'd always known that she'd held a special place in her father's heart and that he loved her dearly. He had lived every day of his life showing her just how much.

Now a part of her understood Jesse's need to know about Craig and why he'd taken her refusal to confirm or deny Craig was his child so personal.

"I never got the chance to thank you for what you did today," she said softly.

He looked at her as if surprised by her words of thanks. "You're welcome."

She cleared her throat. "Are you sure you don't want a cup of coffee?"

"Yes, I'm sure." A thought then struck him. "Do you have any pictures?"

Carla raised a confused brow. "Pictures?"

"Yes, pictures of Craig when he was a baby? Photographs of the first two years of his life?"

Carla couldn't help but smile. "Yes, I have more pictures than most people since Sonya's hobby is photography. Would you like to see them?"

"Yes, please."

She nodded and walked across the room to where she kept her

numerous photo albums. When she brought them over to hand to Jesse, he stood up laughing as he took the armload of photo albums out of her hands. "Hey, you weren't kidding, were you?"

"Nope. It's gotten so bad that all we have to do is reach for a camera and Craig automatically smiles. He is so conceited."

Jesse continued laughing. "He is also a very beautiful child. You should be proud of him."

His comment made her smile. "I am." She then looked at him and he lowered his head to look at Craig's baby picture that had been inserted into one of the album's covers. "And you should be proud of him, too, Jesse. We made him together." For some reason she couldn't stop the chuckle that escaped her throat. "Can we produce or what?"

He shook his head grinning. "Yeah, we can definitely produce."

When their gazes met and held for what Carla thought was an uncomfortable moment, she took a step back and said, "I think I'll go check on Craig. I'll be back in a moment."

"All right."

When Carla walked across the room she glanced back over her shoulder. Her breath caught and her heart swelled when she saw the look of pure happiness on Jesse's face as he slowly began flipping the pages to the album to begin a photographic journey into his son's life—a part that he had not shared. And at that moment she regretted that she had assumed the worst about him and had not contacted him when she'd found out she was pregnant.

And a part of her wondered if he would ever completely forgive her for it.

༄ *Chapter 26* ༄

Grey pinned Brandy with his dark glare. "Why of all times are you being difficult now?"

Brandy turned from the kitchen counter and gave him a dark glare of her own. "Because I have too much to do around here than to roll over and play dead, Grey. What you're asking me to do is impossible. I own this hotel and the biggest event of the year is taking place. We have reservations for over a thousand rooms this coming week. Now is not the time for you to suggest that I go visit my relatives in Macon."

And before he could get another word out she said, "Besides, I'm not as convinced as you that Jolene had anything to do with this. It doesn't make sense. I was the injured party three years ago, not her. I didn't sleep with *her* fiancé, dammit, she slept with *mine*. So she has nothing to be pissed about and definitely no reason to want to do me harm. And," she continued, holding up her hand to stop him from saying anything still, "everything you've told me is speculation. Everyone I know has been a suspect, all my employees and even my close friends. Although I don't consider Jolene a friend—in fact I could care less if our paths never crossed again—you're trying to paint her as a looney-tune and one thing I do know is that she's an intelligent woman with plenty of sense."

Grey cursed silently. He balled his hands into fists at his sides. He had stayed up practically all damn night on the phone and the computer with his friends in D.C. as well as the other investigators at his firm in Atlanta as they tried to piece together what they felt was a viable suspect. Over breakfast he had been completely up front with Brandy. He'd told her how Jolene had been forced to resign her position at BCC because of the videotape scandal and how she had worked at UCF for only a short while before the videos had shown up there as well. They had not been able to locate where her social security number was being used which meant she was either not working or working using someone else's identification. None of those things set right with him and his men, and they agreed that the best thing to do until they tightened the lid on things was to get Brandy out of the line of fire. In other words, persuade her to leave town for a few days since it seemed Jolene was somewhere in the area.

The only problem with that suggestion was the fact that Brandy wasn't budging.

"I was sent here to protect you, Brandy."

"Then do it, Grey, but do it the way you've been doing it and that's from a distance. I don't need you to be glued to my hip now. I have a hotel to run and I'm talking about a huge amount of revenue that's about to flow in due to the Florida Classic. Now, if this conversation is over then we—"

"Dammit, Brandy, this conversation is not over," he said, crossing the room at lightning speed and grabbing hold of her shoulders. "If Jolene Bradford is the person who sent those messages that either means she has access in and out of this hotel or she has an accomplice. How do you know that Lorenzo didn't make her privy to information about this hotel when the two of them were lovers? How do you know she's not sleeping buddies with someone here on your staff, and how do you—"

"Grey, please be reasonable. That videotape was shown almost three years ago. Why would she wait until now to do anything to harass me? It doesn't make sense."

"When people take it upon themselves to lash out at other people for whatever reason, it never makes sense, Brandy. If you won't leave then I'm asking that you follow my orders to the letter."

She glared up at him. "What orders?"

"That you let me know where you are at all times, every second of the day." He wished that he could lock her up in the suite and throw away the key until this matter was resolved.

She sighed deeply. "I've been doing that anyway, Grey, ever since the tone of that last message. Please don't think I'm not taking any of this seriously, because I am. I just don't intend for it to stop my life and my business. I'm not a coward and I won't act like one."

Brandy could see Grey's frustration. She could feel his impatience with her and his need to assert his dominance over her. But more than anything she also felt his intense desire to keep her safe, to keep anything from happening to her and a part of her wanted to believe it had nothing to do with the job he'd been paid to do but that it had everything to do with what the two of them had shared since the night they had crossed the boundaries and staked their claims.

A long, tense moment passed between them and then Grey reached out and pulled her to him and she felt the impact of his hard body pressed against hers. The dark, intense glare in his eyes suddenly turned heated, hot, scorching. His hands slowly moved down her shoulders, past the line of her back and waist to cup the firm curve of her bottom.

"No one will hurt you," he said thickly, from between gritted teeth. His words were absolute, definite, clear.

Then his mouth came down on hers with a hunger that took her breath away. The air surrounding them suddenly became overheated, heavy with the nuance of a sexual power neither Brandy nor Grey could control. Her body constricted with a sizzling stroke of heat when his tongue captured hers possessively, pleasuring her mouth in a way that only he was capable of doing.

With today being the day when most of the guests would arrive, there was a chance she was needed downstairs but going anyplace was the last thing on Brandy's mind and evidently his. He suddenly wedged his feet in between hers, drawing her knees apart, spreading open her legs. Then she felt his hand move and quickly lift her skirt.

He continued kissing her while she heard his zipper being eased down and then she felt her skimpy panties being ripped off her. Before she had time to react, Grey broke the kiss and whispered. "Wrap your legs around me."

He lifted her into his arms and she obeyed, placing her legs around his waist, tight. As soon as the swollen folds of her moist femininity touched his hard, aching erection she buried her face against his shoulder. She felt every nerve in her body, every single muscle, tighten in anticipation when she felt his hard, engorged flesh get in position at the entrance of her mound.

"I want to come in you, again."

His words, whispered softly, erupted her passion and she gasped when he thrust into her, his hardness filling every single inch of her body. He took a few steps and when she felt the hard, solid wall against her back, her fingernails sank deep into the blades of his shoulders. He then proceeded to take her with a hunger and fierceness that had her crying out in pleasure as his body began thrusting in and out of her. She met his every thrust, her body just as hungry, just as greedy as his.

Passion, the mind-boggling, gut-wrenching kind, the get-your-fill kind, took away her ability to think. All she was capable of doing was feeling the way his body was entering her, withdrawing, then entering her again, while their tongues tasted, mated. He held her body in place, her back braced firmly against the wall as he continued to pleasure her, make love to her. And then she felt his shoulders tense beneath her fingers. He broke off the kiss and threw his head back. His nostrils flared and he thrust into her, pinning her against the wall with the force of his arousal. And then she felt him come as the hot molten liquid that he enjoyed giving her, releasing into her body, mingled with her own, flooding her insides.

His eyes locked on hers the moment her inner muscles gripped him, held him, milked him for every drop of semen his testicles could produce. She wanted it all, everything, inside of her. Her legs around his waist tightened.

Their bodies arched. She intended to have it. He intended to give it to her.

"Brandy!"

"Grey!"

Their names were screamed from their lips simultaneously; the atmosphere surrounding them drenched with the scent of sex. He leaned down and recaptured her mouth. Their tongues tangled as a potent, overpowering rush of passion washed over them, around them, through them, and at that moment they both knew how it felt to go up in flames.

The next two days went by in a whirl at the hotel with the number of guests who'd begun arriving and checking in. To make sure everyone had sufficient accommodations, the hotel had increased its staff even more, which didn't sit too well with Grey, although he understood why. An increase in staff made things rather complicated for his investigation. One person he'd felt confident in marking off the list of suspects had been Wilbur Green. One night Grey had run into the man sitting at the bar drinking. Off work and deciding to relax somewhat, Green had also loosened his lips and told Grey about his pending divorce and how he felt his wife was trying to take him to the cleaners. Grey was satisfied that had pretty much explained the reason behind the phone call Brandy had overheard the month before.

A phone call that Grey received from his contact at the local Bureau later had compelled him to call a short meeting with his investigators who had joined him at the hotel the week before. Brandy was presently in a staff luncheon meeting and one of his men, who were pretending to be a waiter, was keeping close watch on her. What bothered Grey the most was just how easily his people had been hired by the hotel with false identification and credentials. Brandy assumed her employees were getting a thorough screening before being hired and he was finding out that was not the case.

"Earlier this week I noticed Sam Perrin in the private elevator, the one that goes to the administrative offices and Ms. Bennett's private floor," Apollo Guisto, one of Grey's top investigators, remarked. Apollo had gotten a job with the hotel as a highly skilled repairman who was assigned to work on the elevators and air-conditioning systems.

Grey glanced down at his list. With so many employees coming and going, it was hard to keep track of all the names at times. "Perrin? That's the kid who's a bellman, right?"

"Right. He's about twenty-one and from what I understand, a student at a local college here."

Grey nodded. Perrin had been the same person who Brandy had mentioned having bumped into once in a deserted hall when he first arrived. At the time Grey hadn't found anything significant about that since a profile he had ordered indicated the young man was a hard worker at the hotel, as well as a good student in school. "Did he mention why he was in that elevator?"

"No, in fact I saw him about to mess with the security system when I walked up. When I asked if anything was wrong with the system, he brushed it off saying that he had stepped on the wrong elevator by mistake. But that didn't explain what he'd been about to do to the security box."

Grey nodded. "I think we should make sure we keep a close eye on Perrin."

The other men in the room nodded. "Let's meet again tomorrow unless something develops that we all need to know about," Grey said, checking his watch. Brandy's luncheon would be over in less than ten minutes and he intended to be right there in plain view when she walked out of the meeting room.

Another meeting was called later that day when one of Grey's men had something to report. "Sam Perrin quit."

Grey lifted a dark brow. "He quit?"

"Yes, he called in earlier today and said he won't back. He's not even giving two weeks notice."

"Did he say why he was resigning?" Apollo Guisto asked.

"According to what I heard, he claimed he was getting behind in his studies at school. And there is something else. Something I think is major."

Grey met the man's gaze. "What?"

"A little investigation has revealed that Sam Perrin and Jolene Bradford know each other, very well."

Grey sat up straight in his chair; his gaze was intense when he got the man's meaning. Jolene had to be at least twelve years older than Perrin. "Are you sure?"

"Positive. In fact they lived together for over six months."

"Are they still living together?"

"It doesn't look that way. My sources say she moved out a month or so ago but that Perrin was pretty damn smitten with her."

Grey sighed deeply as he stood. He still didn't know Jolene Bradford's whereabouts and that bothered him. "I want to know everything there is to know about Perrin including every aspect of his job while he was here. And I want Jolene Bradford located. I'm going to get a photograph of her so we can be on the lookout in case she makes an appearance here at the hotel.

Swearing softly, Grey spun on his heel and strode out of the room.

A hour or so later Grey entered the suite to find it dark and quiet. Evidently Brandy had gone to bed already. He'd had one of his men stationed right outside the door all the while he'd been in a meeting. He wasn't taking any chances especially after receiving the last note, the one he hadn't told Brandy about yet.

He shuddered at the threat that had been made, this one a little more explicit than the others. It claimed that when he was through, no other man would want Brandy. Again it had been signed *The Man*, but now that Grey knew the writer was a woman—a woman who believed all the ills that were befalling her were Brandy's fault—he knew he was dealing with someone who was not in their right mind, and the only thing on that demented mind was revenge.

Earlier that day, a friend of his, a former agent, had paid a visit to Jolene's parents in South Carolina. They claimed they had not heard from their daughter in over eight months. They'd also told the agent that when they had seen her last, she had not been herself but they didn't believe that she would deliberately hurt anyone.

Removing his jacket, he relieved himself of his gun and holster. He carried both into the office and placed them in a drawer. He couldn't help but remember the first time Brandy had seen his revolver. For the longest time she had stared at it like she'd never seen a gun before. Then her eyes had looked up at him as if expecting some sort of explanation as to why he was carrying such a lethal weapon. But now whenever she saw it she didn't seem to think twice about it.

He rubbed a frustrated hand along his taut jaw. His shoulders felt tense, which was usually a good sign that something, although he didn't have a clue as to what, was about to happen. He was glad he and his team had uncovered so much in a relatively short period of time but didn't like the fact that their prime suspect could not be found. That meant she could be just about anyplace.

Without any reason to suspect the hotel's security manager any further, Grey had taken Perry Hall into his confidence. To say Hall had been upset to learn that threats against Brandy had been made right under his nose and that he hadn't been apprised was an understatement. And then to find out that he himself had been a suspect had almost been the last straw. But Grey hadn't had the time or the inclination to deal with hurt feelings. His main concern was seeing that Brandy was protected and he needed Hall's cooperation.

The man knew the layout of the hotel better than anyone and had the manpower to aid in keeping Brandy safe. After getting over his initial shock, Hall had been helpful in showing him the location of all the security cameras and agreed to have his men hook up a few others in various strategic places. He also agreed to let Grey use some of his men to monitor the cameras on a constant basis. The man had found it hard to believe the possibility that Sam Perrin was involved in anything. He claimed the young man was a "good kid" who kept to himself and did a good job and was friendly to everyone. But then on the other hand, Hall didn't discount the possibility that Perrin could have been the one delivering the messages since he'd had the opportunity to do so.

Grey didn't want to think about Perrin or Bradford any longer. He only wanted to think about Brandy and immediately headed for her bedroom.

Silence greeted him but so did her scent. His gaze was drawn to the woman lying in the large, inviting bed. The covers had been pushed back out of the way and his breath caught when he saw that she lay on the silken sheet naked. At least the sheer flesh-colored nightgown she wore made her look more naked than clothed. She was lying on her side with the front of her facing him.

The glow of light—from a nearby buildings—that shone through her bedroom blinds illuminated her form. His gaze took in all of her, her full, luscious looking breasts with the dark nipples, tiny waist, sexy belly with the gold navel ring he'd seen the first night they'd made love, and her long, sleek, and gorgeous legs. But the part of her he couldn't take his gaze off was the thatch of dark hair between her legs. That particular area of her beckoned him, aroused him. And he thought of the hours he'd spent in that spot the past couple of days and just thinking about it made his erection throb harder, made his need for her that much stronger.

Driven by a desire that rammed through him with uncontrollable lust and an erotic hunger, he yanked off his clothes and flung them to the floor. It was difficult to breathe but he forced air from his lungs as he walked to the bed and came to a stop. He inhaled her scent as his mind flared with the thought of getting between her thighs.

A sound he suspected was his heavy breathing made her slowly open her eyes and she looked up and met his gaze. She ran her gaze over his naked, aroused body before letting her eyes settle on that part of him that was fully aroused and shamelessly throbbing for her.

Brandy's gaze slowly returned to his as she shifted her position to lie on her back. Their gazes locked. Held. And the heat transmitting between them was almost unbearable.

Hot. Blistering hot. Passionately hot.

Simultaneously, they drew in short, tight breaths at the same time as he placed his knee on the bed to join her there. She immediately raised up to meet him, coming into his arms, drawing his head down to hers when her arms wrapped around his neck, joining their mouths into a kiss.

Their tongues tangled, tasted, as an urgent need filled both of their bodies. Grey gently slid his hands beneath her, lifting her to him, to his body, to his erection, finding that area between her thighs that was hot, damp, ready.

Needing it, desiring it, obsessed with having it.

And seconds later when he entered her, he growled deep within his throat, wondering how one woman could bring him to this: an irresistible need to bury himself inside of her, to pump into her, to come in her. A part of him wanted to pull back and pull out. He didn't want to be that overwhelmed, overtaken, totally consumed with a woman. This was more than he'd felt for any woman, including Gloria. His mind closed out thoughts of Gloria and what she'd done to him, how she had betrayed him in a way no wife should ever betray her husband.

Instead he wanted to concentrate on the woman whose body was now joined with his. The woman who had the ability to drive him wild, the power to make him want to forget things he should remember, and who possessed the ability to satisfy every need within his body.

Not a single word was spoken between them as they mated in this special way. It was a way that took their wants and desires deeper, and made their passion for each other stronger. It was a way that had no restrictions, no reminders of past pain, and no regrets. The only thing they wanted to concentrate on was each other and the flame that was erupting into a full-blown fire.

Grey knew that when he uncovered the person threatening to hurt her and it was time to go he would carry this, her generous acceptance of what they shared, with him always.

Brandy Bennett would have a permanent place in his heart.

❧ *Chapter 27* ❧

"Mommy, Daddy says that big boys don't wet their pants."

Carla tried to hide her smile as she glanced at her son over her glass of milk. "He did?"

"Yes, and he said I should try not to do it."

"And will you?"

Craig nodded his head up and down before his attention was again drawn to the cereal box in front of him. Carla sighed deeply. Jesse had managed to do in less than a week what she'd almost given up as a losing battle—Craig and his potty training. Mrs. Boston had reported that there had not been wet or soiled training pants since Jesse had talked with his son.

His son.

The words seemed to hover in the air around her. It had been over a week since Jesse had made the decision to not only let her keep her company, but had made sure it could never be taken away from her. Her employees were ecstatic to know they would be keeping their jobs, and so far none of them had mentioned or questioned Jesse being Craig's father. These days they only had nice words to say about the man who only a week ago had all of them sweating bullets.

"Mommy, will Daddy come here today?"

Carla met her son's intense gaze. She knew that Jesse had not missed a day coming to visit Craig, although the majority of time he came while she was at work. Whether that time was more convenient for him or whether he was avoiding her she wasn't sure. But still, his presence was there in her home even when he wasn't. When she got home in the afternoon she had to contend with Craig's relentless babbling of all the things he and his daddy had done that day. Then there were the reminders that a man had been in her home.

The scent of him would linger in the air long after he left.

"Mommy?"

She blinked, realizing she hadn't answered Craig's question. Although she wasn't privy to Jesse's schedule, she didn't see where this day would be any different than the others. A part of her wondered just how long Jesse would stay in Orlando since she knew he had a business waiting for him in Los Angeles.

"Yes, Craig, I'm sure he'll come, but you can't expect him to come visit you every day."

"Why?"

"Because he has work to do."

Craig vigorously shook his head. "No. My daddy said he loves me before work."

Carla smiled. "Yes, but Mommy loves you before work, too, but she still goes every day, doesn't she?"

He nodded. "Yes."

"Then you'll understand when your daddy has to go to work."

The doorbell rang and she saw Craig's eyes lit up. "That's my daddy."

Carla lifted a brow, wondering if what Craig said was true and Jesse was at the door. Mrs. Boston had a doctor's appointment and wouldn't be coming until noon, so Carla had cleared her calendar this morning to stay home with her son.

She hoped it wasn't Jesse since she was still wearing her bathrobe, but before she could stop him, Craig had raced away from the table toward the door. She caught up with him in the living room and her heart tugged at the excitement she saw in his face.

He peeped out the window and saw Jesse. "It is *him*, Mommy. It *is* my daddy!"

Carla pulled her robe tightly together as she opened the door.

"Jesse."

"Carla."

She stepped aside. "Please come in. There's someone here who's excited about seeing you."

She watched as Jesse's eyes lit up the moment he saw his son and she couldn't help the fluttering that touched her heart. A little over a month ago Jesse Devereau had not known his son existed and now the love he had shining for Craig was blatantly clear for anyone to see. His acceptance, his love had been just that easy, simple and heartfelt. And Carla knew it was love. No matter what type of relationship the two of them had, their son would always enjoy the love of both his parents. Together they would look out for his well-being and best interest.

It was one of those rare days in late fall where a coat was needed and Craig had given Jesse barely enough time to shrug out of it before he had jumped into his arms. "Daddy, Daddy, you came today!"

"Of course I came," he said hugging his son to him. Then he lifted a brow and pulled back somewhat. "And how's the potty training going?"

"Good," Craig said eagerly and proudly. "Isn't it, Mommy?"

Carla chuckled. "Yes, it's going good."

Craig worked his way out of Jesse's arms. "I'm going to get my coloring books and colors." And before Carla could remind him he still had cereal left in his bowl to eat, he had taken off.

Jesse chuckled as he watched. "I remember when I use to have energy like that."

For some reason a moment in time came to mind when she'd thought he'd had a lot of energy—the night they'd made love. He had taken her with a vitality that took her breath away just thinking about it. Once he had gotten over the shock that she was a virgin, he had proceeded to give her the best sex of her life.

The only sex of her life.

She blinked when she suddenly realized that Jesse had been saying something. "I'm sorry. What did you say?"

Jesse smiled as he put both hands in his pockets. "I said I'm glad the potty training has improved."

Carla returned his smile. "Yes, I'm glad too, and I really appreciate your help."

Jesse nodded and then his smile vanished. "I was a late starter myself. In fact I can vividly remember getting brutally whipped every time I did something in my underpants. That's the reason the first family didn't keep me."

"Oh, Jesse, I'm sorry," she said, wondering what type of people would not recognize that some kids were slower to learn than others.

"Thanks but I learned to survive."

She nodded. Yes, he had. And along the way he had also learned not to become attached to anyone or anything. People had hurt him. They had let him down. He had grown up depending on and believing in no one. She couldn't help but wonder what had compelled him to let his guard down with her that night they'd met at Sonya's birthday party. Why had he trusted her enough to reach out? To let go? And for a rare moment, to share himself? Her vivid memories—and she still had plenty—reminded her of how he had shared himself with her, his time and his body.

At that moment Craig raced back into the room and any further thoughts of Jesse and that Thanksgiving night slowly dissolved from her mind.

Carla received a call around eleven from Mrs. Boston advising her the doctor's office was running late in appointments and it would be after two before she could get there. Carla had told her not to concern herself with coming over to take care of Craig today because she would be staying at home the remainder of the day. She had placed a call to the office and Michelle had passed her messages on to her and had cleared her calendar for the remainder of the afternoon. Michelle had told her that Brandy and Amber had called, as well as Sonya.

Carla glanced across the room. Jesse and Craig had finished coloring an hour or so ago and were now building something out of Craig's LEGO blocks. She had been sitting quietly on the sofa reading and every so often she would glance up and look at them, their heads together, father and son, as they tackled what appeared to be an interesting project.

"You want to help, Mommy?"

She blinked. Craig had caught her watching. She shifted her gaze from Craig to Jesse. So had he. "Uh, no thanks, although it looks like fun, Mommy will just continue to sit here and read her book."

"What are you reading?" Jessie asked.

She shifted her gaze to Jesse and for a minute wished she hadn't. He looked so good lying on her floor, so comfortable, so at home and so damn masculine. He had worn his jeans and a T-shirt and the clothes fit him like a second layer of skin.

She cleared her throat. "There's some new software out on the market and I thought I'd become familiar with it."

He nodded. "What's it called?"

Carla noticed he hadn't stopped what he was doing with Craig and couldn't help but wonder how his attention could be focused on two things at once. "It's called Cybernate Plus and is supposed to be able to combine a lot of computer applications in one program. Ever heard of it?"

"Yes, and I've already checked it out and it's not as good as they claim. One of my companies is working on something similar that will be better. We hope to have it on the market within a few months."

Carla nodded. She was tempted to ask him just how many companies he had and decided it wasn't any of her business. She switched her gaze from him to Craig. Their son was fighting hard not to fall asleep.

Instead of saying anything out loud, she tilted her gaze to Craig and Jesse's gaze followed. He smiled in understanding.

"Hey, big guy, it's time for your nap."

Of course Craig decided to be difficult. "But I don't want to take a nap. I want to stay here with you and Mommy."

"All big guys need naps, Craig."

"Even you?"

Jesse chuckled. "Yes, even me. Now, come on let's get that nap over with."

"Will you be here when I wake up?"

Jesse glanced quickly over at Carla and lifted a brow. She read his question and at her nod, he said to his son. "Yes, I'll still be here."

Satisfied with his father's answer, Craig placed his hand in his and allowed himself to be led to his bedroom. By the time Jesse returned, Carla was in the kitchen making another pot of coffee. "I can leave if you want me to, Carla."

She turned around and met Jesse's gaze. "No, you're welcome to stay. I just don't want you to feel obligated to spend every waking moment with Craig. I know you probably have other things to do."

Jesse shook his head. "No, not really. I have people in place to run things so I'm fine. Besides, it's important to me that I build a strong, solid relationship with Craig. I want him to know and understand the role I intend to play in his life. I think that's very important, given the fact that we aren't married. It will be a challenge but I want him to know he can count on me just as much as he can count on you."

Carla nodded, wondering why a lot more men didn't think that way. The world would be a better place if they did. There were too many children who didn't know their fathers, and fathers who didn't want to know their children. They were men who had enjoyed their time in the bedroom but didn't want the responsibility of being a father to the child they had created.

"Thank you."

Jesse lifted a brow. "For what?"

"For having that attitude."

He shrugged. "For me it's more than an attitude, Carla. It's who I am. Craig has brought something special into my life. He has given me purpose, direction. He has made me look deep into who I am and what I am. Being with him, spending time with him has helped me to see the mistakes I've made and to be there to encourage him, to teach him and show him how not to make those same mistakes."

Carla nodded. "I'm about to have a cup of coffee, would you like one?"

"Yes, I'd also like to talk to you about something."

"All right. Go ahead and sit at the table and I'll bring the coffee on over." Carla's kitchen was a compact place and she could feel Jesse's presence like a tangible thing. He suddenly made her kitchen feel warm and intimate. She watched him sit down at the table and could tell something important was on his mind and couldn't help wondering what it was.

After pouring two cups of coffee she brought them over to the table and sat down across from him. Earlier, while he had kept Craig occupied, she had gone into her bedroom and changed into a pair of slacks and a loose-fitting top. It was one of her favorite outfits for lounging around the house.

"What do you want to talk to me about, Jesse?" she couldn't help asking before he'd taken his first sip.

He met her gaze. "Thanksgiving. If you don't have any plans for that day I'd like to take you and Craig to dinner."

Surprised, Carla lifted a brow. "You would?"

"Yes."

Carla inwardly sighed as she recalled another Thanksgiving that the two of them had spent together. He had remarked more than once during the course of that evening how special she'd made that day for him. She leaned back in her chair. "Thanks for the invitation," she said grateful and appreciative. "But I'd made plans to prepare Thanksgiving Dinner here for me and Craig."

"Oh."

For the past two years it had been just her and Craig. Both Brandy and Amber usually traveled home to be with their families and it had become a tradition for Sonya to visit her grandparents who lived in South Florida on Thanksgiving. When Craig was born Carla had started her own tradition with the two of them getting up and saying a prayer to thank God for all of his blessings, eating breakfast, then settling down to watch the Macy's Thanksgiving Parade. Then, a little after two o'clock they would eat the dinner she'd prepared the night before.

"If you're not doing anything that day, Jesse, you are more than welcome to eat dinner with us."

He met her gaze. "Are you sure?"

She smiled. The expression on his face reminded her so much of Craig's when he was excited about something. "Yes, I'm positive, and I know Craig would want you here."

He didn't say anything for a long moment then asked, "What about you, Carla? How would you feel about having me here?"

His question jolted her although it shouldn't have. For the past couple of weeks she had done a lot of thinking and had to admit that she had provoked him to go the extremes that he had. They had both made mistakes. "I'm fine with it."

He nodded slowly. "And would you go out with me sometime if I were to ask?"

Carla shook her head. "No, not now. I believe your main focus should be on getting to know your son, which you've been doing. Don't think about adding me in the mix because it won't work."

His gaze raked her features, frowning. "Why not?"

"Because I'm not interested in having a man in my life right now." In that moment, she decided to share something with him that he really didn't have a right to know but maybe then he would understand. "In fact, Jesse, I haven't been romantically involved with anyone since that night I spent with you."

At the curious lift of his brow, she continued. "A couple of months after that night we spent together I found out I was pregnant and not long after that my brother died which threw me into the role of being CEO of Osborne Computer Networks. Then after Craig was born my time was taken up with him. He became my sole interest, my only interest when I wasn't at work. I received offers for dates but I turned them down, preferring to spend my free time with my son. I did go out with Brandy, Amber, and Sonya occasionally and for me that was enough."

Jesse stared at her and she couldn't help wondering what he was thinking. She hoped he understood that she wasn't ready for a man in her life and accepted that.

But Jesse wasn't accepting anything. He looked away when he saw that he was making her nervous. He sipped his coffee, his thoughts churning furiously.

He had been the only man she'd ever slept with? She hadn't been with anyone since?

When she got up from the table to pour another cup of coffee, he released a deep breath. Right then and there he decided he would immediately start work on his most important merger. It was the one that would make his son and the mother of his son a permanent part of his life.

Not too far away, on the other side of town, a secret meeting was taking place.

Sonya walked into the restaurant and glanced around. She smiled when she saw Mike Kelly stand up and wave her over. He was sitting at a table facing the window and she quickly walked over to join him.

She passed a table where a man and woman sat enjoying their meal. When the man glanced up he recognized her immediately. Dalton Gregory's eyes nearly popped out of his head and he began choking on his wine. A waiter quickly crossed the room and began pounding on his back.

Sonya inwardly smiled. Dalton had learned a hard lesson that hell knew no fury like a sistah's fury. He would think twice before using another woman again. Dismissing him from her sight as well as her thoughts, she continued walking toward Mike Kelly.

"Thanks for agreeing to meet on such short notice, Mr. Kelly."

Mike smiled as he took the hand she offered in a handshake. "No problem, Ms. Morrison. You said something about there being an emergency?"

Sonya nodded and sat down. She waited until after the waiter took their drink orders. "Yes. But first I want to thank you. Although you may not admit it, I have a feeling that you may have helped soften Jesse up just a bit. I think what he did in the end was wonderful. Now Carla won't ever have to worry about the possibility of losing her company again. I appreciate your help and for that I will be forever in your debt."

Mike smiled. "In my debt?" he asked, doubting she wanted to be in his debt. The payback just might be more than she would be willing to deliver.

"Yes." She then opened her napkin and placed it in her lap. "But what I wanted to meet with you about tonight was Carla and Jesse and what's going on between them."

Mike raised a curious brow. "And just what's going on between them?"

Sonya frowned. "Nothing."

Mike chuckled at her frustrated look. "Nothing?"

"Yes, nothing, so I thought the two of us should step in."

Mike leaned back in his chair, intrigued. "Step in and do what?"

"Make them realize they want each other."

"And you think that they do?"

Sonya looked at him like he was dense. "Of course. So what do you think we should do?"

Mike chuckled. "Nothing."

Sonya blinked. "Nothing?"

"Yes, nothing. Jesse can handle things on his own."

"Well, he couldn't before. Without our help he'd still be making a mess of things."

Mike shifted in his seat uneasily. She had a point there. When it came to Carla Osborne, Jesse had a tendency not to think straight. "Just what are you suggesting we do?" he asked reluctantly.

Sonya smiled and Mike thought it was the sexiest smile that he'd ever seen on a woman. "I have a plan," she said happily.

Mike chuckled. "I figured you did."

"And it's going to take place on Thanksgiving night."

Sonya leaned across the table and he couldn't help but smell her scent. The scent of a woman. A very desirable woman. "Thanksgiving night?" he asked, barely getting the words out.

"Yes. Are you with me?"

Mike swallowed. Not as much as he would like but he intended to change things, slowly but surely. "Yes, I'm with you."

Sonya smiled brightly. "Good."

⊱ *Chapter 28* ⊰

*A*nother arrangement of flowers, Amber?"

Amber couldn't help but smile at Eileen's raised brow. "Yes, aren't they beautiful?" One thing about Cord Jeffries was that, if nothing else, he was a very persistent man. He claimed the flowers he was sending practically every two to three days was his way of thanking her for the time she had spent in his home taking care of him. But all she'd done was to make sure he had followed doctor's orders. He had not been bedridden so she had not had to wait on him hand and foot. Her presence had merely been there to remind him of what he was supposed to do and what he was not supposed to do. And she had to admit that he had been cooperative but she'd known he'd had an ulterior motive. The man wanted to get with her and she had a feeling he was on his best behavior now because he planned to get downright naughty later.

"This guy must have connections with this particular florist," Eileen added, breaking into Amber's thoughts.

"That's a possibility," she said grinning, while remembering that Dev's girlfriend Briana owned a nursery in town. She straightened the display items that were located near the cash register. Business was slow today. With the huge number of people in town for the big football game this weekend, business had been excellent for the past couple of days; so much in fact that she'd hired additional help. The young girl from one of the colleges was working out well and was a natural with the customers. Amber wished there was some way she could keep her on even when business went back to normal.

"Don't look now, but guess who walked in?" Eileen whispered. Then with a conspiratory wink she added, "I wish a man who looked like that had the hots for me. I would certainly make it worth all the effort he's putting into the pursuit." The older woman then walked off.

Amber's stomach muscles tightened in anticipation. She knew whom Eileen was talking about even before she looked in Cord's direction. Their gazes met and immediately, just that quick, her breathing became choppy and she could feel her nipples pucker against the satin material of her blouse. The man, she had concluded quite some time ago, was living, breathing, walking sex appeal. She didn't like thinking that way; didn't like the way her body responded whenever she saw him and a part of her was appalled by it all. But still, it happened each and every time. While in his home those four days, they had tried to downplay their attraction, focus on other things, so they had spent a lot of time talking about their families or lack of, their days in college and their failed marriages. She had even told him about the baby she'd lost and her desire to have children. And he had shared some painful times with her as well. He'd told her about the woman who had agreed to be his wife but had never played the part. Yes, Amber concluded, she and Cord had gotten to know each other fairly well during those four days. And on the following day when she'd returned home, the flowers began arriving.

Amber remembered the times she had wanted Gary to send her flowers, especially on Valentine's Day. But he'd been of the mind that it was wasteful to spend money on flowers when the best way to express his love was in the bedroom and between the sheets. She had believed him, gullible and stupid as she'd been, until she'd finally realized that Gary had confused love with lust.

And unfortunately, so had she. But never again would she make that mistake. She knew the difference. What she was feeling for Cord was lust, not love. She would never let herself fall in love with a man again.

"Amber." Cord murmured a greeting when he came to stand before the checkout counter. He smiled at her. It was a gentle smile. A sexy smile. "How are you?"

Amber sighed deeply. The man was so heart-throbbingly good looking that a part of her didn't know how to deal with it. She just wanted to go someplace private with him and get naked. He brought out those kind of scandalous thoughts. And it didn't help matters that the air surrounding them suddenly became drenched with his scent. Manly. Robust.

"I'm fine, Cord, what about you? Have you been taking things slow at work?"

He grinned. "As slow as I can and I've been leaving work everyday on time. My secretary doesn't leave me much choice since she makes it a point to start turning out the lights and setting up the alarm system at five on the dot."

Amber chuckled. "Good for her." One thing she had come to realize about Cord during the four days they had spent together was that he was a stubborn man. He'd also been a sexually frustrated man and she had felt it each and every time he had looked at her.

Like he was doing now.

Damn. The two of them were hopeless. Two hopelessly hot people who didn't want to do anything but jump each other's bones, but who were also determined to prove there was more than sex between them. At least that's what he wanted to believe. But with him standing in front of her, giving her silent messages with his eyes, messages that had her panties getting wet by the second, it was hard to buy into what he was selling.

"Would you go out with me tonight?"

Surprised by his question, Amber didn't move for a few seconds as she calculated in her mind if his restriction of "no sex in two weeks" were up. She swallowed when she realized they were not. He had another three days to go. Going out with him would only be torture that neither of them needed. And the risk of temptation was too great.

She shook her head. "I don't think that's a good idea, Cord."

He chuckled lightly. "I think it's the only good idea there is, Amber. Dev may be concerned about me working myself into an early grave if I don't slow things down at work, but I figure I'm going to work myself into an even earlier one if I don't relieve some deep sexual tension pretty damn soon. There are only so many cold showers a man can take."

Amber considered him for a long moment, and then quickly looked around to make sure they weren't being overheard. "So, are you now saying it will be just sex between us?" She needed to hear him say it. She needed for him to confirm that the only thing they wanted from each other was a roll in the sheets. That was the only thing she could handle. She didn't want to think about anything more serious than that.

Cord reached out and placed his hand over her hand that was resting on the counter. He leaned closer. "I want you, but not just for sex, Amber, although I'd be lying if I said that wasn't the main thing on my mind right now. But I want all of you, your mind, your body, and your heart."

She raised a brow. He'd said the wrong word. "Heart?"

His smile disappeared and a serious expression touched his lips. "Yes, heart."

Speaking of heart, hers suddenly thumped as the safety shield surrounding it went up. She could deal with mind and body, but she knew she couldn't handle anything dealing with the heart. That old vulnerability that had kept her from getting serious about a man just wouldn't allow it. She'd made one mistake and didn't want to make another one. "Let's just leave the heart out of this shall we?"

He stared at her, his expression intense. "I wish I could, but I can't."

Amber frowned. "Then maybe you should. Your marriage was no better than mine." She regretted saying the words the moment they'd left her mouth, but it was too late to call them back. At least she was honest and had spoken just how she felt.

He narrowed his gaze. "That may be true, but that doesn't mean I can't move on. I suggest that you do the same."

"I have moved on."

"No, you haven't. You're still holding on to the past and all the things your ex-husband did to you. I think it's time for you to let go."

Amber lifted her chin. "Look, it's getting pretty busy in here again. I really have to get back to work but thanks for all the flowers you've sent."

"Will you go out with me tonight?" he decided to ask again.

"No, and please don't ask again. I don't need the hassle."

He nodded. "All right. And I'm sorry if you think I've been hassling you because that wasn't my intent. Just think about everything I've said, and if you think you might be interested then let me know. You know how to reach me."

And without saying another word, he turned and walked out of the store.

❧ *Chapter 29* ❧

I don't like this, Brandy," Grey all but growled.

Brandy swallowed. She'd figured that he wouldn't, but there was nothing she could do. The mayor had asked that she be present during several functions today when dignitaries of both universities, as well as the coaches, players, and teaching staff, made appearances. As owners of one of the hosting hotels as well as one of the major sponsors, she'd felt an obligation to be there although she knew it would throw a monkey wrench into all the security measures Grey had put in place for today. "This is something I have to do, Grey."

Grey sighed. And keeping her safe was something he had to do. "Do you know all the places they want you to be?"

"Yes, but if you intend to follow me around, then please do so from a distance. Keeping watch over me at the hotel is one thing, but being hot on my tail in public is another. I'm a businesswoman, Grey, and having a lover who appears to be obsessed with keeping me in his sights twenty-four hours a day is not the image I want to foster."

Grey frowned. "To hell with your image, Brandy, protecting your ass is what I'm primarily concerned with right now."

"And you can still do so at a distance, Grey."

"I won't do it at a distance, Brandy, so forget it. I will be accompanying you to whatever functions you have scheduled today as your escort. And if anyone has a problem with that then that's too damn bad."

Brandy swallowed. To say Grey was upset would be putting it mildly. He still was operating under the belief that Jolene was the person out to get her and although she had to admit that theory was a possibility, she just wasn't as convinced as he was about it. However, to fight Grey on any of his plans would be a waste of her time. She narrowed her eyes. "Fine, do whatever you want, Grey, but I don't like it," she said, sounding highly disgruntled and making sure that he knew it.

"You don't have to like it, Brandy. But I am asking you to trust me and to do what you're told with the belief it's for your own good." Grey sighed. He was getting downright tired of having to explain every single thing to her. Why was she determined to be so damn stubborn? He had to admit he liked her stubbornness sometimes, but not when it came to her safety. If anything were to happen to her . . .

He shook his head. No. Nothing would happen to her because he wouldn't let it. Jolene's photograph had been circulated around the hotel and he'd even asked the local authorities for their help. It was time. He had a feeling there was a mad woman on the loose who was set on revenge.

Driven by a need he didn't understand, Grey let out a curse and pulled Brandy into his arms, taking her mouth with a possession, a want, a desire that he recognized even if he didn't understand. Automatically, her arms wrapped around his neck and she returned the kiss with the same blazing passion. Emotions welled up inside of Grey, sharp, fierce. Her taste slid through him and with a deliberation that was relentless; he took his time, giving her a long, hungry kiss that ripped through both of their senses.

When they broke apart he looked into eyes that burned with all the sensuality he sampled again and again and again. He knew that walking away from her and returning to the life that awaited him in Atlanta would be the hardest thing he had to do.

Jolene Bradford looked at herself in the mirror, proud of what she saw. She almost didn't recognize herself and was grateful for the many times she had watched Perrin apply makeup to the film cast and crew. Now, since he had gotten scared and decided he wouldn't help her any longer, she had to go solo. Perrin had felt that putting the fear of God in Brandy was one thing, but doing physical harm to her was another. He had gotten cold feet and defected, leaving her on her own. But Perrin's refusal to help any further was something she couldn't be concerned with. With or without him, today would be the day.

She did a quick check to make sure the vial was secure and tight in the pocket of her coat. Brandy Bennett would finally get hers and it was about time. She had caused her too much pain, embarassment, and humiliation. Thanks to Brandy, those damn videotapes were everywhere and Jolene couldn't even keep a decent job. There was no place she could go, no university where she could teach without those damn videotapes coming out of the woodwork. And then she would lose her students and the faculty's respect. Her male students would slip her lewd notes asking for blow jobs or to meet her after school for a gangbang. It had been nearly three years and the nightmare had not ended and she only had Brandy to blame.

The two of them had a score to settle and it would be done. This was their day of reckoning and Brandy would get to see how it felt to be the center of attention.

Grey's eyes narrowed on Brandy. "Just how many more meetings do you have today?" He couldn't help but admire her energy. They had put in several appearances, which included a breakfast meetings, two luncheons, and a few other meetings as all of the committee's planning for the Florida Classic was finally coming together. The game would be played in a few days and already the St. Laurent was at full capacity. That was good business for the hotel but it only made his job just that much more challenging.

"There's only one more for today," Brandy said as she leaned against him in the elevator. She felt tired, but it was a good feeling. Already she was beginning to feel the excitement generated by the rivalry between the two teams.

"There's a small reception that's scheduled for later tonight at Disney-MGM Studios," she continued. "It's not until nine so that gives us time to go to the suite and shower and relax." She tilted her head and smiled at him. "I think a nap sounds good, too."

Grey nodded as he returned her smile. He saw the sultry invitation in her gaze and knew that sleep was the last thing on her mind, just like it was the last thing on his. No matter how tired he felt, he would always have the energy to make love to her, lose himself in her heat, her sensuality.

They made it up to her suite and as soon as the door closed behind them, and once they were in each other's arms, Brandy couldn't help wondering if she would ever get enough of this man. When he placed her on the bed, she concluded that no, she would not. She pulled in a deep breath and her arms slid around his neck.

Grey Masters was addictive and she was undeniably hooked.

Hours later, Brandy had showered and dressed in a lounging outfit that had been a birthday present from her cousins. She walked into the kitchen. Grey was on the phone and from the expression on his face she could tell he was absorbed in what the person was saying.

"I'll be right there," he said tersely into the receiver before setting it down. He glanced over at her. "That was one of my men. The local authorities brought Sam Perrin in for questioning and he admitted to being the one who delivered those messages to you."

Brandy swallowed a groan, not wanting to believe what he was saying, what he was insinuating, implying. "That means that . . ."

Grey's gaze didn't waver. "Yes. And he admitted that Jolene Bradford is the person who wrote them. He went along with it thinking all she wanted to do was scare you and when he saw she had something worse in mind, he decided to cut out."

Every cell in Brandy's body wanted to scream a denial, that it couldn't be true. Her breakup with Lorenzo had happened almost three years ago and she'd been the injured party, not Jolene. She had been the one who'd been played a fool. "It doesn't make sense, Grey."

Grey quickly covered the distance to her when he saw the hurt and disappointment in her face. He drew Brandy's head down to his chest and skimmed his lips across her cheeks. "No, it doesn't, but the biggest disappointments in life often come from those we want to trust, those we thought we could trust," he whispered, thinking of his wife's betrayal.

"But at least we know who we're dealing with now," he continued. "And we also know she's apparently not in her right mind. She's a violent person, so we need to take every precaution."

Brandy nodded. "What do you need me to do?"

"We'll continue with the same plan we've had in place. I'm going to stick to you like glue at tonight's function as well as any others planned for the rest of the week. A photograph of Bradford has been circulated and we hope we can pick her up before she decides to do any mischief."

Brandy hoped so. A part of her wondered if there was something she could have done to avoid any of this. Right after the wedding Jolene had called her several times to talk and offer an apology, but Brandy, still raw from the pain, had refused to talk to her and had literally dismissed the woman from her life. As far as Brandy had been concerned what she and Lorenzo did had been unforgivable.

"I need to go downstairs and meet with a detective from the Orlando Police Department. We're handling this as quietly as we can, Brandy, I want you to know that."

She nodded. "I do and I appreciate it. You don't think she'll do anything to harm any of the hotel guests do you?"

"No, I think her anger is directed at you. You're the person she wants to hurt."

Brandy shuddered at the thought.

"Lock the door behind me. I've arranged for a security guard to be posted outside the door while I'm gone which shouldn't be any more than ten or fifteen minutes. I've ordered something for you to eat which should be up shortly. I figured you'd be pretty hungry."

A hot blushed heated Brandy's cheek when her mind recalled the vigorous activity that had taken place in her bedroom a few hours ago. "Thanks," she said, appreciating his thoughtfulness. "I could use something to eat."

Grasping the back of her neck, Grey leaned down and placed a kiss on her lips. "I could stay in bed with you forever," he said in a low, caressing and arousing voice.

"And I feel the same way about you, Grey."

Minutes after Grey had left, Brandy wandered restlessly around the suite while she waited for him to return. She pulled out several magazines and even turned on the television but she could not stop her mind from thinking about Jolene.

She sighed when she heard the knock at the door and crossing the room she glanced out the peephole and saw it was a waiter with a dinner trolley. Removing the security locks, she opened the door so the man could wheel the trolley inside the suite. Brandy frowned when she didn't see the security guard that Grey had mentioned would be posted outside.

"Excuse me," she said to the waiter who was wheeling the trolley to the middle of the room, "but did you see someone standing outside my door?"

The man turned around and the first thing Brandy thought was that he was someone she didn't recognize, but then they had hired additional help for this weekend's function, so that wasn't unusual.

"I wouldn't worry about him if I were you."

Brandy's breath caught when the man peeled off a fake mustache then snatched off an Afro wig, exposing shoulder-length air. It didn't take long for her to see that the person standing before her was not a man but a woman. She blinked and when the woman grabbed a napkin from off the trolley and began wiping makeup from her face, Brandy suddenly went cold inside.

Jolene.

Grey paced around Perry Hall's office after listening to the detective's report. The only other thing Sam Perrin could tell the authorities about Jolene's plans was that she had spent a lot of time mixing some chemicals together. When asked where Jolene had gotten the chemicals he'd told them that while working as a biology professor at UCF, Jolene had had access to the university's chemistry lab.

Fear and fury roared through Grey upon listening to the detective describe Jolene's devious mind.

"Uh, there's something I forgot to mention that's a possibility," Sam Perrin said, his voice sounding rather nervous.

Grey stopped walking and met the young man's jittered gaze. "What?"

"Jolene took one of my makeup kits so she might not look like herself."

"Damn!"

No sooner had that one word escaped Grey's lips, there was a knock on the door. Hall immediately granted the person entrance. Apollo Guisto walked in looking angry and upset. "We have a problem, Grey."

Grey's heart began beating rapidly. "What?"

"The waiter who was to deliver room service to your room was found in the elevator unconscious. Someone injected him with something that caused him to black out."

Grey's hands tightened to fists at his side. He quickly crossed the room to Apollo. "What about the security guard I stationed at the door?"

"The security camera we installed on Ms. Bennett's floor has picked up him lying flat on his back near the door. It's my guess the same thing happened to him. It's also my guess that Jolene Bradford is alone with Brandy Bennett in her suite as we speak."

Moving with the speed of lightning, Grey was out of the room with the other men following behind him.

Brandy knew the best thing to do was to not lose her cool and keep Jolene talking. She had to believe that Grey was on his way. She had to believe that. "Why, Jolene? Why do you hate me so much?"

Jolene's laughter was chilling. "Considering everything you did to me, Brandy, how can I not hate you? I admit that sleeping with Lorenzo was a mistake but I paid the price for that indiscretion. My fiancé wouldn't have anything to do with me and everyone treated me like I was dirt. But then when I ran into Lorenzo some months ago and he told me the truth, I couldn't believe you would stoop so low."

As far as Brandy was concerned, no one had stooped as low as Jolene but decided not to tell her that. Although she didn't see a weapon of any kind on the woman, she wasn't taking any chances. "Stoop so low for what?"

"Lorenzo said you planned the entire thing and that it hadn't been a fluke that the videotape was shown at the wedding like everyone thought. He told me that you and those damn cousins of yours planned everything just to embarrass and humiliate us in front of everyone. But you weren't satisfied with stopping there, were you? You had copies of that videotape made and distributed everywhere so I couldn't put what I did behind me. I was asked to resign from three different universities because of you."

"I had nothing to do with those copies, Jolene."

"Lies! I don't believe you. It wasn't my fault what happened between Lorenzo and me. It just happened and I didn't know he was taping us. I lost so much over the years and you were supposed to be my friend."

Brandy's skin began to crawl at how calm Jolene appeared and fear began growing inside of Brandy. "And you were supposed to be my friend, Jolene," she said softly, trying to be just as calm. "How do you think I felt when I watched that video and saw the woman in bed with my fiancé was you? A person I trusted as my best friend, my maid of honor, the woman who was to be the godmother to my children?"

Brandy watched Jolene's face twist in pain at the reminder of what she and Lorenzo had done. "Get real, Brandy. Do you think I was the only woman he was screwing? You trusted Lorenzo too much. I know it was bad judgment on my part but still that was no reason for you to do what you did. And I want you to know how it feels to be ostracized, to stand out and have people whisper about you behind your back. I thought about setting up a tape in here and film you and your boyfriend making out but decided that was too easy. I wanted to get you where it hurt—your face. I used to get so damn sick and tired of you mama bragging about how beautiful you are. And I intend to fix that. If no decent man wants me then no man, decent or otherwise, will want you either."

Brandy watched as Jolene pulled something out of her coat pocket and Brandy took a step back. "Think about what you're doing, Jolene," she said in an attempt to reason with her, although she had a feeling she was wasting her time. "Is it worth all of this? I promise not to press charges if you walk out of here and don't come back. Why mess your future up over—"

Jolene waved an sharp hand in the air, demanding Brandy's silence. "I don't have a future because of that damn videotape. Once anyone sees it I'm nothing more than a laughingstock around campus and my male students immediately consider me as nothing but a slut and try hitting on me. Even Lorenzo treats me like dirt. He came out smelling like a rose because his family has money, but for me it's different. Scandal follows me everywhere and I'm tired of living that way." She moved toward Brandy. Her steps slow, determined. "So it doesn't matter if I'm arrested. I'll go to jail knowing that I've given you a dose of your own medicine."

Brandy moved backward. Her first thought was to try to make it to the bedroom but Jolene stood between her and the bedroom door. "My boyfriend is on his way back, Jolene. You won't get away with this."

The woman laughed. "Oh, yes, I will. Have you forgotten that I'm a biology professor with a minor in chemistry? I've mixed some of the strongest chemicals together that will disfigure your features for life," she said holding the vial up for Brandy to see. "What's in here is some pretty potent stuff. When I'm through with you even your boyfriend won't want you."

Knowing she was trapped, Brandy refused to just stand there and be at Jolene's mercy. Swallowing the panic that rose in her throat, she took off toward the kitchen intending to find something she could use to defend herself. Her heart began beating wildly when she heard Jolene's angry footsteps behind her, close on her heel.

Then the next thing Brandy knew the door crashed open and Grey and a few men rushed in, tackling Jolene to the floor, and knocking the open vial from her hand. It spilled on the floor, immediately eating away at the carpet. Some of it spilled on Jolene's hand and she was screaming as if in tremendous pain. Brandy also noticed that some of it had gotten on one of the men's jacket, which he quickly removed. She stood aside as the men rushed Jolene to the kitchen sink to try and wash off the contact the acid had made to her skin. Brandy closed her eyes when she saw Jolene's hand and the damage that had already been done. Jolene had been right; the chemicals had been potent. Brandy shuddered when she thought that it had been Jolene's plan to throw those chemicals in her face . . .

"Grey!"

Grey immediately came to her and pulled Brandy into his arms. "It's okay, baby. It's over. It's all over." He pressed her head against his chest and inhaled a long deep breath, angry at how close Jolene had come to hurting his woman. He picked her up into his arms and carried her out of the kitchen and into the office, closing the door behind him. He sat down in the wingback chair.

And in his arms Brandy broke down, allowing all her emotions and tears to pour forth. She had just come through one hell of an experience and he understood her need to release her fear, anxiety, and pain. Jolene Bradford had hurt her before and today she had tried hurting her again. Today Brandy had once again seen how someone you considered a friend could turn on you, betray you.

There was a knock on the door."

"Come in."

Apollo stuck his head in. "We've called 911 to take Ms. Bradford to the emergency room. The squad should be arriving any moment," he said.

Grey nodded. "That's fine, but get her out of this suite," Grey said to Apollo as he drew Brandy closer to him. "And tell Hall to get someone from housekeeping up here immediately, and make sure it's someone who can be trusted. I want things to appear like an accident. We don't want to spook any of the hotel guests."

Apollo nodded. "Right." He then closed the door behind him.

"Thanks, Grey," Brandy whispered.

"You're welcome, sweetheart." He then proceeded to gather her closer into his arms and kiss her tears away.

"Are you sure you still want to go out tonight, Brandy?" Grey asked, although he knew what her answer would be. He sat on the edge of the bed and watched her get dressed. He had yet to put on his own clothes hoping she would change her mind about going anywhere tonight. His opinion was that she had gone through a lot today and the best thing was for her to rest her mind as well as her body. But it was apparent that she was determined to stay busy and not let what had happened earlier in her suite deter her plans.

The trip to the police station had gone rather quickly thanks to the statement Sam Perrin had already given. Sadly, Jolene had been admitted to the hospital with third-degree burns on her hands. Brandy had been incredibly brave and he'd been proud of her and had told her so. She had smiled at him and had lifted her chin stubbornly, her internal strength pouring through and said, *"I'm a Bennett and Bennetts are brave."* He'd heard the pride in her voice and couldn't help but admire her strength, her tenaciousness, and her determination to put what she had endured behind her.

Brandy turned away from the mirror and met his gaze. She shivered slightly and wrapped her arms around her middle. "I'm sure, Grey. I have to do this. If I don't then Jolene would have won. I can't let her. She has tormented my life for the past month and I can't let her continue to do so. I have to get back to living a normal life. Like you said earlier, it's over and I have to believe that."

Grey stood and crossed the room to her. "Believe it. The courts will decide what they will do with Jolene. If she's had a mental breakdown like you believe then she will get the help she needs since she didn't actually hurt anyone other than herself."

Brandy nodded. "Are you still coming with me tonight, Grey?"

For a long, suspended moment his gaze held hers, then he asked, "Do you want me to?"

"Yes."

"Then, yes, I'll come. It will take just a second for me to get dressed." He turned to leave then turned back around to meet her gaze. "My flight will leave tomorrow around noon," he added, his voice low and rough.

Brandy inhaled a deep breath. She had always known that he would leave after finding out who'd been sending her those notes but she hadn't counted on it being so soon. "You're leaving tomorrow?"

"Yes. There's a case pending that I have to get back to."

Her shoulder lifted in an attempt at a casual shrug. "I understand." Although she said the words, she really did not. Especially when she thought of the times they had spent together, specifically those intimate times. She would not, she could not believe that he slept with every woman he was paid to protect. A part of her believed things were different between them although he'd never said it.

Grey released a long breath. If Brandy understood then she definitely had one up on him because he sure as hell didn't. He couldn't understand why he felt the need to separate himself from her, to put distance between them, the need to walk away. His jaw clenched in irritation. He knew the reason although now he couldn't admit it. He needed time to think, to be sure. He had made a mistake once with Gloria and finding out the truth about her had damn near destroyed him.

Unable to help himself he crossed the room back to her. His smile was sad as he tucked a finger beneath her chin and lifted his gaze to her and asked, "Can we talk?"

Brandy bit her bottom lip as her gaze reflected emotions Grey couldn't define. "Yes."

She was surprised when Grey sat down on the edge of the bed and tugged her into his lap. He then wrapped both arms around her and pulled her tightly to him. Automatically, naturally, her head went to his shoulder as he cuddled her securely in his arms.

"When I first arrived here, Brandy, my primary concern was to do a job, to protect you and find out who was sending you those notes like your cousins had asked me to do. It was never my intent to become intimately involved with you."

"Yes, but you did," she pointed out.

Grey smiled. She wasn't going to let him off easy. "Yes, and I don't consider what we shared as some sort of erotic rump between the sheets or illicit tryst. Everything we shared, and everything we did to me was special."

"I thought it was special, too," she said quietly, lifting her head slightly from his shoulder to look up at him.

Grey stared down into her beautiful features, features that he knew he would carry in his heart for some time. "You were like a snowball effect and you caught me off guard, Brandy." He shook his head as a light chuckle escaped his throat. "Now I know how Quinn felt the first time he met Alexia. You Bennett women are something else."

Brandy smiled proudly. "Yes, we are."

"Anyway," Grey said, trying to get the discussion back on track, "I tried to do my job but discovered keeping you safe was no longer a job but an obsession. And it got worse every day. Words cannot describe how I felt the moment I realized that you were alone in this suite with Jolene Bradford. I had no idea what she planned to do although Perrin had mentioned to the authorities something about some chemicals she had thrown together. Since she delivered the food, I thought she planned to poison you or something and I literally lost it. I burst in here like a madman, without even thinking of the other possibilities that could be taking place inside of here. What if she had a gun or a knife or something? My bursting into here like that could have given her a reason to shoot you dead."

"Grey," she said softly, interrupting his words. "She didn't have a gun and I'm glad you and everyone showed up when you did." She then took a deep, calming breath. "And you don't have to explain things to me about us, I understand. That first time I laid eyes on you was at Alexia and Quinn's twins' birthday party. I knew you were a loner and then after talking to your sister Quinece and she explained the tragedy that had happened to your wife, and how you lost her, I—"

"I didn't lose my wife, Brandy."

Brandy blinked. "But—but I thought Quinece said she was killed in a car accident."

Grey nodded. "She was. But what none of the family ever knew, because I never told them, was that at the time of the car accident, Gloria had left me and was on her way to start another life with her lover. I found the note she left on the kitchen table when I flew home after getting word of the accident. The way she had planned it, was that I would come home during the end of my job assignment, which would have been about two weeks after she and her lover took off for parts unknown. According to her note, she would have contacted me eventually for a divorce."

Brandy's jaw clenched in anger. "That's pretty damn tacky."

Grey gave her a slight smile. "No, in fact it was rather sad, especially since she never reached her destination. And later I couldn't help but wonder how her lover handled it when he'd discovered she never would."

"Did you ever find out who he was?"

"Yes. He was at the funeral. When we made eye contact, I knew who he was. We didn't say anything to each other but from the devastated look on his face I knew that he had loved her . . . although she hadn't been his to love."

Grey sighed deeply, thinking that he would never forget that day for as long as he lived. "But then," he went on pragmatically, "she was never mine either. Gloria hated what I did for a living, the frequent trips away from home, the secrecy, and the long hours. When we first got married she swore she could handle the life of being a FBI agent's wife, but in the end she couldn't and sought love and passion with another man."

Brandy didn't say anything. Instead she thought of Lorenzo and Jolene's betrayal. Finding out about them had hurt and she could just imagine how Grey must have felt to discover his wife had not been faithful. She sighed deeply. "So where does that leave us, Grey?"

There, she thought. She had placed her cards on the table by asking the burning question of the hour and she wouldn't give him the chance to deny there was an "us." There may be issues that needed to be worked out but there was still an "us" and he might as well get used to the idea.

"I don't know, Brandy. I truly don't know about *us*. I know that I care for you deeply and—"

"That's not good enough, Grey."

Grey blinked. "Excuse me?"

Brandy wiggled her way out of his arms and stood up in front of him and placed her hands on her hips. "I said that's not good enough. Caring deeply for me just doesn't cut it. I want someone who will love me unconditionally, a man I know I can trust, a man who is willing to take on my family, which includes the constant drama with my mother and father, and a man who is willing to father the babies I intend to have. The man I want to love me has a big shoe to fill because I plan on moving into that shoe. I'm tired of avoiding the toe and longing for the middle but avoiding it, too, because of the fear of getting hurt again. I know how it feels to hurt, Grey. Trust me when I say that I've experienced similar pain. But I'm willing to move forward and not look back."

Brandy reached down and took his hand and pulled him to his feet. She wrapped her arms around his neck and skimmed her lips along the corner of his mouth and cheek. "If you want tonight to be the last night for us then that's fine. I won't like it but I'll take it because I discovered awhile ago that I had fallen in love with you."

"Brandy, I—"

"No, Grey, let me finish while I still have the nerve," she whispered softly against his lips. "And because I love you, I'm willing to give you time to decide just how you feel about me. I'm aware that it takes some people a while to come to conclusions about certain things. But I don't plan to wait forever, Grey. I plan to get on with my life with or without you. You are *not* a free man, but I *am* a free woman and I plan to stay that way. Being free means accepting the good things the future has to offer and not dwelling on the things your past life has brought you. I can no longer moan and groan over what Lorenzo and Jolene did to me just like you can't get hung up on what Gloria did to you. Let it go and move on. And when and if you decide to do that . . . and if it's not too late for *us*, I'll be here."

She sighed and decided she had said enough. The ball was in his court. He could play it or lose it and dear God she hoped he would play it. She cuddled closer into his arms wondering what he was thinking while he was holding her so tight, like he never wanted to let her go. She had meant what she'd said. If he decided that tonight would be their last night together then that was fine. Somehow she would find the strength to move on. She'd done it once and she would do so again. She was a Bennett and like her Grampa Ethan always said, you had to be the one to take the reins of your life and seek your own happiness. And everyone owed it to themselves to be happy.

She hoped and prayed that one day Grey would realize that.

Chapter 30

Praise God, I'm glad it's over," Carla said with profound relief in her voice as she hung up the telephone. Amber had called to tell her about Brandy's ordeal with Jolene Bradford and to let her know that Brandy was okay.

"Is everything all right?"

Carla looked over and met Jesse's concerned gaze. He stood in the middle of the kitchen doorway, his eyes glued to her. For a brief moment she had forgotten he was still there. He had dropped by earlier to spend time with Craig before his bedtime. Craig had fallen asleep while his father had been reading him a story and Jesse had been the one to tuck him in.

"Yes, everything is fine. A good friend of mine was being stalked and I just got word that the stalker was caught."

Jesse nodded. "I'm glad to hear that."

"Yes, so am I. I've been worried about Brandy and when I go to bed tonight, I'll definitely be able to rest better."

Jesse swallowed deeply. He didn't want to think of her in bed but was having a hard time not doing so. Every time he entered her home, which had been on a daily basis lately, to see his son, he would have a physical reaction the moment he saw her. And tonight it was worse than ever. He crossed his legs so the lust that was ripping through him and settling dead center in his midsection wouldn't be too obvious. Carla had begun getting comfortable around him, he could tell. She had started letting her guard down more and more. Whenever he dropped by, he enjoyed seeing her as much as he enjoyed seeing his son. And although every cell in his body screamed for him to make a move, he had decided to be patient and take one day at a time, and he could see the results.

He could also feel the need of his frustrations.

He wanted her and wanted to rediscover all those feminine secrets he had uncovered the last time. He wanted to sink his hard shaft into her while kissing her to oblivion. He wanted to—

"Jesse?"

He blinked upon realizing she'd been talking to him. "Sorry, what did you say?"

She smiled. "I said that I talked to Sonya today. She's decided to stay in town for Thanksgiving and came up with an idea."

"What idea is that?"

"She offered to help me with dinner if you can get your friend Mike Kelly to join us."

Jesse lifted a brow. "She wants to invite Mike?" he asked surprised.

"Yes, evidently they've run into each other a few times and she thinks he's a nice guy."

Jesse nodded. "How do you feel about an extra person coming for dinner?"

"I don't have a problem with it and she wanted to know if you would ask him."

Jesse nodded again as he took a couple of steps into her kitchen. "Yes, I'll ask him although I'm not sure he'll come. Mike is somewhat of a loner during the holidays."

Like you, Carla wanted to say but decided not to. This past week had been busy with a lot of legal matters. Craig's last name had officially been changed to Devereau and when she'd seen the name written on the legal document for the first time, she had felt a profound sense of pride that the man who had fathered her child had wanted to claim him. She knew that in addition to the transfer of Osborne Computer Network stock, Jesse had also established a very hefty trust fund for his son. There was no doubt about it, Craig was a blessed little boy and she intended to make sure he grew up knowing it.

"I'm sure Sonya would like it if he were to come," she added when the kitchen became quiet. Seeing him standing in the middle of the floor suddenly made her feel incredibly hot, aroused. Those things were constant whenever he came over for a visit. It didn't take much for her to remember that one night they had spent together, and how easily he had fit between her legs, how tender and caring he'd been upon realizing that she was still a virgin. And his lovemaking had sent the both of them soaring, not knowing at the time that they were in the process of creating a very beautiful little boy. She would never forget how it felt when the weight of his body had pressed hers down into the mattress while he smoothly and rhythmically thrust into her over and over again while making love to her mouth at the same time.

"Carla?"

She blinked and swallowed deeply, quickly composing herself when he recaptured her attention. "Yes?"

"I said it's time for me to leave."

She noticed he already had his jacket in his hand and was putting it on. "I'll walk you to the door."

When they reached the door he stopped and turned to her. "It still may be too early yet, but do you have any idea what Craig wants for Christmas?"

She laughed and when she did a disarming smile curved the corners of his mouth. "Trust me I have plenty ideas of what he wants," she said.

"Then maybe the two of us can go shopping after Thanksgiving."

Her stomach fluttered at the thought of spending time with him without Craig as a buffer. He had suggested that they go out once but she had flatly refused. But now, a part of her wanted to spend time with him. "Yes, I'd like that."

"All right. You can let me know when. I'm sure it will benefit the both of us to get an early start."

"Yes, I agree." Carla cleared her throat and looked at him, her gaze searching his in the foyer's dim lightning. He wasn't making any attempt to leave but at the same she hadn't opened the door for him to leave either. She swallowed deeply when he took a step closer to her.

"I'm glad we agree on that," he said huskily.

"Yeah, me too," she said taking her own step toward him and automatically reaching out and smoothing her hand beneath his jacket, her palm coming to rest on his chest. The contact sent an immediate shudder through him, one that went straight to her. Ultimate awareness, sexual attraction, chemistry reaction . . . all the things she had tried downplaying, ignoring and avoiding over the past weeks hit them dead center—right in his midsection and right between her legs.

"Have I ever told you how incredibly beautiful you look each and every time I come to see Craig?" he asked huskily.

Carla licked at her mouth and couldn't help noticing how Jesse's gaze was focused on her tongue that she was using to wet her lips. "No, you've never told me that."

A sensual smile curved his lips. "Then I'm telling you now. Every time I drop by you look incredibly beautiful."

"Thanks for the compliment."

"You deserve it." She saw his face lowering to hers and of their own accord, her lashes began drifting shut and her lips parted. And then she felt his mouth on hers, taking it with a hunger which was the same hunger she felt, tangling his tongue with hers. He was determined to recapture the intensity of the kiss they had shared three years ago. Even if that was impossible, it appeared that he intended to die trying.

She moaned as his tongue took her mouth on a joy ride through Pleasure Park. A part of her needed to experience this, needed to relive this. And he was giving her everything she needed in full force. And when the palm of his hands touched her backside, bringing her body right smack to his hard erection, she was suddenly overpowered with such an erotic sensation that she felt her body move against him.

In the back of her mind she wanted to pull away. She wanted to think that they were moving too fast, too soon. But then she remembered that it had been almost three years for her. Almost three years without this. And her body was responding to the one person it remembered as giving it ultimate satisfaction.

She finally pulled her mouth from his and groaned deep within her throat when he tangled his fingers in her hair and pulled her head back to taste her throat and neck before recapturing her mouth again. Their tongues tangled, mated, as she continued to come unraveled in his arms and with his kiss.

Jesse sealed the moment between them the only way he knew how— the only way that seemed appropriate—with a kiss that would open some doors for them while at the same time permanently closing others. The bad memories of the past were behind those closed doors where they belonged, and where he intended for them to stay.

He released her mouth and continued to hold her in his arms. Tonight the depth of their feelings had thrown them and there was no turning back.

❧ Chapter 31 ❧

Shutting off the shower, Amber dried off with a huge velour towel. After lotioning her body and applying some of her favorite perfume, she quickly dressed in a bra and panties then wiggled into one of her favorite dresses.

Deciding not to put on any pantyhose, she slipped into a pair of comfortable flats. A few minutes after applying makeup, she smiled at her reflection in the mirror. Although she had spent the last twenty minutes making herself look pretty damn good, she didn't have a single place to go.

Brandy had given her tickets earlier that week for the Florida Classic's Battle of the Bands, where the bands from the two rival universities would be competing on the football field tonight. She had attended the event the prior two years and had enjoyed herself immensely, but she didn't want to go there tonight.

She'd thought about going to see the new Halle Berry movie but decided it was a chick flick, one she would enjoy seeing with Brandy and Carla, or with her sisters when she went home next month for Christmas.

She also ruled out the thought of going to dinner alone since she wasn't in the mood. She had spoken to Brandy earlier and she was in just as dismal a mood since her bodyguard had left yesterday. Although Brandy hadn't said much about the guy, Amber had a feeling that the relationship had ended up being more than a business one. That thought kicked off an idea in Amber's mind and she quickly decided that instead of finding someplace to go, she would visit the nearest Blockbuster and rent one of her favorite movies, *The Bodyguard*.

Leaving her bedroom she picked up her purse and grabbed her car keys off the counter. Her evening seemed a little brighter now that she would be spending it with Kevin Costner.

A half hour later Amber sat in the driveway and listened to the smooth humming of her car engine. After leaving Blockbuster it seemed her hands had a mind of their own and instead of heading back home, she had gotten on Interstate 4 and within minutes she'd found herself pulling into Cord's yard.

It had been a week since he had come to her store, a week since he had delivered his ultimatum. Either she was willing to move in the same direction he was headed or she wasn't. She still wasn't sure what her position was on that. Every time she thought of getting serious with him she got scared and remembered how things had been with Gary. All she knew was that she had to see Cord tonight, and talk to him.

After shutting off her car's engine she began having doubts that she'd made the right decision about coming, at least without calling first. What if he had company? What if he was asleep, since the house looked pretty dark? What if he was still royally pissed with her and didn't want to see her?

Refusing to sit outside in her car any longer, Amber decided to face whatever Cord dished out. She opened her car door and got out. Sauntering up his walkway seemed like the longest stroll of her life and it didn't help matters that her heart was beating a thousand beats a minute. But she was determined to see him. And then?

She didn't have a clue.

Cord lay in bed, listening to the sound of Brook Benton croon about a rainy night in Georgia. The music was playing on the radio and having nothing else better to do, he had turned it on the moment he had gotten into bed.

He tried to think of a number of things, especially Dev's announcement earlier that he intended to ask Briana to marry him and had purchased the engagement ring that day. Dev wanted a short engagement, in fact he was pushing for them to marry New Year's Eve day so they could ring in the new year as man and wife.

Cord was definitely in agreement with that and had told Dev that marrying Briana before the year's end would definitely be a tax advantage. But Cord knew income taxes were the last thing on his best friend's mind. Dev was in love, undeniably so. He had found the woman of his dreams and wanted to make things forever.

Forever.

Cord didn't see anything wrong with forever with the right woman and immediately thought of Amber. Amber with the beautiful eyes, voluptuous hips, and full curves.

Although she wasn't ready to accept anything serious between them, he knew in his heart that she was the right woman for him. It didn't matter that he had known her for a little more than a month. What did matter was that there was something between them and it was something he refused to dismiss even if she wanted to.

He shifted in bed to find another comfortable position when he heard the doorbell ring. Deciding that it couldn't possibly be Dev and Briana since Dev had driven down to Daytona to propose to her on the beach, Cord wondered if it was another buddy of his, a fellow accountant, who dropped by occasionally to shoot the bull and drink beer.

Getting out of bed, he slipped into his pajama bottoms and made his way toward his living room. Whoever it was, he hoped they didn't intend to stay long because he definitely was not in the best of moods.

Cord had breathed in her scent the moment he opened the door. "Amber? What are you doing here?" he asked, totally surprised to see her. His breath caught on a surge of pure happiness at the very thought that she was here, standing in his doorway and looking as sexy as any woman had a right to look. He swallowed deeply as he waited for her response. He had never been unsure of himself with any woman but with Amber he felt an emotional vulnerability that he'd never felt before. Before him stood everything he'd ever wanted and everything he needed, but he knew he had to convince her of that. Her ex-husband had done a number on her and he had the job of making things right. He knew at that very moment that his life would not be fulfilled until she was a part of it.

"I'm sorry, I should have called first, Cord, but—"

"Nonsense, you didn't have to call first. Please come in."

Her gaze left his face and moved to his naked chest. "You were in bed?"

"Yes," he said hoarsely. "But I wasn't asleep. I was listening to music."

"Oh." Amber's gaze stayed glued to his chest. This was not the first time she had seen him without a shirt but every time she saw him she couldn't help but appreciate just how beautifully made he was; dark chocolate coloring, muscled chest and shoulders, flat stomach, patch of hair that tapered down past the waistband of his pajamas . . .

"Would you like to come in?"

Amber swallowed and lifted her gaze back up to his. "Yes, if you sure you don't mind the company."

"No, I don't mind at all." When she was completely inside he closed the door softly behind her and leaned against it and looked her up and down. She was wearing a very sexy looking dress and it showed all her voluptuous curves. Sighing deeply, he left his place against the door and strolled across the room to her. "Would you like something to drink?"

"Uh, no, but thanks anyway."

He nodded. He looked into her eyes and what he saw left him completely breathless. She had that flushed look, that aroused look, that "take me to bed" look. At least he thought she did but decided that he needed to make sure.

"Let's go into the living room and sit down," he said softly, taking her hand in his. "There is something I want to talk to you about anyway."

Amber lifted a brow but didn't say anything as he led her into the living room. She sat down in the first chair she came to, a leather loveseat. "So what is it that you want to talk to me about?"

Cord sat down on the sofa and faced her. He wanted to talk about sex but decided it wouldn't do good to rush into that kind of topic. Sex was something you eased into, in more ways that one. So he decided to throw her off base, mess with her mind, then later work his way to her body. He was tired of playing fair. He loved her and by the end of the evening she would know it and accept it. She would also realize that he wasn't going to give up on her.

"I want to talk to you about *Tax Tips*," he finally said.

Amber blinked. "Tax tips?"

"Yes, now is the time for you to think about ways to save your tax dollars for this year before it's too late."

Amber blinked again. Saving tax dollars was the last thing on her mind. In fact she frowned at the thought that Cord even wanted to talk about taxes. It was bad enough that she had the hots for him tonight and what made it worse was that he appeared oblivious to that fact.

"Have you paid your property tax bill yet?"

Amber lifted a brow. "Yes, why?"

"That's good. That way you can claim it on this year's tax return," Cord said with a smile.

Amber raised her eyes upward. *Whoop-dee-doo*.

"And I suggest that you make any charitable contributions before the end of this year. Clean out your closets and donate anything you no longer want or need to a nonprofit thrift store—and get receipts for those non-cash contributions or for cash contributions of two-hundred and fifty dollars or more."

Amber stared at him wondering if he was serious—not about the information he was telling her, since she believed it was true—but the mere fact that he was spending time even discussing such things with her. They were alone. He was half naked. She was fully clothed but she was getting hotter by slow degrees. Maybe she needed to get his attention or if nothing else, take his mind off the subject of taxes.

"And what about stocks, Amber?"

She shrugged a shoulder. "What about them?"

"Do you own any?"

"Yes," she responded, slipping out of her shoes.

"If any of them decreased in value this year, you might want to sell them before December 31, and use the loss to offset other capital gains."

Capital gains? She would show him the ultimate in capital gains, she thought. "It's rather hot in here, Cord. I think I want something to drink after all. May I have a cold glass of water?"

"Sure," he said standing. "I'll be right back."

"Thanks."

By the time he returned with her glass of water, Amber had the three top buttons of her dress undone and was sitting back in the chair looking all innocent and serene. He brought the water over to her and she eagerly took it out of his hands and took a huge gulp. He sat down next to her in the loveseat and she looked at him with a soft smile after drinking the entire glass. "Boy, I needed that," she said, handing the glass back to him.

He placed it on the table beside them. "And what else do you need, Amber?" he asked, tempted to lick away the excess water that was left on her lips.

"What I don't need is more tax tips, Cord. That's not why I'm here."

He nodded, inwardly pleased with the approach he had taken. Now they were getting down to the real nitty-gritty. He leaned back in the seat. "And why are you here, Amber?"

She quickly looked away for a moment. He had asked her that very thing when she'd first arrived but she had avoided answering him. "I think we still need to clear up some things?"

Cord shrugged. "What is there to clear up? You made yourself pretty clear the other day. Just because I told you that I wanted more than sex you pretty much freaked out."

"I didn't freak out."

Cord smiled. He thought she looked pretty damn sexy agitated. "Yes, you did. So I reached the conclusion that you enjoyed living in the past and weren't ready for a future with any man, and that you liked living a solitary life. Is that true, Amber?"

She bit her bottom lip, wondering how she intended to answer him. At one time she had thought that, but now seeing him again was helping put a lot of things in perspective. "Yes, I thought it was true but I'm not sure about anything anymore."

Cord nodded. "There's a saying that the foolish person seeks happiness in the distance and the wise person grows it under their feet. I want us to grow happiness under our feet, starting now. What do you say about that?"

She sighed deeply. "I think that maybe you're right and we should give things a try."

Cord's mouth creased into a smile. "I agree." He looked at her and the three buttons she had undone. "So, instead of giving you tax tips, I'm going to give you sex tips."

She stared at him. "You know some?"

"Yes," he said huskily. "I happen to know a few."

"Really? What are they?"

He reached out and began undoing the rest of the buttons on her dress. "Always take advantage of opportunities."

"Okay," she said softly. "I can agree with that one. What else?"

He met her gaze and smile. "Always make sure you have plenty of condoms on hand."

She chuckled at that one. "And do you?"

"Yes, plenty."

She nodded. "Is there another tip you want to pass on?"

"Yes." He stood and she watched as he went back to the door and checked it. He then returned to her. "Never get naked unless you have a chain latch on the door, especially if someone else has entrance to your home, and it just so happens Dev has a key."

Amber nodded again. "Are you planning to get naked, Cord?"

"Yes." He then offered his hand to her, helping her to stand. "And I plan to get you naked, too."

She watched as he undid the strings of his pajama bottom, letting them ease down his leg over his enormous erection. Amber swallowed. He was fully aroused and his shaft protruded boldly, proudly, and valiantly from the apex of his thighs.

Cord smiled when he saw she was checking him out. "Now it's your time."

Amber had never stripped for a man and didn't know how she felt about doing such a thing. But the look in Cord's eyes was reassuring. He wanted her; all of her and he wanted her just as she was. She slipped the dress from her shoulders then shimmied it down the rest of the way until it lay in a pool at her feet. Then came her bra and panties.

Sighing deeply she stood in front of him like he was standing in front of her, stark naked. "Any more tips, Cord?"

"Yes." He reached out and took her hand in his. "When the situation warrants it, establish the fact that there is a difference in making love and having sex. Tonight I will be making love to you, Amber, and not having sex."

Before she could say anything, he led her into the bedroom and beckoned her to the bed. Joining her there he leaned down and kissed her, sampling her taste and making her ache in the same way she was making him ache. He only stopped kissing her long enough to put on a condom. When his weight settled upon hers she began moving rest-lessly, passionately beneath him.

"Cord, I need you."

"And I need you, too, sweetheart."

He nuzzled her neck, he plied small bites at her throat, nipping and branding her his. And when he checked to see if her body was ready for him, he smiled. She was definitely ready. He nudged her legs apart with his knee. He met her gaze, knowing she may be doubtful of his true feelings now but in time she would see just what she meant to him.

"I love you, Amber."

"And I love you, Cord. I really do love you."

"Ah, Amber." And then he eased into her, a slow process that made him feel the heat of her all the way to his toes. Her words had sounded wonderful to his ears and he went deeper inside of her, almost to the hilt, needing the connection and then he slowly withdrew, and then slid into her again. He kept up the process, the rhythm, the torture, over and over again, each stroke adding more meaning to the one before it, releasing a flood of sensations that the both of them shared.

"This is happiness." He said the words, a whispery rumble from deep within his throat. He was determined to go slow even if it killed him and decided he was definitely dying a prolonged death. The plea-sure was powerful, intense, and strong and he kept going until he couldn't go anymore. When the explosion happened it ripped out both of their souls, their hearts and their bodies.

Amber's fingers sank deep into Cord's shoulders and she let out a huge scream, before Cord could cover her mouth with his. The sound was earthshakingly, painstakingly sensual. Anyone hearing it would know it was a scream of sexual pleasure and not of pain. And Cord decided to let her rip. It was the first orgasm she'd had in over two years and she deserved to blow out her vocal cords. Her scream tore threw him; it gave him intense joy hearing it, and he held on as her body writhed beneath him in intense pleasure as he penetrated deep, again and again. Their bodies vibrated uncontrollably with the force of their climax.

Moments later they lay locked into each other's arms, not able to move, barely able to breathe. Cord pulled her into his arms and in a forced whisper with a smile tilting his lips, he said. "The last sexual tip, the one I failed to mention, is to try and keep the noise down when making love in consideration of the neighbors."

And then he kissed her, sealing the love they had both pledged.

❧ Chapter 32 ❧

 y the time Jesse escorted Carla into the house and shut and locked the door behind them, she was nervous all the way down to her toes.

After dinner, the two of them, along with Craig, Sonya and Mike, had gone to Universal Studios to watch the lighting of the Christmas tree. Afterwards, out of the clear blue sky, Sonya had announced that she and Mike wanted to take Craig to the Magic Kingdom tomorrow and asked that he spend the night with her. There was no reason to worry about clothes. Since he spent a lot of time at Sonya's place anyway, she had plenty of clothes there already.

Carla had been tempted to tell Sonya that she needed Craig home to serve as a buffer between her and Jesse. Without her son in the house, there was no telling what his parents might get into.

Especially tonight.

Even with Sonya and Mike around them, the sexual tension between them had been strong. Every time she looked at him she remembered that day when he had kissed her. And then there was the fact that it was exactly three years ago tonight that they had made love and conceived their son.

Thanksgiving Night.

"Carla?"

She whirled around and gazed across the room at Jesse. "Yes?"

"Am I making you nervous?"

She swallowed deeply. "No, I'm fine."

He stared at her for a long moment. "Are you sure?"

"Yes, I just miss Craig already."

Jesse smiled. "So do I."

Carla shrugged. "Sonya will take real good care of him. She always does."

Jesse met her gaze. "You look good tonight, Carla."

She blushed at his compliment, especially since she wasn't wearing anything special, just a pair of jeans and a pullover sweater. "Thanks. Would you care for something to drink?"

He shook his head. "Not now, maybe later." He crossed the room to stand in front of her. "Do you realize it was three years tonight when we had our first date?"

"Yes."

"Do you know how much I wanted you that night?" he asked, his voice low and seductive.

Carla's stomach tumbled in a wave of intense desire. She decided to be completely honest with him. "Probably as much as I wanted you."

He took a step closer, appreciating her honesty. His hazel eyes were slightly glazed. "And do you know how much I want you tonight?" he whispered.

She nodded. "Probably as much as I want you."

She met his mouth when it came down to hers and rested her body against his. Their tongues began mating, slow but not gently. They were hungry for the taste of each other. He was devouring her mouth and she was devouring his.

His hand ran down her back and cupped her behind, bringing her firmly against his erection that pressed against his jeans. But that wasn't good enough. He didn't want clothing separating them.

He broke off the kiss and pulled back just enough to look into her eyes. "Tell me what you want, Carla," he said huskily, hoping that she would and that it would be the same thing that he wanted. "Tell me."

She wrapped her arms around his neck and met his gaze. "I want you to take me to bed and make love to me," she whispered silkily. "I need you, Jesse. I need three years worth of hot, mind-blowing love-making. That's what I want . . . from you."

Jesse's breathing deepened, his nostrils flared and adrenaline rushed fast and furious through his veins. He reached down and lifted her into his arms and quickly carried her into the bedroom and placed her on the bed. Without wasting any time he undressed her and when she lay completed naked before him, he stood back.

Deftly. He unsnapped his jeans and proceeded to take them off. He planned to love her just the way she wanted to be love . . . three years' worth. He took the time to put on a condom, then thought that the last time they had used one she had gotten pregnant anyway, and decided if she got pregnant again that would be all right with him. He wanted other children. He wanted other children from her.

When he joined her on the bed and touched her, she moaned out his name. He needed to taste her all over and moved his mouth everywhere over her sensitive skin, tasting her breasts then working the tip of his tongue down her belly and between her thighs.

"Jesse!"

Her body was hot and he tasted her heat as she twisted mindlessly against his mouth. Her fingers dug into his shoulders but he didn't feel any pain, just pleasure.

"I need you inside of me, Jesse!"

He obliged her request and slid his body over hers as she spread her legs apart. Without preamble and without wasting any time, he entered her. He needed to be inside of her just as much as she needed him to be inside of her. A low, primitive growl rumbled up from his chest as he continued sinking deeper and deeper into her. She was tight, wet, snug, and he wanted it all. He wanted to be sheathed so deep inside of her and never come out. He felt himself moving back and forth and she arched her hips to receive him, all of him. Her moans became a song of pleasure that played on his senses, increasing the pleasure they shared.

And moments later when he gave one last hard thrust, she screamed his name, the same exact moment he screamed hers. And they shattered into a million delirious sensations that took control of their minds and bodies, sending them into waves and waves of pleasure.

And they both knew that this was just the beginning.

❧ *Chapter 33* ❧

$\mathcal{B}$randy smiled when she finished opening her gift, a joint venture from Carla and Amber. Her smile widened when she looked at the skimpy nightgown they'd bought her as an early Christmas present. "And just what am I supposed to do with this?" she asked, holding it up to take a closer look. She was glad the three of them were locked away in Carla's office, which gave them plenty of privacy.

"If you have to ask then you're in worse shape than we imagined," Amber said laughing.

A teasing frown touched Brandy's face. "Hey, no fair. Just because you two are getting *some* on a regular basis these days is no reason to be mean," Brandy said, pushing the gift box aside. She then looked at Carla. "And I noticed you went out of town a couple of days ago."

Carla leaned back in her chair and smiled brightly. "Yes, Jesse and I went away for the weekend. We flew to Barbados and had a wonderful time."

Amber chuckled. "Yeah, I can just imagine how good a time you had. Who kept Craig?"

Carla smiled. "Sonya but she had some help from Jesse's friend Mike." Although she decided not to say anything, Carla knew that

Sonya and Mike were now an item, a very hot item. They were seeing each other on a pretty regular basis and Mike stayed over at Sonya's place occasionally. This was the happiest she had ever seen her friend and wished her the best.

"Will Craig be getting a brother or sister anytime soon, Carla?" Amber asked grinning.

Carla's smile widened. "We're trying to be careful but decided if I end up pregnant again we'd get married right away."

Brandy raised a brow. "And if you don't end up pregnant?"

Carla grinned heartily. "Then we'll have a July wedding."

Brandy and Amber were out of their seats screaming with joy and exchanged hugs with Carla. "Oh, Carla, that's wonderful. Have you told Craig yet?" Amber asked, happily.

Carla chuckled. "Yes, but he doesn't understand since Jesse has become a permanent fixture around our house anyway. I enjoy waking up with a man in my bed."

Amber smiled dreamily. "I know the feeling."

Brandy gave them a pretended pout. "Well, I don't know the feeling so let's change the subject. Amber is getting married in the spring and now you're getting married in the summer. I guess I have to save up to buy wedding gifts," she said chuckling.

Brandy began rewrapping her gift. She would be leaving in a few days for Macon to attend her father's birthday party and then a few days later she would join her cousins, Taye, Rae'jean, and Alexia with their families as they celebrated Christmas at Alexia and Quinn's huge get-away cabin in the Tennessee mountains.

"Brandy, have you heard anything from Grey Masters since he left?"

A shiver of pain coursed through Brandy with Carla's question. It had only been three weeks but it felt more like three months. She met Carla's gaze. "No, I haven't heard anything from him. I guess he's trying to forget me like I'm trying like hell to forget him."

She then sighed deeply and said, "Hey, I refuse to turn this into a pity party. It's a time to celebrate the both of your good news and I'm happy for each of you. And since this is an official sistah circle meeting, I think I have the perfect principle and when I came across it, I immediately thought of us."

Amber lifted a curious brow. "What is it?"

"A ship in harbor is safe but that's not what ships are for." Brandy swallowed deeply. "The three of us are like ships, and for two years we've pretty much stayed in harbor, not wanting to venture out into the turbulent and choppy waters. But we've finally decided to hoist our sails. We've recognized that we're strong, sturdy and dependable. We have weathered the storms and now we're confident that we can withstand anything that comes our way; an iceberg, tidal wave or even a hurricane. And what makes it so special, especially for you two, is that you have good, strong men at the helm to guide you, protect you and take care of you. The two of you were made to love, and I'm so glad you found special men who love you in return."

Amber wiped a tear from her eye. "And it's my prayer, Brandy, that you find someone to love you as well. I believe in my heart that there's someone out there for you; a man who will love you unconditionally and treat you with the honor and respect that you deserve."

"And I agree," Carla said, wiping a tear from her eyes as well.

Brandy smiled and she grabbed hold of her friends' hands and held tight. "If it's meant to be, then it will be."

❧ Chapter 34 ❧

Christmas Eve night

*B*randy stepped outside on the porch and inhaled the scent of the mountains. She loved this part of the country, its ruggedness and its solitude and appreciated Alexia and Quinn for inviting her.

After the surprised announcement her parents had made at her father's birthday party a couple of days ago, she needed to spend time here to recover from shock. After thirty-three years her parents had decided to get married on Valentines Day. Brandy shook her head. Heaven helped them all. Valerie Constantine becoming Valerie Bennett was definitely too much to think about. But she had to admit her parents actually seemed happy.

"We were wondering where you ran off to," someone said behind her. Brandy immediately recognized Taye's voice. She turned to meet three pairs of curious eyes. She smiled. "I thought I'd come out and appreciate the stars for a while. Are the little ones in bed?"

Rae'jean laughed as she leaned against a wooden post. She had only a couple more months left in her pregnancy. "Yes. It was easy to convince them that Santa only came after they went to sleep."

Brandy nodded. "And the teens?" she asked referring to Taye and Michael's daughters, Monica, Sebrina, and Kennedy.

"They're upstairs listening that CD Alexia gave them," Taye said shaking her heads. "You better be glad that you were given one of those detached cottages, Brandy. Some of us will be sleeping with ear plugs tonight."

"Hey, don't complain," Alexia said laughing. "I could have given them the first item on their Christmas list which was a nude photo of Maxwell."

Brandy shook her head. It seemed like her little cousins were growing up. "Will the adults still be opening their gifts tonight?" she asked. Alexia had made a suggestion that the grownups opened their gifts tonight so nothing would take away the kids' excitement in the morning.

"Yes, that's why we came outside to get you. It's time, before Michael, Ryan, and Quinn get busy putting together that swing set out back, so we want to open the gifts now."

Everyone went inside and as soon as the men were herded from the kitchen, they gathered around the tree. Alexia began passing out gifts, and when she handed Brandy a huge box, she said. "I was told to ask you to open that one first."

Brandy met Alexia's gaze and her cousin gave her an innocent shrug. "All right," Brandy said, placing the other gifts she'd received aside. The box was prettily wrapped and she hated opening it, but she did so anyway. It appeared that every eye in the room was on her.

After opening the huge box she began removing globs of tissue paper and uncovered another box, this one a shoebox. She smiled thinking that one of her cousins had been thoughtful enough to get her the pair of boots she'd been talking about buying these past few weeks.

When she opened the shoebox she lifted a confused brow. They were men shoes; and a very expensive looking pair. Included in the box was a sealed letter that was addressed to her. She nervously opened the envelope.

Brandy,

You once said that you wanted someone who would love you unconditionally, someone you could trust, someone who was willing to take on your family and someone willing to father your babies. You also said that person had a big shoe to fill because you planned on moving into that shoe. Well, here are mine. I'm not only offering you my shoes but all my love as well. It's been hard without you this past month and time away from you has made me realize that you were right. It's time for me to move forward and not look back and I'm ready to do that. I know all the things you want and I want them too. I love you and I'm asking that you share my shoes and I promise to love you, protect you and cherish you until the day I die. If you believe my promise, if you accept my love and everything I've written, please take a step outside the door.

Grey

Brandy wiped the tears from her eyes as she glanced around the room. Everyone was quiet as they watched and waited to see what she would do. Brandy gathered the shoebox in her hand. "Excuse me, I have to go outside," she said nervously, quickly heading for the door. "I'll be back in a minute."

Behind her she heard Quinn chuckle then say. "Don't count on it. He's a Masters."

Brandy stepped outside and closed the door behind her. She glanced around. It was dark and there was a full moon in the sky. Then she saw a movement and Grey appeared, out of the shadows. She was so glad to see him that she dropped the shoebox and ran into his outstretched arms.

He caught her and held her tight to him. "I love you, Brandy," he whispered against her ear. "I love you so much. I didn't realize how much until I left. I tried to fight it and couldn't. You're mine and I will never let you go."

Brandy reached up and placed her arms around his neck. "And I love you, Grey, and I will never let you go either, and I will proudly share your shoes."

A huge smile touched his lips. "That's what I needed to hear." He then reached down and swung her up into his arms.

"Grey! What are you doing?"

"I'm taking you to the cottage. I have something else for you there."

Brandy smiled. "Umm, more shoes?"

He looked down at her and his smile widened. "No, more Grey."

Brandy grinned. *More Grey.* She definitely liked the meaning behind that.

✥ Epilogue ✥

Ten months later

The savvy sistahs walked into the plush restaurant and a number of heads turned and looked their way. Individually as well as collectively, they received admiring glances and lingering gazes. Other women silently complimented the way they were dressed—glamorous, elegant, and stunning. They were gorgeous, sophisticated, high-class sistahs. Savvy sistahs. Women who knew what they wanted, women who were accomplished in everything they did.

Women who were cherished by the men who loved them.

Brandy Bennett smiled upon seeing the attention they were getting. She glanced at Carla and Amber. Their friendship had begun two years ago on this very night, and they were here to celebrate as well as to reflect. With the power of prayer, the grace of God, and a firm belief that they were truly worthy of love from good men, they had stepped out on faith.

And their faith had seen them through the worst times.

Their men would be joining them later since the women had asked for an hour alone to chat and catch up on things. There had been so many changes in their lives and they no longer lived in the same town. Brandy had turned the running of the St. Laurent over to Kathie when she had returned from abroad, and had opened a bed and breakfast in

Atlanta where she currently lived with Grey. They had married on Valentine's Day, when her parents had decided not to mess up a good thing by getting married. Go figure.

Carla was the jet-setter, traveling with her husband and son, but she still considered Orlando her primary home. Taking a cue from her husband and his business success, she found herself delegating a lot of her duties at Osborne Computer Network. She enjoyed spending time at home taking care of Craig and Jesse and only went into the office a couple of days a week.

Amber still had her bookstore and had opened two others. Cord was keeping her accounting books straight, and he still provided her with plenty of tax tips . . . among other things. Their first child was due in six months.

After being shown to their seats, a waiter came and took their drink orders. "Milk," all three of them said smiling. Brandy had just found out she was pregnant that day and Carla was due to have her baby around the same time as Amber.

When the waiter returned with three glasses of milk, the women joined hands at the table, bowed their heads, and prayed, thanking God for bringing them to this point in their lives and for giving them the strength to endure all things. They also sent special thanks out to God for their men.

Then they made a toast. "To us, the savvy sistahs, and to our undying friendship and continued success in all our endeavors," Brandy said. "And most important, to the men who love us."

Smiles curved their lips as they drank their milk. They had always been there for one another and they always would be. Their minds reflected on the principle they had shared in the car on the way to the restaurant that was found in I John 3:1. *Let us not love merely in theory or in speech but in deed and in truth—in practice and in sincerity.*

And with their husbands, the men they loved, the extraordinary males that God had sent into their lives, they were always putting their love into practice.

READING GROUP GUIDE

1. Do you think, considering their past relationships, Amber, Brandy, and Carla were justified in not wanting to seek serious relationships with men?

2. Do you think the three women offered support for one another? Why or why not?

3. Of the three savvy sistahs, who do you think had the biggest issues? Why?

4. Do you think Brandy's relationship with Grey moved too fast? If so, why?

5. Do you think Jesse was justified in wanting to take Carla's company away from her since she refused to cooperate and tell him what he wanted to know?

6. Should Carla have notified Jesse about her pregnancy regardless of her assumption that he was involved with another woman?

7. Do you think Amber was overly cautious when it came to developing a relationship with Cord Jeffries?

8. Do you think Sonya was justified in her jealousy of Brandy and Amber? Should she have felt threatened by their friendship with Carla? Should she have made an attempt to get to know them better?

9. Who did you think was Brandy's stalker? Why?

10. Were you satisfied with the way the story ended for all three sistahs? Why or why not?

**For more reading group suggestions visit
www.stmartins.com.**